Another Crescent Moon

Josh Cook

Better Than Starbucks Publications

Another Crescent Moon

Copyright © 2023 by Joshua Cook

All rights reserved. This book or any portion thereof may not be reproduced or used in any manner whatsoever without the express written permission of author and the publisher except for the use of brief quotations in a book review or scholarly journal.

First Printing: ISBN 978-1-7376219-7-3

Cover image: Dream by WOMBO

Better Than Starbucks Publications
3094 Adkins Forest Lane, Tallahassee, Florida 32322

". . . but the offspring of the inferior, or of the better when they chance to be deformed, will be put away in some mysterious, unknown place, as they should be."

—Plato, *Republic*, Book V

ONE

My power chair's been good to me for years. It'll have to be for several more. Medicaid only covers a replacement once a decade, and if it breaks down in the meantime, I'd rather crawl than go back to life in the manual, when I'd be stuck in front of cable news for hours without recourse.

In those days, I was an even bigger burden on my staff. They always had more pressing things to do than wheel me to the toilet, like finishing their nap or scrolling their feeds. When they'd finally find the time, it'd be too late, but still they'd push too fast and ram my legs into the walls. Some of the bruising on my shins is permanent. In the end, one of them suggested I be seen for an electric. The clinic didn't have a chair that fit my bony frame, so the technician sized me up for this one, then made it special-order. It's the most comfortable I've ever had, the first where I'm not slouched and weirdly angled between the wheels. The headrest keeps my neck in place, so for the first time in my life, I see the world as most people do. There are even days the seat feels like a pillow for my backside. But the best part, without question, is the joystick, which I lean on as I blast to the table, sideswiping BJ and knocking the spoon from his sunspotted hand.

"Youch!" he cries, sliding his glasses up his eagle's beak of a nose. "Watch where you're going, Cliff. Who gave you a license to drive?"

I raise my hand as best I can and grunt remorsefully.

"No hard feelings," says my housemate. "I'll always be your friend, no matter what. Just try to be more careful next time, will you?"

This is all part of our daily routine, a recurring sketch that brings a little flavor to the tepid oatmeal Thomas, the overnight staff, feeds the guys for breakfast. It began as an accident. I wasn't paying attention and I collided with his chair. When it dawned on him the next time was on purpose, BJ swore he'd report me to the authorities. I didn't put it past him. He's always telling Brad, our house manager, about somebody's indiscretions. But over time, he's become a surprisingly good sport.

Thomas doesn't even smile as he raises my shirt, cracks open a can of

Ensure, plugs the syringe into my feeding tube, and pours, hastily, as usual. The milky liquid slops over the syringe's edge and splashes on my stomach. If he'd give me a napkin, I'd try to clean it up myself, along with the mucus that formed at the base of my tube as I slept. Both will have to wait until this evening's shower. This, too, is part of the routine, one of the many it's hard for me to understand, much less accept. There's no day program today, so we're hardly in a rush. But Thomas's shift is almost over, so he pretends he hasn't noticed.

His bite dangling over the table's edge, BJ aims his empty spoon at Lem. "And as for you, old buddy, if you don't stop humping your bed like you do, it's a goner."

That's what wakes me up most days. When he goes at it, Lem's old box springs groan like metal banshees. Staff only wash our sheets when they feel like it, which is close to never, so normally our bedroom smells crusty and faintly alkaline. I know Lem can't help it — when you're in the mood, you're in the mood — but today it tore me from a dream about the woman from the Silver Lining Inn & Suites commercials, and I haven't forgiven him yet. Not that he knows or cares, and actually, I prefer it this way. Of the four of us who live here, Lem's the biggest and the strongest. If he weren't so gentlehearted, he'd have me and BJ in headlocks. Instead, he remains silent — like me, he can't talk, though not for the same reasons — and jabs one more impressive spoonful into his mouth.

"I'm not kidding," BJ says, scratching the dark hair on the sides of his head. Sunlight through the window behind him forms a halo around his bald crown. "You only broke your last bed a few months ago. They don't grow on trees, I say. And you, Rickey, why don't you eat up already? Thomas worked real hard to make our oatmeal. You haven't even touched yours yet."

Even though it's not his job, BJ's heart's in the right place. He knows Lem and Rickey need direction. At least this way someone's giving it. Thomas is so focused on the window — Francis, who works the day shift, is late relieving him again — that I could crush his toes under my wheels before he even knew what hit him.

Rickey blinks. Below his stubbly beard, his small hand trembles like a caffeinated finch, a side effect of all his medications. He's in his favorite T-shirt, the one with fireworks, flying saucers, and two words, SUPER RICK, in big, explosive letters on the chest. He brings his hand down to them and holds it there as if prepared to take an oath.

"Wanna cookie," he says, his voice soft and slurred. "Wanna pop."

Twenty years I've lived with these guys and I've never heard Rickey say anything else. It's not that he doesn't know other words — he understands what other people tell him — it's that as far as he's concerned, these are the only three worth speaking. Left to him, the kitchen would be an arsenal of soda pop and snickerdoodles. The trouble is, his taste for sweets has tempted him to break our house rules, as it did when he raided the kitchen one night and stuffed macaroons in his sock drawer. When Brad got word, he called it *maladaptive*. After speaking with Rickey's behaviorist, he put locks on our cupboard and fridge doors and gave staff the keys. One day, not long afterward, no one could find Rickey anywhere. The two staff on duty searched the place in a panic, not out of fear of his safety, but because they'd been paying less attention to him than to the shows they'd been streaming on their laptops. One of them was on the phone with Brad when Mrs. Mason rang our bell, holding Rickey by the hand. She'd caught him slinking through her kitchen with a can of RC Cola and a box of Chips Ahoy. Luckily for him — and our staff — she was patient and forgiving. She even let him keep the drink on the condition that he apologize for breaking and entering. He told her, "Pop," and smiled, which, for her, was close enough.

Unlike my bit with BJ, Rickey's act still amuses Thomas. "Regretfully, Super Rick," he laughs, "that is out of the question. It's only breakfast. Snack time is at three. That's when you have your cookie and pop, Mr. Man."

The thing about Thomas is that while he hasn't learned to interpret my gestures, it's become a lot easier for me to understand his accent.

"Three o'clock, Rickey." BJ nods so hard his glasses fly off, landing lenses-first in his wet breakfast. He plucks them up and puts them on, all smeared with oatmeal. "We all get one cookie and one half-pop apiece. Except for Cliff, of course."

"That's right," says Thomas. "Cliff will just have one Ensure for snack. But for now, you must all be on your best behavior. Mr. Brad will be here shortly."

"But it's not Monday."

Monday is when Brad collects the contact notes and timesheets.

"I know, but today Brad is training new staff." Thomas starts my second can before what's already in the syringe has had time to clear. "He's finally found someone to take Paul's place."

He wasn't long with us, Paul. Then again, most staff don't stick around for more than a few months. They usually resign by choice, but with him, it was different. About a month ago, on what was at that point the year's hottest afternoon, he drove us to the Tomlinson Square Mall. Knowland Residential prides itself on taking us on "outings" — pizza parties, trips to Howler's Fun Zone, dinner and a movie at the dollar theater. We thought we'd spend an hour rambling from shop to shop, maybe tossing a loose nickel in the big wishing fountain by the escalators. But when we parked, Paul got out and left us in the van, which only locks, per Knowland's policy, from the outside. We spent that hour trapped like canned Vienna sausages in an oven set on high. As we broke into an ocean's worth of sweat, BJ tried the doors and

Lem began to howl and pound the windows. His thumping and wailing grew louder whenever somebody walked past, but they'd look inside — if they bothered at all — and squint, then shrug, then head into the store where Paul was trying out new titles on the GameStop demo unit. By the time he came back, we reeked of piss and shit and were all on the verge of heat stroke. BJ wasted no time letting Brad know what had happened. It might be the one case since I've known him where his reporting made a difference. Paul wasn't just fired. He was arrested. The story even made the local news. Viola Hart of Channel Eight interviewed John Knowland, the CEO, who assured her that the staff was "one bad apple" whose actions weren't "reflective of" the company's "core values." For the first time in years, John Knowland came to see us, here, at our place, and burst into tears on our front porch. Then he put us in a circle, his face all sad and pale and wet, and promised to make us "whole again before the end of Quarter Three." Rickey's parents were there, too, the old pushovers, on one of their rare visits. He's the only one of us whose family is still involved, however slightly. They believed Knowland's every word and even thanked God for the mercy of Paul's having cracked the van's window.

"What's his name, the new guy?" BJ says. "Where's he from? Is he friendly? Has he worked as staff before? If he has, was it for Knowland, or another company? Does he know about my creams? If not, you must tell him, I say. If I don't get my creams, then my skin gets all rashy."

As Thomas finishes the second can, more Ensure dribbles down my belly and oozes toward my navel. "Calm down, please, sir. Of course, he'll be trained on your creams. It's company policy, yes?"

"I should hope so. His name?"

Thomas unplugs the syringe, caps my tube, tapes it up, and pulls my shirt down over my congealing breakfast. "I don't know. We've never met. But I'm certain of this: if he knows what's good for him, he'll be nothing like Paul."

"I should hope not." BJ wipes his mouth with his sleeve. "And I should also hope he remembers my creams — look, you there, Lem, stop that. That's my breakfast, pal."

The big guy has set his empty bowl to the side and gone for the glob I knocked from BJ's spoon. He hasn't had his shower, so his hair, longish, dirty-blond, and unevenly cut, sticks up at strange angles, giving him the air of a police-detained Nick Nolte. He balls the oatmeal in his fist and frowns at BJ, the stains on whose lenses are like another pair of eyes.

"Wanna pop," Rickey says.

Lem shoves the blob into his mouth, sits back, and chews, gazing triumphantly up at the ceiling.

BJ slaps the table with both his veiny hands. "What a disgrace."

"I think Francis will be happy," Thomas says, running his hand over his small afro. "He's been working by himself for a whole month, and I can see how he could use the extra help."

With the bottom of his shirt, BJ rubs his lenses, streaking them with little swirls of Quaker Oats. "Yeah, well, so could I."

"But Francis, especially. You all can be a — how do you say — a handful."

"I'm not a handful. I'm a person."

"You don't say," says Thomas absently, glaring through the window at the drive.

)

Brad never knocks. He just stumbles through the front door cradling his dusty laptop, looking like it's been a month since he last slept. He's in the same ill-fitting button-up he wore on Monday. Behind him, in strolls Francis, who seems hungover, and who's thirty minutes late. Thomas grabs his bag and asks if he got stuck in traffic yet again. He says *traffic* like it's code for something else.

"The very same," says Francis, locking his neon-green Dodge Challenger with yellow lightning bolt decals on either side.

"The very same is why I'm late for my next shift." Thomas works nights for us and days for another residential company.

"Please accept my most humble apologies."

Thomas charges out without another word, holding the door open for a man I've never seen before. As Brad waves him into the living room, he waves at us, taking in our home's one decoration, the word JOY carved from a slab of balsa wood hanging from the front wall in the foyer. In a black T-shirt, jeans, and the thinnest sandals I've ever seen, he looks to be in his forties and has his hair cropped short and faded toward the back. On his left cheek lies what looks like a small scar. No one's ever come in on their first day bearing Knowland's New Employee Handbook. I've always assumed new staff have thrown their copies in the trash as soon as training's over. But the new guy's got his pressed against his chest like a clutch of sacred papers.

"Hello," he says softly, his accent thick but different from both Thomas's and Francis's in a way I can't quite place.

Brad's never talked about being in the military. As far as I know, he never has been. But he's always had his hair buzzed like a drill sergeant's. It's graying, like my beard and Rickey's, but Brad's has probably resulted more from job-related stress than age. He's made it to his third year as a house manager, in charge of our place and four others just like it. The work obliges him to be on-call twenty-four-seven, in case of an emergency, such as the one Paul caused, or if a staff decides to quit mid-shift or just straight-up doesn't show. Inarguably the position is demanding. Most people don't last a year in it. When someone sticks around for three times that, I can almost see why they'd believe they'd make the cut in basic training.

"What's this doing here?" he says, ignoring the new guy and pointing to the side table, where the staff log sits. It's where staff are supposed — this being the operative word — to write down anything the next shift needs to know or might find helpful. "Doesn't this binder belong on the shelf?"

No one responds. Maybe the question is rhetorical. But Brad has more important matters on his mind and his computer. The laptop's a massive thing, a relic of a time when streaming was what water did and tablets were for hieroglyphs. Issued by the company, it only works when it's plugged in, and *clunk* is the only sound it ever makes. *Clunk* when he flips it on, *clunk* when he shuts it off, *clunk* when he sets it on our wooden coffee table, dust rising up around it like Charlie Brown's disheveled friend.

"Also, unless I'm mistaken, Francis," Brad goes on, blowing the cloud into the corner, "this is your third late in as many weeks. I hope we're not having those problems again."

"Traffic jam on the highway." Nostrils flared like two deep holes dug into earth, Francis towers above and smiles down on his boss. "I am truly sorry, but there was nothing I could do. I got here as soon as time allowed."

"That's weird. I didn't see anything about a backup on the news." Brad takes his phone out to look it up, but it's the old flip kind the agency issued him and has no Internet. "In any case, maybe it's time you start checking the morning traffic reports. That way, you can leave home earlier, or find another route here, if you need to. I'd really hate to have to bring HR in on this."

His employee's grin snakes ever outward. Francis knows HR won't get involved. With staff like him, they never do. Brad likes to talk tough and even issue threats of termination, but he'd never fire anyone unless he had no other choice, as with Paul. For Knowland Residential, retaining staff has always been a challenge, to say nothing about finding them to begin with. Plus, if Brad canned him, he'd have to work Francis's shifts at least until the new guy's been fully trained. For him, it's more important to have warm bodies around than good ones. At least that way he's less at risk of losing his mind.

"I understand." Francis plunks down on the couch and changes the channel from the weather we've been watching to cable news.

Brad's gray eyes ripple with their first resolve since he sent Paul packing. This is our place, after all. We should be the ones to decide what's on TV. He champions "client preference" during trainings, but never when it matters, and it seems I'm not the only one who knows this. Brad's forehead wrinkles and his gaze narrows, suggesting thought that leads to bold, decisive action. Today might be the day he lives up to his own standards by exercising his authority and advocating on our behalf. In other words, today might be the day he does his job.

But then those eyes meet Francis's, still smiling from the couch, and their strength dissolves like sugar in a tall, cold glass of water.

"Everyone," Brad says. Head hanging low, he points at the new guy. "This is Ayodele. He'll be shadowing Francis today. We hope to have him on with you guys full-time very soon."

Beaming, BJ edges forward. "Pleased to meet you, Yodel. I'm Benjamin Joseph Green — BJ, for short. Now, about my creams —"

"We'll get to that," says Brad, welcoming the distraction. "For now, we've got some housekeeping to do."

"Please, Mr. BJ, call me Ayo. But what, if I may ask, is on your glasses?"

BJ takes them off and studies their smears. "Looks like oatmeal to me."

"Your glasses — is that where you keep the oatmeal in this house?"

"Maybe," BJ smiles.

"Don't you think maybe we should clean them up?"

"I certainly wouldn't want to impose, Yodel, not on your first day and all." But BJ's already presented them to the new staff. Ayo sets the handbook on the coffee table, takes a tie-dyed handkerchief from his pocket, and wipes them clean.

"There you are, sir," he says. "No more smudges now. Those scratches, though, are permanent, I fear."

"No biggie, as they say. I can see just fine enough," says BJ, bumping up against his old recliner.

"That happy guy is Lem," Brad says. On the couch, Lem rubs his belly, crusty oatmeal and a smile on his lips. "Next to him is Rickey. Watch out for those two, or else."

"Duly noted."

"And this is Cliff, our Resident Cool Dude."

Every time he says this, Brad makes the hang-ten gesture in my face, and I smile and nod, since I can't extend a middle finger.

Ayo folds the hanky up, returns it to his pocket, and puts his hand out to me. "It's nice to meet you, Cliff. I look forward to our time together."

Wheeling back, I study Ayo's face, my own scrunched up in disbelief. No one's said anything like this in years. If they had, I might've laughed, what after a decades' worth of subpar staff and John Knowland's endless chain of broken promises. How can you trust someone who makes a pledge and then, whether from fear, forgetfulness, or having other fish to fry, never delivers? And yet, and with only the occasional, blatant exception, my housemates have never seemed to mind the company's design for our lives. It makes me wonder if I'm overthinking it or if something else is deeply wrong with me. But then the moment comes when, instead of sticking up for us, Brad rolls over at the slightest push from Francis, and I remember how I came to be so doubtful in the first place.

"Don't worry. I don't bite." Ayo's voice is quiet and measured. It's steeped in sadness, which is reflected, too, in his eyes. His smile's not enough to hide it, but I don't get the sense he's trying to.

Ayo stands before me, hand still out. Playing along, I grunt and raise my own as far up as I can reach. His palm is much warmer than I expected it to be, and despite his voice's subtle confidence, his grip is even more nervous than mine. The scar on his left cheek is no bigger than a mail stamp, faded, midnight blue, and shaped like a waxing crescent moon. He leans down to my level, cocks his head, and makes to speak when Brad, yanking up his computer, taps him on the shoulder and coughs.

"Let's get on with it, Private." This is what he calls all new recruits. "Please, follow me."

Ayo retrieves his handbook. "I'll see you later, gentlemen."

"Good to meet you, Yodel, and don't forget about my creams."

"You have my word, BJ, and Cliff, we'll talk more later."

Brad marches him down the hall to the spare bedroom he's requisitioned as an office, then shuts the door. We fall silent, and Francis's show cuts to break. There's an ad for life insurance, then one for gold, then one for cash for gold, and then the one where the old man in the orange polo orders constipation suppositories from the convenience of his phone. The box arrives, he tears it open, and, his smile broader than a Walmart floor plan, he shoves one up his rear end to his wife's great satisfaction. But when this nightmare finally ends — until the next time — my eyes go wide and my heart skips several bars.

I thought I'd seen them all before. Most of my life is spent right here, watching commercials. But this one for Silver Lining Inn & Suites is new to me. Its star strides through the lobby. Her hair's dark curls bounce off her blazer's shoulders as her heels go click, click, click on squares of marble. The long line at reception parts for her without complaint, for she has unsheathed her ArgentCare® Rewards Card, making the clerk's eyes swell until they pop out of his head. Through the hall, up the elevator, and all the way to her suite's door, she's hounded by admirers and paparazzi who care more about that stupid piece of plastic than what she thinks or how she feels. Powerless to stop their questions or the imbecilic flashing of a thousand camera phones, I wallow in a slough of guilt and rage until recalling that

1. The scene was likely filmed some months ago, meaning it's all over and there's nothing I can do, and
2. It's not for me to save her. She can do that for herself.

Which is just another of the many reasons I've fallen for her like I have.

It's only when she's ducked into her suite, having escaped the mob's parasitic clutches, and locked the door behind her that she transfixes me with the green whirlpools of her eyes. They suggest unfinished business — our last conversation was cut short by Lem's screeching bed — and I wonder if she wants me to pick up where we left off, as I was torn awake before I had the chance to ask her name. I do this now, with my eyes, but she's shifted gears, drawing attention to her room, its spaciousness, the giant bed with its soft, blue sheets, the loaded, mahogany mini bar, the full-sized fridge in one corner, and the hot tub in another. As she nods at each amenity, her hair dances like twin waterfalls at night. Then she turns and whispers the only words I've ever heard her speak outside my dreams:

"I deserve better. Why shouldn't you?"

"Ah," I grunt. *If only.* But she's already gone, replaced not by Lem's box springs but by Silver Lining's logo, a dark cloud with the sun shining behind it.

Francis has the show on where the two bald guys in suits, their noses in full gin blossom, rail at each other from either end of an impossibly long table. Immigration is the topic of their next segment, and their views are as divergent as their heads are similar. The bald man on one side thinks we should welcome immigrants. Not only do they make our country stronger, but we also owe it to them, whose own lands we have "effed up" over decades through our "pigheaded policies" and our support of "tinpot dictators." The bald man on the other side laughs so hard he nearly chokes to death. Only after hacking up an intact and spit-shiny M&M does he respond. Far from making our country better, he croaks, immigrants have brought it to its knees, which, he then speculates, into the camera and with a wink, is exactly where his hairless foe would like to see it. Over fierce objections and calls for his immediate resignation, he then proclaims his thesis: immigration "is diluting our great culture beyond recognition, and it's time we put an end to it for good."

The whole thing is foul enough to make Francis look up from the game on his phone. "Stupid man, stupid pronouncement. You can't escape such idiocy these days" — forgetting that you can, with the click of a remote — "but make no mistake. People believe men like him. They hold this country's highest offices. If they get what they want, there will be no staff for you — no Francis, no Thomas, not even your new Ayodele."

"It's *Yodel.*"

"Whatever, BJ. It's all the same. If he gets his way, you'll only have Brad to help you out and wipe your bum."

I'll grudgingly admit Francis has a point. Most of the staff who've ever worked with us have come from abroad. Some have been better than others, but none as bad as Paul, and he was from Cleveland, I think. The hardest part is getting used to their accents, pronunciations, the stress they put on syllables where we're not used to hearing it. But this has never bothered me like it might other people. It's not so easy to understand me, either. What I've learned from living here is that if they do a good job, it doesn't matter where staff come from or what they sound like, and that the ones who do a good job are the exception to the rule.

"I wipe my own bum, amigo."

"I'm aware of that, old man." Francis grins not at BJ but me. "I was talking about Cliff. He can't do much of anything, can he?"

Except this, I wail, and put my chair in reverse, plowing into the side table's corner and spinning it clockwise from the wall. The staff log slips off the edge and plunges to the carpet. I shift gears and rumble over it like a monster truck over an Oldsmobile. The binder's metal spirals moan pathetically, straining, cracking, and finally surrendering to my weight. I've turned our living-room floor into the scene of a war crime, a sprawling grave of torn and wheel-smudged pages, on top of which stands BJ, spouting tears.

"Clifford David Emerson," he shouts. My full name is printed at the top of most of my documentation, which he's had a peek at over the years, in violation of at least a half-dozen laws and Knowland policies. "You've ruined everything. How's staff supposed to write in here now? Why, you just wait until the authorities hear about —"

I don't wait for him to tell me what will happen when they do, or for his calls for Brad to banish me forever from this place. Per our routine, he'll soon regain his composure and forgive me, pointing out that what I did was wrong while emphasizing his commitment to our robust, eternal friendship. For the time being, I wave defeat and my apology, circle my chair the other way, and, careening over layers of crumpled paper, leave the living room for somewhere quieter.

In the foyer, something pulls me to the sidelight windows flanking the front door. They're not curtained, so sometimes I'll sit here a while if I need to be reminded there's a world beyond these walls. But with its pristine asphalt and herbicidal lawns, Saltpeter Street is less a world than a protective bubble. Everything about it screams *conformity.* The only thing that makes our house stand out from the others is the composite ramp Knowland installed next to the steps of the front entrance. While it's been a lifesaver to me, it's a red flag for anyone on the hunt for their dream home. It and the van — full-sized and solid-gray with no conspicuous markings — are the sorts of things a couple asks about before they sign the mortgage, like lead pipes, faulty wiring, or whether the guy from two doors down's a sex offender.

"That's right," Brad booms through the door down the hall. He's a much louder talker in training mode, and his tone suggests he spends a lot more time here than his usual fifteen minutes a week. "He might not look like it, but he's a crafty one, that Rickey."

He shares the story of Rickey infiltrating the Masons', then bursts into laughter as deafening as it is practiced.

"The point is," Brad says, "keep an eye on him at all times. Normally, people with Down's Syndrome are much bigger. Rickey would be, too, if we gave him pop and cookies every time he asked. Take a look at his behavior plan when you get a chance."

Ayo says something I can't make out.

"No need to go over it today. Just review it on your downtime. Francis has been with these guys a while. Talk to him if you've got more specific questions. For now, let's move on to Cliff."

He does these things so often I've learned my part by rote. First, there's the special pride he takes in my being the only one in this house without an *intellectual* disability. "The other guys aren't always with it, as you'll see — Lem, especially — but when it comes to Cliff, well, he's sharp as a tack." He loves applauding my ability to comply with simple orders — around here, they call them "goals" — such as *Come and get your meds* and *Don't you wander off, now, in this giant grocery store.* But when he dives into my past, he strikes a mournful note. My diagnosis, cerebral palsy, presented when I was two. As a result, I've never walked, and because of my dysphagia, I can't swallow and so will never know what food tastes like. "Times were different back when he was growing up. There weren't the treatments kids have access to today. That's why Cliff can barely move. He's been that way forever. It's why they placed him in SPED classes. Obviously, it's not where he belonged, but what can you do?" He sighs, his voice growing indignant. He's reached the part of my story where my parents gave me up and I was sent to Sinai Grove. "The things they did to patients there were just barbaric. For your well-being and mine, I won't get into them today. If you're interested, you can probably find the gory details on the Internet. What matters is that word eventually got out. It made national headlines, which forced their hand up at the statehouse, and they shut the whole place down within a year. But if it hadn't been for those reporters, who knows what might've happened? Sinai Grove might still be operational. Scary stuff to think about." There's a pause for brief reflection on the scary stuff, and then, right on cue, Brad cheers up. After everything I'd been through, I finally found my way to Knowland Residential and this nice house on Saltpeter Street, where I've flourished ever since. "Here, Cliff lives a full and healthy life." And here, at my journey's climax, Brad used to play inspiring brass-horn music, but at some point, his iPod died, and he hasn't replaced it yet. "We keep him and the guys as active and engaged in their community as possible. They get out for walks when the weather's nice. We throw parties every holiday up at the office. And then there's Memory Makers, our day program, where they spend three days a week. Laura, who heads it up, has turned it into something really special. Ask the guys. They all love it. Lots of opportunities for social-ization with peers through games, movies, and sing-alongs, which I'm pretty sure are everyone's favorite . . ."

The last time we had a sing-along, I felt like snapping Lem's glitter wand in two and ramming the jagged halves into my ears. We all have things that test our patience and grate on our souls. Two of the top five on my list are "Skip to My Lou" and "Baa, Baa, Black Sheep."

I barrel back to the living room, where BJ has the binder in his lap. He dries his tears with one of its rent pages.

"This is terrible," he says, and scowls at me through clean but crooked glasses. "I hope you're happy, Cliff. This book's a goner."

I grin. He covers his eyes with the sheet.

"This is no laughing matter."

"It will be all right," says Francis. "Brad will bring a new one. Don't worry your big head about it."

"Still, it's the principle of the thing. What'd this poor binder ever do to —"

"Mm-hmm." Francis has turned back to the TV.

The two bald men now disagree about whether Tommy Horner, a member of the U.S. House of Representatives, should be kicked off his committees for being caught on camera calling an opponent the *r*-word. The first bald man believes the slur is as "offensive to people with disabilities as the *n*-word is to African Americans." He doesn't, however, feel the punishment fits the crime. The House should take it a step further against Horner and expel the "thin-skinned bully" from Congress. The second bald man laughs again, then chokes again — this time so hard a producer has to run out and perform the Heimlich on him. A handful of half-digested M&M's on the long table later, he gets to his point, which is that a bunch of "Twitter trolls with nothing better to do" are "blowing the whole thing out of proportion." They need to "grow up" and stop searching for stuff to get mad at, stuff like what Horner said, stuff that, in the long run, "just plain doesn't matter. It's a harmless little word, for Christ's sakes," he coughs. "You all should calm yourselves and learn how to take a joke."

Sometimes, when I was at Sinai Grove, the people whose job it was to care for us would use that harmless little word. They'd use it when they put women's makeup on our faces just for kicks. They'd use it at night, if we refused to go to sleep, when they burned our arms and legs with cigarettes. They'd use it, too, when they squatted, shat in buckets, and then fed it to us for dessert. They never gave me any, though. If I'd choked to death, they would've had a real situation on their hands. But that didn't stop them from bursting in one night, the smell of vodka on their breath, and force-feeding some to Robert Elvidge, my roommate, before they sodomized him with his cane. I don't know what he'd done to deserve it, but I know they took turns. There were two of them. The one who wasn't going would just sit back and smile at me. They knew I couldn't speak a word of it to anyone. What they didn't know was that, in doing what they did, they'd perforated something. The next day, morning staff found blood in Robert's stool. They took him to the ER, he didn't come back, and a few days later I got a new roommate. I don't know what became of Robert, or whether he even survived, but anyone who's interested can probably find the gory details on the Internet.

TWO

When the bald guy show ends and *The Deal with Firth Bronzer* comes on, Brad returns with his laptop cradled in his arms like an infant. Behind him, Ayo looks like all new hires do after these trainings, his shoulders drooped and eyes glazed over from Brad's information blitzkrieg. If anyone ever asked me, and if I could, I'd advise splitting these trainings into two sessions, which would make a lot more sense given our extensive needs. But Brad's priority is to get staff in our home and on their feet as soon as possible. At this point, they'll sometimes realize they're being thrown to the lions with what amounts to a toy sword and call it quits, bursting out the front door and down the ramp without so much as a *Goodbye*. Others strut around like experts, like sudden PhDs in Cliff, BJ, Lem, and Rickey studies. But most come out of training with that tired air that says, *Here goes nothing*. It's written all over Ayo's face until he surveys the vast expanse of ruined paper on the floor. He looks at me — not in reprimand, but as if to ask why — and starts picking up the pages and setting them on the tray over my lap.

"Cliff and I," he says, "will get this cleaned up, Mr. —"

"Brad!" BJ dashes in from the bathroom, where he's been crying snotty rivers into a roll of toilet paper. "There's been a massacre in here, I'm sad to say."

"I can see that, bub." Slowly, casually, Brad leafs through the staff log's remains. "What happened, guys? Who did this?"

Glasses uneven like unbalanced scales of justice, BJ, his own arms full of paper, nods at me. "Who do you think? There's only one man in this whole house who drives a death machine."

"Cliff?" Brad grips my arm. "Don't tell me this was you."

I shrug.

"There's no denying it." BJ drops the paper to the floor. He's in a T-shirt, but he rolls his sleeves up anyway, a move he learned from the detective shows we used to watch. "I saw you with my own two eyes." He stomps around the room, huffing and thrusting his shoulders about.

"Easy there, fella. I'd rather you not dislocate anything. Besides, a broken binder's not the end of the world. I'll bring in a replacement next —"

Brad's phone bursts into the digitized version of "Taps" that serves as his ringtone. He unfolds the ancient device and presses a button.

"Go for Brad." This is how he answers all his calls. "Hold up, Victor. Easy breath, even tone, like we talked about last time. Good. Tell me again. Who did what?" Brad listens with squinched eyebrows to the staff who works at one of his other group homes. "Teddy Loftis. Got it. Exposed himself. Yikes. To seven elderly women during the lunch-slash-reading club they're having at IHOP. You're right, that's not good. One of them's on hold with the police? Yes, that makes it even worse. All right, Victor, here's the plan. No matter what, you must get Teddy's pants on. This is your top priority. He will resist, but if you tell him there's McDonald's in the car — yes, I know there isn't, but desperate times call for desperate — no, it's desperate, but not unprecedented. He's pulled this stuff before. Never at IHOP that I recall. At Howler's, once or twice, at last year's Christmas party, and, if memory serves, there was an incident at church a while back — the point is, I'm headed your way." Brad makes to end the call, then brings the phone back to his face like a sergeant would a walkie-talkie. "Oh, and Victor, I almost forgot. Whatever you do, if you see a Channel Eight news van, keep your distance. This is no drill. You tell them nothing. Zero. Zip. Not a damn word. Channel Eight is not your friend. This is as important as getting Teddy's underoos back on inside that IHOP. Make sense? I'll be there soon. Brad out."

His conversations with his kids end slightly differently: *Dad out.*

"Teddy *Loftis!*" BJ uppercuts the air, making his glasses go yet more slanted on his face. "If it's not one thing, it's something else, I say. Don't save him, Brad, I beg you. He deserves everything he's got coming to —"

But Brad's already at the door. "I have to run, you guys. Francis, hold down the fort. Remember to show Ayo the med pass, Cliff's feeding tube, and the Hoyer lift, too, if there's time. Sorry to cut things short like this, Private, and good luck. You're going to need it."

He slams the storm door shut and disappears.

"Next time I see Teddy," BJ growls, "I'm going to give him the old what-for."

"What does that mean?" Ayo says.

"It means Cliff is off the hook for now. Enjoy it while you can, I say, but mark my words. I'm watching you."

He points two fingers at his eyes and then one of them in what he thinks is my direction.

"Mr. BJ?"

BJ spins around, away from Ayo, and says, as sweetly as a cardinal on the hunt for morning love, "Yes, what is it, Yodel?"

"I'm wondering how you can see anything with your glasses hanging down in this manner."

"I see everything clearly," he says, flumping down onto the arm of his recliner.

"I'm glad to hear it, I think. Are you feeling better now?"

"That remains to be seen. I'd be fine if it weren't for Cliff and Teddy's wicked antics."

"I doubt it was their intention to bother you." Ayo dredges up another batch of twisted paper and sets it with the others on my tray. "Cliff, we'll throw this out later. Okay?"

"Maybe it wasn't Teddy's intention, but you'd be hard-pressed to say it wasn't Cliff's."

"How can you be so confident of this?"

"Why," says BJ, "just look at that satisfied smile of his."

"I see that smile." Ayo returns it with his own crescent-shaped grin. "It's a good one."

"Not if it's made at my expense."

"What if it's not? We don't know what's on Cliff's mind. He could be thinking of so many different things. Couldn't he?"

"I guess. He could be thinking about anything, like how that death machine has spelled the end of several things."

"Oh. Mr. Brad didn't tell me —"

"Don't worry. I'll explain. You might want to sit down, though." But BJ plows ahead without giving him the opportunity. "That man" — aiming a finger at my chair — "has even crushed staff's phone before."

Ayo jacks an eyebrow up. "Is that so?"

"It is. Is there nothing you'd like to say in your defense, Cliff?"

If only I could.

If only I could, I'd tell them this staff wouldn't change me. Every night, after dinner, he'd lie on our couch and play games on his phone. The other guys didn't mind much. When they had to use the bathroom, they could do it on their own. As for me, I'd squirm for hours in my slowly drying mess, both front and back, grunting for his help, which he'd studiously ignore. I just didn't understand it. All he had to do was clean me up and throw on a fresh Depends. Instead, shift after shift, he chose to play games. One night I decided that was it. When he, whose name I don't remember but was probably Jaylin, got up so he could use the bathroom, his phone dropped from his pocket to the floor. The way it crunched beneath my wheels was as satisfying as I imagine a bite of fresh potato chips might be. In retrospect, I don't have any regrets, and Jaylin didn't stick around much longer after that.

"I didn't think so," says BJ, sadly.

Emerging from his hangover on the couch, Francis stretches and pats Rickey on the shoulder. "That's why I like Super Rick the best," he says through a deep yawn. "No drama and no problems with this man. All he ever wants is his cookie and his pop."

Rickey's eyes light up with explosions even brighter than the ones on his shirt. "Wanna —"

"I know, I know. Don't worry, little man. Snack time will be here before too long."

"Speaking of Rickey," says Ayo, "maybe now's a good time to read his plan."

Francis condones most of his coworkers' behavior. The only thing he couldn't stomach, as far as I can tell, was Paul's last act with the company. The mall happened on a day Francis had requested off. When Brad broke the news, over the phone during his next shift, and asked if he'd be willing to work solo for a few weeks, Francis promised he would, for our sakes, then chucked his French fries at our wall. The face he made that day is the same one he gives Ayo for taking Rickey's binder down and paging through it on the carpet.

"Let's see here." After Ayo gets several pages in, BJ, breathing more steadily, hops out of his recliner, clears his throat, and hoists his index finger toward the dusty ceiling.

"Excuse me. I've something to say." Whenever he does this, I can't help but picture him in laurels and a toga. "Cliff, you and I have known each other for so many years I've lost count. We've had our ups and downs, to be sure, our good days and bad — most of the good brought on by me, and the bad by you, but I digress. The point is, I know you well. You're not a bad man, deep down in your heart, no matter what you do, no matter how high you spike my blood pressure. I know you couldn't help it when you crushed the staff log to bits, though I wish you could explain exactly why you did it. While it isn't right, regardless, I still forgive you." He inches forward and stands there gallantly. "So, whaddya say we let bygones be bygones, old pal, and start acting like buddies again?"

He extends his hand until it hovers above mine. I reach up. He clasps it. The handshake is solid, genuine, and a little too moist for my taste, but it always makes me smile. Now it does the same for Ayo, too.

"Very nice," Ayo says, folding the book in his lap. "I like that you two can work through your differences."

"It's a living." BJ ambles back to his recliner. "I like to let Cliff know we're pals, even if we don't see eye-to-eye on everything. Or most things. I'll always be grateful for him, and Lem and Rickey, too. Just like I'm always grateful for Brad and Thomas, and for you, Francis, too, because you're always there to help us, every day, with your hard work."

"Mm-hmm."

"And I'm grateful for you, Yodel, too."

"Thank you, BJ. I'm happy to know you, and I'm thankful to finally be here in America."

BJ thinks a minute. "You just got here, huh? How was the trip?"

"It was very hard. It took a lot of work and time and patience. But the effort and the journey were well worth it. Otherwise, I never would've met you gentlemen, now, would I?"

"That's true, as they say. So, it took a long time, eh? Why's that? Did you come from the moon or something?"

Ayo laughs and rubs the scar on his cheek. "Not quite, but it was pretty far. The plane ride was actually the quickest part. The longest and most difficult was making sure I had my paperwork in order."

Francis listens selectively. "That's even truer."

"Well, I'm sure happy you made it. Why'd you leave, though, in the first place?"

Ayo's brown eyes burst with the intensity of memory. "It was time for a change," he says. There's a power in his voice that wasn't there before, a conviction forged from metal in the fire of a deeply embedded history. It's like he's speaking both for himself and on behalf of someone else, someone who can't, or couldn't, share on their own what they've been thinking. "Back home for me, BJ, it is much different from America."

"You don't say. How come?" BJ sits up, has a furtive look around, and then, shielding one side of his mouth with the opposite hand, he whispers, "Is it because they don't have any Wendy's?"

"No, actually, there are several. There are McDonald's, too, for better or worse. They've been there as long as I can remember, since before I was born, probably."

BJ mops up forehead sweat with his shirt's bottom. "Thank the Lord. You had me worried for a second."

"I apologize. I didn't mean to do that."

"No biggie. I'm still wondering, though . . ."

"What is it?"

"Well, if where you're from has both a Wendy's and a McDonald's, how's it different from America?"

Ayo shifts his weight and looks away, past me and BJ, through the glass sliding door that leads to the backyard. Its blinds open, it affords a sunlit view of our small, concrete patio. Four green, plastic chairs are strewn across it, which wind had long ago laid on their sides. At one time they encircled the matching table that we haven't used in years and on top of which reposes a weather-beaten dwarf holding a sign that reads HOME SWEET GNOME. Ayo's eyes are on it, but he's seeing something else, something far away — a past, perhaps, he thought he'd put behind him, a truth that won't be blotted out by distance.

"Well, everyone," he says, as if he didn't hear the question, "what are today's plans? Anything fun and exciting? Or just a walk around the block, maybe?"

BJ rubs his little paunch like it's a genie's lamp. "Well, snack time's at three, of course. Only one cookie and one-half pop apiece, and that's it, Rick, you hear me?"

In between Francis and Lem on the couch, Rickey smiles at his hands as he mouths cookie ceaselessly.

"That goes for you, too, Lem. Don't snatch my food again. You got it?"

But Lem just keeps squinting at the ceiling, his hair jutting out like wires exposed through a hole in the wall.

"Snack time is at three," Ayo nods. "Anything else?"

"You're looking at it," Francis says, focusing on the TV.

Firth Bronzer, host of *The Deal with Firth Bronzer,* wears dark suits and checkered ties that make you dizzy if you look at them too long. He's the network's only anchor with a beard, in which he takes the greatest pride. Neither is he alone in this: *Mutton Chops Monthly* has voted it "TV's Best-Manicured" for five of the last seven years. For four hours every weekday, Bronzer delivers news of our impending doom in honied tones made vaguely bitter by his bland, unblinking gaze. After running through the headlines, he brings on seven greasy pundits and lets them lurch around his table as they debate our world's most pressing questions. At issue on this day is the pop star Aughbreighanna Adelaide's new haircut: what message does it send? How will the stock markets react? Does it pose a national-security threat, and if so, should we nuke the shit out of it? It's the last question that proves the most divisive, bringing the group almost to fisticuffs. Francis watches with delight. He slaps his knee and goes, "Hoh!" when Bronzer observes, not incorrectly, that the discussion is "really taking coif."

"Hoh!" BJ repeats, giving his own leg a mirthful smack.

Standing, Ayo looks at Francis, then returns the binder to the shelf. "Do you like this program, BJ?"

"Well, sometimes, I guess, maybe. I don't really kn—"

"Sure he does," says Francis. "We watch it every day."

❭

BJ shuffles back into the living room, wiping his forearms.

"Thanks much for the creams, Yodel. I feel fresher than a baby in a scented bubble bath." He flops back down in his recliner, angellike. "Oh, and thanks again, too, for that good dinner. Those mashed potatoes really hit the spot," he says, and burps.

"My pleasure, sir." Ayo's head appears from behind the opened door of our hall's med closet. "Rickey, it's your turn now, my friend."

Rickey inspects his hands on the couch. To his left, Francis, streaming a movie on his personal laptop, wears only one earbud, the better to hear Brad barge through the door if he decides to come back unannounced. On our TV, a different flock of pundits squawks about how the nation's values are being eroded by novels and history books.

"Go on, then, Super Rick," says Francis, distantly. "Time for your medications."

But Rickey just stares at his hands, as if waiting for them to be filled. Only when Francis pushes him up does he begin to dawdle toward the hall like a deshelled turtle on its way to its execution.

"Godspeed, Rick," says BJ, then to us, or maybe to no one in particular, "Boy, what a busy few Fridays we have coming up. This week, it's Howler's, and next week, it's the big cookout for Fourth of July."

They throw one every summer up at the company's office. Bringing me so close to barbecue without letting me have any would be considered torture in a decent world. Between the food and the fireworks, John Knowland always marks the occasion by delivering his annual speech about how Independence Day means even more to "us" than to most Americans. In addition to our constitutional liberties, we also fete it up for all the smaller, easily overlooked freedoms we've discovered in our own lives — learning how to cook, finding new friends, or getting hired for our first-ever job, which is supposed to lead to more financial independence — thanks to the support of Knowland Residential and its tireless and dedicated staff.

"Mm-hmm."

"Speaking of Howler's, Francis, don't forget that paper I gave you yesterday from Memory Makers. We're gonna need ten big ones for all the food and fun. I've already planned it all out, see." BJ stands, lifts his chin, and puts his arm out, palm-up, a regular Cicero in the comfort of his own Forum. "This Friday, when I'm at Howler's, I'll have some spicy nachos, drink a Diet Coke, and try my hand again at ring toss. And if I win a bear, Francis, I might even make a special gift of it to you, as my way of saying thanks for all your help with us."

"Mm." Francis doesn't even look up. From his earbud comes the tiny, tinny sound of two people screaming at each other.

"But it won't just be from me, you know," BJ says. "That bear will be a present from everybody — me, Rickey, Lem, and even Cliff, too. He might not show it, Francis, but I can tell he's just as thankful for you and all our other staff as I am."

He throws me an eager nod, waiting for my confirmation. On TV, the blowhards rant and wag their fists around like plump, peach ping-pong paddles.

"Are you now, Cliff?" Removing his one earbud, which still quietly shrieks, Francis leers. It's the same face staff at Sinai Grove would make when they wanted me to know they knew I couldn't breathe a word of their abuse to anyone. Just as they did, Francis knows I can't tell Brad about how last week he made BJ do our laundry by himself so he could come in here and watch his shows. Always wanting to be helpful, BJ did as Francis asked.

He made a good job of it, too, with several notable exceptions — we found the washcloths in Rickey's sock drawer and Lem's underwear in the bathroom closet — but his back's not what it used to be, and those full hampers did look pretty heavy. But the thing about BJ is that even if he were aware he'd been manipulated, he probably wouldn't care, and Francis knows this better than he knows himself.

"You are, Cliff, aren't you?" BJ pleads. "You're as thankful to have Francis here as I am?"

Even if I had the words to try and disabuse him, I don't know if I'd use them. I fake a smile, raise my hands as best I can, and move my bowels in silent protest.

"That's the spirit, old buddy. No need to be shy about letting our staff know how much we appreciate —"

"Very good, BJ. No more talking now."

"Sorry," BJ whispers, sitting down. "I guess you're busy writing notes."

"You're a smart man," Francis smiles. "Why, hello again, Rick."

Rickey moves much more quickly than before, reclaims his seat, and resumes his vacant gazing at his own hands.

"You're up, Cliff," says Ayo from the hall.

Against the wall of the med closet, next to the Bristol stool scale chart, loom stacks of pills in bubble packs, each one labeled with our names on strips of masking tape. Ayo takes the tallest one and shuffles through it, checking each of my fourteen medications against the orders in the log. I've forgotten their names, which in any case are unpronounceable. Most of them are for my CP. They don't improve it, necessarily, but they do a decent job of keeping it from getting worse. The rest tackle their potential side effects: nausea, vomiting, GERD, constipation, dizziness, basically everything they rattle off in those commercials for new meds, except for impotence, I guess, and sudden death.

With the pill crusher, Ayo pulverizes this evening's doses into a bright and multicolored powder that looks like sand art in a bottle. He dumps it all into the water he's prepared in a measuring cup, stirs the mix together with a spoon, then lifts the bottom of my shirt, uncaps my tube, and pops in a clean syringe. When he pours, he makes sure, as Thomas never does, that most of it has cleared before he adds more from the cup. Ayo does this in silence and with unexpected skill. Francis showed him how to use the tube at snack, but not — as Brad had asked him to — how to administer our pills. This leads me to believe he's done this kind of work before.

After flushing the tube with water, he coils it against my stomach and covers it with gauze, taping it in place beside my navel. I pat it and award him a trembling thumbs-up. He marks the pass off in the log, shuts the closet door and locks it, then sniffs the air and frowns.

"I think it might be time for a change."

In my room, he shuts the door behind me. So Ayo won't have to carry me too far, I scoot in close beside my bed and set the brake. There's a Hoyer lift against the wall next to the closet, but because I'm so small — the last time Angie, Knowland's nurse, weighed me, I was at eighty-six pounds — staff never use it. Ayo grabs a towel from the closet and unfolds it across the mattress. He picks me up with ease, like he might a CPR dummy, sets me down gently on the towel, and lays my head down on the pillow he pulls over. Throwing on a pair of latex gloves, he slides off my sweats and then my soiled Depends, chucking the latter in a plastic shopping bag, and asks me if I'm ready with his eyes.

As I'll ever be.

"Good," he says, opening the box of wipes.

When most staff do this for the first time, they'll flinch, frown, or try to fortify themselves against my flimsy, wilting dick. You'd think they'd be more frightened by the bruising on my legs, but this never seems to bother them as much. No, it's the sight of my sad manhood that conjures up their deepest, darkest fears — of what isn't for me to speculate, but I wouldn't mind knowing what else they thought they'd find down there. Evidently something other than what could be mistaken for a "damp packing peanut" as one staff said one night, thinking I'd find it funny too. I wasn't one to let him down, so I laughed with him for a while. Then, as he was wiping me, I loosed a lumpy turd into his hand.

"It might feel a little cold. Sorry about that."

This is all Ayo says for a while, never changing his expression, his movements just as natural and regular as they've been all day. He neither goes out of his way to ignore my nakedness, nor brings any gratuitous attention to it. It's simply there, it's who I am — as if, given the choice, I would've gone with what I've got — and he accepts it as such, without comment. Which is not to say it's not uncomfortable for him. I'm no mind-reader but this is an inherently weird situation. If the roles were suddenly reversed, I'm not sure how I'd act if I had to wipe a stranger's bum. I'd like to believe I'd treat him the way Ayo's treated the four of us, with dignity and respect, like it's his job to help us and he'll do it no matter what.

In this way, then, he works. The wipes are off-brand and can be a little rough, but Ayo uses two at a time, toweling carefully, first with one side, then the other, before pitching them into the bag, repeating the process so many times I lose count. I went a lot more than it felt like. When this happens, staff usually half-ass the job — pun intended — which makes for a long night in bed. This won't be the case tonight, at least. Even better, he says nothing until he's finished. Chitchat during changing time is worse than small talk with the dentist.

"There we are," he says. "Are you ready for a shower?"

Let's do it.

He wraps a clean towel around my torso, then lifts and sets me in my chair. I hear the crinkle of the plastic bag as I zip toward the door, but Ayo doesn't move to open it.

"Cliff."

He's still standing by the bed, his hands full of my waste. "May I ask you a question?"

By all means.

"I'm new here, so I hope this is not — how do you say — overstepping my bounds." He comes to me, his voice a whisper. "But I am curious. That man, Francis, the way he works with you. It seems a little . . . lazy, I think. Does he always act like this?"

Fresh from orientation, all new staff come in with Knowland's mission statement imprinted on the blank canvas of their minds. The whole thing's posted prominently on their website. It's lofty stuff, real inspirational, especially the parts about the agency's

> unwavering commitment to provide quality services and supports to individuals with developmental disabilities through a unique, person-centered approach that emphasizes our clients' rights to 1) be safe and healthy, 2) participate in preferred activities, 3) enjoy equal access to their communities, and 4) live lives that aren't just happy but *worthwhile.*

These words guiding their every action, staff put in a lot more effort at the beginning. They take their jobs — they take *us* — seriously. They treat us like we're people, engage in conversation just for the sake of it, even take us out on walks or drives. Even Francis was this way when he first started. So was Paul. But if they stick around a while — usually a couple weeks, but sometimes it's just days — the inevitable happens. By watching staff who've been here longer, they learn how things operate in practice, and they adapt. Before long, they're doing less, talking less, and spending more time on their phones. Aside from their house manager, they might go months without seeing anyone who works up at the office. This part isn't their fault. It's not like the directors spend any time with us in our own homes. Only John Knowland ever comes out, and only then if things have gotten so bad they've made the evening news. What results is a disconnect between what the people up there think is going on and the way things really look "out in the field," as they call it. The agency's webpage is a nice metaphor for this. It teems with pictures of kids with Down's Syndrome winning at checkers or earning their diploma as their staff cheer from the sidelines, smiles big as boomerangs. Not one contains a single person actually served by Knowland. They're all stock photos from online. Other providers — the competition — even use some of the same ones for their own websites. Of course, it'd be as likely as a miracle to see a single company share the truth: a snapshot of their staff sprawled across the couches of forgotten, sterile houses, streaming movies on their laptops with one earbud hanging out.

Since I can't say any of this, I just frown and nod.

"I was afraid of that." The look Ayo gives me isn't angry. More disappointed than anything, it suggests he'd been hoping for something more but had also steeled himself because he knew deep down that reality tends to frustrate even our lowest expectations. "I don't know what else to say except it makes me sad. But what of that? I'm only on my first shift. I can't imagine how you must feel, having to live it every day."

It's probably no different from how he's feeling, is what I'd tell him, maybe a little deeper, but not as sharp, if only because I've adapted to it. But with this realization comes a new pain, raw and burning, that of the scab pulled off the wound and the alcohol poured onto it.

"May I say one more thing?"

I blink and wait.

"You deserve better," Ayo says, leaning down to my eye level. "You all do." He gestures at the door. "I don't know if those guys are aware of it, or whether they even care. But you do, Cliff. Don't you?"

No one's ever said this outside of the Silver Lining Inn & Suites commercials. Posed by Ayo, it's not as sexy, but much more genuine. He says it not because he has to — it's not like his job requires it — but because he chooses to. Not even John Knowland bothered to say as much on our leg of his post-Paul apology tour. If he had, it probably would've made things worse.

"Don't you?"

I shouldn't have to think about my answer. This is more of a no-brainer than a thick coat on a three-degree day. Yet here I am, mulling it over, doubting everything I've ever thought about myself and my situation, if for no other reason than experience has always proved me wrong. Sure, it could be worse. Sure, it could be better. But at least this is no Sinai Grove. We haven't been abused. We haven't died of thirst or hunger. Aside from the occasional, flagrant exception, our staff meet our most basic daily needs. Maybe that's why BJ feels so grateful for them. If that's the case, then maybe I should stop complaining and be thankful for them, too.

I don't kn—

Through the door comes BJ's voice, loud and happy. He's singing Garth Brooks in his recliner, pouring out a warbled tale in rhyme of all the friends he has in low, low places. Classic country is his passion, and he's not a half-bad singer. They let him showcase his talents every Fourth at Knowland's barbecue. He looks forward to it as much as he does Christmas and has mentioned it at least three times a day for the last month.

"Not now, BJ," Francis says. "Can't you see I'm watching this?"

"Whoops. Sorry about that."

Ayo's still hunched over, waiting with his hands on his knees.

"Don't you?" he repeats.

My nod this time is stronger, more confident, and final, as if I've never been more certain of anything in my whole life.

"Thank you, Cliff. That's what I thought. What I don't know is why no one else agrees."

You and me both, I tell him. *So, whatever you do, don't adapt.*

THREE

Laura's done her best to help us feel like Memory Makers isn't stuck between a pawn shop and a laundromat way out on Broadmoor Street. It was a task worthy of Hercules or any HGTV show. The office park is in the heart of one of the poorest neighborhoods not just in Tired Oaks or in our state, but in the whole Midwest. Its building's chestnut bricks have long since faded to a shade best described as "baby-shit." Through the parking lot's thick cracks muscle weeds of every species, while dying flowers reflect on their mortality in the mulch that lines the walk. Out there, it smells like fungus, as if the whole place sprouted overnight from the floor of a cave. But in here, it smells like cotton candy, and Laura's painted everything bright yellow — so bright it almost blinds me every morning I wheel in. Even so, I do my best to let it slide. Yellow was her son Ethan's favorite color. He had cerebral palsy, too, but was diagnosed with other complications, and passed away when he was six.

"Got your lunch, Cliff," she says, returning from the kitchen with my two cans of Ensure. She stops at BJ's table, though, and mirrors his rotten look. "What's with that poopy face?"

"I'll tell you what. It's Henry Wray. He thinks that just because Everett is blind, he won't notice it if Henry steals his meatloaf. Well, maybe Everett won't, but I sure will, and I won't let it happen on my watch."

He and Henry stare at each other hard across their tables, like a sheriff and an outlaw in a Wild West showdown. Henry doesn't even blink. He doesn't talk, either, but with a face like that, he doesn't need to. His condescending grin speaks for itself. *I am patient and tenacious,* it says. *Your vigilance cannot outlast mine. I'll bide my time in the shadows for however long it takes and eventually, inevitably, I will triumph.* He's never given me reason to doubt it. Per his behavior plan, he should always be in his staff's line of sight. But one day, a while back, at his place, they looked away for a split second. This was all he needed. An hour later, he reappeared near the Dairy Queen on State Road 819. Henry's only mistake was that he didn't look both ways before crossing Tired Oaks' biggest road. If it hadn't been rush hour, he would've been "street pizza," as Brad likes to put it when he tells the story. The truck was barely moving — not fast enough to kill, but with force enough to knock a grown man head-first to the asphalt. That's how Henry got his lazy eye and why the left side of his face is slightly flatter than the right. But on that day, as on every day, he'd let nothing hold him back. He sprang up like a phoenix and made straight for the DQ, which is where the paramedics found him minutes later, his forehead bleeding, grappling with the cashier over somebody's parfait.

"This is your last warning, friend." BJ smacks his fist into his palm. "I suggest you think about your next move very carefully."

A lawnmower plows past the window. Its roar gives voice to Henry's silent rage.

"What's this about my meatloaf?" says Everett, sixty-eight. The collar of his polo shirt is all out of whack, and his eyes, foggier than ever, are aimed in the opposite direction of BJ.

"Don't worry, Everett. We've got this." says Savannah, one-half of Laura's staff support, as she wipes strawberry Go-Gurt from Alec Hayman's T-shirt. It reads I'D RATHER BE SAILIN' above a cartoon boat drifting off into the sunset. "Henry's a grown-up, just like you. He can make his own choices. If he decides to make a bad one, Blake or I will take care of it. But I really like that you called him 'friend' BJ. Even if we get mad at each other sometimes, we're still all friends here. Aren't we?"

Henry side-eyes Savannah, mentally noting, perhaps, to find out where she lives and take a crap on her front porch.

"That's right," says BJ. "That's why I'm helping Everett — because I'm his friend. I'm everyone's friend, don't you know?"

"Even me?" Blake's voice is exaggerated, a register higher than normal. In his yellow top, he's little more than a happy and pale floating head until he steps, like a ghost, from the wall. He claps BJ's back and takes a knee beside Henry, whose lone taco cools slowly, unbitten, on a white paper plate.

"Of course, even you," BJ mumbles through his sandwich. "You and me, Blake, we go way back. Remember?"

By *way back,* BJ means since last summer, when Blake and Savannah first started. They're both still in college, and I wouldn't be shocked if after graduating, they go on to host their own PBS Kids show. But they've maintained their good cheer only because they work here and not in residential. Not only are they the only staff at Knowland who aren't bombarded with requests to pick up shifts: they also have the weekends off. It'd take less than an hour in one of Brad's homes to wipe the smiles permanently off their faces.

"I sure do, bud, and I'm glad to know you, too. How about this taco, though, Hen? Do you want to take a bite yourself, or do I need to do the airplane?" Blake scoops the food up, and making *whooshing* sounds, flies it back and forth near Henry's face. If Henry's tempted to strike, he's Zen about not showing it. His eyes, though, flash with silent, secret warning: *Cut the shit or I'll burn your house down with you in it.*

I share the sentiment, if not the wish for violence. Sometimes this place does help me forget myself for a while. It gets me out of the house and gives me a chance to see different faces. But, like Henry, I've never felt like I fit in at Memory Makers. Imagine: you're a forty-six-year-old man with a mind no different from your staff's who dreams of being treated as such. But your body doesn't work like theirs do, so you can't tell them this. You can't tell them anything. Because they don't know you — how could they? — they adopt the same approach to you that they use with all their wards. It works with them, mostly. Why wouldn't it work for you, too? So, when Laura finishes your first can, flashes you yet another Carol Brady smile, and says, "All done with number one! Now for number two, just for you, you, you," all you can do is nod and try to disappear, hoping to God that Stella Scofield hasn't noticed.

But in vain. Stella's gaze has laid heavy on me since I first rolled up to the table. She no longer tries to hide it behind her blonde, uneven bangs, no longer loves, or thinks she does, in secret but openly declares it every time we see each other, which is at least three times a week. Her hot-pink Minnie Mouse shirt has been burning holes in my eyes for seven minutes. I've been studiously avoiding her for eight. But what I'm learning is, evasion's not enough. She either doesn't get that I'm not interested or doesn't care. Us, together? Cliff and Stella? It'd just be weird. I'm old enough to be her father — she's all of twenty-three — and while many guys my age might jump at the opportunity, that I'm not one of them is probably the one thing I know with total certainty.

"Just for *you, you, you,*" she says. "How's your lunch, Cliffy? Good, I hope?"

The upside of the days when the mowing crew's out there is that it makes it easier to pretend I haven't heard her. I try to touch my ear and look confused, but her eyes are pure and searching, her chipmunk cheeks all rosy with her smile. She brushes her bangs aside and says, "I said, how's your lunch? That's what I said. So, how is it, Cliffy?"

"How is it, Cliffy?" says Willa Maple, who at seventy is Laura's oldest client and whose words are always someone else's. Her hands are blue with bruises from when she smacks her wheelchair's arm, as she does now, with a cackle, as if to stress a witchy punchline.

Fine, I guess? What else is there to tell her, even if I could? That the Ensure is cold and wet and I can't taste it? That the splash around my navel won't be cleaned until tonight, when Ayo helps out with my shower? It wouldn't matter what I said, anyway. Stella's reaction would be the same: a wink, another smile, a coy tilt of the head paired with the twirling of those jagged bangs, and the blowing of a wet and empty kiss.

"I thought so." Stella reaches for a handful of different-colored Goldfish crackers. "It's not just good, it's good *for* you. Well, you keep enjoying your lunch, Cliffy, and I'll be right here if you need me."

Freighted with a guilt that only fattens over time, I turn away. The likelihood of me ending up with anyone is zero, practically, but if it ever happened, I'd want both of us to want it. Stella's a great person and an even better friend, but to me that's all she'll ever be, and this wouldn't change if she colored me a million paper hearts. When she gave me the most recent one last Tuesday, during crafts, I could've screamed at her to go back to work at Burger King. When they'd hired her, it was a dream come true for both of us. She even stopped in one day, all dressed up in her work uniform, and told us about it. I'd never seen her prouder than when she gushed about wiping ketchup from the tables and sweeping French fries from the floor. For the first time in her life, she was making her own money — *the big bucks,* she called it — but naturally the best part was that she got her lunches comped. Everything was going great until two months ago, when a guy from corporate flew in for an audit. I never met him, so I can only assume he was all of thirty-two, wore his name tag like a presidential medal, and tucked his polo into the khakis he'd ironed the night before in his hotel room while listening to Macklemore on Spotify. He took one look at Stella with her smile and her broom and said, "Redundant." Then he and the shift manager waited until she'd wiped up someone's vomit from the drink machine to break the news. While they appreciated her attitude and work ethic, the sad truth was that her services were no longer required. The guy even tried to frame it as a gift, asking her to think of it as a "permanent vacation." That was when she slapped him in the face. She was back here full-time a few days later, her anger having cooled to quiet sorrow. She looked like her staff had had to pull a Humpy Dumpty on her heart. But she's been doing better lately and has long since gotten used to being here again. It helps that no one ever talks about it. Doing so would only make her sad. So to let her know — assuming I could, with complete clarity — that I don't like her in that way would be to break her heart irreparably, would make me feel like garbage in bad need of taking out.

"Lem, sweetie, slow down on those Fritos," says Savannah, tying her strawberry-red hair back. Having dumped the whole fun-sized bag in his mouth, Lem feasts like it's his last meal. "One at a time, okay?"

"You'd better not choke over there, big guy. If you do, we might not play Trouble later, and if we don't play Trouble later, I can't help Cliffy push the bubble."

Lem drops the bag and licks the salt from his lips. He puts his fingers in his mouth and sucks them clean, one at a time.

"There are napkins if you need them." Laura nods at the stack on our table. The squares are small and bright and have characters from the movie *Frozen* printed on them.

Lem declines politely. The mower thunders past the window.

"Bough!" says Alec Hayman. This is all he ever says. Though he looks to be in seventh grade, he's been here since last summer, when he aged out of the school system. His family's still tangentially involved, but he's lived in a Knowland home since he was about fourteen. Like my parents, who weren't equipped to handle my cerebral palsy, his found themselves incapable of taking care of Alec, with his severe autism. We've been dealt hands that are so different in some ways, yet so similar in others. We're both trapped inside these bodies of ours, mine speech and function-deprived, his in sensory overload, like two sides of a misshapen coin. Our diagnoses have rendered us incomprehensible to others. I have no words at all, while he has only one, that blunt, all-purpose *bough*, which he emphasizes and inflects in different ways depending on his mood. It's impossible to know what's going on inside his mind by simply looking at his face. I don't think even he knows half the time. Set into a close-cropped head that's almost too big for his frame, his eyes are wide, deep, always inscrutable. With them, Alec sees things only he can. He hears and feels in heightened ways, as if invisible antennae projected outward from his skull and picked signals up from galaxies Carl Sagan only dreamed of. In another time, people might've said he was a changeling, and his parents might've thrown him to the wolves. Today he has a goal to wipe his own bum and sees a speech therapist once a month.

"Bough!" he says again, those eyes of his dilating.

"I'll be, Alec," BJ says. "Sounds like you're having more fun than I did at Howler's last week." His head drops. His lips purse. "But why shouldn't you be? The ring toss bested me yet again. Francis will just have to wait a little longer for that bear."

Savannah dabs fresh Go-Gurt stains from Alec's chin. "Has he been to the restroom?"

"I don't think so." Blake is shaking a spoonful of beans in Henry's face.

"I haven't taken him," says Laura, setting down the spent Ensure can and capping my tube. "Would you mind, Blake?"

"You bet."

But when Alec *boughs* again, everyone gasps. Without thinking, Laura dashes to the kitchen, knocking over both my empties, and Blake and Savannah fill their pockets with handfuls of *Frozen* napkins. Everybody knows the drill. We have to run it almost monthly. Initiating it, Blake sneaks up behind Alec and gently grasps his shoulders. Like baby geese, his more compliant peers follow Savannah to the safety of a yellow corner.

"This way, bud," Blake says. "Here, I'll help you up."

Alec's hearing, like Francis's, can be selective. His eyes are satellites, bright and fixed on something only he's aware of, his mouth curled up into a wolfish smile. Blake has mentioned how he played football in high school.

He had to hone his reflexes and prepare both mentally and physically for his opponents. Drawing on that training, he anticipates the boy's surprise maneuver. But Alec's hand is slick and delicate, swift as an eagle swooping in for the kill, and there it goes, straight down his backside, rooting through his classic three-stripe shorts.

"Oh, Pete's sakes, not again," BJ yowls, shielding his face with a paper plate. "Shame on you, Alec. Everybody, duck and cover."

"Here we go," Blake says, and with a grunt pulls Alec up.

On his feet, the boy tears his hand from his shorts. Clutching the feces like a live grenade, he hums softly between deep breaths, daring God Himself to stop him.

"Bough!" He stomps the floor in rapture. His footfalls punctuate silent sentences of defiance.

"Gosh," says Laura, coming back from the kitchen, her arms full of towels and wipes and disinfectant. She unloads the supplies onto a table and guides old Everett, who's been wandering in and out of Alec's line of fire, to the corner where the others cringe in fear.

"Don't do it, Alec. We're your friends, remember?"

"Come over here with us, BJ, where it's safe," says Savannah as she wheels Willa to the others.

"I'll be there in a jiffy."

"There you go. Behind me, please. You stay there with Everett. Stella, Rickey, Lem, let's follow BJ's lead, all right?"

"Wanna cookie."

"Later, bud. We just had lunch. C'mon, Rickey, Stella, Cliff, this way — you too, Henry."

Henry remains motionless in his seat. Lem dives under the table and covers his ears with his big hands.

"Over here, Cliff, quick!"

"Don't worry, Savannah, I've got my Cliffy covered!"

Stella leaps up from her table, hightails it to mine, clasps my chair's seatback, and starts pushing from behind.

"Gugh!"

Blake grabs the napkins in his pocket. A glop of upraised stool has broken loose and landed on Alec's forehead, trickling down his face like overheated hair dye.

"Here, use these," says Laura. "Napkins won't do crap for that. Pun intended."

"Gracias, chief."

"Cliff, Stella, let's go now, please, with the others."

Maybe it's because the view's good from where I'm sitting. Maybe it's because I'd rather not have Stella's help. Maybe it's both, or something else entirely, but I can't find it in my heart to move, much less take my hand off the brake. Even if I put the chair in drive, it weighs two-hundred pounds. Though Stella hasn't forced it half an inch, she isn't giving up without a fight.

"Augh! Graugh!" Her perspiration smells like fish and bubble bath. "Jeepers, Cliffy, for someone who's so tiny, you sure are really heavy."

"You sure are really heavy," Willa says.

Alec's swaying side to side, checking Blake's efforts to mop the mess up from his face. As Laura holds him steady from the front, the thin brown river wends its way down the boy's neck and underneath the fraying collar of his sailboat shirt. The more he struggles, the softer his voice gets. His grip on the grenade relaxes, his smile fades, and the look on his face turns less ferocious. He lets out a tired sigh, and with a final, beaten Bough, begins to squeeze the turd and pack it like a ball of dirty snow.

"There we go. Good job." Blake pats Alec on the back. "Let's get you changed."

They trudge off toward the restroom, Blake guiding from behind. There's a softball-sized bulge in the back of Alec's shorts. Lem emerges from his hole, a Frito pinched between his salty fingers. He throws his head back and drops the chip into his mouth. The only sound is of it being slowly, sweetly crunched.

Soon BJ's voice rises above it. "Huzzah! Three cheers for Blake." Pumping his fists above his head, he knocks his glasses loose. That's where they stay, hanging unevenly from his face, as he breaks into and leads the group in "For He's a Jolly Good Fellow."

But at the last *deny,* as Blake opens the door to the restroom, Alec gets his second wind. Twisting free, he reels around to face us. His howling echoes off the walls like thunder in the brightest of skies. Blake goes to wrap his arms around him, but Alec ducks and shimmies back toward the tables. Laura and Savannah fan out on either side, inching ever closer on their tiptoes. Oblivious to their slinking, Alec dances one way, then the other, chanting softly, shaman-like.

"Bough!" he says, taking a big, slobbery breath. "Bough, bough, bough!"

Then he hoists the turd into the air and lets his eyes fall right on mine.

I manage to say, "Uh."

Alec never makes eye contact. Not with anyone. Enthralled and tortured, he's always staring off into the space between this world and another. Absorbed in the fevered brilliance of his gaze, I'm as frozen as the picture on Blake's napkins. Alec's eyes — they flicker with the fervor and the weight of total freedom. It's strange and terrifying. My gut tells me to move. Still, I have to wonder what he's seeing, thinking, feeling. I have to wonder what we'd talk about if we'd been born with voices.

"Now," Laura shouts.

She and Savannah dart in like defensive tackles, but Alec's a crafty quarterback, ducking and dodging, diving and darting around their out-stretched arms. He's a regular Tom Brady, though Alec's ball most likely has more air in it. In his wake, the two women hug each other, having butted heads during their seize attempt. Blake edges past them, plotting his final play. Feet set apart, right hand on the floor in scrimmage stance, he hears the whistle blow and rockets forward, arms chugging, cheeks puffed out. Veering around one table, then another, he leaps over a lunchbox and lunges at Alec, who stands against the yellow wall, still facing me.

"Bough, bough, bough, bough, bough, bough, bough!"

Just before Blake reaches him, the boy lets the feces fly. It slices through the air above our heads, the filthiest Hail Mary. Blake makes the tackle as Laura takes down Everett, who's broken loose and strayed into the turd's flight path. Savannah throws her arms around BJ and Rickey. Lem slips back under the table. The thing has almost no rotation on it. It soars across the room, arcing upward, ever upward. Someone laughs, and below a cooing Laura, Everett whimpers. Blake has Alec on the floor, too, pinning him in a firm hold. Over the boy's moaning, Stella calls my name. I sigh at the urgency in her voice. Against the yellow walls, the clump is like an airborne Reese's egg. Even Alec stops squirming to watch its progress. It reaches its maximum altitude—no more than an inch below the ceiling—and hangs there briefly before beginning its descent. Stella shouts for me again, but I'm still paralyzed, half in wonder, half in fear, both of Alec and of where the turd is headed. It could be chance, it could be fate, or maybe he meant for this to happen. The way he looked at me was with such purpose. But if that's the case, I'm at a loss. I've never done him any harm. Even if we'd wanted to, we never could have exchanged an unkind word. The truth is, I like the little guy. He minds his own business, mostly, and he's one of the few here who can make me really laugh. When he's lobbed his waste before, it's always been at the floor, at the wall, or on rare occasions, at staff for prompting him to eat his veggies. But there it is, the angry dump, sloping down and screaming toward my face.

"My Cliffy! Never fear, I'll protect you!"

Stella hurtles out from behind me, the Hail Mary only feet away. She brushes past me on the right, lets out a battle cry. Two feet. BJ groans and hides his eyes. Stella trips over my footrest but manages to pivot left and hurl her arms out. One. The Reese's egg smacks hard against her forehead and splatters through her jagged bangs, oozing its not-quite-peanut-butter yolk from cheek to chin.

"Augh," she says, running her fingers through it.

"Stella." Laura brings the towels and disinfectant. "My gosh, are you all right? No, Blake, you stay there, or better yet, get that boy to the restroom. Savannah, go and see if there's an extra change of clothes somewhere."

Blake hauls the frazzled Alec to the toilet, shutting the door behind him as Savannah jogs off toward the little room next to the kitchen with a washer-dryer unit.

"I think my old work uniform might be back there somewhere." Stella rubs her stained cheek into her shoulder, turning the hot pink of her shirt a rancid brown. "On second thought, never mind. I don't want to wear that. It just brings back bad memories."

"We'll find you something, dear. Don't sweat it." Laura mops Stella's face with a *Snow White and the Seven Dwarfs* beach towel. "You just sit there and let me get this out. Yeck, it's chunky, isn't it?"

"Like guacamole," Stella says, "but I won't eat it. That'd make me sick, and if I got sick, I might miss some of my precious time with Cliffy."

"Stella," Laura says, adopting the stern tone she saves for the imparting of invaluable life lessons, "I know what you were doing. You were protecting Cliff. I'm sure proud of you for being brave. We talk about that sometimes, don't we? About having courage?"

"We sure do. I used all the courage in my body to save my Cliffy's life."

"Of course, sweetie. I admire that about you, and I know Cliff does, too." Laura takes Stella's clean hand and cuddles it. "But I'm worried that you also put yourself in danger. I know you like to watch out for your friends, but please, don't you ever do that again. I don't want you to get sick or messy. Besides, it's not your job to take care of each other. That's why I'm here, and Blake, and Savannah. Understand?"

"Yes, but I was right here, and you were way over there, and I wasn't about to let anything happen to my boyfriend. Don't you see? I'll do everything I can to keep him safe, every time I get the chance."

Laura is now toweling Stella's shoulder. "How about that, Cliff? Every time she gets the chance. I'd say this girl's a keeper, wouldn't you? I think he does, lady. Check out that smile."

If only I could tell her — but even then, I probably shouldn't. It'd be too late, in any case. Across the room, in the chair where he remained throughout the chaos, Henry Wray grins subtly before he shoves the last of Everett's meatloaf in his mouth.

FOUR

Ayo stops the cart to towel his forehead with his tie-dyed hanky. Four soup cans slide off the toilet paper, thudding hard against the floor, and all the strangers in the aisle turn and stare. The chicken noodle rolls past Rickey's foot. He steps and slips on it, but Ayo catches him in time and holds him upright by the shoulders. As Lem twists a ghoulish booger from his nose and licks it, a man in a black blazer sighs and announces that he's sick of seeing grown men acting like they're children and that he'll come back later, when we are gone, to get his Trix.

"It seems we are an inconvenience." Ayo sets the soup back more securely in the cart. "That's the third time someone has said that just today."

"Don't worry, Yodel," says BJ, doing the maze on the back of a box of Cap'n Crunch's OOPS! All Berries. "It happens all the time. You get used to it."

So it does, and so we have. But it's changed over the years, the general reaction to four adult men laying waste to grocery aisles. Unlike the guy in the blazer, most people show us a lot more patience than they used to. Sometimes they'll even start a conversation up, especially if they have family or friends who get supports, like we do. It's not as often anymore, thank God, but for a few years we couldn't leave the house without some well-intentioned couple claiming that they "saw" us now because of *Rain Man.* But the nicest part about these days isn't that fewer people use the *r*-word. It's that when they do, their children shut them down with righteous mastery.

Ayo looks at BJ over the box of cereal. "Should you, though?"

BJ's thumb turns a tight corner, one step closer to the Cap'n's shiny treasure. "Whaddya mean, should I?"

"I mean, should you get used to something that's an affront to your dign—"

"A little help here," moans Francis, wobbling around the endcap with two large cases of Ensure. After it's stacked up at the bottom of the cart, Ayo checks the grocery list.

"Let's see. We have Cliff's Ensure and the oatmeal, the lunchmeat and Lem's Fritos, the peanut butter and the cheese —"

"Are my creams still in there, too?"

"Of course. They're not going anywhere."

"They'd better not, but in times like these, you never know."

"Sir, in the week I've been with you, have you ever gone without your creams?"

"No," BJ says, peering out from behind the box. "But better safe than sorry, as they say."

"Fair enough."

"Hey, I got it! The treasure is all mine."

"Congratulations," Ayo says as BJ does a celebratory jig. "I never for a minute doubted your maze-solving abilit—"

"What else do we need?" says Francis.

"Mostly, the things for Friday's barbecue. Buns, ground beef, pork chops, pop."

"Pop." Rickey draws out the vowel, savoring the very idea of a drink.

"Don't worry, little man. We'll get your pop." Francis lets fly with the smile he's kept suppressed since his return. "But first, Cliff, don't you want to buy your Stella something for the cookout? A card confessing your true love? Or perhaps an engagement ring?"

"Who's this Stella?" Ayo asks. "I've never heard of her before."

"She is Cliff's sweetheart," Francis winks. "You must have seen those paper hearts he comes home from day program with."

"Of course. I didn't know they were from her."

"Stella cuts them out herself because she loves him. Cliff pretends he doesn't like it, but only because he'd rather we not know his true affections." Francis returns my frown with an even bigger smile. He hugs himself and starts smooching the air. "Oh, Stella! Stella!"

He careens out of my way at the last second. My chair slams into the shelves, toppling cereal boxes like high-rises in an earthquake.

"Augh!" BJ shields his face with his own box. Cap'n Crunch says, "Not again. Do something, Yodel!"

"I'm open to suggestions as to what something might look like."

"Put an end to the death machine once and for all!"

Backing up, I run over a fallen box. A thousand Cocoa Krispies explode beneath me.

"You break it, pal, you buy it!"

"Let's stay calm," Ayo says. "Everything will be all right. Are you okay, Cliff?"

I nod.

"Good. And you, BJ?"

"I'm fine," says Cap'n Crunch, "but I can't say the same for that poor cereal."

"Someone will come and clean it up. How about you, Francis?"

"Never better." His eyes dance with deep and secret laughter. "But in times like these I wonder whether Cliff, like Rickey, might need a behaviorist."

"I think someone might need a behaviorist," Ayo says, and he grabs the cart and pushes it with sudden, renewed strength.

☾

After Paul, the company decommissioned the van he'd locked us in. The replacement pulled into our drive the same day Knowland came by to apologize. It's a model identical to the last in every way except it smells like someone's hosed it down with bleach.

Francis drives slowly, one hand on the wheel and the other on the toothpick in his mouth. He bops his head in time with the radio's top hits, his eyes concealed behind red lenses. Since Ayo started, he's kept the volume at a reasonable level, but he hasn't changed the station from his favorite, the one that plays the same three tracks about rainstorms and killer bees and tough love on a loop. For the first time in a while, I hear BJ singing over it. Not that this is any better. It's not even the same song. The Fourth has been on his mind all day, so not only is he belting out the national anthem. He's also punctuating every line with his best imitation of a crash cymbal. It's enough to make you want to jump out through the window and be turned into street pizza.

"Very good," Francis says above Ayo's and the singer's own applause. "All done now."

BJ balls his hands up into fists and slugs the air. "I don't know, Francis. I think I'm only getting started. What say I treat you to another masterpiece? What'll it be, fellas: 'God Bless America' or 'When Johnny Comes Marching Home'? Or would you rather have a break from all the patriotic fare —"

"That sounds good to me."

"— to hear my number-one crowd pleaser?"

"Which one is that?" Ayo says from the passenger's seat.

"'Skip to My Lou,'" says BJ, smiling.

"How about we take a break from all the songs, forever?" Stopping for the red light, Francis has a long staredown with BJ through the rearview. In the mirror, his shades are twin planets from another universe. BJ pushes up his own glasses, which he knocked loose with that last punch.

"Okey-doke, as they say. 'Skip to My Lou' it is."

I groan and flail against my belt. Lem agrees. He stops his restaurant-gazing, spins to face BJ, grimaces, then passes the vilest gas he's had since Ayo cooked asparagus.

"Man, that was a big one," Francis laughs, rolling down his window all the way.

"Jeez, Lem. Why don't you tell me how you really feel?"

BJ whirls the other way, toward a billboard that shows Mean Barry Dean, the personal injury lawyer, smashing a stack of medical bills with an oversized sledgehammer. We breeze past our dentist's office, the clinic where I was fitted for my chair, and the IHOP where Teddy Loftis exposed himself to that ill-fated book club. Brad told us the police had been sympathetic — one officer had a daughter who lives in a home like ours — but that the manager had taken the opposing view and banned Teddy from the premises for life.

Past the mall and just before the Silver Lining Inn & Suites, Ayo turns around, smiling and holding his nose. "So, I've never been to an American barbecue before. What are they like?"

"They're fantastic, I say. Food, friends, and fireworks. What more could a guy like me want?"

"I'm glad you're excited for it. I am, too, though maybe not as much as that man."

Outside Bowlby's Furniture, that man is dressed up as Uncle Sam. He's been out here most days for a while, twirling a plastic sign like a baton. High up in the air, it says:

GOING OUT OF BUSINESS SALE!
EVERYTHING 50% OFF

A sharp gust fells his red, white, and blue top hat and blows it into State Road 819. The guy runs out and grabs it, hustles back to the sidewalk, and starts humping the hat's head-hole with a sneer.

"I'm even more excited than he is, Yodel. Why, it's not every day you get to have a cookout and see your friends. Everybody's going to be there — Brad, Laura, Savannah, Blake, Everett, Willa, Ed Vernon, that old grump, and maybe even Alec Hayman, if he doesn't throw his you-know-what all over the place."

BJ is right to be upset about the boy's uncultured turd-hurling. After that last incident at Memory Makers, I'm still a little shaken up about it myself. But it's not like, in this system, such behavior isn't par for the course. Sometimes I wonder if life is any different for "normal" people on the outside who are able — in theory, at least — to express themselves in better and healthier ways. But if how they act online is any guide, they fling much more shit than we do, and much more innovatively, at that.

"You forgot to mention Stella," Francis says, "who will be very sad, Cliff, that you didn't get her an engagement —"

"That young man, Alec, may not be there," says Ayo, cutting him short. "I heard Brad say they sent him to a hospital."

"Serves him right. You can't throw your excretions all over God's creation and not expect to face the consequences." BJ's mouth contorts in scornful shapes. "But that still leaves Henry Wray, who'll have to face the music if he tries to steal my dinner, and it won't be a pretty tune, believe you me."

Ayo unfastens his belt and squeezes his way to the back of the van, where he fixes a few grocery bags that've fallen over around my feet. "Don't worry, sir. There will be no thievery of pork chops, bratwursts, hamburgers, or those little cheese-filled wieners we just picked up. Francis and I will make sure of it."

"Mm-hmm."

BJ's doing what I think are supposed to be judo chops. "And so will I."

"There should be no need for that. I trust we'll all be very happy, maybe me, especially. This is my very first Independence Day in America. I'm looking forward to spending it with you gentlemen."

"The feeling sure is mutuable," says BJ.

"Mutual," Francis says.

"You know what I mean." BJ slaps his thighs. "Maybe you're right, Yodel. Maybe I should focus on the good stuff. After all, this is my favorite holiday, if you don't count Thanksgiving, Christmas, New Year's, Labor Day, Flag Day, St. Patrick's Day, Juneteenth — that's the new one I learned this year — and most importantly, all of August, which is, of course, my birthday month. But the special thing about the Fourth is, it's the one day of the year we get to celebrate our freedoms."

"May I ask, BJ, what does that mean to you?"

BJ starts to speak, then closes his mouth tightly and thinks a while. "What does what mean to me, Yodel?"

"Your freedom, sir. What you're celebrating. It means different things to different people. I'm just curious. What does it mean to you?"

"Lots of things, I guess. It means I get to make my own choices."

"That's great to hear. What choices do you make?"

"Hmm. Well, good ones, always good ones. I choose to be a kind and friendly person to all my friends and even strangers."

"Except when someone eats your pork chop," Francis says.

"That's only because Henry has it coming." BJ winds his fist up like they do in old cartoons. "As I say, if he thinks he'll get away with that, he's got another thing —"

"Would you tell me, if you don't mind, what other choices you've made all by yourself?"

BJ leans back and stares up at the van's ceiling. "Let's see. I also pick out the clothes I want to wear." He pulls the chest of his T-shirt up and out so hard its threads start ripping. Printed on it is a large bald eagle's face, fearsome and alert, superimposed over the New York City skyline above the words

NEVER FORGE**T**

When he lets go, the collar's stretched down to his nipples.

"I most definitely won't," Ayo says.

"Won't what?"

"I won't forget, my friend. How could I? I remember that day vividly. It was most tragic, even though I was so far away." Ayo pauses, shakes his head at something deep inside it. "Still, the fact remains, BJ: you have exceptional sartorial taste."

"You're not the first to say so."

"I wouldn't imagine. So, you choose to be a good person, and you pick your own clothes out every day. Is there anything else that freedom means to you?"

"That's probably about it," BJ says, sounding unsure.

"What about other choices you might make? Decisions about other aspects of your life?"

"You mean, like, when I want to go to bed?"

"It could be that. It could be anything at all. Like what you watch on your TV during your free time." Ayo looks at Francis, then back at BJ. "Do you do that, sir? Choose the shows that you all watch?"

"Sometimes. Usually, it's Francis. But that's okay. He works so hard with us that every now and then he needs a little break."

"Yes, it's true. We all need breaks," says Ayo. "I have to say, however, that I am a bit confused."

The yellow light in front of us turns red, but Francis hits the brakes much harder than he needs to. We all jolt forward, then recoil. Everybody, thankfully, is belted in — I doubly so, buckled to my wheelchair, which is in turn strapped to the floor.

"You are confused?" Francis snaps his toothpick in half and flicks it out the window. "About what?"

"About all these freedoms, these choices. Who owns the television at your place, BJ?"

"It's ours, of course."

"Who do you mean by that?"

"Me and Rickey, Lem and Cliff. We paid for it in cash."

"I thought so. When something belongs to you, such as a television, who do you think should get to choose what plays on it?"

"Well, when you put it that way, I'd have to say it should be —"

"He just told you, didn't he?" Francis hurls the words like Molotov cocktails. "He just said he doesn't mind what plays. Besides, I wouldn't change it to a channel they didn't like."

"So, they like watching the news."

"I think so, yes. Anyway, it's good for them to be informed about the world. Don't you agree?"

"Sure," Ayo says, "if that's what they want."

Francis adjusts the mirror for a better view of himself. "I'm certain it is. No one's complained before. For that matter, no one's ever said a single word about it until you started working here."

"I can't imagine why."

The light goes green. Francis yanks his shades out of the rearview, sets them on the car in front of us, and starts sucking on a fresh toothpick. "That's probably a question for another day."

"Another day, then."

"Um, excuse me, but I have a question, if you don't mind."

"We've had a lot of those for one afternoon, BJ. Why don't we wait until tom—"

"No," Ayo says. "You can ask now, if you want."

"I do, see, and it's like this." BJ thumps the exposed chest above his stretched-out eagle shirt. "Since you already asked me, and seeing as you're new and everything — not just to Tired Oaks, or to Knowland Residential, but to America, the whole country — I was just wondering, well, what does freedom mean to you, Yodel?"

"That's a great question." Ayo's gaze falls on the first-aid kit between his seat and Francis's. "Actually, I think you've put me on the spot a little bit."

"Sorry about that. Must be a touchy topic. I know in some places they don't like us for our freedoms."

"No, not at all. I love this place. I grew up in my country hearing about America, about how you're freer here than anyone has ever been, anytime or anywhere. Where I'm from, BJ, it's not exactly like that."

"So you don't have a Wendy's there, after all."

"No, we do, just not as many. But where I'm from is much smaller, and very different." Ayo stares into the cityscape on the front of BJ's shirt. "More than anything, I wanted to come here, to the United States. It wasn't easy, as I've said. It took a lot of time and thought and work. I even had to take a test."

"Yikes! It's a good thing I didn't have to do that."

"Consider yourself lucky," Ayo smiles. "But I studied hard. I learned so many things about this place, its people, and its freedoms. It only made me want to see it even more. The thing about it is . . ." He trails off, seeing something visible only to him, just as it was on his first day, something distant, troubling, something —

"Well, what is it?"

"What is what, my friend?"

"The thing you were saying. Remember? About America?"

"Right. Sorry. The thing is, before I arrived here, I had this whole idea of how everything would be. What it would look like, how it would sound and smell, the sights I'd see, the friends I'd make —"

"Such as me."

"That's right. Such as you. I also had this idea of what freedom would look like — what it would feel like. You understand? But it was all inside my head. Until I stepped off the airplane, I could do nothing but imagine. None of it truly became real until I set foot on the ground. So the thing, BJ, now that I'm in America, is that after all that time, thought, work, and study . . ."

Looking straight at Francis, he falls quiet.

"I'm *listening.*"

"Is that after all that time, thought, work, and study, there is still so much for me to learn."

❯

Rickey holds his cookie like a clearance badge. It vibrates in his small, unsteady hands. He's yet to take a single bite, preferring to prolong the moment. His Dr. Pepper, too, stands untouched on the table in front of him. The ice melts as Rickey mouths sweet nothings to his store-brand snicker-doodle.

"Thanks again for our snack," says BJ, licking sugar from his lips. "This sure is delicious."

"It wasn't I who got it for you." Returning from our kitchen with a dishrag, Ayo steps over the mass of grocery bags still on the floor. "It was Francis. You should be thanking him."

"Where is he?"

"On your couch, watching your TV. Don't you hear the news in there?"

It's the two bald men with gin blossoms. They're holding forth at the same time about whether paper straws are a barbarity the likes of which we haven't seen since Auschwitz.

"Well, thanks anyway, Francis, for everything you do."

"Here we are, then." Ayo rolls up my tube, then tapes it back down on my stomach. Before lowering my shirt, he takes the rag and cleans the globs around my navel.

Thanks for that.

"No problem," he says, waving off my surprise. "It's not so hard to understand if we take the time to listen. Hey, you there, Lem. That's one great-big pop mustache you've grown. Here are napkins if you want to wipe it off."

Giving himself a quick shave — not with the napkins but the tablecloth — Lem springs from his chair and lumbers to the window, where, crooning incoherently, he watches two squirrels engaged in a jittery mating ritual on our front lawn.

"Don't forget your dishes, sir."

But Lem won't hear of it until the critters scurry up the Masons' giant oak.

"Listen, Yodel, I've been thinking," BJ says, between sips, "about how this is your first July the Fourth."

"It is. The first of many, I hope."

"Me, too. But I can't help wondering: if they don't have it where you're from, what do they have instead?"

Ayo wraps the rag around my empty can. "We have our own Independence Day. It's just not July the Fourth. Also, the way we celebrate is a little different from the way you do things in America."

"What, they don't have fireworks?"

"No, there are fireworks, but they don't go on for days."

"Well, that's no fun at all."

"Maybe not. But I had some good times, still, when I was younger."

BJ buffs his glasses with the tablecloth. "You can still have fun when you're a man. Take it from me."

"This is true, and I tried. It was just that, as I got older, I didn't have as much time for fun anymore."

"Had to join the old workaday world?"

"You could say that. What happened was, things changed. Over there isn't like here in other ways, too, so . . ." Ayo looks out on our bare lawn and Saltpeter Street beyond it. "My brother needed help, and it was up to me to care for him." There are things outside, now, that only he can see. "Yes, BJ, it was a lot of work. A full-time job, and then some."

BJ gathers his dishes. "I hope your brother's feeling better. I guess he must be if he came here with you."

Ayo smiles sadly, climbs over the plastic bags, and strides back into the kitchen. "It seems these groceries won't put themselves away. Would you like to help me out?"

"It would be my greatest honor." BJ salutes him with the hand that holds his plate.

"Excellent. You might have to show me where some of these go."

Ayo throws the rag on the counter, pitches my can into the trash, then parts the bags like Moses the Red Sea. But instead of taking the new path, BJ hikes first one leg, then the other, over the jumbo rolls of Charmin and a pound of fresh ground beef. After he puts his glass and plate in the sink, he pulls a dozen eggs out of a sack and sets them gently on a shelf in the fridge.

"Are you sure that's where those go? I thought the eggs went over here."

"Over where?"

"Here, in the garbage disposal."

"Foh!" BJ gapes at Ayo, then at the eggs, then at the deadly, yawning mouth below the faucet. "That's not right, Yodel. Only garbage goes in there."

"I'm afraid you have a point. The fridge seems like a better place, after all, doesn't it?"

"I'd say."

"I'm sorry if I startled you, my friend." Ayo holds the milk up like a liquified white flag. "I was only joking, trying to have a little fun, you see, as a grown man."

BJ tugs his shirt and scratches his bald head. "If you wanted to have fun, why didn't you just say so?"

"Maybe," says Ayo, looking at me through the doorway, "I didn't know how."

"It's all right. I forgive you."

"Thanks again for your understanding and your help."

"Shucks, don't mention it."

Gradually, methodically, and one item at a time, they chip away at the bags. Ayo follows BJ's lead, waits for his guidance on where each new purchase goes: the milk beside the juice, the oatmeal with the cereal, the salsa by the ketchup, the apples in the bowl. BJ's a natural in the role, his voice rising and falling in singsong, as benevolent as it is managerial. He plops the soup on the counter and reveals its destination as the far cupboard. When Ayo unlocks the door and slides in the cans, BJ conveys his highest praises. Today, he says, the ground beef should go on the fridge's top shelf. That way we won't forget it for the cookout.

"Good idea. But what about this lunchmeat?"

"It goes right there with the cheese."

"Above or behind it?"

"Underneath it, if you please."

"The buns, the sauce, the hot dogs? Should we put these on the shelf?"

"Put the buns next to the bread and I will get those dogs myself."

"Looks like we're almost finished. All that's left is Cliff's Ensure, the stuff that's for the closet, and . . . BJ, I see that you're —"

"Don't worry, I've got this." He has the Charmin on his head. "These are going to the bathroom, but I wish I had a sled."

As BJ shambles down the hall, Ayo waves me into the kitchen. On the way, I accidentally bump the table, knocking Rickey's cookie from his tiny, nervous grasp. It lands on his plate and breaks in two. I moan an apology, but he just plucks the pieces up and hobbles off toward the living room, his lips parted in an enigmatic grin.

"Here, Cliff."

Ayo locks the refrigerator door and stands in front of it. At his eye level, secured to the freezer with a magnet that says KNOWLAND RESIDENTIAL, is a fistful of multicolored paper hearts. He takes it down and riffles through the shapes. My name, written in all caps in thick, black marker, looms large in the center of each one. Floating around the letters are scores of smaller hearts of varying colors and sizes, cut from construction paper and attached with Elmer's glue.

"These are what Francis was talking about? What Stella makes for you?"

"Eh."

"They sure are colorful." Ayo cuts them like a deck of playing cards. "It's very nice of her to put so much effort into these. She likes you a lot, I'm afraid. But you, Cliff — you don't reciprocate."

I purse my lips and shake my head.

"She's just not your type, eh?"

Not so much.

"As you say." He holds them out to me. "Here, take them."

Why?

"You'll see. Please. Give me your hand."

I reach out as far as I can. Ayo lays the stack down, then helps me ball my hand up, crumpling the paper like an invoice in my fist.

"I don't know a thing about Stella. She seems like a nice person, very loving. We need people like that in our lives. But it can be problematic, can't it, when we don't feel the same?"

To say the least.

"I understand. I feel for her, too. It's no fun, having a broken heart. But what matters to me is what matters to you — what you want, or don't. Please, follow me."

Stella's hearts bleeding in my hand, I go with him across the kitchen and stop where he does, at the trash. Ayo steps on the pedal that opens the lid. He'd replaced the liner before we left for groceries, so it's empty, mostly. As I gaze down into the abyss, down at my preference, it gazes back up, into me.

"In they go, Cliff," Ayo says. "If that's where you want them."

So it is. I hold them out over the void and squeeze through the sharp pain that soars up my arm like an arrow. Then, slowly, I unclench my fist, releasing the colored wad one finger at a time. Falling as one, the mangled hearts land at the void's bottom with an anticlimactic little *pfft*.

"That'll do it." Ayo slams the lid and sets the lock. "Anything else you'd like to throw away for now?"

Maybe there is, now that he's mentioned it. But for the time being, I just want to tell him thanks. This I do with a nod, which he misses. In the same moment, BJ returns from the hall, hands held high and counting time like the conductor of an opus.

FIVE

Francis's reflexes are more feline than human. When the front door opens without a knock, he says "Gotta go" to his girlfriend, closes the Zoom app, and shoves his phone back in his pocket before Brad has set foot in the foyer. He's not the first staff to do this — or to slide his laptop under the couch, or to wake from a nap at the faintest creak — but he is the first whose coverup skills approach perfection. If it weren't so aggravating, it'd be admirable. The one part of the job he still takes seriously is pretending he takes the job seriously.

"I hadn't thought about it that way, but you're right," he says as Brad walks in. "I appreciate your perspective, BJ. It's so unique."

In his recliner, BJ wakes and, seeing our house manager, wipes drool from his chin with his eagle shirt. "Good morning, O Cap'n, my Cap'n."

"Morning? It's almost 1700 hours, pal. It'll be dinnertime in just a few." Brad's laptop goes *clunk* on the carpet, and BJ nods and falls back asleep. "What's this perspective I was hearing about?"

Francis motions at the TV. "We were talking about that man's new grooming choices."

With the House voting on whether to strip Representative Horner of his committee assignments, Firth Bronzer has devoted the last ten minutes of airtime not to his use of the *r*-word — the reason for the vote — but to the congressman's brand-new neckbeard, which he debuted this afternoon on his slow walk into the Capitol. It's the first such facial hair worn by a sitting member in more than a century, Bronzer notes. He brings on two seasoned strategists from either party to parse out the beard's meaning. But each question leaves them only more divided. How will it play with Horner's base? What implications will it have for foreign policy? Most crucially, how do suburban white women feel about it? The debate grows heated quickly and culminates in one man whipping out a dagger and the other throwing on brass knuckles. Ever the peacemaker, Bronzer jumps between them and warns, his finger wagging, "If you two don't cool it, I'll have to leave it hair."

Francis laughs and slaps his knee. "'Leave it hair.' I love it. That's why we tune in every day."

"So, what was BJ's take?" Brad asks.

Francis is glued to the TV. "What was the what?"

"You know, about the neckbeard. What were BJ's thoughts? I'd ask him, but he looks so peaceful over there."

As BJ snores, slobber oozes from his chin to his stretched-out collar.

"Oh, right. What he said was, uh, that he'd like to grow one. Yeah, that's it. A great-big beard just like that man's. Can you imagine? Old BJ the lumberjack?" As Brad laughs, Francis rises and looks down on him. "But what are you doing here? Is there a problem?"

The flicker of resolve in Brad's gray eyes vanishes as soon as it appears. "Actually," he says, checking his watch, "I just dropped in to see how Ayo's doing."

"You can ask him when he's done." Francis plops down in his couch spot, next to Rickey. "He's giving Lem a shower at the moment."

Right on cue comes Ayo's voice, urgent and muffled. "Please, Lem, come back. We're not done yet."

The bathroom door swings open on its grating hinges. Clumsy, heavy footfalls echo down the hall. When Lem comes out the other side, he's running, in the nude, and dripping water everywhere. His penis is giant and erect, and his balls jerk every which way, like a little punching bag. He disappears into our room as Ayo bursts in with a bath towel on his shoulder.

"He just took off," he says, trying and failing to hide a smile.

Francis nods appreciatively. "When you're in the mood, you're in the mood."

"Ain't that the truth," Brad says. "He's not getting dressed until he's ready."

"By which point he'll need to be bathed again."

From our bedroom comes the metallic roar of Lem's old box springs.

"You can say that again." Brad sits on the floor. "I'm just grateful he does this only at home, unlike some other people I know."

"Teddy *Loftis,*" BJ growls groggily.

"Hey there, bud." Brad takes his glasses from their case and puts them on. Their foggy, scratched-up lenses reflect his laptop's screen twice over. "You finally awake?"

"Not that I wanted to be." BJ removes his own pair to better rub his eyes. "I can't get a wink of sleep around here with Lem going at it like that."

"Is it happening more often?"

"No more or less than usual," says Francis.

The box springs groan in Lem's familiar rhythm.

"Good. I was worried we might need to bring on a behaviorist."

"Speaking of which," Francis grins, "I think maybe it's time to have one meet with Cliff."

"Oh? What's going on with my Resident Cool Dude?"

"Well, you already know he crushed that binder."

Pulverized and paperless, it's still up on the shelf with Rickey's behavior log.

"I do. What else has he —"

"Today, he attacked me at the grocery."

"The death machine has struck again. This time in public!"

Brad whips his flat-topped head toward me. "Is this true, Cliff?"

I shrug.

"Don't lie to the Cap'n. You even smushed a box of Cocoa Krispies."

Brad's face goes grave, but I can't take it seriously, and not just because of the increasingly aggressive moaning from my bedroom.

"It could've been worse. He missed me by a mile. But the fact is, he could've hurt somebody." Francis fights a soulless smile. "I'd be lying if I said I'm not afraid for my own safety around here."

Brad frowns and types something. "Well, I'd be lying if I said that doesn't bother me. Any idea why he'd do this?"

"I have no clue," says Francis.

"No clue? Really?" Ayo twists Lem's towel in knots. "Are you sure you're not aware this never would've happened if you hadn't —"

The metal shrieking stops abruptly. Lem lets out a blissful grunt. The bedroom door swings open and he briefly reappears on his jog back to the bathroom with a gooey, ghostly crotch.

"Disgraceful," BJ says. "When's a man supposed to get a moment's peace?"

Brad's warm chuckle suggests he asks the same question every day. "Would you mind checking on the big guy, Ayo?"

Ayo nods and leaves without a word.

"Give him another shower while you're back there," Francis says.

Brad makes the face reserved for when he reads important emails, his forehead puckered and his mouth squinched up. Seeing this, Francis takes his phone back out and makes the face reserved for when he plays *Baby Jesus vs. the Unbelievers.* He showed it to me once. You're the little Lord incarnate, swinging a golden cross at angry hordes of atheists who use logic, facts, reason, and snark to try and disprove the existence of God. I'm not sure why he likes it so much. It's his only source of work-related stress. By the looks of it, the game is just as tense with the sound off as it is blaring from his speaker.

"Boy, I sure am getting hungry," BJ says. "What's for dinner, Francis?"

"Mm-hmm."

"I don't think I've had mm-hmm before. Is it like Hamburger Helper?"

"Mm."

"Sounds delicious. I hope it's ready soon. My tummy's growling like a Bandersnatch."

Brad looks up. Francis doesn't.

"A Bandersnatch, huh? If dinner's on, I don't smell it. Why don't you get something started, Francis?"

Francis hacks a limb from a zombiesque freethinker. "BJ, go pick something out. I'll be there shortly."

"Sure thing, boss," says BJ, tromping off to the kitchen.

Leaving it at that, Brad resumes his broody email reading. I'm trying to decide which is worse, his leadership abilities or Knowland's confidence in them, when an orchestral barrage erupts on the TV. The words BREAKING NEWS appear against a sea of red, which then parts to show Firth Bronzer, giddy as a tween with backstage Bieber passes. The Horner results have just come in: 218 for, 217 against removing him from his committees. A real nail-biter, it must've been, but it's one of those small victories worth relishing, especially now that Representative Vaught, who cast the deciding vote, has since claimed she was confused when she pressed YEA instead of NAY. In her defense, they're both three-letter words, and rhyme, to boot, making the decision that much more perplexing. But it's too late, Bronzer says with a chef's kiss. There are no mulligans once the tally has been certified. Horner shall sit no longer on the Education, Ethics, or Judiciary committees. He shall only be permitted to keep representing some five-hundred-thousand constituents in his small, Midwestern state until his term expires or he is voted out of office. "Yes, he may be down," Bronzer says, "but he's not out, and he's got a few choice words for his colleagues on both sides of the aisle."

The feed cuts to the steps outside the Capitol, where Horner seethes behind a lectern, surrounded by the press and a contingent of his most passionate supporters. I'd forgotten how grotesquely far apart his eyes are, how his face looks like it's carved from Roquefort cheese, how his hair is like a pewter dome topping the bloated, empty temple of his head. He bleats into the mic with all the bluster of a man who's been asked to leave a Little Caesar's for refusing to wear a mask.

"To be honest, folks," he says, his neckbeard holding up a mottled scowl, "this doesn't surprise me in the least. Fact is, deep down in my enlarged, ice-cold, just-begging-for-a-triple-bypass heart, I knew this day would come. I've spent my whole life without a filter, a lack I've weaponized to maximum effect over the years. I was never like the two-faced cowards in those chambers back behind me. I was the guy who told God's unvarnished truth with a wink and a dog whistle, and at times a little tip of my ten-gallon cowboy hat." Though he's not sporting any headgear, Horner reaches up to where the brim would be and mimes a gallant doff. "It didn't matter who you were, where you hailed from, or whether you were black, white, green, blue, or any of the other hues my staff have begged me not to say on live TV: you could always count on me to speak my mind." The press murmurs. The cameras flash. The crowd around him nods in furious agreement. Someone up front raises a placard adjuring the congressman in red and blue Crayola to

TELL IT LIKE IT IS

"Ain't that what I'm doing?" he says, pointing at the guy, then swinging at the air. "Ain't that all I know how to do? The way things used to be, it was an advantage. People liked the way I talked. They enjoyed all my unprompted, pie-eyed rants. Remember that time I said of Malala, and I quote, 'Hell, no, I wouldn't tap that, not even in a rubber'?" Not only does the throng remember. It wildly approves. The people cheer and punch each other in the mouths. Some of them do crotch chops. One man lifts his hands up to the heavens and begins to speak in tongues. The twelve-term representative exults with them, then his broad shoulders drop and his expression turns aggrieved. "But those days are long gone, folks. All the slurs and epithets you used to hurl like party favors are suddenly *verboten*." He asks if he can have a moment and wipes away a tear with his suit jacket's sleeve. "I swear to God, my friends: sometimes I think about what's happened to this country, and it makes me want to puke." The reporters *ooh*. His supporters boo. He pounds the lectern and says, "I just don't understand it. The world used to be much simpler. When I was growing up, and well into my adulthood, that little word I got in trouble for today was just another word. It wasn't good or bad. It had lots of different meanings. We didn't use it only for the kids who rode the little bus. My friends and I, it's what we called each other when we'd make a bonehead move. It's also what we called the stuff we thought was dumb, like doing homework or recycling. That's why I used it to describe the distinguished gentleman from Texas" — he means Rep. Ploughman, with whom he'd debated border security on the House floor — "after he admitted he didn't 'get' how blanketing the Sonoran Desert in Micro Machines would put an end to our immigration problem." He glowers at two giggling journalists. "Yuk it up, you little shits, but it stopped the two bad hombres in *Home Alone*. What makes you think it wouldn't stop two million in real life? Think about it." Nobody seems to. "How can an illegal make it all the way across the desert if he's constantly tripping over little army tanks? Answer: he can't! My plan's success is just a matter of numbers and logistics, which begs the question: what do you call someone who doesn't grasp its genius? There are a million words in our language, friends, but only one suffices." He looks right into the camera, right at me from five-hundred miles away, and then he says it, the full word, slowly, deliberately, prolonging its two vowels with folksy fervor, his cheeks all puffed-out like an overweening blowfish. The two journalists stop giggling and gasp. Most of his supporters elevate their lighted Bics and close their eyes, as if in supplication for an encore.

"You heard that right. I said it again, this time on live TV." A few women toss their underwear toward the lectern, and soon the whole crowd follows suit, draping the congressman in layers of threadbare Hanes and Always panties. "I've got no qualms about repeating it a thousand times if that's what it'll take to win this battle — because make no mistake, folks, that's what it is. A war. A fight unto the death for our most fundamental freedoms. My opponents, these little Pol Pot cosplayers who want to silence me — you think they'll stop with my committees? Hell, no, they won't. My committees are only what they've stripped from me today. Tomorrow, it'll be the leather chair I stole from Ploughman's office. Friday, it'll be my right to reheat fish in the work microwave. What about the day after that? And after that? Where does it end? When does it end? You all know as well as I: it only ends when they're satisfied, when they've drained the last drop of liberty that flows through our veins like mercury through the tuna I nuked for lunch. So if it means standing up to them for both my independence and yours, then yes, I'll say that word again. But first I'd like to speak directly to those trying to suffocate our freedoms with the hospital pillow of common decency." The raving laundry pile leans hard into the mic, from which hangs a leopard-printed bra and thong set. "You'll never make a fool of me," it promises, staggering and stomping on the steps like the amalgamation of every child's worst nightmare. "Just because your pressure tactics stifle some of us doesn't mean they'll have the same effect on Tommy Horner. Let me put that in plain English: you're tangling with the wrong son of a bitch. I won't roll over or back down, and if I go down, it'll be swinging. I'll fight you back, I'll fight you hard, and you can bet your tactful ass I'll fight you to the bitter end." Slipping off his softcore shroud, Horner sends the undies flying every which way. Some land on the lectern, others on the marble steps behind it, and still more light upon the heads of his admirers, many of whom, now naked from the waist down, put on these precious windfalls and wear them like their own.

"Let me be clear," the congressman says into the bra and thong set. "The people who took offense at what I said, they aren't the ones who have what I've been told are now called 'disabilities.' I've got nothing against those folks, the true" *r*-words, he says. "Why should I? They've never done me any harm, if you don't count Reggie Bibbit, who once stole my Oatmeal Creme Pie during lunch in sixth grade. Holy smokes, that got my goat. Socked him real good for it, too." But all the other *r*-words, he says, "have been spared my righteous wrath. They're not watching this at home, stewing in their skid-marked SpongeBob sweats. They've got better things to do. Last I checked, their turds won't throw themselves. So, no, I've no ill will against the folks with 'disabilities.' It's the ultra-woke kale munchers who claim to speak on their behalf I've got a problem with. You know who I mean. Those anal-retentive buzzkills whose Twitter bios read like itemized nut-allergy lists. Get a grip, dinks. Nobody cares if you can't eat pecans." He struts and frets across the Capitol steps, doing that thing where you clasp your hands above your head and shake them, first on one side, then the other. "They're the ones who have it coming, and it's time we give it to them, loud and clear.

What do you say, my friends? Who's with me?"

After a wave of exaltation that sees its members either dancing, fainting, or kneeing their neighbors in the stomach, the crowd pulls itself together and unites behind a single purpose: to tell its mortal enemies what's what. Following Horner's lead, they all turn toward the camera — toward me — and break out in their one-word chant, emphasizing its long e, grinning like the people in those old photos of town lynchings. Behind them stands the legislator, his smile broader than the rest, ignoring the reporters' shouted questions as he punches left and right with each of the word's syllables.

"There you have it," says Firth Bronzer, rubbing his hardened nipples through his suit jacket. "Representative Tommy Horner defends his right to 'tell it like it is,' standing defiant in the aftermath —"

I peel my hand from the armrest — I've been gripping it so tightly it's stuck — and wheel around. Francis is laughing the same way he did at the grocery, with just his eyes. He slaps his knee, then Rickey's, then winks at me and says:

"How about that, Cliff?"

But the urge doesn't hit me until I turn to Brad, who, still reading emails, has missed everything. His laptop's so bulky that it catches on my footrest and travels with me through the room, leaving its owner in the dust as it clonks against the side table and flips vertically. My wheels spin until its plastic casing cracks, its hinges bend, its metal insides fizzle and die like a romance on reality TV.

"What the hell is this?" says Brad, rolled over on his stomach with his hands behind his head.

What do you think? I reverse. The computer topples backward, landing on the carpet with an airy smack. Francis hops up and views the wreckage, clicking his tongue against his teeth.

"What the hell is right," he says and slides past Rickey, who's staring at the back of his hand like a man reaching the apex of an acid trip. "That poor laptop is —"

"A goner," BJ cries, rushing back in from the kitchen in a chef's hat. He scoops the device up, and, moaning softly, hugs it like the body of a dead, beloved pet.

Brad's face foams with stifled fury. "What the hell is wrong with you?" He almost grabs my joystick hand but thinks better of it. "What makes you think this is okay? Smashing the binder's one thing, but going after people and their laptops? That's not cool at all, dude. I'm of a mind to get John on the phone himself and see what he thinks about —"

The hallway echoes with Lem's stomping and soon he's standing there again, but fully clothed. Fists above his head like he's been doing deadlifts, he lopes off to our room and slams the door behind him.

"What did I miss?" Ayo says, the now-wet towel slung over his should-der. "Oh, no. What happened here?"

"Whaddya think, Yodel? The death machine has struck again!"

"Cliff? You are responsible?" As he crouches by my side, my face heats up. "Why would you do this?"

"That's the million-dollar question," Brad pants. "I was busy over here. You guys notice anything beforehand?"

"Not I." Francis flaunts that silent smile. "I was writing contact notes. Did you see what happened, Super Rick?"

"Wanna cookie."

"You didn't even eat the one you had for snack."

"I was getting dinner ready," BJ says, hand to hat. "I didn't hear a thing except the news."

Francis picks up where he left off on *Baby Jesus*. "Then it seems this little outburst came from nowhere. As I said, it might be time for Cliff to see a behaviorist."

"You can say that again." BJ stresses his words with a left uppercut.

"I think you're right. Let me see if I can get someone on the horn."

Ayo stands up to his supervisor. "If I may, I didn't finish what I was saying earlier —"

But Brad's already left the room, his phone at one ear and a finger in the other, barking orders like a general on the eve of battle.

SIX

K nowland's office is on the edge of Tired Oaks' burgeoning brunch district. For decades, most of Central Street's old buildings had stood vacant and abandoned. But one morning, that all changed. Their brick facades had been washed, their windows cleaned, they'd been given names like Fly by Night and Axe to Grind, and they began to smell like breakfast, attracting hipsters like moths to a flambé. When Francis swings the van's door open, I get a whiff of pancakes, avocado, and something Brad once called "craft beer-scented beard balm" so strong it nearly knocks me out.

Francis hops in from the back, unbuckles me, and grabs the lift's remote. "Out we go," he says, and hits the button, lowering me to the asphalt.

He hasn't told me why we're here. He hasn't needed to. But this doesn't mean I have to make it easy for him, either. I putter off and drift into the parking lot, a loose balloon without a string. He raises the lift, locks the van, and takes the ramp up to the entrance.

"Let's go, Cliff. We're going to be late for your appointment."

He punches the metal plate with the guy in the wheelchair on it. I sputter forward, stop, reverse, then move toward him again, and reverse. The door closes on its own. Francis hits the plate a second time and rolls his eyes.

"Step on the gas, will you? We both know you can go much —"

I burn rubber to the ramp, but as I ascend, I slow down, inching ahead at Rickey's pace, mean-mugging him all the while. Halfway up, I reverse. Francis facepalms as I coast to the walk, then climb the ramp, then descend, then go up again, and descend, my face as solemn as my muscles will allow.

"Are you drunk?"

He knows I'm not, but not that I have been before. It's a story you won't find in my file, one of the many that will die with me. It only happened once — that I remember — on an especially slow night at Sinai Grove. One of the staff brought in a fifth of vodka. After pounding most of the bottle, he and his colleague splashed a little down my tube. I'm not sure how or whether they'd calculated the amount. It was enough to get me tipsy, but not enough to make me vomit. If it had, it would've spelled the end of their careers in the human services field. The whole thing lasted about an hour. I remember feeling strange at first, as if I were floating halfway between Heaven and Hell. This soon gave way to giddiness, then a sense of liberation. Instead of making me a buffoon of even greater magnitude, as they'd hoped, my drunkenness shielded me from their laughter. It couldn't have done much else. Pissing where I sat was nothing new, I had no words to slur, and stumbling to the floor wasn't an issue. As my own broken laughter joined and then trounced theirs, the two men slowly realized they'd handed total control of the situation to someone who had no other way of fighting back. It must've come as the bitterest of insults. I can think of no other reason why they never did it again.

If only.

"I'll push you if I must," Francis says, slapping the plate a third time.

I've gone crooked on the ramp. My chair's back strikes the handrail with a thick, plastic *pronk.* My head recoils against its rest and my arms shoot up in involuntary surrender. Francis moves in behind me, but I lay on the joystick, correct myself, and blast forward through the door just as it's closing.

"What has gotten into you?" he says, following me inside.

As usual, Christine's at the reception desk, drinking coffee from a mug that says YOU'VE GOT TO BE CRAZY TO WORK HERE, BUT IT'S SURE WORTH IT.

"Fancy seeing you here, Cliff. Where's the rest of the brigade?"

"Gone to day program." Francis signs us in on the visitor's log. "Cliff has the morning off. He's come to see Mr. Greg."

"Greg just got in. He should be in his office. Last one in the back hallway." Christine sips her coffee like a bird drinking from its bath. "He didn't say he was expecting anyone."

"Probably he's keeping it on the downlow."

Christine nods. "On the hush-hush."

"That's right. Cliff and I are on a top-secret mission."

"Then I'll keep it just between us," Christine says, closing an imaginary zipper across her lips.

I wave and whiz off around the corner. In the first room down the hall, another basic orientation for staff is underway. One of the other house managers is teaching CPR via roleplay, and just for kicks, I guess, he's laying into a new recruit for declaring the scene safe when it wasn't.

"But I checked twice," the trainee says timidly. "I didn't see any dangers."

"Sure, there were no dangers, except the truck that came from nowhere and jumped the curb, so here you and Lloyd are, lying dead on the sidewalk, your bones crushed by a Ford F-150. Congratulations, New Guy, on a job well done." The house manager pauses, then adds, "Not!"

Lloyd's the practice dummy they use for these things.

"You didn't say anything about an F-150."

"And I won't be there to point it out when you and a real Lloyd are on a stroll three weeks from —"

The nurse's office is next. I wait for Everett's staff to guide him out. When I brake, my wheels squeal, and Angie looks up from her clipboard.

"How's it going, Cliff?" she says, lowering her browline glasses down her wrinkled nose. They're new and go well with the white that she wears all year round. "What a nice surprise. I didn't think I saw you till next week."

Francis creeps in and grabs my wheelchair from behind. "We're here for something else. Probably he's stopping by to say hello."

"No shit?" Angie says.

This is why I like her. She's too young to retire and too old to care about pretense, meaning she's one of the few who work here with the balls to speak from the heart. She's not afraid to challenge anyone, not even Mr. Knowland or — and crucially — herself. I don't mind taking health advice from someone who chain smokes and mainlines coffee because Angie would be the first to tell you that, like Charles Barkley, she doesn't want to be your role model. But my favorite thing about her is her ability to get under Brad's skin like a splinter. It never gets old, his hangdog reaction when she calls him Colonel Flattop to his face. He's tried to stop her, going so far as to file a complaint with Knowland himself. Alas, it's hard for residential agencies to land good nurses for the pay they offer — Angie's told me as much — so they've got no choice but to keep her on the books. It's basically the same reason they don't fire staff like Francis, except in Angie's case it has my full support.

"That's right," Francis says. "We're on our way to Greg's office."

"Oh?" She drops her pen and shoves the clipboard aside. "I wasn't aware there was a behavioral problem."

"There have been some unfortunate developments. Don't worry, though. It doesn't concern you. As far as Cliff's health goes, he's in perfect, tip-top shape."

"Tell me something I don't know," she says. "Well, whatever the issue is, I'm sure Greg will take good care of it."

"Of that I'm certain. Let's go, Cliff. We're already late as it is."

Before I go, I appeal for Angie's intervention with my eyes. She sighs and looks away. There's nothing she can do, and we both know it.

"I'm glad you're so confident of Greg's abilities." Angie stands and grabs her purse, takes out a lighter and her cigarettes. "Just like you'll be glad to hear, Cliff, that I'm confident of your ability to be yourself, no matter what."

On her way out, she squeezes my shoulder. I whirl to her and wave. *I hope to hell you're right.*

☽

Down the back hallway, I slog past Gil the finance guy and Linda from HR, both too busy to chat, which is all right with me. The next few doors are closed. From behind them drift the voices of house managers on their phones, begging staff to fill their open shifts.

"You're only a speed demon when you want to be," Francis says, sliding in front of me.

He stops at the entrance of the room at the far end. Inside, the lights are off. Two slabs of plastic laminate project outward from one wall, forming what passes in these shared offices for desks. Only John Knowland, the department directors, and Angie — because she wouldn't take no for an answer — get a whole room to themselves. At the slab closest to the window sits a man I've seen around sometimes at company events. He's my age, maybe a little older, and has his hair spiked in the manner of boy bands from the late nineties. Except for the white rings around his eyes, his skin's the color of expired apple cider. His cologne's a toxic combination of pine sap and jackal scat. He's the kind of guy who shakes your hand too hard and says things like, "It's a date, then," and "How ya doin', champ?" In khakis and a turquoise button-up embroidered with peacocks in full plumage, he has his feet up on the desk beside his laptop. On it, a giant baked potato between two earphone cushions holds forth against the tyranny of seatbelts.

Francis knocks on the doorframe, holding his nose. "Mr. Greg?"

The guy jolts up, slams shut the laptop. "Who wants to — oh, hey, Francis. Good to see you. It's been a minute."

"It has. How's that grouch Ed Vernon doing?"

Francis worked with Ed before he started at our place.

"Actually, Ed's not my client anymore." The tanned man fiddles with a stack of Post-it Notes. "Turns out he and I just aren't the best fit."

"I'm sorry to hear that, though I can't say I'm surprised. Turns out Ed might not be the best fit for anyone."

"Well, hopefully his new behaviorist's a better one, at least. That guy needs all the help he can get."

"I know someone else who needs all the help he can get."

"Oh yeah? Who's that?"

Francis hikes his thumb at me. "Mr. Emerson back there. We had a meeting set for ten?"

"Right." Greg checks his watch. "Oh, right. Hey, Cliff." He flashes me a soapy smile, exposing teeth almost too perfect to be real. "How ya doin', champ?"

"He'd like to apologize for being late." Francis waves me inside. I stay put, my eyes watering enough to drown hydrangeas. "He's been a stubborn one this morning. Probably he got up on the wrong side of the bed."

"Don't sweat it. Hell, I was late to my own wed—"

The cell phone on Greg's desk wails like a fire horn. Francis reaches for his ears. Frowning, Greg sends the call to voicemail, then motions at the other chair, where Francis takes a seat with some reluctance.

"Brad said he spoke to you about it." Francis fights tears, too, and gestures at the window. "Would you mind cracking that?"

"You guys are hot already? I keep telling John the A/C needs looking at." Greg cranks his window open. It looks out on the spot where the Red Branch Library had stood for ninety years until it closed a couple months ago for lack of funding. One afternoon in spring, a crew arrived and razed the building. They're out there now, hammering away at the future site of Bells & Whistles, the district's third new brunch place in as many months.

"Cliff and I are both obliged."

In the same way a broken clock is right twice a day, Francis has rare moments when he can't help but tell the truth.

"You bet." Greg swings his feet up onto one of his clients' plans. "I spoke to Brad, but he didn't get specific. Honestly, he was so mad, I could barely understand him. Between us, it sounded like the president had just closed his LEGO Gitmo base."

"Please, what does that mean?"

"He's never told you?"

"Not about that."

He's never told me, either.

"Then I've said too much already. If you really want to know, you'd better ask him yourself. You didn't hear anything from me, though."

"I'd rather not."

I would if I could.

"Perfect. You sure you don't want to come in here, Cliff?"

Not even when the smell of his cologne dissipates. I send him a look I hope tells him as much.

"He will, eventually. He might still be confused about why we're here."

"Join the club, hey? But seriously, folks. Let's talk about that. Sometimes, in addition to their primary diagnoses — intellectual disability, say, or in your case, Cliff, CP — the people we serve experience certain, let's say, challenges that prevent full integration into their communities. These range from the very simple, such as anxiety in large groups, to the more complicated — think physical aggression or trichotillomania — and can last a lifetime or for just a couple weeks . . ."

Greg keeps going but doesn't tell me anything I don't already know. Besides, his button-up's embroidered peacocks are making it even harder for me to take him any more seriously than Brad. As for the birds, they're not identical. Some have red feathers, others blue. Some call for mates while others pose aggressively, their wings spread as if in flight. But the objects of their anger and desire aren't depicted. Fucking or fighting, these birds are chasing phantoms. If there's a deeper meaning to this, it's better left for Greg to sort it out himself.

"The good news," he says, "is that when you hit these rough patches, there are guys like me to help you through them."

Then he flashes me a grin so oily you could fry potatoes on it.

"That's what I like to hear." Francis gives the slab an eager slap. "Our friend is truly going through a rough patch. It's strange. Before, Cliff rarely had behaviors. Then, suddenly, they started happening almost every day. Since he can't speak like most of us" — at this, the faintest smile flutters on his lips — "we're really at a loss to know what's going on, much less what to do about it. But at this rate, it's only a matter of time before this man hurts somebody."

"Mm. These new behaviors — what do they look like?" Greg grabs his phone, taps, then pulls the same face Francis makes while playing *Baby Jesus vs. the Unbelievers*. "Go ahead. I'm listening."

Francis whips out his own device, launches the same game, and rattles off my recent sins, from the binder to Brad's laptop to my failed attack on him in public. Embellishing my fury with Homeric artistry — "Cliff unleashed a hellish howl that sent poor BJ cowering behind his Cap'n Crunch cuirass" might be my favorite — he totally omits his part in birthing it. "I feared for my life as I never had before. I've worked with many clients who can be belligerent. I witnessed war and death when I was young in my own country. But never have I seen such rage as was in Cliff's eyes yesterday. It was like staring down the very Devil in the oatmeal aisle."

"Sweet Baby Jesus." Whether this is directed at Francis or the zombie game remains unclear.

"Luckily, no one was hurt, not even Cliff, after the dust had settled. I wish I could say the same for the Cocoa Krispies."

They both pause their battles, bow their heads, and hold a brief moment of silence for a box of cereal.

"I've been working with behavioral issues for almost twenty years. You know this, Francis. I've seen foul misdeeds that run the gamut: physical aggression, self-harm, property destruction, public masturbation, the commission of lewd acts in an IHOP, if you can believe it —"

"I believe it."

"I even had a guy shove an entire straightened paperclip up his urethra once." We all wince and go *Eugh* at the same time. "Sorry about that," Greg says, not really sounding like it. "I only bring it up because I thought I'd seen it all. But running over an old laptop like a possum on the highway is one that's never crossed my desk before. I'm not saying it's right, Cliff, but it's original, I'll give you that." It's not me so much as my chair that Greg looks up and down. "Necessity really is the mother of invention," he snorts.

"Maybe, but Cliff has had that chair for some time now. He's never used it to attack a man before, at least not at this frequency."

"Interesting," Greg yawns. "Have you noticed anything else out of the ordinary? Is he acting out in other ways?"

"Not that I've seen. It's not like he can do much of anything else. But as I say, he was a stubborn one getting here this morning."

Greg curses under his breath. "Give me just a sec." He taps his phone harder, his tongue oozing from his mouth like a tentacle from a monster den. The Christ Child's love for mankind may be infinite, but not his hit points. "Balls." He puts the phone down and his tongue back where it belongs. "Anyway, I know Brad's still mad about that laptop, but the fact is, it's just stuff. There's a huge difference between breaking stuff and breaking people. We can always get more stuff. Brad's probably already found a new computer. People, on the other hand, are living, breathing creatures and aren't so easily replaced."

"That's what I've been trying to tell Cliff. Staff don't grow on trees. It's hard enough for companies like this one to find them. If the clients kill the few good staff they do have, they'll have no one left to help them out."

"Seriously. Talk about biting the hand that feeds you."

"Or crushing the hand that wipes you," Francis smirks.

Greg silences the fire horn almost as soon as it goes off again. "Let me ask you this. You were present at each of these incidents. What happened leading up to them? Did you notice anything different, anything that might've provoked Cliff or rubbed him the wrong way?"

"No, nothing." Francis spins to face me, his smile tripling in size. "Cliff was receiving the same level of quality care as always."

"There've been no abrupt or unplanned changes to the routine?"

"Nothing of the sort. We stick closely to the schedule Brad created for the guys. Memory Makers and grocery shopping keep them busy through the week. If there's a company event, like tomorrow's cookout, we might go to it for a while. But I think they mostly like to relax at home in front of the TV."

I let out a tiny Ensure fart.

"In front of the TV — that's where Cliff had two of his behaviors?"

"Mm-hmm."

"Do you remember what they were watching at the time?"

Instinctively, Francis soars to his feet, flaring both his shoulders and his nostrils. He lifts his chin. He thumps his chest. He looks down on Greg from his full height and says, "What difference does that make?"

"Holy smokes. Easy there, compadre. I didn't mean to pry. I was really just more curious than anything."

"What for?"

"How am I supposed to help Cliff if I don't know anything about him?"

Slowly, Francis sinks back to his seat. "Right. I understand. Sorry about that. It's just that I'm very protective of these guys. I'm not used to giving the private details of their lives to just anybody."

Pushing hard, I break more wind, but it drifts out through the window without their noticing.

"No need to apologize. I get it, and I'm glad you're there for them. A lot of our folks have no one but their staff in their lives, nobody else to advocate on their behalf. But you don't need me to tell you that."

"No, I don't, but you're right. People like Cliff, especially, need someone to speak up for them. They can't do it on their own." Francis turns around, winks, and pats me on the head. "We were watching the news both times he had behaviors. Firth Bronzer and the show that runs before him, where the bald gentlemen yell at each other for an hour. I can't remember what it's called —"

"*Mass Debating,*" says Greg. "One of my favorites."

"Yes, that's the one. Lem enjoys it the most, maybe even more than I, but the other guys do too, even Cliff. If we go a few days without it, I've found we get all tense and agitated."

"Same here." Greg looks past me, through the doorway, then leans closer to Francis, one elbow resting on the slab, and whispers his next words. "The world's a big, chaotic, infuriating place, and most people — let's be honest — can just plain suck it. But *Mass Debating* makes everything more bearable. Sure, it's just a couple jerks going at it long and hard until something explodes, but when it's over, I feel so unburdened. I don't know how. I don't know why. It's sometimes difficult and always messy. But *Mass Debating* is like a safety valve for urges that if released in other ways would do a lot more harm than good." His right eye twinkles, then his left. "But then there's always that weird guilt that comes afterward, like you're drenched in a great filth that won't ever wash away. *Never again,* you swear, and mean it with the fullness of your heart — until it happens again, and again, and again. Yes, never again: the one promise you've broken so many times you've lost count."

"Yeah, no," Francis cringes. "We just like to watch those mofos tussle."

"But that's exactly it. That's the part that reels you back in, keeps you glued to your chair, your hand squeezing the remote like a —"

"Let's move on."

"If you insist."

"I do." Francis takes a box of toothpicks from his pocket and shoves one between his teeth. "So, what's your advice for Cliff? What can we do to get him back to normal?"

"I wish I knew," says Greg, blowing a raspberry from his mouth and the grin from Francis's.

"I don't understand. I thought we came here for your help."

"You did. And I'm giving it. But bringing someone like me on board is a whole process. These things take time if they're to prove effective."

"We've been sitting here for almost half an hour."

"Yes, but think about it. You've seen behavior plans before —"

"Super Rick has one."

Greg processes the name. "Mr. Wanna Pop?"

"The very same."

"Whew. That guy is something else."

"That guy is my favorite."

"Anyway," Greg says, "you know the deal. Plans like his aren't English 101 papers. They're not written overnight. They've got to be accurate and comprehensive, both in terms of the client's history and their present situation. They have to offer strategic alternatives to the current set of behaviors, much like I rely on *Mass Debating* instead of, well, you know —"

"We've moved on —"

"The point remains. A good plan requires all these things and more, not least of which is the correct formatting, including Knowland's logo centered at the top of the first page. Which would you prefer, Francis: a plan today that just exacerbates the situation, or one a month from now that's a whole world more helpful in the long run?"

"Fine. I get it. A good plan can't be rushed. But I hope you can see things from my point of view. As I've said, I'm worried both for Cliff's safety and everyone else's. Something very bad could happen if he doesn't change his tune." He shoots me a worried look. "Is there anything we can do for him in the meantime? Any meds you can prescribe to calm him down?"

"If only it were that easy, but in most cases, that's not the way things work anymore." Greg's tanned face goes all nostalgic. "We can look at adding medications, but that, too, will be a process. We'd have to go through the proper channels, see a psych, and get them approved by Knowland's human rights committee. Not to say we can't do this — at this point, all options are on the table — but it'll be at least a couple weeks before I can give you anything concrete. That said, you should know that Cliff's case might be more difficult than most."

"Why is that?"

"Look, you said it yourself. Nothing seemed out of the ordinary leading up to these recent incidents. You're providing the same level of care as always, supporting Cliff and the guys to follow their routines. If something else is going on — say, he's trying to tell us something through his aggression, which, who knows, he very well might be — it's not like we can just pick up on it like we might with someone who uses spoken, or less violently nonverbal, language. Have you ever —" Greg directs this at me, then thinks better of it and turns back to Francis. "Do you know if he's ever used a comm board?"

"A what?"

"A communication board. An alternative to regular speech or writing. It could be something as simple as a piece of laminated paper with letters he could point to."

"No, not since I've been working with him. Brad said they tried it once, but Cliff's little hand, it jerked too much this way and that. He couldn't keep it pointed at one letter long enough for Brad to figure out the message."

A broken clock is right twice a day. Brad once taped a sheet of paper full of letters to my tray. "Go on, then," he said, nodding at it. "Tell me something. Anything." The message he received was *MPYA LQ,* instead of what I'd intended, which was *BITE ME,* and that was the end of that.

"Fair enough." Greg whistles disappointedly. "Guess I've got my work cut out for me."

"So, what happens next?"

"What happens next," says Greg, stuffing his laptop in a bag, "is I head down the street and get some hot wings in my belly."

"I mean with him."

"Right." Greg throws on a pair of sunglasses, then a fedora. "You two will be up here tomorrow, won't you? For the cookout?"

"I didn't think we had a choice."

"I'm pretty sure you don't."

"Then we'll be here, I guess."

"Great. I'll start meeting with Cliff tomorrow. We'll have sessions once a week. I'll visit at home, mostly, but I might also make some trips up to the day program. And oh, the most important thing: I'll need to speak with the other staff who work with him, residential in particular."

"That won't be necessary. Aside from Brad, I've worked with Cliff the longest. I know him better than all the other staff combined."

"I'm sure you do. But you're not with him all the time, so —"
"So?"

"So, maybe they've noticed things you haven't. Things that only happen on overnights, say, or when you're in the kitchen making dinner."

"I have BJ do that," Francis says, forcing me deeper into the hall. "But I understand. Before you act, you need to see the whole picture."

"Exactly. We'd prefer not to do more harm than good."

"We certainly would prefer that."

As Greg throws his bag around his shoulder, Francis stands above him in the doorway. "Come to think of it," he says, "there has been a change to Cliff's routine you should probably know about."

"I'm listening."

"Last month, the guys got locked in the van for a whole hour at the —"

"Tomlinson Square Mall. I know. It was all over the news. God, the things some people think they can do to our most vulnerable." Greg checks his watch again. "Still, no one was hurt, I gather."

"Angie checked them all out. Fortunately, no one suffered any medical problems as a result of Paul's gross negligence."

"If I remember right, the staff was fired, and John went out to the home and apologized in person."

"He did. It was a most kindhearted gesture."

"I'd expect nothing less from him." Greg grins, his teeth glinting like mirages in a desert. "So how's that still an issue? Sounds like John did everything he could to make things right."

"It's not an issue anymore. Cliff's behaviors only worsened last week, when Paul's replacement started working in the home."

"Well, it's pretty common for our folks to test the boundaries with new staff, to try and see what they can get away with. I have one guy who likes to tell newcomers he's supposed to have McDonald's for every meal. I doubt you'll be surprised to learn they sometimes take him at his word until I set them straight. If something similar is going on with Cliff, it's probably just a matter of making sure the new guy knows where to draw the line and how to hold it."

"I don't think that's what it is."

Greg backs up and bumps against the desk. "Why?"

"Never mind. It's probably nothing. Thanks for your time, Mr. —"

"Tell me."

"Sorry?"

"When we're dealing with behaviors, no detail is too small. Anything can trigger them — the slightest look, a change in seasons, a favorite jacket that doesn't fit the way it used to. Hell, this old fedora's been the cause of at least twelve violent outbursts." Greg removes it from his head and wonders why. "The point is, you need to look out for the little things if you expect to help this guy in any meaningful way. If you've noticed something different, no matter how insignificant it may seem to you, it's best to let me know."

"If it seems I'm being cagey, I apologize. The truth is, I don't want to badmouth my coworkers, especially if they're still learning how to do their jobs. Who knows? Maybe it really is nothing. It's also nice to have someone else on shift with me, seeing as how these gentlemen can be, well, you know . . ."

"A handful."

"Yes, that's it. A handful. So, I hope you understand why I might be reluctant to discuss the way the new staff has been handling things."

"Absolutely. Conflict is hard, and nobody wants to feel like they're getting their colleagues in trouble. But you should know that you can tell me anything without fear of backlash or reprisal. Since Cliff can't speak for himself, it's up to you to be his advocate. That's why we pay you, at least. We'll have him feeling better much more quickly if we address this problem head-on and from the get-go. But I also understand if you need to take some time to think it over, so feel free —"

"I believe Ayo's approach to Cliff is rather unorthodox."

Greg lowers the sunglasses down his nose. "Ayo. That's the new staff?"

Francis nods.

"Interesting name. Don't think I've met him. His approach — in what way is it unorthodox?"

"It mostly has to do with the routines we've established. He seems to think things need to change. He doesn't understand that we do things a certain way for the guys' own good, to provide them with consistency and a healthy environment where they can achieve their goals. It's like he's trying to shake things up on purpose. I'd rather not guess at his motivations. You'd have to ask him about those yourself. But from my perspective, probably it makes him feel a little powerful. It's for that reason I'm afraid he might even try to help Cliff cross those lines you spoke of earlier."

The smile Francis cracks at me is small and says, *I dare you.*

"Wow." Greg writes something down on a Post-it. "That's great information. You've given me a lot to think about. We'll plan on once a week starting tomorrow, Cliff, and Francis, you've got my number if anything comes up in the meantime."

"Definitely. Thanks again for your help. I look forward to working with you and making Cliff feel so much better."

"That's what it's all about," Greg says. His fire horn goes off again, and this time he just lets it blast away.

SEVEN

O n the west side of the office lies the grassy space the company uses for events, whether or not weather permits. It's large enough to accommodate a couple hundred, but I'd say there are maybe eighty of us, all told, seated around its plastic tables with Old Glory flags in little pots for centerpieces. Every year, I recognize fewer and fewer faces. There's always a whole new crop of staff, but Knowland's also pushing hard for growth, so there are as many clients here I don't know as I do. Most of them are younger, male, and have their T-shirts smartly tucked into their drawstring shorts and their ears buried under noise-canceling headphones. Loud sounds might bedevil them, but the heat certainly doesn't. At a quarter past six, it's still in the high eighties. Manning the grills, Brad, Knowland, and Gil the finance guy take frequent breaks to wipe their brows with towels that say WATCH OUT! COOKY'S COOKIN'. They must not have found the time to change out of their khakis into something more appropriate. I'd be feeling a lot worse myself if Ayo hadn't thought to dress me in my shorts.

"Come get it while it's hot," Knowland says into a bright-red bullhorn. "And believe me, folks, it's hot."

The three of us in wheelchairs — Ed Vernon, Willa Maple, and I — are parked on the walk near the building, a perfect spot to take in the dueling smells of roasting meat and bug repellent. Knowland banned our chairs from the grass last Easter after Ed chased the guy who wore the bunny costume into traffic. His wheels tore clumps in zigzags around the lawn, whose rehabilitation took a month and nearly four grand from the company's rainy-day fund. Ezra Hinds, the house manager Knowland had forced into the role, gave his resignation from the safety of a tree without yet having taken off the bunny suit.

"Keep your pants on, Jean-Bertrand," Ed says, thrusting a burly, arthritic finger at his staff. "It won't happen again. Besides, the Easter Bunny isn't here, in any case."

Jean-Bertrand brushes something from his multicolored cotton shirt. "I realize that, my friend. I'm just reminding you in case you see a real-life rabbit and feel the urge to strike."

"And I assure you that won't be a problem as long as real life-rabbits refrain from poking me in the chest and telling me to smile."

"Very well. All I wanted was to make sure we're on the same page."

"Oh, I think we are. See? I've even got the page right here."

Ed reaches into his pocket, pulls out his middle finger, and slowly lifts it up to Jean-Bertrand.

I only see Ed at bigger gatherings like this, and I wish it were more often. I don't know why, and he'll never know it, but his obscene gestures and his furious, wrinkled face make these outings more tolerable. He tried out Memory Makers once but lost his cool during a cutthroat game of Uno. After Blake's attempts to calm him with his PBS Kids voice led to the contents of Ed's lunch box being volleyed at his head, Laura asked that Ed be taken home and not come back. I took it much harder than he did.

"Enough of this," says Jean-Bertrand. "Are you hungry? I'll go make us both some plates."

"Of course I'm hungry, chucklenuts. Why else would I be here?"

"What would you like? Pork chops? A hot dog?"

"A good, old-fashioned cheeseburger will do. Extra tomatoes and onions, hold the mayonnaise and —"

"And the lettuce. I know, I know."

"Then why'd you ask?" Ed says.

But Jean-Bertrand is done with this discussion. "The things we have to put up with sometimes, eh?" he says to Ayo.

"What about the things we have to put up with?" Ed says as his staff leaves for the grills. "Get a load of this. Last week I asked that man as politely as I could if he'd mind stopping by the grocery for some shells and cheese, the kind my doctor's always telling me to cut back on before I tell him where he can shove it. As simple a request as any, or so you'd think. But guess what he came back with?" He makes a face like he's found poop that wasn't flushed. "A box of that organic hippie shit. I wouldn't touch that stuff with the mouth of my worst enemy, who, by the way, is Jean-Bertrand himself."

"Nice to meet you, too," Ayo says.

"I don't know about that."

"Fair enough." Ayo pats the cooler in his lap. "What about you, Cliff? You ready for dinner, too?"

I'm good just watching for now.

All day, BJ's been reminding us of what he plans to eat: half a pork chop, half a hot dog, a small bag of Lay's, and one cup of Diet Coke. But he hasn't so much as gone for his plate yet. Or, rather, he's been distracted a dozen times along the way, stopping and chatting with everyone he sees, asking how their lives and families are, and reminding them that later he'll be singing karaoke. He's wearing his ballcap with the bald eagle on the front, and whenever he greets someone, he doffs it, bows, then asks the person if they'd be so kind as to help him find his glasses, which have slipped off into the grass. Angie's his most recent victim. She makes sure he can see again, straightens the hat up on his head, and takes off toward Central Street for yet another smoke.

"Hippie shit," says Willa.

"Language, please," says her staff, a woman I've never seen before, who then points up to the sky.

Willa points at her, then up at the sky, then starts cackling remorselessly. Her staff huffs and looks away, at the future site of Bells & Whistles. Though the crew has gone home for the day, their giant machinery remains, standing idly in the dirt like sleeping dinosaurs. Their heartbroken, industrial screeching has been replaced by the constant and mostly conversational hum rising from the tables spread out in front of me. Every so often a car crawls by on the street beyond them, the hazy faces inside staring at us with a mixture of perplexity and pity.

"Here we are," says Jean-Bertrand, returning with two packed paper plates.

"Thanks a bunch," Ed growls. As he bites into his burger, a splodge of ketchup bursts loose and splashes just above the surly lion's head on his T-shirt, below which reads THIS IS MY HAPPY FACE.

"I'm so glad we could make it." Ayo sits back and smiles. "This barbecue is everything I dreamed of and more."

I'm about to agree, despite the lingering heat, when Stella appears with her staff from around the building's corner. I haven't seen her since Ayo helped me throw her paper hearts into the trash. My chest wells up with a sudden, sinking feeling. It's not quite accompanied by guilt, which gives me hope, but soon it's undercut by knife-edged fear. Chucking the hearts out without her being there was one thing. Standing up to her is something else entirely. I nudge the joystick and creep behind Ayo, praying he'll shield me from her prying gaze.

"You okay, sir? You seem a little —"

"Evening, Cliff."

Before I've placed the voice, a hand squeezes my shoulder from behind. Rising above it is Greg's head, *sans* fedora, but with a smile so glossy it's blinding. Spanning the V-neck of his T-shirt is a gold chain from which hangs a giant G encrusted with what have to be fake diamonds. I've heard Brad complain enough to know that behaviorists get paid more than anybody at the company save John Knowland, but not even on their salary could they afford so many precious stones.

"Good evening," says Ayo, standing.

"How ya doin', champ?"

If Greg's wearing cologne, the barbecue has mercifully canceled out its stench, but on his breath I can detect the smell of cheap, domestic whiskey.

"Fantastic. I don't think we've met." Ayo extends a hand and introduces himself.

"Greg Gabhart, MSW, LCSW, and as of yesterday, this cool dude's behavioral consultant."

"Oh yes, I heard Cliff was meeting with someone."

"I've heard about you, too, actually," says Greg, his eyes like twin incisions. "Most of it, as I remember, wasn't good."

Ayo doesn't step so much as he's knocked back several paces. "Excuse me?"

"Cliff and I had a long, insightful talk, and let's just say that when it came to you, he had a few choice words to share." Greg slaps his knee and laughs, but neither I, nor Ayo, nor even Greg's own eyes join in. "I'm just razzing you, my guy. Cliff has no hate for you — that I know of. I realize you haven't been with us long, but if you don't know yet that he can't, well . . ."

"That he can't what?"

"You know." With his finger, Greg marks an X across his burnt-orange wattle.

"I'm sorry. I still don't get it."

"You know," says Greg, gesturing again, but slower.

Ayo makes a face that says ?

Pulling him aside, Greg is confident I can't hear him whisper. "Good grief, man. Know that he can't speak. If you don't know he can't speak, then maybe you shouldn't be working —"

"I'm aware Cliff has a condition, and that because of it, he makes his feelings known in other ways." Though Ayo isn't nearly as tall as Francis, his expression — eyes wide, brows furrowed, upper teeth buried deep into his lower lip — has the same dwarfing effect as his coworker's height. "I thought that's why he went to see you in the first place."

"It is. He did. Calm down, though. Sweet Baby Jesus. As I told Francis, it's all part of a process, and helping him is going to take time. But we need to keep it down when we talk about him like this. Nobody wins if he gets any more worked up than he already has been."

"Sure, because if that happened —"

"Then it would ruin all the fun," Greg says at full volume, coming back to me. "And nobody wants that, do they? Listen, Cliff, I'd been planning on talking to you some about the work we'll do together, but on second thought, maybe now's not the best night to get our party started, after all. I don't know about you guys, but I'm here to have a good time." He watches Ayo shake his head and sit back down. "How does early next week sound? If you won't be at home, I'll come visit you at Making Memories."

"Memory Makers," Ayo corrects.

"Potato, tomato," Greg burps. "What do you say, Cliff?"

I shrug.

"It's a date, then."

"He makes his feelings known in other ways," Willa says.

"Hey there, Willa. I'm Greg. Remember me?"

Willa stares at him with her yellow eyes and pale, gaunt face, and shrugs.

"She doesn't remember a damn thing," Ed says, ketchup dribbling from his chin. "But I do. You're the peckerhead who wouldn't let me go to Waffle House on days when I said *ass* or *shit* or *fucking.* I kicked your ass to the curb faster than shit fucking flies through a goose."

"That was me, all right." Greg silences the fire horn in his pocket. "How's it going, Ed?"

"Much better now that I'm working with Portia, who doesn't try to tell me what to do like some business-casual Big Brother."

Portia is also Rickey's behaviorist. She's over at his table now, saying hi. I'd have gone with her, too, if I'd been given a choice.

"And I see she's doing a great job of it."

"And you can lick my taint by the light of the moon."

Greg makes like he's about to punch something, but halfway through the motion changes course, flattens his hand, and runs it through his spiky hair. "I think it's time for a plate. Good to meet you, Ayo. Let's chat more soon. Catch you later, Cliff. Ed."

"*Arrivedouchi,*" says Ed.

Having finally made it to the grills and back, BJ shakes his fists at Henry Wray, who, despite the full plate in front of him, is fixated on Stella's pork chop.

"Something's wrong with that man's tan," Ayo says, reflectively. "I don't know what it is, how it happened, or especially why someone would do that to himself, but something foul's happening there. I feel it in my heart like an eternal truth."

"You'd better get used to it. That's his look all year round." Ed throws his plate into the grass and licks his fingers. "Orangutan chic's what I call it. At least tonight he isn't wearing that dumb hat."

"Count your blessings," Ayo says.

"Damn straight. Last time I saw him, I burst a few capillaries. You know, Jean-Bertrand, and it pains me to say this, but I'm a grown man, and it's time I admit it. I think I owe you an apology."

His staff smiles magnanimously. "Gracious me. I never thought I'd see the day, but I heartily accept. Thank you, Ed. I'm glad you've matured to the point where you see how your words can sometimes hurt —"

"No, no. Slow down, partner. I'm not sorry for that whatso-flippin'-ever."

"Then what are you sorry for?"

Both Ed and his lion glare at the staff. "For misspeaking earlier. I told these guys you're my worst enemy, so I owe them an apology as much as I do you. I'm sorry, you two. The truth is, Jean-Bertrand's not my worst enemy. He's only my second-worst. The man topping the list is that slippery assbag who just left us."

Jean-Bertrand turns around. "Mr. Greg?"

"That's right." Ed wipes his head, smearing his face with ketchup like sunscreen. "I hate that bronze bastard even more than I —"

"But he only worked with you for one day, long ago."

"It doesn't matter." Ed squeezes his hands into fists. "All it took was one look at him to be reminded of that day — the way he spoke to me, tried to tell me I couldn't do the things I liked, and how he did it all with that same shit-eating grin on his face. Mark my words, Jean-Bertrand. If he comes back over here, both he and that tan will regret it."

Ed grunts, takes a swipe at the air, and because he's unbuckled, nearly slides from his chair to the walk.

Nimbly, with graceful urgency, Jean-Bertrand hurries over, hauls Ed back up to a sitting position, then straps him into the chair.

"Let me get this straight," he says, wiping Ed's brow with a napkin. "The whole point of your rant is that you hate me slightly less than you've been letting on. Does that sound about right?"

"More or less, yes."

"Believe it or not, that makes me feel somewhat better."

"Believe it or not, that wasn't my intention." Ed's eyes go all weird, then he winces. "Hey, Jean-Bertrand. Listen. Come closer, please."

The staff leans forward, his ear near Ed's mouth.

"I think I just," Ed whispers, "well, you know."

"You just what?"

Ed falters, coughs nervously. "You *know*."

"How is it," says Jean-Bertrand, "that a man of so many words becomes so terse all of a sudden?"

"I just had an *accident,* goddamn it. Can you help me get changed?" Ed punches the air. "There. I said it. I used my words. Happy now, Pencil Dick?"

"I've never been better. You know why?"

"No, and I don't care."

"I'm happy, Ed Vernon, because despite your foul language, you tried to ask nicely for assistance. It's much easier to get what we want when we're respectful to each other, isn't it?"

Ed turns away and nods.

"Very good," says his staff, taking his bag up from the ground. "I suppose you'll allow me to help because I'm only your second-worst enemy."

Ed takes out his middle finger again, holding it up like a treaty. "I'm pleased to report that we're on the same page."

"My friend, I couldn't have said it better myself."

Side by side, they head into the building, their shadows soft and blurred beneath them, like water under a bridge.

)

The sun begins to set behind the trees across the street, turning their leaves to silhouettes against the darkening expanse of cloudless sky. Mid-daydream about the woman in the Silver Lining commercials, my stomach starts to growl. I roll in front of Ayo, who's been listening to BJ karaoke to the patriotic songs now playing on the stereo by the table with the condiments.

"Time for dinner, then?"

Yes, please.

He stands, picks up his bag, and has a look around. "Let's go somewhere more private."

I follow him past Willa and Ed, who fell asleep after he'd come back from being changed. Up the building's walk, Ayo hums along with BJ's garbled take on James Brown's "Living in America."

"In here," he says, opening the door to the office's back hallway.

Inside, the cool air hits my skin like water, but it's not this that makes me shiver. I've never been here after-hours, when everything's so empty, dim, and quiet. It's like driving through the city in the middle of the night, or visiting an ancient, haunted house. I'm half-expecting the Ghosts of Staff Past to emerge at any moment from the walls, bewailing the shitty jobs they did in mournful, vowel-soaked moans. But whether they were fired or handed in their two weeks' notice, everyone who's ever worked here has simply moved on with their lives and out of ours. Ayo and I, on the other hand, head deeper into the building, down the hall toward Greg's shared office. He stops when we reach the narrow table on the wall next to the restrooms.

"Here's good, don't you think?" Ayo sets the bag down on the table and removes the supplies, then raises my shirt, inserts the syringe, and pours. "Are you having a good time?"

My stomach gurgles its assent.

"I am, too. It's been a learning experience for me. So has everything else. There's one thing, though, I still don't understand. I'm hoping maybe you can help me with it."

I'll try my best.

He looks back at the dying sunlight that spills through the long windows on either side of the door. The can cupped in his palm, he bends down and leans closer to me, his face serious and searching.

"What is a taint?" he says.

I smile and shake my head.

"Does that mean you don't know or that it's better I don't know?"

Well . . .

"Better I don't know?"

I nod very seriously.

"Okey-doke, as they say." He empties the rest into my stomach. "It's all right if some mysteries remain unexplained. That's part of the beauty of life, don't you think?"

He waits for my nod, then wipes a stray glob from my belly before he starts the second can. The air conditioning pauses for a break and we fall silent, listening to BJ belt out "God Bless the U.S.A." in its entirety. It only takes that long for the sky to darken from its melancholy bronze to a sanguinary red that turns the scar on Ayo's cheek the deepest violet. I consider asking how he got it — as far as I know, no one has, not even BJ — then decide that it's all right if some of life's mysteries remain unexplained.

"Do you know what that man told me yesterday?" Ayo says, nodding at the song.

What's that?

He angles the can up and holds it there. "He said" — Ayo cracks the slightest of smiles — "that he has, and I quote, 'the voice of an angel.'"

Oh, Lord.

"What, you don't agree?"

"Meh."

"Between you and me, I probably agree only sixty percent. Still, I'm happy for BJ. I'm very proud of him. There's something in that music, and in himself, that he loves. He's not afraid to share it with those who have ears to hear. And you and I, Cliff, we have ears to hear, don't we?" His face becomes more thoughtful. "Whether we love it, too, is a whole different story, but I'm pretty sure he doesn't care. What he's doing, in his own small way, is giving us a dose of life's beauty as he sees it."

I've had the same feeling before, but I've never been able to put it into words.

Ayo flushes the tube with a bottle of cold water. My stomach murmurs in thanks as both we and the music go quiet. Lost in thought, Ayo cleans up my navel, tapes gauze over my tube, and, draping my shirt back in place, tosses the empties into his bag, where they land with a *clink*. I pat my belly and wheel toward the door, waiting for him to come open it. When he doesn't, I turn back around, my arms raised. He's still standing there by the table with the same piercing look on his face. The A/C roars back to life like someone revived from a coma.

"Can I tell you what I'd like to know even more than what a taint is?"

Of course.

"I'd like to know," he says, "what would make you as happy as our friend when he bursts out into song."

The streetlights wake up just in time to catch the final chorus of BJ's animated cover of "Pink Houses," and several begin flickering by way of applause. Soon they're joined by a strong third of the barbecue's attendees. His hands full with a loaded plate, Brad whistles his brief plaudits, dripping baked beans on his way to sit with Francis, Rickey, Lem, and the gold-chained Greg. He catches sight of me before I have the chance to roll behind Ed, then whistles so loudly it makes most of the young clients lurch back and forth with death grips on their headphones.

"There's my Resident Cool Dude. Come say *aloha,* why don't you?"

As Ayo leads the way, I drag my wheels, swerving around the grills carefully to avoid their propane tanks. I'm preparing to give Brad credit for at least not making the hang-ten sign when he shoots his arms out, palms down, and, curling his lip up like Elvis's, pretends to surf the Big Kahuna.

"Aloha," he says.

"Aloha," says Ayo.

"How ya doin', champ?" A chili-sauce chunk jolts loose from Greg's dog. He seizes the blob in mid-air, then slings it mouthward like a chameleon with a cricket. With each chew, his features expand and contract in little fits of painful bliss. Before he swallows, he bends forward for another mouthful. At the table behind him, there's a staff I've seen around a couple times and —

And Alec Hayman. He's wearing the same sailboat shirt he had on Tuesday, its chest swamped with the saliva that still dribbles from his chin. His skin is pale as an old curtain. His arms hang limply at his sides. His eyes are glazed and droopy, drained of the freedom that lit them up like wildfires earlier this week. Though they're fixed on, if not necessarily seeing, his plate of untouched food, his staff makes no attempt to help him eat. Instead, he swipes at his phone, making the face people do when they're scrolling their feeds.

"You guys enjoying yourselves?" Brad says.

"Of course." Ayo smiles at Rickey, who's examining his bite of macaroni salad like it's a dirt sample from a distant planet. "It's everything I dreamed of and more."

"Great to hear, Private. Get a plate yet?"

"I plan on it."

"We just shut down the grills. Better hurry before everything gets cold."

"It's all right. I'm in no rush."

"No rush, no rush," Greg repeats, musically but off-key, then takes a long drink from a metal bottle. "In what way is this everything you dreamed of?"

"His dreams are very weird," says Francis, shoving his empty plate to the center of the table.

Their faces dimmed by shadows, Brad and Greg chuckle softly while

Lem rams coleslaw in his mouth with his bare hand.

"Maybe they are, maybe they aren't." Ayo steals a chair from Alec's table, plants it in the grass beside the walk. "Either way is fine by me. As I've told these gentlemen, this is my first July the Fourth. I've dreamed about America my whole life: its people, places, sounds, its very meaning. I doubt you can imagine what it all looked like in my head, a land so different and much freer than my own."

"I can," Francis says.

"Because you came here, too, from somewhere else, like I did. But you've been here a while. As for me, I'm still learning everything about this place."

"Perhaps also you're still dreaming."

Ayo sits up, staring Francis in the face. "Which would mean, what, that you're the one who's awake?"

Francis returns the glare, starts to respond, but then just smiles scoffingly.

"Anyway," Brad says, "if you're having fun now, just wait until you see the fireworks. It's going to be quite the show."

"Is it ever," says a voice behind me, rich and deep. A large hand claps me on the shoulder like it did the day its owner came to our house after Paul had locked us in the van. Its grip both firm and fretful, it stays there until John Knowland steps around and stands tall next to me. "How's everybody over here?"

To see his face, I have to tilt my neck so far it hurts. Devoid of tears, unlike the last time I saw him, his blue eyes beam below his sandy bangs, which are longer than you might expect a man my age, much less the CEO of any company not named Virgin, to wear them. His chiseled cheeks are raised in a benevolent smile, and his beard is flecked with wise, white hairs. He's still wearing his apron over his royal-blue dress shirt. Checkered all the shades of green and splotchy with barbecue stains, it has a winking, dancing leprechaun embroidered on the chest. *KISS ME, I'M IRISH,* it says.

"Very well, sir," says Ayo, shaking his hand.

Knowland clenches his palm as tightly as he did my shoulder and introduces himself.

"Yes, we met last week," says Ayo. "You came into orientation and talked of the importance of the work we were about to do. About how Knowland Residential 'separates itself from the competition by helping folks live lives that aren't just happy *but worthwhile.*'"

"Sure, I remember," Knowland says, studying the scar on Ayo's cheek with his special brand of artless curiosity. "I hope something stuck with you, proved helpful in some small way. All I try to do is set the tone for your careers. You may have spent a week up here learning the basics, but it's when you get out there, into these guys' homes, that the real magic happens." Below him,

Brad and Greg grin viciously. "How are things working out so far? Cliff hasn't bit you yet, has he?"

Knowland wipes his hand across his apron, then he turns to me and winks.

"No, he hasn't. I'm still getting to know everyone, but I think we're off to a good start. What would you say, Cliff?"

I smile and nod.

"That's so great," Knowland says. "It always warms my heart to hear it. I'd rather take the extra time and match our folks with compatible staff than throw in just anyone because it's more convenient. Around here we take care of people, not rocks."

His empty gaze on his plate, Alec makes a low, humming sound. His staff, who pocketed his phone the moment Knowland strolled over, dips a spoon into a pile of cold beans, then brings it up to Alec's drool-drenched lips. Drowsily, the boy pushes it away, spilling the beans into his lap.

"I couldn't agree more," Francis says. "As a matter of fact, Cliff and I just met with Greg yesterday to discuss how we can improve his quality of life."

"Is that so?"

"It is." Francis waits for Greg to elaborate, but with a mouthful of pasta salad, the behaviorist can do little more than offer up a string of swollen, squirrely nods. "We talked about the issues Cliff's been having lately. Greg's going to create a plan to help him through this rough patch. Isn't that right, Cliff?"

"You must've heard about the laptop, John," Greg says, finally.

"I'm sorry to say I did." Knowland makes a sorry face to prove it. As I bury my chin into my shoulder, he lays his heavy hand down on the other one. "We all have bad days, though. We wouldn't be human if we didn't. But here's the thing, Cliff. You've got a great team put together." He nods at the table, where Brad licks sauce from his upper lip, Greg stuffs his face with more pasta salad, and Francis is either swatting at flies or practicing semaphore. "It's their job to make sure your bad days don't turn into bad weeks, months, or even years."

In the growing darkness, Brad's gray eyes look black. "We get paid to care for you, Cliff, and not, as John said, a rock, or a boulder, or a pebble, or a stone."

Lem closes his eyes and lets out a spicy fart.

"They're absolutely right, champ, even if they're starting from a flawed premise."

Knowland takes out a little comb and runs it through his beard. "Flawed? In what respect?"

"In this one." Greg scrapes up the remnants of his food and takes one final bite, smiling nostalgically. "When I was eight, all I wanted was to be in charge of something. My parents were in charge of me, my teacher was in charge of class, and my pastor was in charge of the entire congregation. Even Richie Portis, the neighbor kid, was in charge of his dog. It was like I was the only person in the whole world without responsibilities."

"I remember those days," says Francis, "except I wished they'd never end."

"Looking back on it, I wish I had, too. I might've enjoyed them more fully had I known how short they'd be. But the grass is always greener . . ." Greg sighs and shakes his head at me. "I wanted duties, obligations, and the power, however slight, that came along with them."

"Hear, hear." Brad smacks the table. "I felt the same way. I wanted to be someone the other kids could look up to and trust. That's why, in fourth grade, I applied to become a safety patrol."

Knowland returns the comb to his pocket. "I didn't know that about you, Brad. I bet you were a natural in the role."

"I thought I would be, too, but Mr. Winkle, who headed up the patrol, disagreed. I was the only one who didn't make the cut."

"Preposterous. Why?"

"I won't bore you with the details. Suffice to say I exhibited 'a problematic zeal to wield authority' over my peers. He was also concerned I'd bring unwanted attention to the school, which was already reeling from allegations that a group of students — led by me, as it happened — had beaten up our civics teacher. On the other hand, Winkle also believed that my misguided passion would one day lead to an exemplary career in law enforcement."

"So why aren't you an officer?" Francis says.

Brad gazes sadly at his fingers. "I didn't pass the entrance exam."

"Well, that's their loss and our gain," Knowland smiles. "Every cloud really does have a silver lining."

Ayo raises an eyebrow.

"I get it, though," Greg says. "You want to prove yourself to others, especially at that age. It hurts when they don't think you're up to the challenge. That's how I felt when I asked my dad if I could have a dog, just like Richie Portis. He looked down at me from his great height and laughed. 'Listen, little champ,' he said, 'owning a dog's a whole world harder than it sounds. A dog's a living creature. You've got to feed, walk, and bathe it, play with it and love it, and care for it when it falls ill. It's a tall order, and I'm just not sure you're ready.' I was devastated. But you've known me for a long time. You think I'd give up on my dreams so easily?"

"Not if there's any more story to tell," says Knowland.

"'Just give me a chance, Pops,' I said. 'You owe me that much, at least. I'll show you I've got what it takes and then some.' He was skeptical — who can blame him? — but he admired my tenacity and said it was contagious."

"Still is," Brad says, yawning.

"He said I'd get my chance, but that first I'd have to start with something smaller. That very afternoon he drove me to the store and bought me, not a pet, but a Pet Rock." Greg slaps his knee and chortles. "Remember those things?"

"Remember Pet Rocks?" Knowland is misty-eyed. "Do I ever."

"I named him Stony Orlando. Glued little googly eyes to him, wrapped him up in a tiny blanket before putting him to bed at night. Fed him pea gravel three times a day, took him for walks around the neighborhood in the palm of my hand. Caring for him was my number-one priority, and I took more pride in it than anything else I'd ever done, including the spitball I'd pegged Mrs. Rowsdower with on the first day of second grade." Greg looks pensively into the distance. "He taught me a lot, that little guy did, not just about responsibility, but about friendship, love, and life itself. Crazy as it sounds, he planted the seed for what would later blossom into my career as a behaviorist."

Lem lets fly another fart.

"I've known you for years, Greg, but I've never heard that part of your story," Knowland says. "Thanks for sharing. I always love learning about the different paths we took on our way into the field. No two journeys are the same. It's not like, as kids, we dream of staffing group homes when we grow up." He turns his head to one side, Obamalike in the wake of the joke, as the table's laughter runs its course. "Usually, we fall into these careers by accident. Some of us have family members with a disability. But no matter how they started, each of our stories shares a common thread: the desire and dedication to improve the lives of people who, for reasons beyond anyone's control, least of all their own, can't do it for themselves."

His remarks hang like clouds above us, over the tables' muddled conversations, the crickets chirping in the distance, and the fire horn that blares from Greg's pants' pocket.

"So," Brad says, "did you get the dog or what?"

"You bet I did. A puppy, a beautiful yellow lab. I named her Pawn."

"Then it all worked out in the end. But what happened to the rock?"

Greg leans back and sniffs. "I tried to teach Pawn to play fetch with him. She never took to it, so I chucked old Stony through the window of a neighbor's house."

"Mm-hmm."

"Wanna pop."

"Most of it's still in your cup, Super Rick."

"Wanna cookie."

"Maybe you should eat your burger first," says Brad.

Knowland smiles. "Have a bite, Rick. It's good, if not good for you."

"It's so good." Francis rubs his belly. "You should try it, at the very least. Look at it there, the whole world on a platter. Don't take it for granted. Not everybody has the luxury of savoring a big, delicious burger, fresh from the grill and loaded with all the fixings. Think of the starving children, Rick, and those who can't eat solid food."

Then he grins at me with just his eyes.

Ayo's the only one who frowns. "Don't you think maybe . . ."

"Don't I think maybe what?" Francis says, taking a toothpick from his box and gnawing hard on it.

"We'll talk about it later, I'm sure." When Ayo speaks again, his voice is tremulous. "May I ask, gentlemen, whether Cliff is the only one here tonight who can't have solid food?"

"Don't quote me, but I believe so." Knowland scans the sea of tables. "Doesn't look like anyone else with a tube showed up. Why do you ask?"

"I'm just thinking about how all these people enjoying their burgers must look to someone like Cliff, who, as Francis has just pointed out, can't do the same for reasons beyond anyone's control, least of all his own."

"What is your point?" Francis says.

"My point is, is there something else we could do to make his night worthwhile?"

Sloughing his greasy apron like an exoskeleton, Knowland folds it twice before he drapes it over an empty chair. "I can think of nothing better than the fireworks. Can you guys?"

"I can't." Greg blinks and takes a drink from his metal bottle.

Hand to chest, Brad says, "Those bad boys will make it worth everyone's while."

"Will they ever. How does that sound, Ayo?" Knowland asks.

"That sounds great to me, but I think we should ask Cliff himself, and actually, I had something else in mind, as well."

"How's that?"

Ayo's voice grows even shakier. "Forgive me if I'm speaking out of turn, Mr. Knowland. I'm still learning how things work here, not only in this company of yours, but also in this country. I don't want to —"

"Please, there's no need for that. Here at Knowland, we value all forms of diversity. In fact, we'd like to call ourselves the leader in the push for more inclusion in our state's residential agencies. Why, take a look around." Between the staff, who are mostly black and brown, and the client base, which is mostly white, "We've got a healthy mix of backgrounds going on," Knowland says. "Our staff come from everywhere, from South Africa to Cleveland. Of course, the numbers aren't exactly where they could be, but they're more reflective of the country's racial makeup than they've ever been before. What do you think? That's pretty good, right?"

"Sure, I guess?"

Knowland's face suggests Ayo might as well have slapped it. "You guess?"

"I'm sorry. I don't know what else to say."

"Say whatever's on your mind. If you see something I don't, I want to hear about it. Consider it a work in progress. I'm wide open to suggestion. It takes a village, and all that. Now, I know you're new, so you may not be aware of our past efforts to promote diversity. I'd be glad to fill you in, if you have time."

"Mr. Knowland, I —"

"This year we had our first MLK Day celebration, where we invited everyone up here to watch Dr. King speak on our big plasma screen. Didn't have the greatest turnout, but hey, you've got to start somewhere. Then, in March, we brought in a guy who did a day of racial equity training for our office staff. It got more violent than I'd expected, but we learned a lot about the world, and a little too much about ourselves along the way. Oh, and last month, I wrote an article on Juneteenth for my 'Knowland's Notes' newsletter. Did you know that slavery wasn't abolished in Texas until two years after the Emancipation —"

"I did."

"Oh. Well. Of course you did. But most of us had no clue before last month's 'Notes.' So you can see how I might've felt like we were really making progress." He pulls his beard so hard he rips a clump of flaxen hairs out. "But what I'm hearing from you — and I'm inclined to defer to your expertise on the subject — is that we could and should be doing more."

"All I meant was what I said, sir. I don't know what else to tell you. They sound fine, these initiatives of yours. But I'm sorry, I fear I can't be of further assistance with these questions." Ayo nods at me. "No offense, but I believe I'm much more useful helping Cliff."

"Right. Sure. Fine. None taken. Let me know if you change your mind, though. I want to have a Kwanzaa thing this winter, and I'd love to pick your brain about it."

"I don't — yes, I think we can discuss your ideas. But perhaps another time. For now, I'd be pleased if you'd listen to my own about making Cliff's night more worthwhile."

"I'm always up for that," Knowland says, and checks his watch.

"It would be contingent, obviously, on his approval. But I thought it would be at least worth giving him the option. What do you think, Cliff?"

I'm all ears.

"Here's what I'm thinking. Again, through no fault of his own, though it is for his own safety, Cliff can't have a burger, or even the smallest bite of one. But would it be possible, do you think, to give him something approaching the next best thing?"

Knowland paws the hairless portion of his beard. "The next best thing?"

"Yes. Cliff can't have solid food," Ayo says, pointing at the table with the condiments in their bright bottles, "but what if we offered him something he can manage, say, the tiniest amount of barbecue sauce, right on the tip of his tongue, just enough to give him a sense of what everyone else gets to taste? What do you say to that, Cliff?"

The last time I had anything by mouth, I must've been eight or nine. Not long before my parents gave me up, a babysitter fed me a dollop of what even I knew was the blandest possible variation of Gerber baby food. Though I didn't choke, I almost died of excess boredom.

Hell yes, please.

But Knowland, Brad, and Greg have their gazes in their laps. When they respond, it's in turn, each completing the other's thought.

"I —"

"Don't —"

"Know —"

"If —"

"That's such a good idea." His elbows on the table, chin resting on his knuckles, Brad maintains all the resolve that withers under the slightest glance from Francis. "It sounds nice in theory, but the real question is whether it'd be safe."

"I understand. I only bring it up because I've known people like Cliff who've managed it."

"Sure, and that's great for those who can, but the fact is, they're not Cliff. We don't know how he'd react. If it made him sick, or if, God forbid, he choked —"

"Brad's right," Greg says, sharing a secret look with Francis. "On top of that, we should remember those sauces contain lots of sugar, which is a major behavioral trigger for these folks. Given Cliff's recent incidents, it's probably best to avoid introducing any new variables into his equation."

"We could also get ourselves into a heap of legal trouble." Knowland's leaden hand falls on my shoulder again. "It's secondary to the issue of Cliff's safety but is nevertheless something to keep in mind. We can only follow what's approved in our guys' plans. If things went sideways, the blowback would be horrific. The last thing we need is Channel Eight harassing us again so soon after that misfortune at the mall." Everyone nods ruefully. "That said, Ayo, I like how you're thinking outside the box. We could always use more of that around here."

"Bough," Alec whispers from the next table over, then falls asleep.

"Brad, what if we brought this up at his next doctor's appointment? He could refer Cliff for a swallow study. It's worth a shot, and who knows? This time next year, Cliff might be knocking back Sweet Baby Ray's by the capful."

"I'll see what I can do."

"Perfect," Knowland says. "Sorry, Ayo, and you, too, Cliff, that we couldn't give you a more favorable response."

"Good try, though." Francis doesn't cover his mouth when he belches, and it smells like charbroiled ass on the fire pit of Hell.

Alec's staff pulls the catatonic boy from his chair and is dragging him off to the parking lot when Knowland leaves our table for the grills with poise and purpose. He stretches his neck, cracks his knuckles, and does a set of bicep curls with his red bullhorn. When he speaks into it, his mellow baritone echoes off the trees across Central Street like the voice of God from deep inside the last forest left on Earth.

"It's so great to see everyone."

"The feeling sure is mutuable."

Knowland bows in gratitude. "And it was our pleasure, BJ, to be regaled yet again by your karaoke performances."

"Speak for yourself, you soaring dick."

"I love you too, Ed, and I know you'd rather get back to the fun than listen to me droning on. So, since brevity is the soul of —"

"Shit, just get on with it, will you?"

"With pleasure." Waving to the crowd, Knowland misses Ed's masturbatory gesture. "This weekend, all across the country, both in and out of doors and in and behind bars, we Americans are gathering to celebrate our liberty. Our independence. Liberty," he repeats with equal emphasis on each syllable. "Independence. These aren't just words to us. They're ideals to be lived up to, dreams to be achieved. That's why, when you ask your fellow Americans what these words mean to them, you'll get a whole host of responses. You'll hear a lot about our rights — to use all sorts of slurs on social media, for instance, and to bear an armory, and to choose our leaders in elections half the country deems corrupt."

"Well, they are," somebody says.

"Oh, go jump in a lake," says someone else.

"Take it easy, both of you." Knowland lifts a calming hand above them. "There's a time and a place for such debate: three hours past our bedtime in the comments section of an article no one's bothered to read past the headline. Tell me, does this look like that to you?"

Both disputants grudgingly admit it does not.

"I didn't think so. In fact, let's take a moment to reflect on and be grateful for our right to disagree with each other — and our leaders — in the first place. Remember, it isn't like this everywhere. Some of our staff know this from hard experience." A lot of them, including Ayo, respond with solemn nods. "Sadly, the rest of us tend to take these rights for granted, to our own peril. But that's not what I'd like to talk about tonight."

"Oh, thank Christ," Ed says.

Knowland sweeps his gaze from one side of the green space to the other.

"No, I'd rather speak to you of another kind of freedom, one we think of even less and take even more for granted. It's not as sexy as what you'll find in the Bill of Rights, but it's equally important, if not more so. Without it, the lofty notions laid out in our founding documents would be impossible. I mean the freedom to make sure our basic needs are met, to go about our daily lives, and to make full use of our communities. Being born in this country — or coming here from another, less fortunate, place — doesn't automatically guarantee us equal access to this freedom." The blaring of a siren swells from down the street. Knowland waits until the ambulance is gone. "Our clients are living proof of this. You, the folks it's our honor to serve, were all born with special challenges. In whatever form they've taken, they've kept you from living the lives you've always dreamed of. But this doesn't mean those lives are unrealizable. It only means you need some extra help to get to where you want to be. And that, folks, is where we come in."

Arms akimbo, Knowland smiles. A burst of wind blows through his sandy hair.

"How, exactly, do we come in?" he says. "It depends on who you are, what you need, and what you want. Some of you require physical support, assistance to make meals, reminders when it's time to take your medications. Some of you need staffing round the clock, others just a couple times a week. No matter who you are, no matter your abilities, you rely on us to ensure your health and safety. That's our top priority. Once we've seen to it, though, we don't stop there. Our work is just beginning. We take things a whole step further, and it's this that separates us from the competition." Knowland thrusts his chin into the wind. "People who don't know about this field sometimes ask me what I do. It's not as easy a question as you might think. Our product isn't tangible. We don't make cars. We don't sell coffee, though we may drink it by the ton. No, our focus is on something you can't count in the same way: the quality of someone's life. What makes for success or failure? Again, it all depends on those three things: who you are, what you need, and what you want. By my yardstick, there's no greater success than knowing it's you who've chosen what your life will look like every day. So, what I tell those people when they ask me what I do is that I'm in the business of offering choices, both the major, life-changing ones, such as where to live and who to live with, and those which are much smaller but no less important, like where you go for fun, what you plan to eat for dinner, and even what you watch on your TV."

"Well," Ayo says softly.

"In other words, we give you, in our own small way, the freedom to wake up every morning and know the day ahead will be worthwhile." Knowland's presidential pause lasts so long Ed falls asleep again. "What makes this so enjoyable, why I and your staff stick around — it sure as hell isn't the money, believe you me."

As he and his employees share a laugh, Angie rises from her seat and takes the path she's worn through the grass to her next cigarette.

"No, it's not the money. It's because you give us the privilege of making sure you get the same chance to lead lives as independent as the rest of ours. That's why I started this company twenty years ago. It's the only thing that's kept me going these two decades. It's what motivates your staff and guides them as they work their shifts. I say 'work' and 'shifts,' but these are just terms of convenience. I think your staff would all agree there's so much more to what they do than 'work,' that a day they spend with you isn't a 'shift,' but a reward. A more perfect way to put it is to say they're helping you achieve your dreams."

It's not when he tears up, or even when the crowd erupts in cheers, but when Francis begins playing *Baby Jesus* that I can't take it anymore. I lay on the joystick and fly toward him. But the chair where Alec sat and his drool, still puddled on the table, stop me at the walk's edge. I close my eyes and try to disappear. But I have ears to hear and can't avoid John Knowland's voice. His words float across the blank space of my mind like plastic bottles on the surface of a lake.

"I don't know how many times I've seen one of you obtain an independence no one, not even you, thought possible. Life is hard enough, but you were born with the odds stacked even more greatly against you. The world you entered didn't make it any easier. Often, it only made things worse. Some of you spent half your lives or more in institutions. We can't erase the pain those places caused, but even if we could, say, with the snapping of our fingers, we shouldn't. If we forget the way it used to be, we risk returning to those dark days. Heartbreaking as your stories are, there's so much we can learn from them. They're examples of what we, the people charged to care for you, should avoid at every cost. In those places, you had no freedom whatsoever. They were little dictatorships led by small men, tiny tyrants whose hearts were full of malice. I saw this for myself" — he chokes up at the memory — "and I knew I had to set right what I could. That was the seed of this small company. I think — I hope — this seed has blossomed into a tree upon whose branches you can flourish. I think — I hope — that among its tender leaves you've found what freedom means to you, and that you've had the chance to make your own choices, to take risks, and, yes, to face their consequences, good or bad, great or small. If you don't feel this way, even if it's only one of you, then we've failed, and in my mind we're no better than the men who ran those institutions."

He stands tall above the silence, the bullhorn at his hip like a patrolman's service weapon.

Brad jumps to attention and salutes. "But we are, though."

"We are," says Greg, rising, too.

"We are," someone says on the far side of the grass.

The feeling's echoed by another staff, then another, then by several behaviorists and house managers, all standing and inspiring more to do the same until half the congregation is on its feet.

"We are," Knowland smiles. "We are, indeed."

The muffled sequence of the night's first fireworks bursts softly in the distance.

And then Willa raises her bony hand and says, "Lick my taint by the light of the moon."

Her staff's admonitions are drowned out by a wave of anxious laughter.

"Well, on that note," Knowland says, "I'd like to dedicate these to all of you."

He motions Brad up as a couple other house managers roll the grills behind the building. On the way, Brad squeezes my arm so hard it hurts.

"Let's have you guys back up some." Knowland plops a box of mortars on the concrete. "I'd hate to see you blown to smithereens."

"I wish I could say the same of you."

"You're such a ray of sunshine, Ed," his staff says.

Ed raises a butt cheek and unloads a fart on Jean-Bertrand. Waving it off, he leads Ed one way down the walk while Ayo and I take the other, around the fireworks, which Brad lines up in little rows, inspecting them like a general taking stock of his artillery.

"Are we ready, everyone?" Knowland says.

"Light 'em up!" someone yells amid applause.

Knowland stoops around a mortar, clicks a lighter, sparks the fuse, then hustles away, saluting broadly.

"Here's to independence!"

The fuse flares and hisses. The flame devours it as Knowland counts down through the bullhorn: *Five, four.* Everyone who can covers their ears and tenses up in dizzy expectation. *Three.* The smoke's a hellish orange in the fuse's light. *Two, one.*

"Fire in the hole!" says BJ. And then —

And then, nothing.

Well, not quite nothing. There's a lot more smoke, and the mortar's tube starts coughing, sadly and sickly. It sounds like, *Puhhh.*

Then the ball pops out and arcs off to one side before connecting with the pavement with a soft, pathetic *pronk.* I've seen something similar before, in those training videos staff have to watch, where one guy's choking and another does CPR to clear his airway of an ample chunk of ham.

Knowland goes to it with caution, shielding his face with the bullhorn. He decides the scene is safe, then says, "Well, that didn't go as expected."

Ed is doubled over in his chair. "You think?"

"I hope they're not all like that. Shall we try another?"

The answer's a near-unanimous yes, Ed and I the only ones dissenting.

Brad uproots a different mortar and plants it in the place of the defective one, then jogs back to his spot and kneels beside the seated Rickey, who's studying his burger. As long as he had food to contemplate, Rickey wouldn't notice if the whole world went up in flames.

"Here we go," Knowland says, lighting the fuse and speed-walking to a safe space. "Five, four, three, two, one, and —"

And again, nothing. The tube hacks like an old smoker until spitting up the shell a little higher than the last. The ball lands in the grass and rolls to Knowland's feet in a small cloud of smoke and anguish.

"I must apologize," he says. "I don't know what else to say. We just picked these up two days ago. There's no reason why they shouldn't . . . I mean, it's not like they're expired or anything. Is it? This is . . . I don't have the words, I'm afraid. This is . . . this is . . ."

"A disgrace," cries BJ, mopping his tears up with his shirt collar.

"Seconded and carried," Ed manages through hoarse and steady laughter.

"Perhaps." Knowland squats down on the lawn, rests his head in his hands, and thinks. "Or maybe there's another way of looking at this."

"Hey, if it helps you sleep at night —"

"I'm serious. Think about it."

"I will not."

"That's your right, my friend."

"I'm not your friend," says Ed.

"Either way, I'd prefer not to view this as a disgrace but as a setback. If I've learned anything from my time in this position, it's that a setback is just an opportunity for improvement. Here's what we'll do, everyone." Knowland tilts his chin up to the stars. "We're going to try it again."

"Well, you know what they say," Ed coughs. "The definition of insanity is doing the same thing over and over and expecting different results."

"But first, let's light these smaller ones. We probably should've done them to begin with, but we learn from our mistakes, don't we?"

"Speak for yourself, you soaring dick," advises Willa.

"We'll kick things off with these." Knowland holds aloft a box of what are called black snakes but, when lit, look more like ashen mallard dicks. "But they won't get any higher than the pavement, so if you want to see the magic, come on up."

As a handful of clients, with BJ at the lead, march to him like the ragtag band of patriots in *The Spirit of '76*, Ayo taps my shoulder. It's so dark now I can't make out his scar, but his enigmatic smile shines brightly against the night.

"What would you say to a little walk?" he says, nodding toward the street.

Away from here?

"Not too far. Just around the block. I could use a break from all the noise myself."

I point back at Knowland and the others. This is Ayo's first July Fourth celebration, after all. He's been looking forward to this moment for a week, and —

"I don't think we'll be missing anything. They might not even get those little ones to work. Besides, if I'm wrong, the sky is vast," he says, sweeping his arm up at the black expanse. "We don't have to be right here to see it. I'll be back."

He jogs to Brad, who's up the walk, sorting explosives.

Hold on. But he can't hear me. *Shit.* Given Brad's — and Greg's, and Knowland's — response to Ayo's last request, there's no way he'll grant us *furlough,* as I'm assuming he'll call it. We should've just up and taken off. We're both grown men. We don't need Brad's permission. Or so I'd like to think.

But Brad just nods, flicks a popper to the pavement, and, reveling in its puny snap, flings another. It'll be nice to get out of here for a while. Between the smoke and the heat, this place has become a bit too reminiscent of the netherworld for my taste.

Ayo salutes as he returns. "Let's do it."

We're halfway to Central Street when a voice calls out behind me. "Cliffy!"

My heart plunges toward the bottom of that plastic-littered lake. I'm prepared to blast away when Ayo stops me. Something in his look suggests now's as good a time as any to stop running.

"Wait up," Stella says, and before I know it she's jumped in front of me, panting, sweating, and sporting her best T-shirt, the one with Billy Ray on it. The picture is from when he had that princely nineties' mullet, and he's been photoshopped such that instead of a guitar he bears a string of uncooked hot dogs. Behind him hangs the battered Stars and Stripes and a majestic timber wolf, head raised moonward in mid-howl. Below all this, in glossy, golden lettering, it says

YOU CAN'T SPELL SAUSAGE WITHOUT USA

and I'm so deeply thinking, once again, about how true this is that at first I don't hear what Stella's saying.

". . . I'm so sorry I didn't come say hi earlier, but I've been so busy over there with my friends. The food was so good, wasn't it? It was so —" She looks down, at my stomach. "Oh, I'm sorry, Cliffy. Never mind. Just, whatever you do, promise you won't tell BJ about what happened to my pork chop."

"Hi, there. I'm Ayo. And you must be —"

"Stella Scofield." She whips her arm out, elbow unbent, and shakes his hand. "Cliffy's girlfriend." Her eyes reflect the streetlamps' fickle light like shooting stars.

"Ms. Stella. I'm glad we've finally met. I've heard a lot about you."

Stella tosses her head to the side and gives her jagged bangs a flirty twirl. "Oh? I can't imagine why."

"It's true. I've heard so much. I feel as if I've known you for a while now. But I do have one question, if you don't —"

"We haven't set a date for the wedding yet." She speaks swiftly, confidently, with a sudden, swelling warmth. I get the sense that, in her head, we've discussed all this a thousand times. "We agreed to take it slow, didn't we? There's no rush. We've got our whole lives ahead of us. But don't worry, Ayo. We'll let you know as soon as we decide. Who knows? Maybe Cliffy'll end up asking you to be his best man."

I groan.

"I see, and I'd be honored. But truthfully, Ms. Stella, the nature of my question had more to do with what happened to your pork chop."

"Oh." Stella's bangs fall back into place. "Well, what happened was, Henry Wray was sitting next to me. I should've been paying more attention, but I was so busy talking to my friends about the wedding that I forgot to. That's when he saw his chance and swooped in on my pork chop like a vulture. He gobbled the whole thing up before I even had time to say 'Jack Robinson.'"

"I've heard about this Henry, too." Ayo clicks his tongue against his teeth. "It seems the scoundrel's struck again."

"He sure has. Don't hold it against him, though. That's just what he does. If he didn't, he wouldn't be Henry, he'd be someone else. Laura says we all have something that makes us special. I guess it's swiping pork chops that makes him special. Besides, it wasn't a big deal. I just went back to the grill and got another."

"He didn't steal that one too, I hope."

"No, which doesn't mean he didn't try. Still, it worked out in the end. That's why I say, please don't tell BJ. It'll just make him angry, and I don't want that, especially tonight."

"Those are great points. We won't mention it to anyone. You have our word."

"Thanks." Stella waves to let her staff, an aging, pear-shaped, white woman in thick glasses, know where she is. "You guys aren't leaving already?"

"No, we're just on a little walk."

"But the fireworks haven't even started yet."

"They'll be going on a while. We don't plan on being gone for long.

They're only doing the small ones now, anyway."

"I hope Mr. Knowland gets the big ones to work later." Digging her hands into her pink shorts' pockets, Stella kicks the pavement. "It'll be really sad if he doesn't."

Up the walk, Brad, Knowland, BJ, and the group, their faces brightened by their sparklers' orange light, stand in awe of basic chemistry.

"It would be most regrettable."

"It sure would. But even if he doesn't, I'll still be happy."

"Your replacement pork chop was that good, eh?"

"Yes, but not as good," says Stella, patting my knee, "as getting a chance to see Cliffy."

Then she blows me a long, saucy kiss.

Ayo gives me room to act. When I don't, he attempts a change of subject. "I thought it would cool down with the sunset, but it's just as hot as ever, isn't it?"

"Hey, you know what?" Stella says, not taking the bait. "I'm already getting bored with those old sparklers, and those other runts they're setting off aren't any fun, either. Tell you what, Cliffy. I think I'll join you on your walk. Don't leave yet, okay? I have to let Pauline know where I'll be."

I'd rather you —

But she's already gone.

I sigh and spin around toward the parking lot. My chest tightens and my heart keeps sinking. My forehead's washed in a sweat like glacial meltwater. I try and wipe it but can't reach.

And then Ayo's tie-dyed hanky meets my brow and mops it all away. His face looks like the cloth feels, soft and deliberate. It says infinitely more than any spoken language could. When he's finished, he stuffs the hanky in his pocket and just stands there. I have a feeling he won't speak until I have.

I'd rather she not come with us.

"What's to be done about it?"

That's where I was hoping you'd come in.

He smiles. "I know this is hard for you, Cliff. You're a kind person. You don't want to hurt her feelings. You've found yourself in a dilemma." He breathes in the smoky air. "At the same time, we both know what has to happen, sooner or later. You don't want things to stay like this forever, do you?"

Hell, no.

"In that case, you must voice your desires." Ayo crouches, palms on knees. "I'll help you, Cliff, if you want it. But you must take the lead. Okay?"

I've always understood this, even as I've tried to avoid it like a virus. Stella only acts the way she does because I let her. Instead of sharing my true feelings, I've always pretended to be something I'm not, secretly hoping she'd drop it and get over me all on her own. Ed was right about the definition of insanity. I can't keep doing what I'm doing and expect different results. By that yardstick, I've been crazy my whole life. The question is whether I'm finally willing to do what it takes to be sane.

"Huzzah!" BJ's standing in the center of his group, lifting a lit sparkler like Lady Liberty her torch.

I'm giving him my best thumbs up when Stella scampers back without her staff.

"Pauline said it's fine if I go around the block," she gasps, "but I shouldn't be too long, or she'll get worried, and when she gets worried her blood pressure goes through the roof, and when her blood pressure goes through the roof she has to take her pill, which would be fine except tonight she left her pills back at her lover's place."

Ayo's face goes all askew. "Um."

"Um, what?"

"Um, Ms. Stella, how do you know that?"

"Because Pauline told me. We're as close as close can be." Stella crosses her index and middle fingers. "Pauline tells me everything, like how much she hates her husband, what having minnow paws is like, and how big her lover's manhood is. Would you believe it's this —"

"We get the idea."

"I asked her to show me a picture, but Pauline said that's where she draws the line. She's got *scruples,* see. *Moral standards.*" Across the lawn, her staff shows another client just how big her lover's manhood really is. "At least, that's what she says. Anyway, you guys ready, or what?"

My eyes burn. I try to grunt, but all my energy is focused on not crying.

"What's the matter, Cliffy? You look possessed by evil spirits."

Ayo nods. I shake my head.

"What's that supposed to mean?" Stella says, receding several steps.

"What it means, Ms. Stella, is that Cliff would like it to be just us two on the walk."

Her laugh is shocked and humorless, like someone still unconvinced there is a knife thrust in their gut. "That's a good one, Cliffy. I always knew you were funny, but that might be the best joke I ever—"

It's not a joke.

"He says he isn't joking," says Ayo. "Cliff would like some time alone."

"But he's not alone if he's with you."

"I'm his staff. I'll be there to keep him safe."

"He'll be safer if I come, too. It's like they always say, safety in numb—"

I said it's not a joke.

My eyes are bleeding tears. Wiping her own, Stella takes another step back toward the crowd. "You're not — you're not joking, Cliffy?"

I lean my head against its rest and shake it one last time, twisting the knife in a big circle. She chokes on her next words, then gives up on them, her face contorting, first in disbelief, then agony, then raw and endless rage. I can't say I was hoping for the best. But neither was I expecting her to tear me into pieces with her eyes.

"If you didn't want me, Cliff, all you had to do was say so."

I —

But she's already racing back to Pauline with her arms up high and flailing. When she gets there, Stella hugs her and buries her face in her shoulder, and Pauline regards me from across the lawn with the contempt reserved for traitors.

"Perhaps that could've gone better than it did."

Perhaps.

"Stella's a nice person. I don't like seeing her like that. It hurts, doesn't it?"

Acutely.

"But she can't expect you to be someone you aren't. Likewise, you can't expect her to know the truth if you don't tell her. That's why it's important to let others know how we're feeling. This can be hard for anyone, regardless of how they communicate. And yet you did it. I'm proud of you for that. It's a show of independence a thousand times more powerful than setting off some little fireworks."

I give him my best shot at a bicep flex.

"Hopefully, she'll come to understand and the two of you can be friends. You'd like that, wouldn't you?"

I nod hard and mean it.

"Good," he says, throwing his hand up at the street. "Are we ready, then?"

On the way out, we meet Angie, returning from another smoke break. She coughs through her smile at us. "Evening, Cliff. I should know your name, too, but I'm sorry, I don't —"

"Hello, Ms. Angie. I'm Ayo."

"I recognized your face from training." She shifts her weight and slings her purse around her other shoulder. "How are things in the home? How are the guys?"

"Things are going great. The guys are well. We're still getting to know each other, but I feel like we've established good relationships. I enjoy spending time with everybody, especially this man right here."

I shoot her the biggest thumbs-up I can muster.

The doubt fades from her face like breath from a mirror. "Good. They've had a rough time of it lately, the four of them, but it's nice to know they have someone at home they can trust."

"I don't know if I can say they all trust me completely."

Angie cocks an eyebrow. "BJ's still reminding you about his creams."

"Yes, even though I've never once forgotten them, he never fails to mention it, and then says —"

"'Better safe than sorry, as they say.'" Her impression's almost as good as the real thing.

"That's it. That's exactly it."

"Word to the wise: if you're expecting him to stop with that at some point, don't."

"I wasn't planning on it. But that's all right. It gives BJ a sense of control over his life. Who am I to take that away from him?"

"Great question." Angie nods at me. "Well, that makes me happy. All you guys deserve staff who can appreciate these things. As Cliff will be the first to tell you, that's not the way it works out most of the time."

"We have talked about it some — wait, what do you mean, most of the time?"

Angie reaches for her cigarettes. "I mean just what I said. Most of the time, that's not how staff feel. They don't enjoy working with these guys. Not from what I see, anyway. You said it yourself. You and Cliff have talked about it."

"We have, a little bit, as far as what goes on at his place. I wasn't aware it was a greater problem than —"

"Oh, it is, and has been for a long time."

Ayo looks up at the rising crescent moon. "But what about the mission statement? What about the things Mr. Knowland spoke of tonight?"

"Welcome to the real world," Angie laughs. "I see these guys every day. Staff bring them up here monthly for their vitals checks. After we're finished, if they can have it, I'll give them a stick of gum. 'A little something for your trouble,' I tell them. It doesn't seem like much, but you wouldn't believe how such a small gesture can really make somebody's day."

"I believe I can."

"God, I wish I had something that made me that happy. It wouldn't matter what." She spins her cigarette between her thumb and index finger. "It'd keep me off these — for a while, anyway. But those little flavored sticks of resin mean the world to our guys, and they want to share their happiness with someone. Who do you think that someone is, Ayo?"

"It would have to be their staff, wouldn't it?"

"Ten times out of ten. And what do you think those staff are doing nine of those ten times?"

"Knowing what I do about the way things are at Cliff's, I'd have to say probably they're looking at their phones."

"That's exactly it. You're one keen-eyed judge of character."

"No joking? I didn't think there'd really be that —"

Angie shakes her head.

"But nine times out of ten? That seems like way too many."

"I don't keep a precise tally, so I can't say it's scientific, but I can promise you the majority of staff aren't present, mentally, to share in these guys' happiness." She slides the cigarette between her lips but doesn't light it. "Things are no different when I go out to their homes. I take it your experience also bears this out."

"Unfortunately. I'm not there all the time, so I can't say it's always the case, but the other staff who works with me on second shift is very, let's say, useless."

I nod hotly.

"Is he the guy sitting next to Rickey over there?"

"That's Francis, all right."

"Don't quote me, but it looks like there's a game up on his phone — and a most stressful one, at that."

"*Baby Jesus vs. the Unbelievers.*"

"Beg pardon?"

"The game," Ayo says. "He showed it to me one night. Playing as the Christ Child, you do combat with a mob of infidels —"

"I get the idea. What evades me is why someone would so willingly subject themselves to it."

"I haven't the foggiest."

"And look at that. Brad sees him, too, but lacks the balls to let him know it's unacceptable."

"That's why I haven't talked to him. I can't be sure he'd do something about it."

"That makes two of us."

We watch in silence as the figures set off firecrackers and other small incendiaries. Although the blasts are almost uniform in color, sound, and size, everybody seems contented, far from bored. Their shadows appear against the office building in the brief but constant flashes of bright light. There's Brad's on one side, thick and domineering, looking downward. On the other, Knowland's rises high above the rest, head aimed toward the sky. The shadows in between are murkier, more indistinct. The sight is both eerie and beautiful, a tableau you might find on either Hell's or Heaven's walls.

"Ms. Angie?"

She tears the cigarette from her lips. "Yes?"

"May I ask you a question?"

"Of course."

"What would you do in my place?"

"What do you mean?"

"I mean, given what we've talked about," says Ayo, "is there anything more I can do if Brad won't help?"

Angie holds the smoke up to her mouth again. "I've already told you what I'd do."

"You have?"

"Yes. Think back a while."

"You'd give everyone a stick of gum."

"Not everyone. Only those it won't cause problems for."

"Which would seem to be most people. But for someone like Cliff, who probably can't have —"

"The gum is just a thing. A variable. It stands in for something else. Something deeper. That's why I think these guys get such a kick out of it. I could give them anything: a cookie, a mint, a plastic toy, a quarter. It wouldn't matter. It'd make them equally happy. The important thing is it makes them feel special."

"I think I understand, Ms. Angie."

"That makes one of us." She tucks the smoke back in the box and the box into her purse. "Anyway, I'll get off my soapbox. I just needed a break from all the noise. Looks like you guys do, too."

"It's a lot of fun back there, but yes, we decided it was time for something different."

"Enjoy it while you can. Guess I'll get back and watch Colonel Flattop and Chief Soaring Dick play with fire."

As I slap my knee, Ayo says, "Who are they?"

"It's probably better you don't know."

Ayo's upper lip folds over his lower one. "All these words I've never heard before. There's still so much for me to learn."

"You could say the same for all of us." Angie coughs into her fist. "But listen, Ayo. No matter how much you learn about this place, don't you ever dare change how you work with the guys."

Ayo nods. "You have my word."

"Good. You'd better not, or you'd have me to deal with."

"Your bad side is the last place I want to be."

"I've learned to take that as a compliment," Angie smiles. "And Cliff, you'd best remember, too, that all you need to be is yourself, no matter what."

I flash her another thumbs-up. As she heads back to her seat, Ayo looks at the moon, a silver grin on the face of the sky. There's a fizzling sound, then another spate of small explosions, and the group by the wall erupts in fresh surprise.

"One moment, please," says Ayo.

He trots back toward the building. The breeze slows in the branches of the trees across the street, the voices at the tables on the lawn have all gone quiet, and the shadows on the wall are now a single, darkened mass. In the distance, mortars thunder, laying siege to the night sky.

I take a deep breath. It's almost funny how quickly and eagerly new staff change the way they work with us. No matter where they've come from, no matter their country or culture, they've never had issues adapting to the realities of how Knowland Residential operates, not in theory, but in practice.

I'm glad Angie said what she did to Ayo, especially about how, if he changes, he'll have her to reckon with. But I don't think that, in Ayo's case, she needed to say anything. I don't know how or why, but I can see it in his eyes and in his smile. I'm not afraid that he will change his ways with us. I can't remember the last time I felt completely safe with someone who's supposed to take care of me. I'm not afraid he'll do anything to put me or the guys in any danger —

"I'm sorry." A gust of wind brings my staff back. "I realized I'd forgotten something. You still up for this?"

We reach Central Street and hang a left, heading south on the sidewalk. The area is thick with smoke, but mercifully, the restaurants have all closed for the night. At least we won't have to suffer that sriracha craft-beer beard balm stench.

"It's finally cooling down some, isn't it?"

Yeah, it's nice.

We move side by side, my wheels thunking over fissures in the walk. The street's well-lit and otherwise empty. In the midst of faraway explosions, a steady stream of drunken voices flows from out-of-sight backyards.

"Look, Rygert," one of them says, "I'm not saying you're wrong. I'm just saying that, if satellites can pinpoint our exact location on this planet and we're willing to give up every last detail of our lives to social media, how are any of us really, truly, genuinely free?"

"And all I'm saying, dude, is what can we do about it? Nothing. Zero. Zip. Not a damn thing. Life's much easier when you don't worry about stuff you can't control."

"He's right, you know," Ayo says.

Who?

"Whoever was talking to Mr. Rygert back there. What was his question? How can we be truly free if we're being watched all the time?"

As someone who's supposed to be watched most of the time, I'm not sure how to respond.

"I realize your experience is much different from most people's. Those guys back there, they don't have staff whose job it is, on paper, anyway, to keep them safe from harm. They don't need to ask permission to drink beer and have fun."

Are you sure that's what they're having?

"To each his own," Ayo grins. "Maybe they are. Maybe not. My point is, our world is such that, even here, in this country, we surrender aspects of ourselves to someone or something else more powerful. In return, we receive things like the joy of scrolling our feeds or a safe and healthy life. We'd like to think they come from people acting in our best interests. What Rygert's pal was asking, basically, was, *Do they, though?*"

My chair thuds over another crack.

"I'm asking the same question of Mr. Knowland," Ayo says. "You have, too, Cliff. Haven't you?"

So many times I've lost count.

A few blocks from the office, he quickens his pace and steps in front of me. Close by, someone cries out for a drink. Bottles clink in a toast, a round of mortars sounds, and the wind blows a Black Cat wrapper across the street ahead of us.

"I don't know what's gotten into me," Ayo says, "but I can tell you when it did: when Francis taunted you with Rickey's burger, and after that, when Knowland said it'd be wrong for you to have this. You're a grown man, Cliff. You don't need their permission to make choices."

He reaches in his pocket and removes his tie-dyed handkerchief. Glancing over my shoulder, toward the barbecue, he kneels beside me and lifts the hanky. Lying on it are a plastic spoon inside a wrapper and a tiny takeout tub of dipping sauce.

"As I told them, I've known people who had trouble swallowing, just like you, but who could manage a small amount of sauce, pudding, or ice cream on their tongue. I wouldn't be doing this if I thought it might endanger you."

I believe you.

"So, here we are," he says, holding the tub up. "I'd like to offer you the choice and let you make it for yourself."

My first thought, again, is Hell yes. But then, if Knowland found out, he'd fire Ayo, at the very least. If I choked, or even if I didn't, he'd frame this as neglect at best, abuse at worst. Like Paul, Ayo could be arrested, charged, or even deported, and we'd be right back where we were with only Francis —

"I see you're conflicted. Honestly, I'd be surprised if you weren't. But listen. If this is what you want, what other people think about it doesn't matter. I don't plan on telling anyone. Whether you decide to is up to you."

Why, though? Why are you doing this?

"Forgive me, but are you asking why I'm —"

Yes.

"Because, Cliff, I'm thinking of what Ms. Angie said about making you happy, and of what Knowland mentioned, too, about having the freedom to take risks. I believe she meant what she said. As for Knowland, though, and call me crazy, but I don't think he was being honest."

I manage a weak smile.

"One thing I've learned, even if almost too late, is there's a difference between caring for someone and caring about them. The first takes a lot of work, but in the end, it's not so hard. Anyone can do it if they have to. Francis, for example."

My smile grows a little.

"Caring about someone, though, isn't so easy. It can't be done with mere physical effort. You must exert yourself in other ways." Ayo lays a palm across his chest. "You have to feel for them. Understand? Not in the sense that you're sorry for them, or that you pity them, but in the sense that all the time your heart has space for them. It's like . . ." He searches for the right word but comes up empty. "I'm sorry. That's about as close as I can come to putting it in English. All this to say that caring *about* someone means much more than passing out medications, or helping with a shower, or standing tall above a crowd and making speeches into bullhorns."

Huzzah!

"And sometimes, caring about someone means putting yourself in harm's way. I know what I'm doing, my friend. I know I could lose my job for this."

I'd rather you wouldn't.

"But I wouldn't have brought you here if I weren't willing to face the consequences. That's my decision to make. I also understand that, terrible as they sound, those consequences come nowhere close to what you'd be risking." He moves the hanky, tub, and spoon to his other hand. "I've done this many times before. I'm very careful. But should you agree and something happen, I wouldn't let you . . ."

He's staring at the moon again. I look up, too.

"I like working with you, Cliff," he says. "What I like most about this job is it gives me the chance to make your life a little better. I don't plan to waste that chance. Otherwise, I'd be no better than — how did Knowland put it? No better than the workers in those old institutions."

But we are, though.

We are, indeed.

I make a sound like an exasperated horse.

"I couldn't have put it better," Ayo says. "When someone's words don't line up with their actions, it's hard to trust them, isn't it?"

I nod.

"Do you trust me, Cliff?"

I nod again.

"Enough for this?"

I catch myself this time. Playing it safe sounds pretty good. We wouldn't have to worry about the consequences. We could just go back to the cookout and pretend like nothing happened, and I could leave the sauce's flavor to my imagination, keeping it, along with Silver Lining's most prestigious guest, in my dreams, where it belongs.

But he wants this as much as I do. I'm about to ask him why he'd risk everything he's worked so hard for, his employment and his very right to be here, for anyone, least of all me, when I decide maybe it's better I don't know. I should be satisfied just knowing he wants to make me happy. Still, it shouldn't have to be this way, that the few who really care feel like they've got to risk their jobs, or worse, to do them right.

"If you don't want to," he says, "that's okay. We can go back —"

I bring my arms together and clap my hands. I look down at the hanky, and at Ayo, and I nod.

"Are you sure?"

Let's do it.

"Okay, then."

He frees the spoon from its wrapper and peels the lid from the tub. It glistens in the funnel of orange light above our heads. The neighborhood has fallen to a haunting silence. Humming, Ayo gently dips the spoon into the tub and draws out a drop of sauce no bigger than a pearl. My mouth waters. My heart hammers through my shirt. The moon grins mischievously, defiant of the laws that keep it hanging there but no less governed by them.

"Remember, Cliff, if something happens, I'm right here."

I open my mouth and extend my jumpy tongue.

"Here's to independence," Ayo says, setting the sauce down gently. And then —

And then — nothing. No tang, texture, flavor, nothing but a small, wet weight, as if I've caught a single raindrop in a downpour. I can't say I'm surprised, but I should've considered this a possibility. It might've helped diminish this strange disappointment. The tub's not labeled, so it could've been that Ayo chose something bland at random without knowing it. Or it could be that my tastebuds have atrophied after decades of disuse. Either way, it's not worth dwelling on — and at least it isn't baby food. My expression unchanged, I close my mouth and let it sit there.

Ayo steps back and wipes the spoon with his hanky. "Well? What do you think?"

I wiggle my tongue and shake my head. The sauce remains flavorless and light.

"Not so good, then?"

"Nnnh."

"Not so bad?"

My lips purse.

"So, neither good nor bad?"

I nod.

"It isn't much at all," he frowns.

I nod harder.

"Well, that's too bad. One might even say a bit anticlimactic." He folds his hanky slowly, returns it to his pocket, and inspects the spoon. "I'm sorry, my friend. This might be the one thing I wasn't expecting. Maybe I should've picked another kind of sauce. But the important thing is you tried. You made your own choice. You should be proud of yourself for that. I am."

I try nodding, but all my energy is focused on not crying.

"If you like, I'll clean your tongue, if you'd rather not take the risk of swallowing it."

I sigh and put my tongue out. It isn't twitching anymore, but what I manage to say still sounds less like *Ah* than *Eugh.*

Ayo hoists the spoon into the air. A ball of light reflects off its white bowl, then disappears as he brings it to my face. A tear breaks free and slides down my cheek as the spoon lands on my tongue.

And then the explosions go off.

One chain bursts above us, too close to have come from anywhere but the office. It's so loud that Ayo shudders, drops the spoon, and stumbles back. I don't have to turn around to see it. The blasts obliterate the darkness, coloring the sky a surreal gold, then white, then red and blue. They hiss and boom and crackle and fade and are replaced by new eruptions, just as blaring and as bright. Ayo watches as a child might, and as I did once, when I was so young I thought they were in honor of the birthday of the world. Only when I smile do I realize that I, too, have become childlike — and that it's not because of these explosions, but the others. The ones no one, not even I, can see, because they're all inside my mouth.

Building gradually, like music brought to crescendo over several bars, the taste unfolds across my tongue, raw and beautiful, full and pungent, thick as the smells still emanating from the grills. It spreads electrically through my body, from my shoulders to my fingers, from my hips down to my toes. I have no frame of reference, nothing to compare this feeling to, but I imagine it must be something like the wild joy in Alec's face when he took his frenzied stand at Memory Makers. Suddenly, the way his body jerked and eyes went wide makes perfect sense. I twist against my belt. I flap my arms. I'd kick the air in ecstasy if my feet weren't strapped into their rests. Instead, I rock side to side in my chair's fitted seat, my smile waxing crescent. The whole thing only lasts a few seconds and fades with the sounds of Knowland's mortar blasts, but it leaves me feeling energized and unfettered, as if I've been reborn and liberated all at once.

As the crowd back at the cookout breaks out in raucous cheers, Ayo holds me steady by the shoulders, smiling broadly, but uncertainly. "Are you all right?"

My own grin might as well be etched into my face. I try to straighten up. I hold out my hand, fight through the cramping, and give him a jittery thumbs-up.

"You can taste it, after all? How is it, my friend?"

I nod. Then I swallow. And when I swallow, I don't choke.

Ayo steps back to behold the smoking sky. "I'm so glad," he says, "but I'm sorry it took so long to happen. I don't know what that was all about."

My smile widens. I shrug.

"But you are safe?"

I hold my thumb up higher.

"What a night this is, Cliff. I'd say the walk was well worth it."

He offers me his hand and we shake, his grip much firmer than it was when we first met.

"To independence," he says. "Though I can't promise we'll do this all the time. Probably, you wouldn't want to. Barbecue for breakfast sounds a bit unappetizing."

"Nyah."

"But if there's something else you want, or want to do, I'd like it if you let me know. I'll do my best to make it happen. Does that sound good?"

"Mm."

"It's a plan, then. Maybe even it's our own behavior plan."

This receives my full-throated support.

"Okey-doke." He drums out a little beat on either hip. "Should we be getting back? It might be nice to watch the show with the others."

We move slowly through a haze of colored smoke, my wheels whirring, my body jostled by cracks in the sidewalk. It's only when we've reached the office that my limbs leave off their shaking. At the spot where we met Angie earlier, I hit the brakes and raise my hand. Ayo nods and waits for me. I inhale, close my eyes, and don't think of anything but simply savor the subdued taste that still lingers on my tongue. Another round of mortars rises and explodes, painting the void behind my eyelids a brilliant, reddish gold, and as the noise gives way to silence, BJ's cry cuts through the night:

"Huzzah!"

EIGHT

The morning sun has raised the white flag to a tempest. First, there was that sweet, peppery smell you sometimes catch before one hits. Then the sky through Laura's window turned a jaundiced yellow, the deadbeat cousin of her bright and healthy walls. The wind strengthened, the birds cut short their chirping, and the traffic out on Broadmoor Street all but vanished. Then came the darkness and a cracking rent the sky to pieces, sending Lem and several others scrambling under their tables. When the rain began to fall, it was in slabs so thick it blotted out the sign across the street that reads

Second Chance Payday Loans
Get First Loan at Zero Interest*
(Some^ Restrictions Apply)
*** Ha-Ha, Just Kidding˙**
^ All, Actually
˙ :)

and an hour later, it's not showing any sign of letting up.

"Hey there, Cliff," says Blake with a sprightliness unphased by the foul weather. "Listen, buddyroo. We need to figure out which of these to color next." He sets aside the Shrek he's filled in with colored pencil and presents me with two choices: Woody and Kung Fu Panda. "Well? What do you say?"

I say, "Eh."

"I hear you," he laughs, loudly, in my ear. "Some days you just feel crabby. And that rain's not helping, is it?"

I shrug. Blake pats my knee. He shoves his smile in my face like a salesman would his product.

"How about Kung Fu Panda? Everyone loves him." He said the same of Shrek when I refused to choose between him and the Boss Baby. "I have a feeling he's about to turn that frown right upside-down."

I hope Blake's not a betting man. He should be feeling lucky I can't sock him in the jaw. Last night I had another dream about the woman in the

Silver Lining ads, and for the last twenty minutes he's been keeping me from remembering it with his talk of how we should stay positive even when things are at their darkest. What he doesn't know, what I'd scream into that smile if I could, is that everything was going fine until he plopped down next to me hugging those printouts.

"Don't count on it," says Stella, coloring aggressively, disregarding lines and filling in her characters with black Crayola.

"Stella," Laura sings from the next table, where she's helping Everett with Buzz Lightyear, "you've been making poopy faces all day long. What's the matter?"

Stella scrawls a death shroud over Pooh Bear's likeness. "Nothing. I'm fine."

"Well, aren't we just a glum bunch today?"

"Not I, I'll have you know."

"You might be the only one, BJ," Laura says. "You must still be riding high from your performance at the cookout, which, by the way, was wonderful."

As he puts crayon to paper, BJ's grin is anything but modest.

"I thought so, too," Savannah adds, her red hair all up in a bun. "It was the best part of the night."

Removing Alec's giant head from her shoulder — it's been his pillow since we started coloring, and he leaves it dark with drool — Savannah folds his arms together on the table and gently sets it down on them. This is his first day back since last week's Hail Mary incident, and he might be the only one who doesn't know it. His residential staff basically dragged him in this morning like a drunk friend in dire need of a couch. His dead eyes have opened twice in these two hours. He hasn't said *bough* even once.

"Was it even better than the food?" Blake says with an incredulity whose false innocence borders on the mocking.

"If not better, then just as good."

"You can say that again."

"I'm not one to brag, of course," says BJ, setting aside the finished page and going for another from his stack, "but I do have the voice of an angel."

"You sure do, BJ," Laura says, "and we're glad you're so willing to share it with us."

Stella crumples up the morbid Pooh, chucks him to the floor, and puts her head down on the table. "At least someone had a good time at the cook-out."

"Stella, sweetie." Laura glides to the girl and rubs her shoulder. "This isn't like you. Please, tell us what's the matter. I hate seeing you so sad."

"You might as well get used to it," Stella mumbles through her fore-arms. "This is the new me, the true me, the me who understands that life is agony, happiness is an illusion, and love is the greatest lie of all."

Her new look reflects the sea change in her philosophy. She's dyed her hair the color of her crayon. Her fingernails and eyelashes are also painted black. Her bracelets and her shirt are the same sepulchral hue, and on her chest it says, in letters white and faded and forlorn:

THE CURE

"Oh, Stella." Her sitcom-mother's face swelled up with stifled laughter, Laura kneels beside her. "I don't know what happened, or what's gotten into you, but I can tell you that you won't feel any better if you don't talk about it."

"What's the point of feeling better? Aren't we all just going to die, anyway?"

"Not for a long, long time, and we need to make the best of it while we're here. You know that better than anyone."

"Maybe I did, but not anymore. Please, Laura, just leave me be so I can sulk in peace."

"All right, hon," Laura smiles. "Just know I'm here for you when you're ready."

"Don't hold your breath."

The thunder grumbles like a god who needs to be appeased. Lem ducks back under the table, only to peer over its edge a moment later, a dismayed Kilroy. Across from him, Willa swirls sea green over *Snow White's* evil queen, and next to her sits Rickey, calm as ever, not coloring but blinking at his Cookie Monster sheet.

"I wish Cliff could let me know what's bugging him," Blake says, and slides the paper closer. "He's been out of sorts all morning, too."

Behind the walls of her arm fortress, Stella titters scornfully. "Go figure."

"What's the story with you two? I thought you and Cliff were friends."

"I told you I don't want to talk about it."

"Okay, angel. I'll leave you be for —"

"Fine. You got me, Laura. I'll talk." Stella's head shoots up like cannon fire. "I guess I don't have a choice since you keep hounding me."

"What I said was you can tell me when you're —"

"I did," Stella begins. "I thought Cliff and I were friends."

"I did, too," says Blake.

"And I." Everett nods in the opposite direction.

"Actually, I thought we were more than that." Stella fidgets with her sable bracelets. "But now I know the truth, and so do you. We're not either one anymore, and if I'm being honest, we never really ever were."

"Don't you say that, lady." Laura's wiping the crayon marks Everett made on the table in her absence. "It isn't true, and you know it."

"How would you know? Just because we're here three days a week doesn't mean you know everything about us. Anyway, you asked. Well, I'm telling you, aren't I? Aren't I?"

"Yes, of course you are. I'm sorry. I didn't mean to give you the impression that your feelings aren't important. They're very important to me, your staff, and everybody in this room."

"Not everybody."

"Aw, what did Cliff do this time?" BJ says, his frown tight and unforgiving.

"And how come Stella isn't calling him 'Cliffy'?" Everett asks.

"If you'll just let me talk, I'll let you know." Stella chokes up as she dries the delicate black streams from the white plains that are her cheeks. "I thought Cliff and I were friends. I thought we were more than that. But that all changed on Friday, when he — when he —"

A monstrous crack of thunder sounds, a sudden windblast blows the main door open, and in sweeps the pouring rain — and Greg. Clad not in a raincoat but a sopping shirt of lime-green paisley, he stands in the entrance holding a briefcase, slightly dazed, eyes adjusting to the room's yellow walls. Save for the skin around his eyes, his face is even tanner than it was last week, and clinging to the skin below his lower lip, like a barnacle, is a soul patch that accentuates not his jowls so much as their thick wrinkles. Thankfully, the stench of his cologne, an infernal concoction of Mountain Dew Code Red and canine anal-gland secretion, has been dampened by the rain, but it still hangs faintly in the air like one of the room's elephants.

"Hell of a storm out there," he says. Defying several laws of nature, his spiky hair remains in perfect shape.

Laura squints. "That you, Mr. Gabhart?"

"In the flesh, if I can still refer to it as such."

"Please, come in and dry yourself off. Everybody, this is Greg. Some of you might already know him. He'll be hanging out with us a while. He's Cliff's new friend, which means he's our new friend. What do we say to Greg?"

"Hi, Greg," says everyone, though coming from some it sounds like Gag.

"How ya doin', champs?"

"Good to see you," Laura hums. "I barely recognized you, though, what with that —"

"With this old thing?" Greg strokes the graying shellfish above his chin. "I almost didn't recognize me either. 'Holy smokes,' I said into the mirror. 'Who's that handsome cross between George Hamilton and all of NSYNC?' What do you think?" He slams the door and stands with fists on hips, a Superman in the midst of a midlife crisis. "Pretty fly for a white guy, eh?"

Willa says, "Don't count on it."

Greg takes this in stride as he slithers through the room, his skin glistening, his tongue exposed between two flaky lips. Leering at our coloring sheets, he smiles at the ones who've stayed between the lines, grimaces at those of us who haven't. When he reaches Alec, who's still face-down and slobbering, he raps the table with four knuckles all but crying out for moisturizer. A moment later, the same hand squeezes my shoulder like a snake swallowing an egg.

"Didn't forget our meeting, did you?"

I try to blow a raspberry but end up sounding more like a dying donkey.

"Is that how we talk to friends?" says Blake.

"It's all right. We're still establishing rapport. Cliff hasn't warmed up to me yet, but it'll happen soon enough." Greg releases my shoulder, allowing me to breathe. He steals the empty seat beside me and planks his briefcase on the floor. It's one of those whose texture is like alligator scales, its top half darker than the bottom from the rain. Unsnapping its jaws, Greg pulls out a notebook and a pen, then puts his feet up on the table, crossing them at the ankles. He's wearing canvas slip-ons without socks, and wags the top foot back and forth, flinging water on the bear that Blake is coloring. "So, what's the plan for today?"

"You're looking at it." Blake drags the page his way and smooths the wet spots out.

"Just about." Laura has taken over coloring for Everett, whose crayon marks she couldn't get out of the table. "I was thinking we might take a walk, but it doesn't look like that'll happen anytime soon."

"Doubtful. It's rotten out there."

"Well, it's not any better in here."

"Could've fooled me," says Greg, taking in the glum bunch.

"Today's been tough. In fact, the only one who isn't feeling low is BJ."

"That's right," beams BJ. "I'm still riding high from my performance at the cookout."

"I was there," says Greg. "You sure did sing a lot."

"How'd you like to hear an encore?" BJ rises, hand to chest. "I know 'Ring of Fire' and 'Boot-Scootin' Boogie.'"

"Too bad there wasn't time for those at the barbecue."

"You're telling me, partner."

"Maybe after lunch we'll have a sing-along," says Laura. "That is, if anybody's feeling up to it. But thank you, BJ, for your kind offer."

"Why not now? It might help cheer everyone up."

"That's true, but if you'll remember, before Greg came in, Stella was sharing what's bothering her."

"Is Stella here today?" Greg scans the room. "I didn't see her when I — oh, wow. Wow. Hi, Stella. Wow. I didn't recognize you, what with that —"

"What with what? With all this sadness? All these tears? What with this useless, bleeding heart?" Stella cups her hands below her breasts as if to catch the blood hemorrhaging from her ticker like oil from a fractured pipeline. "With this new knowledge that life is just one long parade of pain and sorrow? With this empty husk that was my body, barren and forsaken? Or with this tattered, broken soul that's been cast into the wild, lonesome, friendless, loveless, and bleaker than a dark November day?"

Outside, the lightning strikes, the thunder rumbles.

"I was going to say with that Cure T-shirt, but those things, too, I guess?"

"You guess? You come in here unannounced and wearing paisley, interrupt me when I'm pouring my heart out, barely recognize me even though I saw you Friday, and even after I explain in no uncertain terms why I look and feel like this, all you can do is guess?"

"Stella, dear," says Laura, "I know you're upset, but that's not the way we talk when we're with fr—"

"I don't have friends! I don't have anyone! All I have is black despair, broad and boundless as the night!"

"Wanna cookie."

Greg is doodling the Mötley Crüe logo in his notebook. "I can come back another time, Laura, if you think it might work better."

"No, I won't hear of it. You scheduled this. You made the trip. You're staying. Besides, if anyone's equipped to handle days like this, it's you."

"Well, the praise is always welcome, and I'd be glad to help if I could, but I don't work with" — Greg nods at Stella — "so I couldn't bill for it. But if she's interested in getting a behaviorist, which probably needs to happen ASAP, I can ask around. Portia might have some openings, now that I think of it."

"I know you're talking about me," Stella says into her palms. "You don't need to make it some big secret."

"What? Me? Never."

"You nodded right at me. I could see you through my fingers."

"No, I didn't."

"Yes, you did. You know, just because I have a disability doesn't mean I'm stupid."

"Of course not, darling," Laura says. "Why would you think that? Nobody said anyone was stupid."

"He didn't have to. I saw his face. Look at him. He's still making it."

Greg sneers like an ersatz Calvin peeing on the words GOOD TASTE. "I am not."

"See, sweetheart? He said he's not. Greg didn't come here to hurt anyone. He came to help."

"I don't need his help."

"You sure need someone's help," Greg whispers.

Stella's hands fly from her face, launching black tears everywhere. "What did you say?"

"Nothing."

"Don't lie to me, Brad Paisley. You said something. I know it."

"No, I didn't."

"Yes, you did."

Greg lifts his hands in surrender. "All right. Guilty as charged. I did say something. The truth is, I didn't want to make you any angrier, so I whispered it. I said I wish I could help you, but as I just mentioned, it's not my job, and clearly, you don't want it. But listen, if the funds are in your state budget and you want to work with Portia —"

"I don't want to work with Portia. I don't want to work with anyone. The only thing you, her, and anyone can do for me is mind your own damn business."

"Stella! Watch your —"

"No, Laura. The girl's right. I've taken this too far. All it's done is made her more upset. We should probably leave her be for now."

"That might be a problem, though," says Blake.

Marking out the hair-band logo, Greg flips his notebook's page. "Oh, really?"

"You're here to work with Cliff, right? Well, he's been cranky all day, too." Blake's face goes all faux grumpy. "He wouldn't even pick which ones to color."

He holds the pages up for Greg to see. The characters all pose in the same way, arms crossed, heads tilted to the left. Their expressions, too, are identical, the eyebrows smugly cocked in the same arch. Each grins as if in recognition that we're all in on the joke. I've been wondering for years just what's so funny. For the life of me I can't figure it out.

Greg mirrors their smirks. In his notebook, he writes one word: *Noncompliance.*

"Why on Earth not?" he says.

"I don't know," Blake says from behind the colored Shrek, butchering the pale-green ogre's Scottish accent. "He'd rather be a sourpuss, I guess. But I'm pretty sure it has to do with Stella. It seems she and Cliff have had a falling out."

"No! What over?"

"She hasn't told us yet."

"All we know," says Everett, "is that she doesn't call him 'Cliffy' anymore."

"Yikes. So that's what it's come to. But I thought Stella and Cliff were tight." Greg crosses his middle and index fingers. "Like this."

"That's what I thought, too," Laura frowns. "That's what we all thought. Why, just last week I was telling Cliff she was a keeper."

Beak poised above his paper, BJ draws with a red crayon. "She saved his life, you know, and would you look how he rewards her."

"Saved his life? That sounds courageous. And well above her pay grade. How'd she do it?"

"You mean you didn't hear?"

Greg shrugs. "What happened, Stella? Did you give Cliff the Heimlich? Call 911? Make him overdose on all your positivity? Hit me with it. I'm ready as I'll ever be. The more you can give me, the better. As I told his staff the other day, I've got my work cut out for me with this one."

"It wasn't any of those things," BJ sighs. "It was something a lot messier."

"I'd be lying if I said I didn't like where this is going."

"Well, too bad for you," Stella grunts. "I don't want to talk about it anymore."

Below *Noncompliance*, Greg writes *Strained relationships with friends*. "It is too bad, because I'm dying to hear you tell the tale. C'mon, Stella. I don't like being in the dark. It scares the ever-loving feces out of me."

"Not my problem."

Laura smacks the table. The sound is damp and empty, like someone knocking on a rotten log. "That's not how we talk to our guests, and you know it. Please apologize to Greg."

"For what?"

"For the way you've been speaking to him since he got here."

Stella crosses her arms. Her shirt now says THE CUR. "What if I don't?"

"Then I'll have to call Pauline and ask her to come get you early. I think she'll agree that yours isn't the kind of attitude we like to see at Memory Makers."

"Big whoop. Go ahead and call her. I won't be missing anything."

"Maybe not." Laura crosses her arms right back at her. "But maybe, if you keep it up, you won't be joining us on our next trip to Howler's."

Leaping from her seat, Stella cries her first tears of the day that aren't for me. "That's not fair, Laura, and you know it."

"Is it fair of you to treat Greg like you have? What has he ever done except try and help you feel better?"

"Is that, um, is that what he's been doing?"

"What else would you call it?"

"Well, it kind of seemed like he was patronizing me and making light of my pain."

"That couldn't be further from the truth," grumbles Greg. "I'm sorry you feel that way."

"You sure don't look like it."

Greg smiles, his mouth wide open, like a water dragon cooling itself off. "Whatever do you mean?"

"I mean, what exactly's going on with your face right now?"

"Stella."

"What, Laura?"

"We don't make fun of the way people look."

"But I'm not. It's an honest question. Is he smiling or trying to catch bugs?"

"Why couldn't it be both?" Everett wonders, his eyes foggy-white.

"Fair question," Greg says.

"Regardless, there's still someone who won't be having fun at Howler's unless they apologize."

"Fine." Stella's shoulders sink. "I'm sorry, Greg."

"Look at him when you say it."

She does. "Sorry."

"And what are we sorry for?"

"FForthewayIspoketoyou."

Greg cups a hand behind his ear. "What was that, precious?"

"For the way I spoke to you," Stella huffs, falling back into her chair.

"And . . .?"

"And?"

"And for calling me Brad Paisley?"

Stella hides her face behind her black-nail-painted hands. "And for calling you Brad Paisley. There, I said it, Laura. Can I go to Howler's now?"

"We'll get to that. Greg, do you accept her apology?"

His camera out in selfie mode, Greg is touching up his forehead with a bottle of spray tan. *Pssh,* it goes, and then he dabs the wet spot with a cotton ball. "It could've been more genuine, if you want the honest truth. But I appreciate the effort and I'm prepared to meet her where she is. Apology accepted."

The room bursts into applause. BJ high-fives his neighbor once, twice, three times over. Willa cackles merrily as Alec, still unconscious, makes a mess in his classic three-stripe shorts.

"Augh," Everett says. "What's that smell?"

"I think somebody pooped," Savannah says.

"No, not that smell. The other one. It's like a dog had diarrhea after drinking Mountain Dew."

"Oh, that. Actually, I kind of like it."

"Me, too," Laura says.

"Well, I don't, and I wish someone would do something about it."

"I'll take care of the human poo, at least," says Blake.

He's helping Alec to the restroom when Greg stands and coughs. "Apology accepted, Stella," he says, "on one condition."

Stella falters from inside her finger forest. "On what condition?"

"That you tell me — tell us, tell everybody — what happened Friday between you and Cliff."

Another peal of thunder sends half the room into fresh panic.

"How did you know it was Friday?"

"I heard you mention it as I was coming in. It seemed like you were having a real moment. I'm sorry to have interrupted when I did. It might be my life's greatest regret."

"Isn't that so nice of Greg?" Laura asks. "He's apologizing even though he doesn't have to. Answering him would be a great way to say thanks."

"What do you say, Stella? Just let me know what happened and we'll call it even-stevens."

"I told you," Stella whispers, "I don't want to talk about it anymore."

"I'm sorry to hear that." Greg scribbles the words TWISTED SISTER in his notebook. "But not as sorry as I am to have to ask you in the first place. The thing is, if I'm to help Cliff, I'll need all the gory details. I'd much rather ask him, but, well, you know . . ."

"I know," says Laura, pouting.

"What you might not be aware of is the hard time Cliff's been having on the home front. There've been mood swings, he's flying into rages for no apparent reason, and, and . . ." Greg looks at the poster on the wall that says PERSISTENCE below a sleeping cat. "But no, I've said too much already. Everyone's having a bad enough day as it is."

"What did he do?" Stella says.

Greg's foot rocks back and forth on the table. "You're asking me?"

"You said Cliff's been having mood swings. What's wrong with him?"

"As I say, buttercup, now's probably not the time." Greg sighs and shuts his notebook. "I'm sorry, Laura. This just isn't working. I'll come back another day."

"No." Stella shoots up, arms at her sides. "You're not leaving until you tell me."

"That's not a good idea. No, I won't do it. Ever. You've established your boundaries. I should respect them — and you. All of you. Consider this my way of doing that." As Greg rises, a glob of mud flies from one of his slip-ons and lands on my chair with a *splat*. "Well, it's been real, y'all, and it's been fun, but I can't say it's been real —"

"You're not leaving," Stella says, her face ablaze, her fists balled up, "until you tell me."

"Heh. I admire your spunk, sweetums. I'm glad to see it hasn't disappeared with your new . . . look. But much as I'd love to, I can't. I've played the tape over and over. It never ends well. There are no positives to telling you how Cliff smashed that precious staff log, how he crushed Brad's business laptop, or how he damn-near killed his staff the other —"

"What?" says everybody, their tidal wave of eyes walloping my craggy coastline.

"Aw, shucks. I've spilled the beans."

"That doesn't sound like Cliff to me," says Everett. "Maybe it was an accident."

This trickle of a guess soon swells into a torrent of speculation that goes on for a whole minute: *Was it on purpose, what Cliff did?* everyone asks. *Or was it an honest mistake? Either way, just what the heck is going on with him these days? Perhaps he's constipated? Even if he is, that's no excuse. Half the room gets constipated once a week. The staff are only there to help him. Why would Cliff try to kill them? And did he use a pair of nunchakus in the attempt?*

"It wasn't an accident," rises a voice above the rest, after a while. "And it wasn't with a pair of nunchakus, either. It was with that — that — it was with that death machine."

Heads whip toward my housemate.

"What'd you say, BJ?"

"I said it was the death machine." His mouth small, his eyes slits, BJ aims a knobby finger at my chair. "I hate to be the bearer of bad news, and it shames me to admit it, but that man's an attempted murderer." Over their scandalized gasps, he tells the room everything he knows, from the time I crushed a cell phone to my demolishing a box of Cocoa Krispies. "Just like a steamroller," he says, blowing red crayon slivers from his glasses.

"Thanks, Beej." Greg nods solemnly. "I know how hard that was for you."

"If you think that was hard, imagine living with the guy."

Laura's got her hands pressed together in prayer. "This doesn't make any sense. It's crazy. The person BJ's described — that's not the Cliff I know."

"Me, either." Everett says.

From the restroom comes a tired, nauseous moan.

Greg reclaims his seat and hikes his feet back on the table. In his notebook, he writes *Disappoints both peers and Laura.* "Who is the Cliff you know?"

"He's been coming here three days a week for years," Laura says. "He's a sweet man. A kind man. When I heard you'd be working with him, I said, 'My God, why?'"

"Really? How come?"

"Because we've only ever seen his laid-back side, his quiet side. He's always smiling. Always happy. He gets along with everyone. He doesn't just engage in each activity. He seems to really like them, especially the sing-alongs, even though he can't, well, sing along." Laura makes a bridge out of her hands and rests her chin on it. "This is just so darn upsetting. Hard to believe. Have you ever seen him acting out, Savannah?"

"Never. I started working here last summer. This is the first bad day

Cliff has had in all that time. He's been a real joy to have around. Most days it's like he's not even here."

"That's why we hope you get him back to normal soon, Greg." Laura shoots me a mournful look. "The Cliff we know would never hurt a soul."

"I thought so, too, until he broke my heart."

Greg grins at Stella through the thunder. Curiously, she smiles back.

"What do you mean, he broke your heart?"

"For Pete's sakes, Cliff," says Everett. "Why'd you do it?"

"No, listen, guys," Stella says calmly. "It's okay now. I'm over it. I just thought you should know because —"

Everett lifts his unseeing eyes to the ceiling. "How in blazes are you already over it? Last I heard, you and Cliff were scheduled to be married any day now."

"Well, not anymore," sighs BJ.

"Jeez. Just when it seemed things couldn't possibly get worse."

"It's all right. Didn't you hear? I said I'm over —"

"Clifford Emerson," Laura scolds. "And after everything she's done for you —"

"What has she done for him, other than save his life?" Greg is snacking on a bag of pretend popcorn. "I'm still dying to know how she did it, by the way."

"Why, she helps him every day," Savannah says. "Like when we play Trouble. Stella pops the bubble, then moves his pieces on the board."

"She even says 'I win!' when it's not true," says Everett.

Greg whistles his surprise. "You weren't kidding, Laura. This girl is a real keeper."

"I'd say," BJ scowls. "Especially after last week, when she took that turd for him."

"What!" says Everett, shocked. "How did I miss that?"

"You were still lying on the floor, when Laura tackled you, remember?"

"Oh, yeah. Thanks for that, Laura. I'm ever grateful."

"You're welcome, dear."

"Holy Moses." Greg whistles again, this time much louder, right in my ear. "This turd, my friends: whose was it?"

Everyone nods at the restroom, from which both Blake and Alec groan.

"Right. So that's how she saved his life."

"I told her she shouldn't have done it. It's staff's job to make sure everyone's safe. But that's what love is like, isn't it? It blinds us to our own well-being." Laura gives the keeper a caring nod. "Thank you, Stella, for sharing this. I'm so sorry you're in pain. If you want a shoulder to cry on, I'm here for you."

"So am I, I'll have you know."

"Thanks, Laura and BJ, but as I say, I'm —"

"And as for you, Cliff, I'm afraid BJ is right. You ought to be ashamed of what you've done, hurting your friends so badly. I think you owe one very special person an apology."

I'm so confused I can't even grunt. One of the few things I've ever really wanted has been for Stella to get over me. Had it happened long ago, it never would've come to this. I never would've felt bad for not wanting her that way. I never would've had to break her heart. Above all, she never would've had to go all Edgar Allan Poe on us. But the weirdest thing just happened, and I have no idea what it means. When she said those words, "I'm over it," which on any other day I would've died to hear her say, my heart exploded like a bomb inside my chest.

"Well, Cliff?" BJ crosses his arms. "We're waiting."

"Look, champ," Greg says, "I know this isn't easy. It's never fun admitting we've done somebody wrong. Add to that the fact that well, you know" — he slashes an X across his vocal cords like he did to Ayo at the cookout — "and it makes for a doubly difficult time." He hauls his sockless feet off the table and scoots toward me, planting his elbows on his knees. "How about this, though. What if you nod to say you're sorry, shake your head to say you're not? That sound good?"

"I don't need him to apologize. I said I'm fine."

"Sounds perfect to me," Laura says.

I just don't understand it. Stella's moved on. She's even said so more than once. This is a cause for celebration. There should be pyrotechnics and a ticker-tape parade. I've never had more reason to be happy — for us both — which is why I can't explain this gaping emptiness, like someone's hollowed out my insides with an ice-cream scoop.

"That's too bad," Greg says, ending the terrible silence. "It seems someone would rather stay at home than go with the group next time to Howler's."

"I'd sure hate for that to happen. I know how much fun you guys have there." Laura curls her lips. "Even you, Cliff. Since I know you're a better man than this, I'm going to give you one more chance. Go ahead, please. Look Stella in the eye, do as we've asked, and tell her you're —"

"Stop it! Stop it, all of you! Why won't you listen to me?" Stella flaps her arms, a defensive mother goose. "I don't need him to apologize, okay? Don't you know it's not his fault?"

"Not his fault?" Greg smiles. "My ears must be giving out. I could've sworn I heard you say he crushed your soul the other night."

Stella retreats to the stronghold of her folded arms. "He did, but he couldn't help himself. It's not his fault. It's just who he is."

"I beg to differ," says Laura. "That's not who he is. Search your heart, Stella. It's only there you'll find the truth."

"That's what I thought, too. But the truth I've found is that I didn't have a clue. I thought I really loved Cliff. I thought he loved me back. It seemed so pure, the two of us together, like something out of a bedtime storybook. At least that's what I told myself. And I believed it, too, with all my heart. That's why it hurt so much when he said I couldn't join him on that walk. My whole world came crashing down, like that house they built on sand in the Bible. It's my fault it fell, though. I put it there in the first place. I believed in an illusion. But I've rebuilt my house now, this time on a rock. I see things for how they really are." Stella's eyes are wet and bright with understanding and relief. "I see that if I really loved Cliff, I would've known how much he's suffered. I would've seen how much he's battled with himself and how hard it's been for him because he can't tell anyone about it. You're right, Laura. I was blinded, but not by love. It was by selfishness. I only ever thought about what I wanted. I didn't care that Cliff wanted something different. I didn't care, because I didn't know, because I didn't see the man he really is. The way he's been acting, lashing out like that, is the only way he has of telling us he's hurting." She brings her hands up to her heart and nods. "I'm not saying it's right. I'm just saying I get it. I'm saying that if I'd really loved Cliff then, loved him the way I do today, I would've listened when he tried to tell me this, respected his decision, and supported him as best I could, even though it wasn't what I wanted. That's what you always say, Laura, isn't it? That when you're friends with someone, you're friends with them for good, no matter what?"

"That's so right, honey," Laura says, drying the rivers of mascara running down her face. "I say it every day, don't I?"

"Just about."

"Bravo, Stella." Greg writes something down and then springs up. "You've made more progress with Cliff in seven minutes than I could've made in seven months."

"I wouldn't go that far," Stella says, fingers fumbling.

"Then don't. I'll do it for you. After that performance, I'm not sure he needs me anymore. What do you think, Cliff? Would you rather work with her, or what?"

Laura says, "Look at that face. I think he's still in shock."

"Wouldn't you be, too," says Greg, "if someone spoke for you the words you couldn't speak for yourself?"

"I don't know what I'd do, except be grateful there were people in my life who cared for me like this girl cares for Cliff."

"Amen to that," Savannah says. "Thanks, Stella, for turning the frown of this bad day right upside-down."

"Any time."

After the cheers, tears, and my peers, led by BJ, singing "For She's a Jolly Good Fellow," Greg tugs his soul patch thoughtfully. "You know, Stella, as indebted as I am to you for helping out, I have to say I'm also super-jealous. How'd you figure out what's wrong with Cliff so quickly?"

"I don't know. It just happened. I wasn't sure at first that what Pauline had said was true. But the more I thought about it, the more it started to make sense."

"What did? What'd Pauline say to you?"

Stella makes a face that says, Like, duh. "That Cliff is gay."

"What!" the whole room blurts.

"Did you say, 'Cliff is gay'?"

"Guilty as charged," Willa cackles.

"Congratulations, pal!" Everett says to the ceiling.

"This is such fantastic news," says Laura. "How did I miss it all these years?"

"Don't feel bad," Savannah says. "We all did."

"But for how long has he been gay?" Everett asks.

"Probably since he was little," says BJ.

"So you'd think," Laura says. "It isn't like he has a choice."

I silently swat at the air.

Everett coughs. "That's not what my uncle used to say."

"That's not what Pauline said, either." Stella says. "Actually, she didn't say 'gay.' She used another word, one I won't repeat in front of friends. I love her to death, but she can be so embarrassing sometimes. Her worldview is, well, let's just say a little backwards."

"So I've noticed.," Everett shakes his head in disappointment.

"But me, I'm much more open-minded. I've learned to accept my friends for who they are, no questions asked." Stella nods at me again to great applause. "I'm really sorry, Cliff, that it took me so long to get you. Even after Pauline told me, albeit in her crude and dated way, I couldn't bring myself to believe her. I still feel terrible about it."

"Don't get down on yourself, hon. How could you have known? You said it yourself. Poor Cliff can't talk about his feelings."

"You're right, but still, I should've seen it. All the signs were there. I mean, why else wouldn't he want a piece of this?" Stella strikes a sexy pose, then laughs at her new outfit. "Jeepers. The last few days have been such a blur of pain and sadness. At some point I must've asked Pauline to take me to Hot Topic."

"You look fantastic."

"Thanks, Everett, but I think I'll go back to my old clothes after today."

"No, thank you, Stella, for being such a great friend."

"And thank you, Cliff, for being honest. Even in the best of circumstances, coming out takes so much courage. That you've managed to do so in spite of all your other challenges is just so gosh-darn inspirational. I'm sorry." Dabbing her tears, Laura smiles at the yellow walls. "After I lost Ethan, I was devastated. God knew I'd need courage to keep going, but I wasn't sure I wanted or deserved to, and anyway, I didn't think I had it in me. But as the days turned into weeks, and the weeks into months, it dawned on me: not only had I found that courage, but that no matter what anybody else was going through, theirs could never be as strong as mine." Coming to me, she wipes cold sweat from my forehead with the back of her hand. "That's what I believed with all my heart, until today."

I writhe around in my seat, trying and failing to escape her touch.

"It's okay, Cliff. There's no need to be ashamed. As Stella said, we'll always be your friends, no matter what. You should be proud of yourself. We're all very proud of you. Isn't that right, you guys?"

Amid the chorus of supportive praise smirks Henry Wray, a demon among angels. He's the only one whose eyes reflect the truth. Stella didn't fool me into thinking she had changed. I fooled myself, like a man lost in the desert pinning his hopes on a mirage.

"I have something to say, please," says BJ, rising. Behind his red-flecked lenses, his eyes shine with love and deep regret. "We've known each other many years, Cliff. We've lived together ever since you left the hospital. Yes, we've had our differences. I never understood why you behaved the way you sometimes did. It stressed me out, how you'd crush a binder or try to murder Francis for no reason. Most of all, it scared me. Things got so bad sometimes I wished you'd go away forever." He shudders at the thought. "What I didn't know was that you were fighting with yourself, and you feared you didn't fit in with the rest of us. It must've seemed like you were all alone in this cold world." BJ thrusts his hand up at the waning storm. "I'm not saying this justifies your bad behaviors. You've put me through a lot of grief, you little stinker. But here's the thing. I tell you all the time, and it's still true. You and I are best friends. We always have been and always will be. I'm sorry for not seeing this in you before. But no matter who you are or who you love, I'll support you, Cliff, completely. We're all proud of you, old pal, but no one's prouder than I am, I say."

The room's acclaim rings like a hundred thunderclaps. Instinctively, my hands fly near my ears but don't reach them. BJ bows, then stoops to pick his glasses up. Laura rushes to her office, comes back with several tissue boxes, and throws them out like Oprah hurling money at her audience. Emerging from his space under the table, even Lem appears to smile.

It's not until the clamor and the rain die, not until the sunlight penetrates the clouds through Laura's window, that Greg's slow clapping bounces off the yellow walls. "How heartwarming is this?" he says, his voice crackly, like someone's who hasn't used theirs in a while. "God, how I wish John were here. Was anyone recording?"

"Sadly not." Savannah drops a wad of tissues in the trash.

"I was so caught up in the moment I didn't even think about it," Laura says.

"That's all right. I'm just grateful to have been a witness. Otherwise, I wouldn't have believed it." Greg grabs and twists my shoulder, as if feeling for the best grip to launch a changeup. "No joke, Cliff, this is hands-down the most fruitful session I've had in all my years as a behaviorist. Think of the ground we've covered in this short hour. Think of the progress. The man before me now isn't the man I saw when I trudged in here, soaking wet. He's gone, replaced by someone new, someone comfortable with himself and with his deepest, darkest secrets." He throws his off-speed pitch, leaving my shoulder damp with rainwater. "The irony is that none of it is thanks to me. All I had to do was watch as our dear Stella stole the show. No, it's true. I came prepared. I had a long list of questions. She asked and answered the whole lot — with one glaring exception."

"What would that be?"

"Isn't it obvious?" Greg slings his notebook into the trash, a disc golf hole-in-one. "Who's the lucky guy?"

He rides the quiet wave of *oohs* like a surfer, arms stretched so that his body forms a *T*, then sticks his tongue out to one side and throws me two hang-ten signs.

"That was my next question, too, I'll have you know."

"I wouldn't doubt it for a second."

"Well, who is it, Cliff?" says Everett. "Don't leave us hanging here like this."

"This is so exciting. Anyone else on pins and needles?"

"I'm on something, Laura." Greg brandishes his lizard smile at me. "For real, though, champ. The cat's out of the bag. There's no point in hiding anymore, no need to run."

"He might not be ready yet," says BJ.

"That could be. See how he digs his chin into his shoulder."

"But when will he be ready, if not now?"

"Probably next week," says Everett.

"But that's so far away."

"No, it's actually a great point," Laura says. "I say we give him time. Some things can't be rushed. If anybody knows this, Greg, it's you and I."

"Mm-hmm. Again, I'm sorry. Our progress might've sent me a bit overboard. You're right, Laura. Sometimes the best thing we can do for these folks is back off for a while."

"Amen to that," Willa says.

"Well, I know you'll probably meet with Cliff much more when he's at home, but we'd love to have you back. You're welcome anytime. He's here three days a week."

"Maybe I will come back before too long." Greg heaves his alligator briefcase over his shoulder like a hunter who's just bagged a kill. "Good to see you, champs. Until next time."

"What do we say, guys?"

"G'bye, Gag!"

"Bye, now." But halfway to the door, he wheels around. "One last question, Cliff, and then I'll leave you be, I promise."

"Don't you think he's had enough for one day?" BJ says.

"He's had much more than that. But I had another thought, and if I don't ask now, I might forget it. You wouldn't want that to happen, would you?"

"I don't know how I'd sleep at night if —"

"Good, BJ. That's what I thought." Greg oozes back to my table. "Besides, it's nothing big. I just want to dot my T's and cross my I's before I write this session up."

"Well, what is it?"

Plopping his briefcase down on Kung Fu Panda, Greg towers over me like Francis grinning down at Brad. "I'll understand if you're not ready, but if you'd find it in your heart to answer me, it'd be most helpful."

"He'd be happy to," says Laura.

"Here's what I don't get, and again, it's probably nothing, but I'd like to clear this up today, if we can. As much as some of us, including me, would rather not admit it, there's a chance, however small, that Stella's wrong."

"That's not possible," Stella says.

"Of course, sweetness. It's probably not the case. But my work involves a lot of guessing, especially with these more nonverbal folks. Before I write a plan, I've got to be as certain as I can that what I think is wrong is right. If not, it'd be like replacing my car's flat with one of these." Greg kicks my chair's front wheel. "Do you think that'd help Cliff feel better?" Stella's silence indicates her disagreement. "That's what I thought, too."

"How can you know for sure, though?"

"Help us out, Cliff. If Stella's wrong, and you're not, well, you know, then what were you and Ayo doing Friday at the cookout? I saw you both escaping into the night as we were setting off the fireworks. Where were you headed, pal? Why'd you leave?"

"They went to take a walk, like I said. That was when he broke my heart, when he said he didn't want me to come with him."

"I see. A little walk around the block. Just Cliff and Ayo, no one else?"

"No one else. I was there. Pauline saw them, too. That's when she said Cliff is probably, well . . ." Stella bites her lower lip. "But what does Ayo have to do with . . . oh. Oh. *Oh.*"

"Why do you keep saying that?" says BJ.

"Why do you think?"

"How should I know?"

"Oh, I don't know. Maybe because you've lived with Cliff for, like, a hundred years already."

"Now, you listen to me. We might be getting up there, but we're not that old, I'll have you —"

"Good grief, BJ. That's not the point. Think about it. You just made a whole flipping speech about how you guys are bestest friends."

BJ takes another bow. "Thank you, thank you."

"That's still not the point."

"Then what could you have possibly —"

"She means that Cliff is gay with Ayo."

"What?"

"That *Cliff* is gay with *Ayo,*" Everett repeats.

"What!" says everybody.

"Way to go, Cliff!"

"Who's Ayo?"

"It's a mystery."

"No, it's not. I know who he is. I also know you're wrong."

"Why would you say that?" Stella asks.

"Because it's *Yodel,* for one thing, and second, he's our staff."

"Oh, yes. Ayo," Laura says. "He and I met for the first time at the cookout. Such a sweet man, he is. So much better than the staff whose place he took."

"Yeah, well, to be fair, switching him out for a Pet Rock would've been a great improvement." Greg stands with one foot hoicked up on the chair, a conquistador peacocking for his portrait. "But I'd rather not bring back traumatic memories for anyone. Here's my point, Cliff. I can see why you might take to Ayo as you have. Compared to the last guy, he must seem great. He doesn't lock you in a van for hours at a stretch. He takes you on long walks on moonlit nights. Who could blame you if your feelings for him turned into something a little more than friendly?"

"Not I," Everett says. "Anyone who'd blame you needs to learn to have a heart."

Stella's eyes are freshly moist. "I couldn't be happier for you, Cliff."

"This isn't right, I say."

"BJ, please, there's no need to raise your voice."

"I wouldn't have to if you'd listen, Laura. Yodel's a kind and caring person, and I love him very much. But it isn't what you think. He's a friend to all of us. That's all it is, though. Friendship. It's nothing more or less than that."

"Maybe," Stella says, crossing her arms. "Maybe for you."

"Not just me. It's obvious for anyone with eyes to see. No offense, Everett."

"None taken," says the old man, looking the wrong way.

Stella points at BJ, her sable bracelets clacking together. "Talk about pot meeting kettle. How can you see anything with that red stuff on your glasses?"

"Red stuff, eh?" Removing the pair, BJ squints, greets the red stuff with a surprised "Oh, yeah," and breathes fog onto the lenses. He grunts and rubs them with the bottom of his shirt, then returns them to his face having only smeared the flakes around some. "There. Now I can see even better."

"You sure?" Stella says. "Looks like you might've gone and made it worse."

"Might I suggest you get your eyes checked," says BJ, groping about in red darkness.

Greg stomps on the chair, scattering flecks of caked mud everywhere. "You know what I think? I think we've speculated long enough. I think it's high time we gave Cliff a chance to speak up for himself. After all, only he can tell us his true feelings."

"How's he supposed to do that? It's not like he can —"

"No, it's not, Laura. But don't forget there's more than one way to communicate. Let's try what we did earlier, when I asked him to apologize. What do you say, Cliff? If the lucky guy is Ayo, let us know by nodding once. If it's someone else, or if we're altogether wrong and you're not, well, you know, then shake your head as many times as you see fit. Capisce?"

"Sounds like a plan to me," Savannah says.

"To me, too, but I can't say the same for Cliff."

"Nor I," says Everett.

"Maybe he didn't hear you, Greg."

"I'm pretty sure he did."

"Look, there he goes again, digging his face into his shoulder."

"And his eyes are shut more tightly than a coffin."

"This is so sad," Savannah says.

"Why is he doing that?"

"Beats me."

"Hello, Cliff? Hello?"

As all their voices become one, filled with a concern that cuts like a blade, I reach out my right hand, feeling blindly for my joystick.

"If you can hear us, just say, 'Ah.'"

"Correct me if I'm wrong, but it looks like he's in pain."

"You might be onto something, Savannah. It's like he's being crushed by an army tank."

"Yeah, except he isn't."

"Maybe he's trying to hide."

"We can all see you, Cliff."

"I can't."

"But you still know he's there."

"Of course I do," says Everett. "I feel his presence in my bones."

"I think I'd rather not know what that means."

"Quiet, everyone," Laura says. "It's okay, Cliff. There's no point in hiding. We're your friends, and always will be, no matter what."

"We'll always be your friends," Greg sings, all out of tune. "We'll always be your friends, no matter what. Open your eyes, Cliff. Like it or not, we're here to see you through this. Not everyone's so lucky to have support that runs so deep. If they did, the world would be a vastly different place. There'd be a lot less pain and sorrow. People wouldn't be so lonely. They wouldn't feel like no one has their backs." His scaly claw falls heavy on my arm. "That's why you need to know we're not mad at you. No one is, not me, not Laura, not even Stella or BJ. That won't change, Cliff, not for anything. We won't be mad at you, no matter who you are, what you've done, or what anyone else has done to you." He squeezes my arm hard and hisses his next words into my ear. "But if you think your silence is protecting anyone, consider this. It might seem like you're helping them for now, but in the long run all it does is hurt them — and yourself."

"I don't get it," Laura says. "What are you insinuating?"

"I'm not insinuating anything. I'm simply asking questions. All I want to do is understand what happened at the cookout."

"I've already told you, like, twice."

"And I thank you much, sweet Stella, but what I'd like to know, and what only Cliff can tell me, is whether something happened on the walk he took with Ayo. Was that all it was, Cliff? Just a walk? A break from all the people and the noise? Or was it something more? Something Ayo might've asked you not to share with anyone?"

I reach out a little farther but come up with a handful of nothing.

"What else could they have done?" says BJ.

"That's what I want to find out."

"They probably watched the fireworks."

"Yeah, like we were doing," says Savannah. "It didn't matter where you were. You couldn't miss them in the sky."

"Maybe." Tightening his grip, Greg stops the blood flow to my hand. "Maybe not. We won't know until he tells us. Is that what you did, champ? Take in the fireworks? Or did Ayo do something he shouldn't have?"

"You mean, like, break up with him?" Stella says.

"I sure hope not." Everett crows.

"For the love of God, Cliff and Yodel are just —"

"Did he, Cliff?" says Greg. "Did he do something to you?"

"I don't like where this is going."

"You think I do, Laura? You think I want to bring this up? You think it's fun for me to find out one of my clients has been —"

"Please don't raise your voice in my day program. I know you're upset and have concerns. But take a look around. Is here the best place to air them? Is now the time?"

"If not here, where? If not now, when? Should we just send him home today and risk it happening again? I doubt this'd be your program for much longer after that."

"It is for now, and these aren't the kinds of memories I want my guys to make. All I ask is that you take this conversation elsewhere."

"I get it. I really do. But this can't wait." Greg kicks his chair out of the way and hunches over at my side. "Level with me, Cliff. If something happened, nod. If it didn't, shake your head. Help me help you, man. Help me help you. The pain is writ large on your face. Tell me the truth and I'll make it go away."

My hand's gone numb in Greg's death grip. He smiles and works his claw into my skin. Somewhere far away, a toilet flushes.

"Just tell him, Cliff," says Laura. "Just tell him and this nightmare will be over."

Tingling, unfeeling, my fingers finally find what they've been searching for.

"Please, Cliff. Do what he says and he'll leave you alone."

"What has he turned you into?" Greg whispers.

I don't feel it as I pull back on the joystick. I don't even feel the anger anymore. All I feel is my wheel rolling over Greg's left foot, crushing his metatarsals like five wishbones at Thanksgiving. Releasing me, he staggers forward, hugs his lifted knee, and hops on his good foot, his teeth bared in a sanitary snarl. He bumps into the table and caroms back toward the chair, a broken pogo stick bouncing in fitful bursts. In the distance, Willa cackles. Just before Greg hits the floor, Laura catches and eases him down, sliding the *Sorry!* box under his head, a makeshift pillow. She mouths her orders to Savannah — *Call 911 and grab some ice* — and quiets BJ's cries for my exile with a raised hand. Straightening Greg's legs, she places his foot on a stray lunchbox. It's bent perversely inward and is outgrowing its shoe. His tanned face twists in agony. His mouth is wrenched up like a mask's. But it's only when the restroom door swings open that he screams.

"What the hell?" says Blake, all out of breath.

Standing in the doorway like an unsung comic duo, he and Alec pant, their arms wrapped around each other's backs. As Blake slumps down and takes a knee, Alec steps into the room, hands folded near his chin. Gleaming with new life, his eyes meet mine. The boy isn't just awake. He is conscious, alert, lucid. It's like he's cut the cord that's kept him tethered to that other, mystic world, whose strange and brilliant images were only visible to him. Our faces are twin stories, one reflected in the other. We read them like two rare, forbidden books.

NINE

The boardroom's walls are white and bare and form a cage for thirteen swivel chairs around a lacquered table. The decisions made here are never reached without solemn disputation about everything from lowering staff's base pay to limiting staff's already-meager health insurance packages. This is also where they fired Paul before he was arrested. If his case goes to trial, the state could hold it in this room. It's the sort of place a jury might spend days debating whether the accused deserves life or the death sentence.

"This can't be right." With a pen, Knowland stabs a hole into his printout of the incident report. "It says here Stella's hair had been dyed black."

"I swear it on my vintage Matchbox Twenty T-shirt, John," says Greg. "It was black as an ill-omened cat. God, how I wish you'd been there. The scene was so jarring, yet also weirdly cute."

In the corner, Francis laughs and sticks a toothpick in his mouth.

Knowland sighs and says, "Poor girl. You must've really put her through the wringer, Cliff."

"To say the least. But by the time the ambulance arrived, she was already feeling better. I think it's safe to say she'll live."

"And how have you been holding up?"

In the two days since our session, Greg's face has gone burnt umber. At first I thought he'd shaved his soul patch, but against his darkened skin it's merely harder to make out. Stare at his chin long enough and you'll find it like the answer to the world's worst hidden-figure puzzle. He scoots back and kicks his cast up on the table, his bare toes sticking out like uncooked pigs in one big blanket. The plaster is half-black with all his coworkers' John Hancocks. Knowland refused to start this meeting until everyone had signed Greg's shattered foot.

"I'm hanging in there," he says, two nipple rings bulging through his rose-pink muscle shirt. "Still in a lot of pain, but the doc says I'll be walking in six weeks. In the meantime" — he points to the folded-up wheelchair on the wall behind him — "let's just say I've been gaining some applicable perspective."

"Well, I appreciate your coming in today — all of you — on such short notice," Knowland says, feeling his beard. The clump of hair he plucked out at the barbecue is coming back in strong. "When I got word of what had happened, I knew this wasn't something that could wait."

"Good thing your mindfulness coach canceled, then."

"Last-minute, too, but better late than never, and my schedule's still tight as a snare drum. I've got lunch with an old college buddy in an hour, so let's get to it, shall we?"

"Of course."

"You bet."

"I've never been more pumped-up for anything." In full fatigues, Brad shoots to his feet, hand over heart.

"And the other staff — Ayo — where is he?"

"In the breakroom. I'll bring him in when we're ready."

"Good." Knowland turns to me. "I gather, Cliff, you know why we've called you in, but don't think for a minute that it's you who's in trouble. Remember, our only purpose is to help you, both through the good times and the terrible."

Everyone nods intensely, like believers at their priest.

"No, it's not our job to punish you. Neither does anyone think less of you for what you've done these last few weeks." Knowland's fingers mesh together like big zipper teeth. "That said, Laura's asked that you not return to Memory Makers for the time being."

"What? Since when?"

"Since this morning. You didn't see the email? She sent it with high importance."

Brad brushes fuzzies from his fatigues. "I haven't had the chance. With Ayo on suspension, I've been helping Francis out around the house. I thought Laura promised Cliff could go back in a couple days."

"That was the plan, but she understandably wants us to get things sorted out first. Most of her folks are still traumatized by Tuesday's events. They won't stop talking about it, and I don't blame them."

"You should hear BJ at home," Francis grins. "All that comes out of his mouth are calls for this man's banishment. Thomas says he's even cursed Cliff in his sleep."

"This is all so sad and unexpected. I'm this close to crying in my morning coffee."

Knowland lifts his sky-blue mug, on whose front, among a patch of painted clouds, rests an empty, cartoon wheelchair with angels' wings attached to either side. Printed just below it, in white and pretty cursive, is some advice:

NEVER IGNORE SOMEONE WITH A DISABILITY

YOU'D MISS AN AWESOME CHANCE TO BE UPLIFTED

On the back, in the same font, it says LAARP, which used to stand for Legislative Advocacy Association for Retarded People — it was founded in a different time — but now the letters denote nothing, like the ones in KFC. Once a year their CEO comes up here, to Knowland's office, shares his gratitude with staff for the great jobs they do with us, and then, under the guise of a request for a donation, shakes them down for ten percent of their next paychecks.

"Do you hear that, Cliff?" Brad says. "Do you understand how much you've disappointed us? How frightened your friends have become of you? How much you've inconvenienced me and Greg? Did you know he had to take a rideshare to get here? That last night Teddy Loftis flashed a youth group at Bob Evans and I had to —"

"Save it," Knowland says.

"All I'm saying is, for God's sake, dude, I'm up to here in crises as it is. If something's eating at you, there are better ways to handle it than —"

"Easy, easy. I get it. We've all been on edge for one reason or another. Why, only yesterday, after I clicked that link in my junk mail, I had a panic attack that lasted half an hour." Knowland pounds the table. His sandy bangs swing like a pendulum to the wrong side of his head. "Five-million dollars wired directly to my bank account! I should've known it was a ruse, just too damn good to be true."

"Don't sweat it, John. Everybody falls for that trick at least once in their lives."

"Twice in my case," nods Francis. "Who doesn't want to think they've won the UK Lottery?"

"Someone not in their right mind, that's who, and that's exactly who I was as I racked my brain for a solution."

"So that's what that sound was. I thought I was going crazy, hearing things. I could've sworn it was a ghost crying out for Miley Cyrus."

"It was no ghost, Greg. It was I, and I was saying 'Wily virus.'"

His face goes tragic as the mask's, an expression Brad, Greg, and Francis imitate like reflections in a funhouse mirror.

"You got it fixed, though, right?"

"Only after I remembered we have a whole IT department. If it hadn't been for Nelson, I'd still be making ransom payments." Knowland slides his hands across the table toward me. "That's why I bring this up, Cliff. Every day, I try to practice kindness, to think of others' needs more than my own. It's what drove me to this line of work decades ago. Trust me, it'd be a whole lot easier, and much more lucrative, if I only thought about myself. But you don't need me to tell you that's not who I am, that's not who these guys are, and that's not the kind of staff I want to send into your home. I surround myself — and you — with caring people. Warm and helpful, selfless people. We don't hire anyone who doesn't demonstrate these qualities. But nothing's perfect. You're no stranger to this. Every now and then some wretch slips through the cracks and causes problems. What I need to know from you is whether it's happened yet again."

Greg wiggles his toes inside his signature-scrawled cast. "If it has, there's no shame in it. It's not only people like you, Cliff, who are easily exploited. Heck, John's the smartest guy I know, and he's just admitted to having become somebody's sucker."

"If it can happen to me," Knowland says, chin angled up, "it can happen to anyone."

"Which is why I don't resent you, Cliff, for breaking my foot in five places and forcing me out of this year's LA Fitness disc-golf tournament."

"What a pity. I know how hard you'd been training for it."

"*Kay Sara Sara,*" says Greg. "To get angry would be taking the easy way out. I'm just glad I can still be of service to Cliff and his team."

"Well, that's the spirit. I'm sure if he could speak he'd tell you 'thanks' a whole ten times over."

"He doesn't have to speak to let me know. I can see it in his eyes."

"Either that," Francis says, "or he's trying to poop his Depends."

"The point is, I'm not here for the plaudits. I'm here to help. Besides, it's hard to stay mad at someone when you doubt it was their fault to begin with. Here's what I'm saying, Cliff. It's the same thing I was getting at right before you, well, you know." Greg runs his fingers over his cast. "We don't think, as Stella does, that you've been acting strange because you're gay."

"Though if that were the case, you'd have our full support."

"It'd make things that much simpler, too. We would've had no need to meet today, and there'd probably be no point in you and I continuing our professional relationship. I don't plan to burst Stella's bubble, though, if that's what you're afraid of. It's not only for her own good that she believes in this illusion. You'll both sleep much better this way, don't you think?"

"Like babies," Francis says.

"Precious dolls. But those of us who care about the truth, like you and me — we aren't so easily satisfied, are we? We understand our problems are large and complicated, and that they won't be solved by such simple, painless answers. That's why I don't buy Stella's theory, and why I have a different, much better one." Greg's face looks hot enough to roast lamb over. "I suspect you've been targeted, Cliff, like John was when he clicked that link, by someone who doesn't have your best interests at heart."

"By a fraud who takes advantage of others' kindness."

"By a predator who preys on our most vulnerable."

"By a thug who's using you for his own twisted purposes." Brad jumps up and socks the wall like a detective seeking justice the hard way.

"Gah," Knowland says, shielding his face with his copy of the write-up. "What the hell was that for?"

"Sorry. I probably shouldn't have done that."

"You're darn right, probably. Good God. You damn-near put a fissure in my sheetrock. One more outburst like that and I'll retract your latest spot bonus."

"It's too late," Brad says, nursing the guilty fist. "I've already spent the gift card's entire balance. How else could I have afforded this righteous get-up?" He stands up straight in his fatigues, salutes his boss, then, growing pensive, sinks back into his chair. "But you're right, John. I've acted rashly, and in doing so have disgraced the honor of this uniform. You don't need to retract anything. I still have the receipt. I'll return the clothes to Cabela's as soon as we're done here. I'd take them off now, but I've got on nothing underneath."

"No, that won't be necessary. None of it. I know how much that little costume means to you. Anyway, you've earned it. Thanks again for picking up my dry cleaning."

"It was my privilege." Brad caresses his long sleeves. "I won't make excuses for myself, but the truth is I'm just so damn worried about Cliff — these new behaviors, the way he's hurting people, the possibility that a part of it, however small, is my fault —"

"Don't say that. There's no way you could've known."

"I wish I could agree. But I oversee the trainings and the day-to-day at his place. I keep thinking about how this could've been avoided if only I'd paid more attention."

"What's done is done, Brad. You can't blame yourself for anything. I don't."

"Maybe you don't, but I —"

"Look, what Paul did at the mall put everyone in a tight spot. Channel Eight sure didn't help anything. That said, we did our best to replace him with someone we thought would restore the guys' dignity. It's possible we were wrong. But the fact is, we don't have the facts yet." Knowland curls his printout upward, turning it into an ark. He points the bow at me and says, "To get them, Cliff, we'll need your honesty. To that end, I have only one question. All you have to do is either nod or shake your head."

"It won't be easy," Greg says. "In fact, it'll likely be painful, but keep in mind that, regardless of the answer, and no matter how much it hurts to think about, everybody here has your back."

They all break out in violent smiles.

"We'll always have your back, no matter what. Before I ask, you should know this is no walk in the park for me, either. It's never fun to think one of our own has been mistreated." Rolling his ark into a tube, Knowland holds it like a scepter and poses like the monarch of a kingdom made of paper.

"But this isn't about me, Cliff. Today is about your well-being. Remember, all I want is your honesty. Understand?"

"Answer him," Brad says.

I do.

"Here goes nothing." Knowland starts to ask, then turns aside and begins softly weeping. "I'm sorry, gentlemen," he says through his fingers. "The mere thought of this is making me *verklempt.*"

"If it's too much, I'll ask him," says Greg. "The whole thing was my idea, after all."

"No, I need to do this. Actually, as the head of human resources, Linda should've launched an inquiry into it as soon as it happened, but since she's out until tomorrow, the duty falls squarely on my shoulders. Her daughter couldn't've picked a better time to have a baby, am I right?" His face paling at the thought of his sad burden, he lurches forward and goes full-on waterworks. "But first," he says, his eyes anguish-red, "give me a moment to collect myself."

Brad goes to him. "Are you all right, sir?"

"Get your hands off me. I'm fine. Never better." His beard splotchy with slobber and snot, Knowland uses his jacket's lapel like a Kleenex. "Too bad I can't say the same for this suit."

"Go home and clean up, John," Greg says. "We can handle this. I'll have a report ready for you by this afternoon."

"I won't hear of it. You know the old saying, 'The captain goes down with the ship'?"

"Are you sure it's the most apropos?"

"Why wouldn't it be, if you got the message?" Knowland sits back and crosses his legs. "My apologies, Cliff. I'd promised myself I wouldn't do this. But as I say, it's so awful, even suspecting someone has taken advantage of you. I've known you longer than most of our clients — twenty years, if my math's right. Do you remember when we first met? It was at Sinai Grove, not long before they discharged you. So much has changed since those days. I hadn't even read your file yet. But I could tell just by looking at you how hard a time you'd had there. You were so broken and hollow, more of an empty shell than a man with thoughts and feelings of his own. God, it makes me sick to picture it." His hand flies to his mouth and he chokes back another cry. "My point is, I knew I'd have to save you from that place and give you the life you'd wanted, one that was real and filled with hope and love and, most of all, worthwhile."

I haven't thought about that day in a long time. Knowland was so much younger then, much less polished, but still just as quick to make great promises. The biggest difference between now and then is that back then we both believed them — he because he wanted to, I because I had to. The alternative was to stay inside that hospital, to keep living as a shell, a dried-up husk blown through a fallow field by fickle winds. What's funny is how I trusted him more than I might have because the first thing he did on seeing me was cry. It seemed so genuine, so unlike anything I'd been used to from the staff at Sinai Grove. He couldn't handle it, he said, knowing how badly I'd been treated. But that would all be over now, he said, if I wanted it to be. He owned a company that cared for folks like me in their own homes. He only hired warm and helpful, selfless people, people who'd get us out in our communities and keep us active every day. For the first time in my life, I'd be respected, treated no differently than anyone else outside those walls. It sounded like a dream, almost too good to be true. I'd been prepared to die in that abyss. Most days I'd hoped for death to come sooner than later. Those tears, though, sealed the deal. They showed me that compassion still existed and sparked a faith I've never had at any other time before or since. John Knowland was my savior, my salvation, my Jesus Christ in a three-piece. He'd take me from that hell and set me up not quite in paradise — not even then would he pretend it'd be perfect — but in a place that, in comparison, would feel at least heaven-adjacent. That's exactly what it was, too, for a while. BJ was over the moon to make a new friend — so was I — and Lem and Rickey didn't seem to mind me, either. The company was small enough that we all knew each other's names. They trained staff on everyone, so if someone had to miss a shift, another could fill it who was already aware of our needs. We did get out more often then, and not only to the grocery, but to places we'd suggested — restaurants, the movies, walks along the river or around the block. Staff would even take us with them when they went inside the mall. But then gradually, as one year turned into another, and another, things began to change. All the hospitals like Sinai Grove were closing, and the agency was growing, both in and outside Tired Oaks. Knowland started coming out to our place less and less often until eventually he stopped his visits altogether. Our staff didn't stick around as long as they'd used to, and the ones who did adapted to the emerging status quo. As their phones grew more sophisticated, their interest in us waned. They began concocting reasons why we couldn't leave the house: it was too cold, too hot, too mild, they were too sick or too tired, or the best excuse of all, which was that they didn't have gas money (Knowland's never made them pay for fuel from their own pockets). The only work they'd do was that which kept us alive, and even this they did on their own time. If it had happened all at once, I think BJ would've noticed. He might even have reported it to the proper authorities, who at that point might've done something to fix it. But ours was a case of four frogs in a pot of water slowly brought to boil. By the time we were scalding, we'd already adjusted to the heat. Besides, it wasn't anything we hadn't all been through before.

"I think he remembers," Greg says, winking. "Look, you guys, he's crying, too."

Francis gnashes on his toothpick. "The poor man."

"Go get Ayo, please," Knowland says.

"Now? I thought you wanted to ask your question first."

"I didn't have to, thank God. Cliff just answered it." Heavy and shrill, Knowland's breath whistles through his nose like a steam engine in the distance. "Bring him in now. It's time he saw the fruits of his foul labors."

"I don't think I —"

"If I have to ask again, Brad, you're going to need that gift receipt."

Hugging himself, or, rather, his new fatigues, Brad leaves the room, shutting the door behind him. Knowland grits his teeth and grabs his phone, and soon Greg and Francis do, too. In a silence so thick I could swallow it, they type, tap, and scroll frantically, their faces only inches from their screens.

"I won't ask your forgiveness, Cliff," Knowland says, not looking up. "I'm not sure I deserve it — not yet, anyway. I know it's something that has to be earned. I'll do everything I can to make things right, to make you whole again before the end of Quarter Four, but the choice lies with you, in the end. Nevertheless, I made you a promise, and I mean to keep it. I'm a man of my word or I'm nothing —"

The door swings back open and in marches Brad, trailed by my staff. Hands crossed in front, Ayo wears a bright-orange dashiki with a kaleidoscopic green-and-yellow pattern emanating outward from the chest. He hasn't shaved in a few days and looks like he hasn't slept in all that time, either. His thin sandals make no sound as he moves to the table and waits. Though his eyes are downcast, they shine with defiance, kindling the same in my own.

"Please, have a seat," Knowland says. "Thanks for your patience."

Ayo sits between Knowland and me. "Gentlemen," he says, gently. "Hi, Cliff."

"Help yourself to an apple?"

"An apple, Mr. Knowland?"

"From the big bowl in the breakroom. You're welcome to one when you leave."

"Oh, yes. I saw them. I thought about it, actually, but I'm sorry to say they've gone bad."

Knowland drinks from his mug. "Already?"

"Unless my eyes have deceived me."

"Huh. All of them?"

"From what I could tell. Brown with spots."

"That's a shame. Shocking, too. I bought them just yesterday."

"Well, you know what they say," Ayo smiles. "One bad apple will spoil the bunch."

"They do say that, don't they?" Knowland scribbles a note on his printout. "Thanks for letting me know. I take it you know why you're here."

"I have an idea. I'm sorry to hear about your foot, Greg. I hope Cliff has apologized for it."

"He doesn't need to. I've told him as much." Greg taps his cast with a pen. "That's why John wanted to speak to you now."

"And why I haven't been working since Tuesday."

Knowland forms a small church with his hands. "When you went through our training," he says into it, "we made you aware of our suspension policy for all staff suspected of abuse or neglect."

"I remember. Is it also your policy to not explain your suspicions until two days after the fact?"

"Excuse me?"

"This is the first I'm hearing I've been accused of anything. I'm just wondering if it's standard practice to keep staff in the dark about why they're not working until —"

"That's my bad," Brad says. "It's harder with Cliff, as he isn't verbal. Since we didn't have the facts, I didn't explain why he'd been taken off the schedule. I just asked him to take some time off. Unpaid, of course."

Ayo raises his eyes. "And now you do."

"And now we do what?"

"Have the facts."

"Enough of them to come to you with questions," Knowland says. "I hope you're ready with the answers."

"I'm ready. I've done nothing wrong. I only wish you would've asked me earlier. We could've cleared these things up right away."

Across the table from him, Francis beams.

"If only it were that simple." Knowland's church crumbles and falls. "But sadly, it's not. We've got forms to fill out and procedures to follow. When we receive an allegation —"

"May I ask, was it Cliff who first filed the complaint?"

"I believe that is none of your business."

"Why not? I'm the accused. Do I not have a right to know who's accused me, and what of?"

"We'll get to that. But first, we've got questions for you."

"Of course. I apologize."

"It's not us you should be apologizing to," Brad mumbles.

"Who, then?"

"Who do you think? The man it was your job to care for but instead used for your sordid and sickening —"

"Brad, I'll remind you of what happens if you punch my sheetrock again."

"Ten-four." He wallops his palm and sits down.

"Thank you. Much as we'd like to sometimes, we can't take the law in our own hands. There are reasons for each of our protocols. By following them, we're not only covering our own butts and making sure our guys remain healthy. We're also taking the high road." Knowland courageously strokes the dried snot in his beard. "This is what separates us from and holds us above those who seek to disrupt our stability."

On the table, Greg's damaged foot seesaws. "It's what makes us men and not beasts. That's why I forgave Cliff for breaking my foot," he says to Ayo. "He knew not what he did, nor what'd been done to him, and lacked the tools, much less the ability, to express himself in a more appropriate way."

"Please, ask me your questions."

"I'll start by pointing out that Cliff has had behaviors in the past, which makes sense, given his history. Lots of our folks, especially those who've spent time in hospitals, have suffered abuse at the hands of their caregivers." Knowland stifles another sob. "Acting out like Cliff has been seems natural, almost understandable, when we consider his unfortunate background. We are what we find ourselves surrounded with, are we not? True, we don't know much about whether or how Cliff engaged in behaviors before us. Sinai Grove didn't keep records on the subject."

"It seems unlikely, though, as back then he would've only had a manual wheelchair."

"Possibly. But we can't know for sure. Behaviors take on many forms. He could've found other ways to vent his frustrations." Knowland picks up and smacks his report. "What we do know is that, since he's been with us, Cliff's tantrums have been limited and sporadic."

"Rare to the point of nonexistence," says Brad.

"So rare," Knowland nods proudly, "that he'd never, until now, needed someone like Greg to help him maintain good behavior. It's a testament both to his resilience and, if you'll allow me to toot my own horn, to our prowess in providing quality care. Not even after what he'd gone through at the mall did Cliff exhibit any maladaptive conduct."

"Um," Ayo says.

"It was only when you came along that things took a turn for the worse. Do you have any guess as to why that might be?"

Ayo sets his hands out flat in front of him. "My guess is you think I'm responsible."

"I don't have to think," Knowland says, "when I know it."

"What is it you know? Lay out your charges. I'll answer them."

"First, why don't you walk us through your process? How'd it work? What'd it look like?"

"My process? Of what?"

"Of gaining Cliff's confidence, Private, and then taking advantage of it."

"Fair enough. I'll start with the first part. I'll tell you how I gained his confidence. Not just his, though. Everyone's. BJ's. Lem's. Rickey's. It was pretty simple, actually, which is not to say it was easy." Ayo shoots Francis a look. "You want to know what I've done to earn their trust? I've treated them and their home with respect. Asked them questions and then listened to their answers. I've given them choices and the time to think them over. Paid attention to their moods. Stayed present for them, engaged with them, even when I'm tired and just feel like checking out. I've done with them the things they like to do. When BJ sings his songs, I might sing along with him, if I know the words and he'll allow it. It's not my place to make him stop doing what he enjoys because it might get on my nerves a little bit. This doesn't happen often, by the way, and only then after the tenth time in a row he belts out old 'Skip to My Lou.' It's my place — and my job — to make sure these men are living good lives. That's all I'm focused on at work. As you've said, Mr. Knowland, what a good life means to each of us depends on who we are. Our clients are no different. What makes some of them happy is more obvious than what makes others happy. BJ loves his music, while Rickey would be delighted to just sit around all day with his cookie and pop." In his pause, even Francis drops his scowl to join the others in a smile. "With Cliff, however, it's not as clear-cut, but one day I'll find the answer and help him get the thing he wants — that he deserves."

"He just likes to look at it," Knowland says.

"Excuse me?"

"Rickey and his cookie. Or his burger. Or whatever else he's holding at the time."

"True enough. I think Super Rick eats with his eyes."

"Wouldn't that be something, if he could?"

"If we all could." Greg licks his lizard lips.

"We'd have to exercise much more than we do now."

"And Cliff could grab a bite with us at last," Francis laughs.

"Hey, a guy can dream, can't he?" Knowland's teeth glisten like sardines inside the tin can of his grin. "If I could snap my fingers, Cliff, and make it happen, you know I'd do it in a heart—"

"Answer the second part," Brad says.

"The second part?"

"Of John's question. Have you already forgotten? What'd it look like, Ayo? How'd you terrorize Cliff? I want every last gory detail."

Ayo stares him in the face and says, "I didn't."

"I'll only ask you one more time."

"And I'll give you the same answer. I can't confess to something I'm not guilty of. If I've done Cliff any wrong, it hasn't been on purpose. All I've tried to do is make his life a little better. More worthwhile. That is the mission statement, isn't it?"

"It is," Knowland says, approvingly.

"And? Are you saying you believe him?"

"I'm not saying anything, Brad, but —"

"But what?" Brad rolls back until his chair bumps up against the wall. "But after seeing what you did in Cliff's eyes and promising to set everything right, you're just going to cave as soon as Ayo says a couple pretty words?"

"Is that what you think our mission statement is? Just a 'couple pretty words' up on our website?"

"No," Brad stutters. "I mean, yes, they're pretty — you wrote them yourself — but there's more to it, something much deeper, than the way they sound when rolling off the tongue. For all that, they mean nothing if our actions don't reflect them."

"Point taken. If we don't back them up in practice, even our grandest declarations come to nothing. That's why I like you, Brad. It's not enough for you to know this all-important truth. Like me, you've got to live it every day. I see the same in you, Greg, and in you, Francis, too. None of you would be here if I weren't sure of this, if I weren't such a keen-eyed judge of character. As such, I'll tell you this. After hearing Ayo out, and after speaking with him last week, I don't think he's the kind of man who'd do to Cliff — or anyone — what we've suspected."

"What were you suspecting? What do you think I've done to Cliff?"

"That's just it. We didn't know. It's not like he can tell us. All we had to go on was Greg's hunch."

"What was this, please, this hunch of yours?"

"Two days ago, I saw Cliff at his day program. My goals were simple: one, to establish rapport, and two, to get a feel for his routine. It was my first session with him, actually. I wasn't expecting any breakthroughs."

"And yet you made a few." Ayo nods at the cast on the table.

"One, at least. But it wasn't I who made it. That honor goes to Stella. I believe you two have met."

"We did. At the cookout."

"Right. I'd never seen someone in such a bad way as she was on Tuesday. As I was telling these guys, you had to be there. The girl was barely recognizable with her painted nails and gloomy hair. My heart went out to her. It ached with her pain." Greg's scorched face twitches at the memory. "At least, it did until she called me Brad Paisley."

Even I discard my frown to join the others in a laugh.

"I'm not finding that in your report," Knowland says, perusing it.

"You won't. It's not. I didn't include it."

"And why would that be?"

"Because I didn't see how it pertained to Cliff's behavior."

"But aren't you always saying that even the slightest detail might help explain our folks' aggression?"

"Of course, but let's be real, here. The chances this had anything to do with it are slim to none."

"And yet there is a chance, however slim, is there not?"

"That's highly doubtful, John."

"Who's Brad Paisley?" Ayo says.

"It doesn't matter."

"It most certainly does. Brad Paisley is one of our finest living country singers. To be compared to him is no great shame."

"I'm not ashamed. I simply didn't —"

"Oh, I see. It's because you wear those paisley shirts sometimes."

I send Ayo a giant thumbs-up.

"It's not that funny, you guys. A little easy, too, if you ask me."

"I'd agree," Knowland says, "if it hadn't been Stella who said it."

"But doesn't that just reinforce my point? Stella's young, she has a diagnosis, and was so devastated that she —"

"Gave you the idea you've been running with since Tuesday. You said it yourself, Greg. The behavioral breakthrough wasn't yours. It was hers. But for that, Ayo would still be on the clock."

"And I'd never have punched John's poor wall."

"At least not for this."

"What is 'this'?" Ayo says, as if holding the word in his hands. "You still haven't told me why you took me off the schedule."

Knowland drums a waltz out on the table. "It's funny, actually, in retrospect, though as you've seen, it surely wasn't at the time. Ms. Scofield was upset because of what had happened at the cookout. It seems Cliff had snubbed her with your help."

"This much is true. Cliff needed a break from the racket, so we took a small walk through the neighborhood. I asked Brad for his leave, which he granted."

"That's correct."

"Stella wanted to join us. You know of her feelings for Cliff."

"And then some," Francis says. "All those paper hearts."

"When she went to let her staff know where she'd be, Cliff informed me that he'd rather she not come. He wanted it to be —"

"And you know this how?"

"What do you mean?"

"I mean how could you tell he didn't want her to join you?"

"I've already said. I asked him and I listened to his answer. Just because he can't speak doesn't mean he can't communicate. I told Cliff I'd help him if he needed it, but that I wanted him to take the lead in breaking the news to her. He was conflicted. He didn't want to hurt her feelings. He likes her as a friend, nothing more. But he couldn't have expected her to know this if he stayed silent." Ayo turns to me, his scar a sharp blue in the boardroom's heavy light. "It was up to him to make his feelings known. Otherwise, as I reminded him, she'd keep thinking, well, that they were to be married soon. Isn't that how it happened, Cliff?"

I nod.

"Well, how insightful is that?" whistles Greg. "Looks like we've got a regular Cliff Whisperer on our hands."

"That's enough. Don't forget we're a team. We might not see eye-to-eye on everything, but we have the same goal in the end: to make sure these guys flourish." Jotting a note on his printout, Knowland gives Ayo a big, grateful nod. "Thanks for your hard work with Cliff. I know it's not easy, and I'm sorry we didn't call you in before. As things stood, we were fearful you'd used him somehow. And to think," he laughs faintly, "it's all because Stella concluded he's gay."

"He still could be." Francis bares his teeth in less a smile than a bite. "Just not with Ayo."

"Is that what you supposed? Is that why we're here? You thought Cliff and I were in a relationship?"

"I'm afraid that, yes, Ayo, this was our assumption. We only had one lead and were obliged to look into it. We owed at least that much to Cliff. Crazy as it sounds, many of the wild allegations made against our staff end up being true. Take Paul. If he hadn't owned up to it, I wouldn't have believed he'd locked the guys in the van."

"I once had an employee at another house," Brad says, "who broke a client's jaw because he refused to go to bed."

"God, how I remember, and how I wish I could forget."

"And another who used his client's SSI funds to cover his own rent."

"I regret to say that's happened more than once."

"Then there was the staff who fell asleep with a lit cigarette in his mouth."

"Luckily, those folks live but a block from Ladder Twelve."

"And the one who took his clients to a drug deal."

"In one of our own vans, to boot," Knowland sighs. "Had it not been a police sting, we might never've learned about it."

"Mychael, his name was. With a *y,* as in, *Why* did we hire him? He was friends with the sad sack who ordered porn on his guys' cable package."

"Which happened at the same site that caught fire, I believe."

"Same house. Different staff."

"The poor men who live there. For a while, they just couldn't catch a break."

"You can say that again. It was the porno guy's replacement who brought his girlfriend to their place and did the deed on their new futon —"

"Thank you, Brad. I think Ayo gets the picture."

"You sure? I could go on for days."

"That won't be necessary," Ayo says. "I understand, and I'm sorry your clients have had to suffer these indignities."

"You and us both." Knowland crosses his legs the other way. "We dealt with them the only way we could have: termination. They were all arrested, too, and some even deported. If nothing else, Ayo, I hope this shows you where we're coming from. While these cases are the exception, not the rule, we've seen them frequently enough to know that, if we're not careful, anything that can happen to our folks will happen to them. I wish we could've left all that behind when the state closed its last hospital, but shuttering those prisons didn't alter human nature. We'll always have good people. We'll always have bad people. Sometimes we'll see a bit of both in the same person." He smiles bittersweetly, taps his temple with his pen. "The best we can do is to stay vigilant, and when the bad sneak through the cracks, to root them out like weeds in a garden."

Brad nods so hard it nearly takes his head off. "It's what makes this the most exhausting job I've ever had, and keep in mind I spent a week driving for Amazon. I'm sorry for punching the wall about you, Private. Though they're very rare occasions, there are times when even John and I have made mistakes."

"Unlikely as it sounds, it's the truth. It's also nothing personal, so don't take it that way, like someone did, apparently, when our Stella gave him an alias."

His face deadpan, Knowland lifts his chin above our laughter and revels in it.

"It's all right, Greg," Ayo smiles. "No one thinks any less of you because of your clothing choices." He tugs the mottled chest of his dashiki. "Many people find my own style peculiar, too, so —"

"That's where you're wrong, champs," Greg says through gritted, gleaming teeth. "Last I checked, this isn't middle school, and your little insults don't bother me. I don't care if you, Stella, or anyone else thinks I look like Brad Paisley."

"It's not so much you look like him as it is you wear those shirts a lot."

"At least once a week," says Brad.

"Sometimes up to four, if Christine's tallies have been accurate, and I'm inclined to think they are."

Greg winces like he's just stepped out into the sun. "Since when has she kept tallies?"

"Since you started wearing them, however long that's been." Knowland counts the time off on his fingers. "I'd say it's going on five, six years now."

"For what purpose?"

"We pool our pocket money weekly, and whoever guesses the right number splits the jackpot on Friday brunch at Axe to Grind."

"I've won seven times this year alone." Brad rubs his belly blissfully. "Again, it's nothing personal —"

"And again, that's not how I'm taking it. Paisley pool or not, I'll keep wearing my sweet shirts until they're frayed or no longer fit." Greg breathes in and puffs his chest out, pointing his nipple rings at us like another pair of eyes. "I'm glad you guys, and the whole damn company, it seems, can have a little fun, even if it is at my expense. I'm man enough to take your slights in stride."

"Then why are you still so darn angry?"

"Because, John" — Greg checks his watch — "we've been here half an hour and are no closer to the cause of Cliff's behaviors than when we started. Correct me if I'm wrong, but I thought that's why you called this meeting in the first place."

Knowland folds his arms over his copy of the incident report. "He has a point, folks. We've dillydallied long enough. I take full responsibility, and I apologize, especially to you, Cliff, though in my defense, I was just so relieved — I'd say we all were — to learn it wasn't your new staff who hurt you."

"I hope you're right," Greg says, "both for Cliff's and Ayo's sakes."

"What do you mean, you hope? Isn't that the one thing we've proved? Or do you have some secret knowledge the rest of us aren't privy to?"

"I have no secret knowledge. As I say, these things aren't easy. But you brought me on with Cliff to sort him out, and that's what I intend to do."

"Fine. Let's do it, then," Knowland says. "Let's do it together, as a team. You've got our attention, Greg. What's on your mind?"

"What's on my mind is that Cliff didn't break my toes until I asked . . . what was it? Oh, yes. What Ayo had turned him into."

"What are you suggesting?"

"Nothing. I'm just looking at the facts. It's possible I'm wrong again — and oh, how I'd love to be — but before joining you in your complacency, there's one more thing I still need answered."

"Go on."

Greg rocks his cast side to side like a swollen metronome. "What I need to know is whether that's really all it was last Friday — just Cliff and Ayo on a harmless little stroll. Or was it something more? Something neither of you wants us to find out?"

"Something more?" Ayo asks, quietly. "I'm sorry, but I don't under-stand."

"Oh, I think you might, though. Your eyes — they've lost their spark. It's almost like I've struck a nerve. Let's dig deeper, then. What are you keeping secret? Don't look at Cliff. Look at me. I'm asking the questions now. What were you guys up to while we were busy with the fireworks?"

"I've told you everything. There's nothing left to relate."

"I don't know, John. What say you?" Greg clicks his lizard tongue against the back of his bright teeth. "I'm no lie-detector test, but it seems to me there's something new in Ayo's tone, a certain *Je naysay craw* that makes me think he's holding something back."

"Please, how am I supposed to answer this?"

"With the truth." Knowland rests his forehead on his thumb and sighs. "Answer with the truth."

"If it was just a walk, why do you sound so guilty? Why won't Cliff look me in the eye?"

"Because you're right," Ayo says, sitting up. "Because that isn't all it was. Because yes, he and I did something we intended to keep secret."

"God almighty." Facepalming, Knowland doesn't see Brad leap out of his seat and thwack the wall with a surprise right uppercut. "What the hell was —"

"That man just put a fissure in your sheetrock," Francis says through his gnawed toothpick.

Brad stands stunned beside the crack, which is no longer or wider than my crooked pinky. "John, I —"

"Sit, Brad. There, that's a good boy." Knowland roots out another gift card from his jacket pocket and flings it to him like a frisbee. "Here's a little something for your trouble."

"I — I don't —"

"Shh. Quiet, now. Listen. It's okay. I get it. You're angry — you have every right to be — and you couldn't help yourself. I'm upset, too," Knowland says, fighting another cry. "I just have a different, better, and more mature way of showing it. Trust me, if I were in your combat boots, I would've done the same."

"These aren't combat boots." Brad gazes down at them. "They're tactical. There's a big difference. I can break it down for you, if you like."

"Please don't." Knowland's voice is cold, assured, and overflowing with unflappable intent. "The style of your footwear, the hole you smacked into my pure-white boardroom wall — these are the very least of our worries."

"So, you and I are good, then?"

"Haven't I already made that crystal clear?"

Brad scrapes up the plastic card and pockets it. "Yessir."

"Good." Knowland turns to Ayo, clicks his pen, and writes something down on his report. "Thank you for telling the truth, finally. Please, continue. What'd you do to Cliff out there?"

Ayo meets Knowland's calmness with incomprehensible composure. He sits with his back straight, staring unblinkingly to his left, though not at Knowland so much as at the future he and I discussed on Friday, on our walk. He said he knew what he was doing, knew he could lose his job, or worse. He said he was willing, nonetheless, to take that risk to make me happy.

So I told him I was willing, too.

I curse myself twice over, both for that and for being born without a voice. If only I could speak, this would all be over in a second. I'd tell them the whole thing was my idea but that Ayo had refused, and so I made him do it. I'd tell them whatever they wanted to hear if it meant they'd let him stay. Better yet, I would fight them with my words. I'd hold a mirror up to their faces and make them take a good look at themselves, letting the truth flow from my tongue like a deluge. They'd no longer have the luxury of ignoring their own failures, or of papering them over with nice bromides. They might even have to change the way they do things around here, so that their mission statement lined up with their actions, and I'd have stood up for myself, all by myself, instead of burying my chin into my shoulder and trying to sink deep into my wheelchair.

"It wasn't like that," Ayo says. "I didn't do anything to him. What I —"

"Bullshit. Why is he attacking everyone if you've done nothing?"

"Let him finish, Greg."

"Thank you, Mr. Knowland." Ayo clears his throat. "As I was saying, I didn't do anything to Cliff. What Brad told me about him, about his history, during my training was most helpful. But I didn't need to read Cliff's file to know he's had enough already done to him to last a lifetime. It's all written there, across his face."

"Mm," Knowland says.

"For his whole life, he's been at someone else's mercy. We all are, to a degree. Each of us needs to be cared for in some way. But not many of us depend, like he does, so entirely on others for our survival. It's no one's fault, least of all Cliff's own. It's just the way it is."

"Why don't you tell us something we don't know, like what you did to —"

"It's just the way it is," Ayo repeats. "When someone relies so completely on us, it's only natural we focus on ensuring their most critical needs are met. In doing so, however, it's easy to forget what you mentioned at the cookout, Mr. Knowland. It's easy to forget that the people we care for have the same deep hankerings and dreams that we do — that life, for them, as for us, is much more than being fed and bathed and given our meds on time — that they, like us, deserve choices and the right to make decisions about how to lead their lives."

"That's exactly what we do," Greg says. "That's what this program was designed for. That's why these folks have plans and goals and staff and guys like me to help them."

"I know that's how this thing's supposed to work. I'm sure that's what it looks like, too, for many of your clients. But in the couple weeks I've been with Cliff, I've found this isn't how things work in his specific case."

Both Brad and Greg laugh condescendingly.

"In what respect?" Knowland says.

"With all due respect, sir, in all the respects."

I turn my head a bit and crack my eyes.

"I'm not saying I agree, but please elaborate."

"Take his goals, for instance. Did he create them on his own?"

"How could he have done that?" Francis says.

"Our clients are as involved in the writing of their goals as they want to be. Some lead the discussions. Others sleep straight through them. I've been to Cliff's meetings before, and I'd say he falls somewhere in between. He sits in on them, contributes what he can, and signs off on each plan before it takes effect."

Brad clasps his hands atop his buzzcut. "John's right. Cliff may not have come up with his current goals, but he sat down with the team as we reviewed them and stamped his signature to show his approval."

"I see," Ayo says. "So, the one that runs — how is it? — 'I will come to the med closet when it's time to get my meds' — that wasn't his idea, but he approved of it?"

"As he has every year since I've known him. It was in his plan before I started. I believe they put it in when he first received the electric. Before, he'd always needed staff to wheel him around, so it was an easy way for him to grow his independence."

"And yet it's still in there, even though he's mastered it."

"Yeah, well," Brad coughs, "we can probably take it out at his next meeting."

"What about this one: 'I will let my staff change me without excreting on them'?"

"That's another from before my time. I think it only happened once, but it led to the staff quitting. We'd like to keep them around, if we can."

"Still, he only did it that one time, years ago?"

"As far as I'm aware."

"Perhaps this is another, then, that you can take out at his next —"

"Is there a point to this?" Greg slaps the table.

Ayo grins. "You mean you don't see it?"

"Why don't you enlighten me?"

Ayo brings his hands together, as if he's holding a large book. "I figured if anybody would understand, it'd be you. You know behavior, yes? Put yourself in Cliff's shoes. Doing these same things, working these same goals long after you've accomplished them — would this be meaningful to you? Would it be worthwhile? How would you feel if someone chose these to be your dreams, and not just once, or twice, but every year as far back as you can remember? Please, I'm asking you to look hard at this man." When Ayo nods, I raise my head and open my eyes all the way. "These goals in Cliff's support plan — do you believe they're meant to help him flourish? Do you really think that's all he wants from life?"

In silence, Brad searches the walls for a clock he knows doesn't exist,

Greg and Francis take out their phones and start playing *Baby Jesus,* and Knowland simply sits there, his face in his report, moving his tongue between his teeth and upper lip.

"I didn't think so," Ayo says. "I think you're aware that Cliff can do, and wants, much more than this. The only thing I've ever done is seen this in him and tried to help him get it. In other words, I've only sought to help him find happiness."

Francis wipes an invisible tear. "How very precious."

"Okay," Knowland says. "If you've tried to make Cliff happy, why not share it with his team? This sounds like a success story, something to be celebrated. We could even put it up on social media. Think of the engagement this could spur, the good publicity it'd bring us in the wake of that disaster at the mall. For crying out loud, man, why keep it secret?"

Ayo flips his hands over and puts them palms-down on the table. "Because I gave Cliff barbecue sauce."

"I thought," says Knowland, after gathering himself, "we told you not to do that."

"In no uncertain terms." Brad wages war against his impulse to go and slug the wall again.

"And for a whole host of reasons," Greg says, kneading his nipple rings, "not least of which was that those sauces contain sugar, a chief cause of behaviors."

"To say nothing of the health hazards posed to Cliff by such recklessness. You know he has dysphagia. You know he can't have anything by mouth. Just because it isn't solid food doesn't mean he couldn't choke on it."

"You're right. We heard everything you said that night. We understood the risks. In fact, we talked them through together."

"What more was there to talk about after we had told you 'no'?"

"At first, I didn't think there was. The issue seemed settled, not that I agreed with you. I hadn't planned on bringing it back up, especially so soon after you had made yourselves so clear." Ayo nods and smiles sadly. "But then I heard your speech. One part in particular really — how do you say — struck a chord with me. You spoke of how you launched this company to give your clients the freedom to take risks, 'good or bad, great or small.' Do you remember?"

"Of course I do. I give the same talk every year. I can recite it in my sleep and still mean every word."

"Even the part where you said that if you don't let them make their own choices and take their own risks, you're no different than the 'tyrants' who ran the old hospitals?"

"I meant every word of it," Knowland frowns, "and I take your point. This is not to say you're right. Far from it. My initial statement stands. Cliff could've died because of you."

"I didn't force Cliff to do anything. I gave him a choice. He thought about his options carefully, then decided it was worth the risk. I didn't give him much, just the smallest amount on the tip of a spoon, and I was with him the whole time. If anything had gone wrong, I would've been right there to help." His eyes softening, Ayo sweeps his arm toward me. "Suffice to say, he didn't need it, though the flavor didn't register at first. It was like his tastebuds were so fast asleep they needed time to reawaken. But when they came to life and he discerned the sauce's tang, he smiled in a way I'd never seen before. I knew, in that moment, that for the first time in his life, this man had discovered the pleasure of taste."

Knowland makes another note on his report and circles it. "I can't believe I'm saying this, but if what you've said is true, it changes the equation just a bit."

"You can't be serious. Regardless of how it made Cliff feel, Ayo still broke the rules. That Cliff survived it doesn't mean it wasn't dangerous."

"Greg's right," Francis snorts.

"I apologize for disregarding your directive. I understand your position and your concern for Cliff's well-being. We have this in common. We care for our clients. While our approaches may differ, our goals are the same. But I won't lie to you. If I could go back in time to that night, I'd do things exactly the same. After his decision to experiment, I'd told Cliff we couldn't do this every day, and I don't think he wants that, in any case. As I said, I believe he wants something much more, and I'd love to find out what it is, if you'll let me. Yet, for all that, you're right. I've broken your rules, Mr. Knowland, and whatever they might look like, I'm prepared to face the consequences."

"You must know that what you've done, even though Cliff remains safe, is still grounds for termination, at the least."

"I do." Ayo takes his hanky from his pocket and wipes the tear flowing down my cheek. "If this is your decision, so be it. I've been through much worse, and I'll manage. All I ask is that you keep in mind what I said about Cliff's desires, that he wants something more from life than what he's getting presently. I believe it's this, more than anything, that's been the cause of what you're calling his 'behaviors.'"

"Such wisdom," says Greg, his teeth shining like floodlights. "Such revelation. Since John's about to give you the boot, you might want to con-sider reapplying as a behaviorist. If they'll have you, we could tackle Cliff together, try to solve him like a living riddle. What do you say to that?"

"Respectfully, I think you and Stella already make a super team."

The brown of Greg's face goes dark red. "We don't kill our clients with dreams, at least."

"I said enough," Knowland booms, his features rotten. "There'll be no irony or sarcasm as long as I head up the company. What good has it ever done us? What benefits have we ever reaped in its rank, unwelcome wake?"

"None," says everybody, in the same remorseful tone.

"I didn't think so." Knowland crumples up his sheet of paper and lobs it toward the table's center. "Besides, no one's getting fired. Not today, anyway. I don't think you aimed to hurt Cliff, Ayo. I don't think your intentions were ill. I'm thrilled that you're trying to help him, but concerned your approach is going too far. That said, you've earned a second chance today. I can tell you want only the best for Cliff, even if your method's been misguided to this point. This is why I'm willing to work with you, provided you agree to work with me."

"Thank you, Mr. —"

"I'd urge you to reconsider, John. We can still nip this in the bud before it's too late."

"I've made up my mind. I expect you, Ayo, to avoid such indiscretion in the future. You'll heed our every instruction, which for you might as well be the law. To begin with, you'll only feed Cliff through his tube from now on. The same goes for your work with the other guys. You'll follow their plans to a T. If it's not in their plans, you don't do it. If we tell you 'no,' you don't do it. If you're not sure about something, you ask. Understood?"

"Yes, sir," Ayo says.

"Think of this as probation. Be thankful for it."

"I am, very much."

"We'll meet again in two weeks to review. I hope to hear only good things at that time. But let me be perfectly clear, Ayo. Fail to comply even once and you're done."

"I understand. Thank you again, Mr. Knowland."

"Don't make me regret this."

"I won't."

"Good." Knowland knocks on lacquered wood. "As for the rest of you, I expect you to remember we're all in this together. This means no more infighting, resentment, sarcasm, or snark. You're all part of a team. Act like it."

"Of course," Francis laughs.

"Roger that," Brad salutes.

"You betcha," Greg grins, his toes jiggling. "By the way, I should have Cliff's plan finished soon. I'll send it out to everyone and visit the house to do training. Here's hoping it works. Otherwise, as I see it, the only other way to keep him and others safe amounts to a regression, of sorts."

He indicates the manual wheelchair folded up against the wall behind him.

"And I'll use this second chance," Ayo says, "to make sure that won't be necessary."

Francis cocks his head and grins, as if to say, *Good luck with that.*

TEN

"Whaddya mean, he isn't gay?"

"Just what I said. I hate to burst your bubble, but Ms. Stella's theory was false. It seems Cliff and Ayo aren't together, after all."

"But that's what I've been saying all along. It's not Yodel he likes. It has to be somebody else."

"Maybe. Maybe not. The truth is, we still don't know yet."

"Then why'd he try to kill you at the grocery? Why'd he break poor Greg's foot into a thousand pieces?"

"That's the million-dollar question," Francis says, face in his phone. "You'd think there'd be a reason, but sometimes things happen we can't explain."

BJ freezes mid-air punch, the gears in his head spinning like clockwork. "Like what?"

"*The Mary Celeste.* Tunguska. Roanoke. To name a few."

"I don't even know what those words mean."

"They mean if you don't calm down, you're going to give yourself a heart attack."

"He'd be the one giving it to me, don't you know." Wiping jelly stains from his blue polo, BJ eases himself into his recliner. "I thought that's why you met today. You were supposed to get Cliff figured out and all."

"I thought so, too, but these things can take time."

"Well, I'll tell you this, Francis. He'd better straighten up fast, or I'm out of here."

"Is that right? Where would you go?"

"Anywhere else would be just fine with me. Brad has other houses. Maybe they have openings. Heck, I'd even suck it up and live with Henry Wray, if that's what it comes to."

"You must've lost your mind," Francis says, after typing out and sending a text.

"It's not my fault." His knobby knees exposed below a pair of drawstring shorts, BJ cranks his leg rest up. "I hope you understand what you're doing to us, Cliff. The pain and the fear you've caused. The sadness and the suffering. Every day it's some new tragedy with you. Sometimes I even worry you might come after me. Why, I only feel safe in my own home because of Francis —"

"Quiet now, old man. The show's on again."

"Sorry."

Back from commercial, Firth Bronzer continues his special coverage of the breaking news out of the Capitol, where, having been ousted from his committees for using the *r*-word, Representative Horner and twelve of his most fervent supporters have staged an insurrection. At least, that's what Bronzer's calling it. The word evokes images of armed and angry throngs, bloodshed and body armor, the violence and the vomit of a collapsing civilization. There's none of this here save the vomit, and that's only because the men involved — they're all men, as far as I can tell — have been drinking steadily since nine o'clock this morning. This is the last thing one might expect from such a peril to democracy. There are no militia here, no bikers, no brawny brutes in battle dress. There's just guys my age in straight-cut jeans and bargain sneakers struggling to stay upright on the Rotunda's terrazzo floor. In this task, the crumpled cans of cheap domestic beer they've strewn across the hallowed space aren't helping. Horner trips on one pulling a man up by the arm and falls on top of him, knocking the guy unconscious under his massive, suited frame. The congressman either can't or refuses to rise to his feet, so that's where he remains, lying face-down on his comatose accomplice as he belches out the chorus to "The Yankee Doodle Boy." All around him, senators and tourists go about their day like any other, stepping over and around the plastered putsch as Lincoln looks on from the vantage of his pedestal.

"Can you believe this?" Francis slaps his knee. "It's a sad day for the country, but it does make for good TV."

"A sad day, indeed."

"Wanna pop."

"What were they hoping to accomplish? What did they expect to change?"

"Not their clothes, that's for sure. Look, most of them have pooped and peed their pants. If they had staff, like we do, they would've brought an extra pair along."

"Mm-hmm."

As the insurgents slip in their own upchuck like old *Double Dare* contestants, Bronzer provides running commentary from the safety of his studio. "If nothing else," he says, his tone enraptured, "this is the nation's first successful *spew d'état.*" "*Sic semper vomitus,*" he declares, when one of Horner's backers does a barrel roll through a pile of regurgitated chicken nuggets.

"That's a good one." Francis laughs through his nose. "'*Sic semper vomitus.*'"

"I wish I knew what's funny. I could use a laugh. But I don't think I can today. I'm too sad Cliff's not better yet."

"I said chill out, BJ. Stop being such a killjoy. For once in your life, look on the bright side."

"My housemate's a hardened terrorist. What's the bright side of that?"

"Fair question. Still, you'll be glad to hear he's staying home from day program for now. You'll be safe from his chair there, if nowhere else."

"Maybe you're right, Francis. Thanks for the good talk. I'll take my peace of mind where I can get it, and I'll enjoy my life while I still can. And even better, Yodel's back."

"Hip-hip hooray," Francis says. "Oh, that reminds me. I forgot to share the most important part of Cliff's meeting."

"I don't want to hear it. The last thing I need is more bad news."

From the hallway, Lem appears, buck naked and glistening. He pauses long enough for us to note his raging erection, then hustles off toward our room, leaving wide, wet footprints in his wake. On his heels, Ayo mops them up with a dry towel, folds it over his arm, and looks to us, his face gleaming with sweat. Before he has a chance to speak, Lem's box springs resume their strident screaming.

"Not again," BJ cries. "Show some mercy, Lem. Between your shenanigans and Cliff's cruelty, I can't take it any —"

"Easy there. You didn't let me finish."

"Finish? I said the last thing I need —"

"It's good news, actually. A silver lining, if you will." Tossing his phone onto the couch's empty cushion, Francis whistles. "Ayo promised us he'd fix Cliff very soon. As he sees it, Cliff has hopes and dreams no one knows about, not even you. Not only will Ayo discover them. He's going to make them come true, like a genie in a child's story. What's wrong, BJ? Don't you hear me? I know Cliff can't jump for joy, but why can't you? This means your days of worrying are numbered. Why aren't you as happy as Aladdin's closest friend?"

"Of course I'm happy, and I appreciate the thought, Yodel, but how, exactly, will you do it? It's not like Cliff can —"

"I told you not to worry." Francis flings Ayo a gnarled grin. "He'll solve this great mystery. It'll only take time and much patience. Until then, everybody feels much better knowing he and Cliff aren't, well, that."

"They'd have known a long time ago, too, if they'd only listened to me."

"That's their problem, not yours. The important thing is that, eventually, they did. But I'm sorry to say I can't share their confidence yet. There's still one question I need answered before I can agree Ayo hasn't caused Cliff any harm."

"He's right there. Why not ask him?"

With the towel hanging limp on his arm, Ayo's a matador facing a bull in the ring. "I'm right here. Why not ask me?"

Francis leans toward him. "You admitted to feeding Cliff barbecue sauce?"

"You heard what I said. You were there."

"Why'd you do that?" BJ's eyes are huge behind his cloudy lenses. "You know Cliff can't have food. He could die if he —"

"It's all right," Francis smiles. "He was only helping Cliff to have fun. For the first time in a long time, or maybe ever, he got a taste of something pleasant, one of life's smaller delights most of us all too often take for granted. Yet Ayo understands he took a major risk, and that Cliff's was even greater. He apologized for it."

"You're right to be angry with me," Ayo says. "I'm sorry for making you worried, BJ."

"He admitted his mistake and promised only to feed Cliff through the tube from now on."

BJ smacks his armrest. "I should hope so. I'm still mad at Cliff for everything, and I still want to move away from here, but I'd be sad if something happened to him, Yodel, and even sadder if it was because of you."

"It's okay. Cliff survived. Despite his condition, he swallowed the sauce with no problems. But that's where my question arises, you see, the one they didn't ask at today's meeting."

"What is it?"

"I want to know if that was the only thing he swallowed, or whether he ingested something more."

Francis turns his smirk on me and makes a heavy gulping sound.

My grunt lengthens into a growl. We both know I can't get to him behind the coffee table, but this doesn't mean I can't send him a message. I grab the joystick and —

"Let me handle this, Cliff," Ayo says.

Francis hops to his feet. "What is there for you to handle? My question was for him."

"That was no question. It was an insult."

Widening his stance, Francis forces Rickey to the far side of the couch. "An insult? All I want is the truth. It was you who broke the rules and —"

"Since when do you care about the rules? You've flouted them since my first day, and probably long before that."

"Heh. In what way?"

"You know what you've done," Ayo says, stepping closer, "and also what you haven't. For that matter, you know you're lucky I didn't bring it up to Mr. Knowland earlier."

"Bring what up? What can you tell Knowland he doesn't already know? He and Brad have never had issues with me. You make it sound like I'm a monster, like I'm the one who poured that liquid down poor Cliff's broken throat. For all your bluster, though, you remain very light on specifics."

"I didn't say you were a monster. I don't think that's what you are."

"What am I, then, in your expert opinion?"

"Just plain mediocre, mostly."

"Who's insulting whom now?"

On TV, Horner slides off his abettor and, lying face-up on the Rotunda floor, gives the finger to a flock of fourth graders on a field trip.

"You wanted my opinion. I'm giving it. You're mediocre. Middling. Average, if even." Ayo nods at the phone on the couch. "What else would you call spending most of your shifts on that thing? It's not an insult. It's the truth. Isn't this what you're looking for?"

"The truth is I didn't almost kill one of my clients."

"Of course not. The thought would never cross your mind, you're so busy ignoring them."

Francis sneers and flares his shoulders. "Why don't we ask them what they think? Would you say I ignore you, BJ?"

"Well, I don't know," BJ stutters. "As I say, I'm grateful for all my staff, but Yodel's right. Sometimes it does seem like you're on your phone a lot —"

"Shut up, old man, and go do your laundry. You've put it off too long as it is."

"Don't talk to him like that. You do what you want, BJ. If you'd like to sit there a while, then stay. Your laundry can wait until later."

"Thanks, but I should probably do it now." Slipping out of the recliner, he shambles off toward his room. At the hallway's entrance, he turns back with tears in his eyes. "I'm sorry if I hurt your feelings, Francis. I didn't mean it. No matter what, I'm still thankful for you —"

"Go away. We need to talk in private."

"Okay, but —"

"Now."

BJ hobbles down the hall without another word.

"Why would you say these things?" Ayo says. "What makes you think you can speak to these men in this way?"

"It's not your concern, little man. I let you do your job. Let me do mine."

"Mm-hmm." Ayo drops the towel and takes another step forward, fists clenched at his sides. "What is your job, by the way? To sit on the couch and watch television?"

"I do more than that, and you know it."

"Apologies. I forgot you play *Baby Jesus* a lot."

"That's not what I meant."

"No? Then you must've meant how you FaceTime with your girl-friend."

"We don't FaceTime. We Zoom. And those are very rare occasions and happen only when there's nothing else to do."

"And also only when Brad's not around."

If my chair had a horn, I'd honk it three times.

"So? Our days here are long." Francis socks his own palm. "We're allowed to take breaks. What do you care how I spend mine?"

"I don't. But neither do I think your breaks should last the whole shift."

"Good thing you're not my supervisor."

"You're right. I would've had you out of here after what happened at the grocery. Wait, please," Ayo says without flinching. "I'm not done yet. If you plan to hit me, I won't stop you, but you should let me finish, at least."

Francis lets his fist fall to his hip. "Go on, then."

"I'm not your supervisor, but I'm someone who cares about these men. I want to see them treated with respect. That's the essence of our jobs, mine and yours. I've tried to do mine to the best of my abilities. Maybe I took things too far when I fed Cliff by mouth. But at least I tried to give him something good. That's more than anyone will ever say of you, Francis. It's why I don't consider what I did a failure. My only failure on the job has been my hesitation, until now, to call you out for failing to do yours."

"And now you have." Francis raises his hands in surrender. "Is that all you wanted to say?"

Ayo laughs. "There are so many things on my mind, but considering our audience, most of them aren't appropriate, so I'll give you the brief, wholesome version. I don't care what you think of me, Francis. You can call me 'little man.' You can call me whatever you want. We're coworkers. We should get along. It'd make our days here more pleasant. If we can't, then so be it. We'll keep our conversations to a minimum. That's probably the best for both of us. But here's the truth you've been wanting so badly. These men deserve better than you." Ayo stands as close to him as the table allows, his shins digging into its dusty bottom shelf. "The thing about it, though, is I'm pretty sure you already knew this."

"What is your point?"

"My point is, if you ever treat these guys like this again, you and I will have serious problems. Do you understand what I'm saying to you? From now on, I only want to see you treating them the way you should've been all along, like human beings."

"And how would you suggest I do that?" Francis says, seeming much shorter than ever.

"It's not hard. Here, let me show you. BJ, would you come back here, please?"

"Just a jiffy." BJ's voice is muffled down the hall. "This laundry's sure giving me trouble today."

"I'll help you later. Will you join us again for a moment? There's something I'd like to ask you."

"I'll be there as soon as I can."

"You're an odd one, you know." Francis falls to the couch with a flump. "I've never worked with any staff like you before. Don't ask me what it is. I can't explain it, but I've seen it in your face since you first started."

Ayo touches his scar, which burns blue in the afternoon light.

"Here I am, Yodel," says BJ, shuffling into the living room, a pair of pajama bottoms wrapped around his head like a ski mask. He gropes around until he finds the wall and stands there facing it. "I think."

"What happened in there? Are you all right?"

"I was doing just fine until my hamper exploded on me, the scoundrel."

Ayo pulls the PJ's off BJ's head. "We'll give it the what-for in a while. But for now I have a question for you and your housemates."

"What about Lem?" asks BJ. The springy caterwauling, which had ceased when Francis leaped off the couch, picks up again, its force redoubled. "Oh, criminently. Never mind."

"We'll let Lem do his thing. He's not hurting anyone."

"Except that bed of his," says BJ, shaking a fist at the gods.

"The thing is, it's his bed, no one else's. He can do with it as he pleases."

"Until he breaks it and has to get another."

"Which is up to him, as I'll remind you. We might not agree with it, but we should respect his choice. My question has more to do with your choice."

"My choice of what?"

"Of what to watch, BJ." Ayo shoots a thumb at the TV. "This is your house, isn't it? Shouldn't you guys be the ones to choose your entertainment?"

"Yes, that would be nice, but as I say, Francis likes to watch his own shows, sometimes."

"I think Francis can watch his own shows on his own TV at his own house. Wouldn't you agree?"

"That sounds real good, of course, but —"

"And you, Francis? Wouldn't you agree, as well?"

Francis grinds his teeth and leans back hard into the couch. "I suppose it is their place and their TV."

"There's no supposing anything. This is their place. This is their TV. They should be the ones to pick what plays on it."

"What if they don't care? They never have before, and —"

"Have you ever asked them?"

Francis pretends to think. "Probably. I don't remember."

"Do you, BJ? Has Francis ever asked if you cared about what's on?"

"I sure would hate for anyone to get in trouble."

"No one's in trouble, sir, especially not you. You're a good man. You care about your friends. You always try to do right by them. What's more, you always tell the truth. That's one of your greatest strengths and most outstanding qualities."

"It's a living," says BJ, beaming.

"I'm glad you're proud of it. There's no reason why you shouldn't be, and there's no reason you shouldn't tell the truth about this. Has Francis ever asked about the shows you'd like to watch?"

BJ scratches his bald, shiny crown. "I don't think so. It always seems like he just puts on what he wants."

"What about you, Cliff? Has Francis ever checked with you?"

I shake my head.

"I see. And you, Rickey?"

"Wanna cookie."

"I thought you might say that," says Ayo. "But I figured I'd give it a shot. Here's what is going to happen, my friends. We're going to have a house vote."

"What's that mean?" says BJ.

"It means I'm going to give you some choices, and you'll pick the one you like best. Whichever one wins, that is, whichever one has the most votes, will be what we watch for today. How's that sound to you? Pretty good?"

"I'd say. That is, if it's all right with Francis."

"It doesn't matter if it's all right with Francis. Remember, this is your house. It's your call."

"Oh, yeah. I almost forgot."

Francis raises a finger of timid objection. "But look here, BJ, on the news, if you would. A congressman has launched a rebellion at the Capitol. Do you understand how serious this is? History's taking place before our very eyes."

Horner finally claws his way back to his feet and staggers to the statue of George Washington, whose pedestal he starts humping like a dog with the hots for a fire hydrant.

"So, that's what they're doing, eh?" BJ whips his glasses off and rubs his eyes. "Silly me. I thought they were having bad behaviors."

"They're doing that, too," Francis says, "but my point is, whatever we call it, as citizens who care about our country, we really shouldn't miss this most remarkable event."

"What we really shouldn't do is not let these men choose for themselves. What do you say, BJ? Cliff? Rickey? Is there something else you'd rather watch than this old man copulating with a sculpture of your most revered Founding Father?"

"Who are you to dictate how things should —" Francis stops as Ayo hikes an eyebrow. "I'm just asking that we wait for this to end before we change the channel."

"Fair enough. That can be one option. Do you have any other ideas, BJ? Anything else for you to vote on?"

BJ pinches his chin. "Well, sometimes we like to watch the weather."

"You mean on Channel Eight?"

"I mean on the Weather Channel. It's all they ever talk about."

"Ah, I should've guessed. It's right there in the name."

"You bet your butt it is, Yodel. Back in the old days, we watched it all the time."

By *back in the old days,* BJ means my first few years here, when the Weather Channel was on most afternoons. The network has always appealed to the guys in a way most things never could. It doesn't deal in abstractions, offering only the concrete, comprehensible reality of what's going on outside these walls. In its clear and simple presentation of its clear and simple subject, it provides BJ, Lem, and Rickey with a sense of comfort, knowledge, and control over their own universe. Even better, unlike the news, nobody ever yells, if you don't count Jim Cantore's live reporting from the eye of every hurricane since 1992.

"That sounds like a great addition to our list. Any other suggestions? Cliff?"

I point to BJ.

"Are you seconding your housemate's choice?"

That's right.

"Thank you. Very good. It's up to you, now, Rickey. What are your thoughts?"

"Wanna cookie?"

"You can't watch a cookie, Rick."

"Why not? Almost every day we look at cookies during snack."

"Yes, but mostly we eat them," says BJ. "You can't eat what's on TV."

"I agree, but democracy is messy, as they say, and it seems to be his choice, so we'll respect it. Here we are, then." Ayo holds his hands out like a pair of scales. "Here are our options. From Francis, the sad state of affairs inside the legislature. From BJ, the Weather Channel, which Cliff has also thrown his weight behind. And from our quiet friend Rickey, we have, as expected, one whole cookie." He raises his right hand. "All in favor of the legislature? Excuse me, Francis, but this exercise is for the men who live here only."

"How's that even fair? We work here. We help them. We should have a say in —"

"Have you already forgotten what I said about how this house is theirs?"

Francis looks away and shakes his head.

"Good." Ayo lifts his left hand. "All in favor of a cookie?"

No one responds, not even Rickey, who's smiling at something far away.

Ayo brings his hands together and extends them outward, palms up, as if waiting to catch a storm's first drops of rain. "Lastly, all in favor of the Weather Channel?"

BJ and I heave our arms up as high as we can.

"There's two for the weather. Is there anybody else who wants to vote?"

Everyone turns to face Rickey, whose smile widens as he peers into the distance.

"Then by a vote of two to zero to zero — the last zero being Rickey's cookie —, it's the weather that carries the day."

"Huzzah!" In my twenty years here, I've beheld BJ's dancing and singing, I've heard him bellow and blubber and bleat, and I've hearkened to many of his finest orations, but never, until this great moment, have I witnessed him doing the dab.

"Are you all right, BJ?" Francis says.

"I've never been better." Clasping his hands in triumph, he shakes them first to his left, then his right. "Though I do apologize, Francis, for not picking your favorite channel. I hope you're not mad about it."

"You chose what you wanted. There's no need to feel sorry. He knows this. You know this, right, Francis?"

"Of course," Francis spits. "You've got nothing to be rueful about."

Lem's bed's rusty keening comes to a sudden halt and is soon followed by a deep, gleeful groan.

"Except for that," BJ says. "Has he no sense of shame?"

"Doubtful. Look, there he is again, still in the nude, on his way back to the bathroom."

"I think it's your turn to wash him up," Ayo says.

Francis considers a rebuttal, decides against it, and heads down the hall with his tail between his legs.

"How does one operate this?" Ayo says, taking up the remote. "I've never seen a gadget so complex. All these buttons, symbols, and colors. It's like something you'd find on an alien spaceship."

"I'll handle this, Yodel, if you please."

Gladly, Ayo gives the thing to BJ, at whose touch Representative Horner, who's just thrown up on Reagan's bronze shoes, vanishes from our TV and is replaced by scenes of people leaving beaches en masse. It seems a superstorm is threatening to slam the eastern seaboard. Jim Cantore's preparing to fly out there and will be reporting live through wind and rain until the weekend's up. Dreadful though the situation is, there's something oddly soothing in the Weather Channel's coverage — the map's multi-colored hues, the anchor's steady inflections, the calm urgency with which she advises those in the storm's path to listen up and batten down.

"Thank you, BJ. I hope they'll be okay, though. That looks to be one terrifying tempest."

"I'd say. I'm just glad we're safe and sound right here in our nice house."

"As am I." Ayo peeks through the back door's blinds, out at the dazzling sunlight. "We won't have to fear a storm today, at least. In fact, it's so nice we could even have our dinner on the patio."

"That sounds great. How about some stir-fry? There are plenty of veggies in there, and some chicken."

"Certainly. Would you mind getting the pan out from under the oven? I'll be there to help in a minute."

BJ nods and leaves the room, snapping his fingers.

"Thanks, Yodel."

"You're welcome, BJ."

"That wasn't me," BJ calls from the kitchen, "but I still thank you all the same."

Ayo wheels around. "You didn't? Who was it?"

"Well, it sounded like Rickey, I think, but he only ever says —"

"Thanks, Yodel," the voice says again.

"Was that you, Rickey?" Ayo goes to him and kneels by his side. "Did you say something to me?"

Rickey's smile is broader than ever, his gaze still aimed far in the distance. He raises a trembling hand and lets it fall to Ayo's knee, which he squeezes softly before turning to him.

"Thanks, Yodel," he says, his eyes bright. "Thanks for the weather."

"It's my pleasure, my friend, and you're welcome."

He grins, pats Rickey's shoulder, and walks with purpose to the kitchen. It's from there that BJ, at the top of his lungs, sings "For He's a Jolly Good Fellow" for him, getting through it several times before his voice begins to crack. Then he just hums it.

☽

The calling of my name pulls me back to consciousness. I flow like a current through the void, toward the circle of blue light, and come out its other side into our darkened living room. The TV's drowsy glow shows empty beaches, but not much else has changed out on the eastern seaboard. In the map down in the corner, the storm revolves ruthlessly around its axis, though its tentacles still have some way to go to Florida's coast. Offscreen, the anchor speaks in the same quiet tones that lulled me off to dreams I wish I could, but can't, remember.

"Cliff."

My stomach gurgles. My eyes are heavy with gunk.

"I'm sorry to wake you."

Through the back door, night is falling fast.

"But everyone else is in bed."

I press the power on my chair. The button turns red as the eye of the storm.

"If you like, I can take you to yours."

Shaking my head, I try to rub the gunk out, but can't reach.

"Here, let me help. Close your eyes, please."

Ayo's colorful handkerchief grazes my tear ducts, first on one side, then the other. I yawn and nod my thanks and we go silent for a while, watching the wind pick up through the TV's palm leaves. Outside, the sky's deep blue gives way to black and a bright multitude of stars.

"It's getting pretty late. You're sure you're not ready for bed?"

"Nah," I say, throwing a finger at the map on the big screen.

"Fair enough. Yet it seems we're the only ones still conscious in this place."

Behind us, Francis sleeps peacefully, curled up on the couch like a big fetus. He doesn't snore but only smiles, his face devoid of the secret contempt that usually accompanies this expression of his in waking moments. It's not the first time he's conked out on the clock. Before Ayo started, when he was working by himself, Francis would pass out in the same position around this time every night. He'd set the alarm on his phone to go off about five minutes before Thomas showed up. It was loud enough for us to hear through our bedroom doors and sounded like a rooster being strangled with a garrote. He knows this is forbidden and that he'd be fired if Knowland found out. In homes like ours, it's a form of neglect.

Ayo squats down at my side like a catcher. "I wasn't too hard on him, was I?"

I shake my head so hard it hurts.

"I didn't think so, either. The man had it coming. But you know this. And look at him now, catching winks like a baby." Ayo grins dismissively. "I'm of a mind to tell Brad about it. What I don't know is whether he'd believe me."

I look at his pocket, where Ayo's phone slumbers, then try my best to mime taking a photo.

"Good point. That would be solid proof. But I'm afraid that even then, he might accuse me of deflection. After all, I'm on probation. I've made it on — how do you say — his shit list."

My smile grows with his own.

"You're right, in any case. I think my message had much more impact than anything Brad could've said."

"Mm."

"I guess we'll see what happens. What I'm hoping is Francis will take my words to heart, not only for your sake, but also for his own. I wasn't joking earlier. If he doesn't change, he's going to regret it."

I purse my lips. *What will be will be.*

"For now, I must apologize for something I regret." He folds his hands together and holds them out to me. "I've done something I shouldn't have.

I'd promised you I'd tell no one what happened on our walk. Today, I broke that promise. At the time, it didn't seem I had a choice. Those men had accused me of absurd and heinous things. I felt I had to stand up for myself, that only brutal honesty could vindicate me. For all that, though, I should've checked with you first. I should've asked your permission before saying a word. I don't want to be like them, Cliff. I don't mean to break my promises. You deserve people you can trust. That wasn't who I was today, and for that I'm very —"

I'm glad you said it.

"I understand, but I must do this, all the same. This is your life. These are your decisions. You should be the one to choose who knows about them and who doesn't."

I nod, we fall quiet, and nothing changes in the world on our TV. The anchor speaks over the wind from her desk as the waves beat the beaches like whips. Anyone still around when the storm hits, she says, won't stand a chance unless they shelter underground. Even then, survival's not a given. Better to get as far away as possible, she says. Better to get as far inland as one can. The whirling mass up on the map is unlike anything she's ever seen before.

"Living in these times is very strange," Ayo says.

You're telling me.

"Though you likely could've said the same in any other time, as well."

Fair enough.

"No, I don't think it matters when we live, or where. There have always been forces that can't help but cause pain. Some of them, like this storm, come from nature. We know why they happen. Science explains them. In themselves, they're neither good nor bad. The storm doesn't know what it's doing, of course. It's not trying to hurt anyone. It is what it is, nothing more, nothing less." Ayo shifts his weight down on his haunches. "There are other things, though, that bring just as much pain, but which make much less sense in my mind. Take the way some people treat each other. Take the way Francis treats you." He looks over at the giant fetus on the couch, who sighs through his childlike smile. "He knew what he was doing the whole time. He meant to hurt you and had fun doing it. For him, it was no different than a game. The attitudes that make someone behave like he's behaved . . ." The sadness I saw in Ayo's face on his first day reemerges like a long-forgotten song. "When I came to this country, I thought I'd left that all behind."

I raise both hands, asking why.

"I haven't told you much of where I'm from, have I? It's so different from this place in many ways, but one of them is not because we don't have any Wendy's."

"Ha."

"As I told BJ, we have several. Sometimes we even go inside them, if we're feeling especially brave. Still, there are discrepancies between our Wendy's and yours. The shape and color of the buildings aren't the same, for one, and where I'm from, their burgers taste a little older, and a little weirder, too. Yet, on the whole, these differences don't amount to much. No one seems to mind them, anyway.

"But there are other, more significant distinctions," Ayo says. "We only became a free people very recently compared to you. There are still many things for us to figure out. It was just a few years ago, for instance, that we passed a law like the one here saying people with disabilities have rights to be respected. This took decades to happen, and even now, the law's not being followed as it's written. The attitudes toward people who, like you, require help remain stuck far in our reactionary past." He stares deep into his memory and shudders. "Some still believe sorcery and sin cause disabilities. This entitles them, in their minds, to treat those born a little differently with derision and hostility."

"Mn."

"But they don't act this way only to strangers. They treat family like this, too, if they feel bad spirits are responsible. They can't or won't give help themselves to those who need it most. Instead, they send them off to hospitals like the one you used to live in. They have no programs there like this" — he indicates our living room — "where the care is provided not in institutions but out in people's homes. Maybe one day they will, but I doubt in our lifetime.

"If they'd had them," says Ayo, still gazing into the past, "things would've been different. Better, I'd hope, but who knows? As things stood, I wouldn't let David be sent away."

Who's David?

Ayo smiles. "He was my brother, Cliff. I see a lot of him in you. Just like you, he was tough. He used a chair to get around, though admittedly it wasn't nearly as nice as this one. He knew what he was up against, and despite everything, he kept fighting. He wouldn't let other people's actions shape the way he felt about himself. He was who he was, and he was proud of it. Also, like you, he had a superb sense of humor. He always made me laugh when I most needed it. I did the same for him, sometimes just to hear it. His laughter made the good days even better and the bad ones not as bad.

"It wasn't easy, being his only caregiver. It was a full-time job on top of the one I had already, and we had no one else to turn to for support. When I took David in, our family abandoned us both. We moved to a new town, as far away as we could. It hurt more than anything, seeing us all torn apart thanks to ideas with their roots in superstition." The anger on his face soon yields to patient resignation. "But if I had to do it over, I wouldn't change anything. David deserved more than that world and its ignorance, hatred, and fear. In my own small way, I tried to show him this — like I try to show you,

Cliff, every day — just by sitting and being with him, as we're doing now. I talked to him and treated him as I would any other human being. It always struck me how simple this was and yet how so many others refused to see it. For them, it was much easier to ignore David's humanity and to treat him with cruelty and violence. But in doing so, they taught me the difference between knowing when to run, as from a hurricane, and when to hold your ground."

Cautiously, I reach out to the scar on his left cheek.

"Yes, I received this on one of the latter occasions," he says, tracing the mark with his finger. "We were taking a walk when some men approached. They weren't men, actually. They were boys, at least mentally if not in age — three little boys out to cause others pain. Not just anyone would do for them, though. It had to be someone who couldn't fight back, someone whose weakness would make them feel strong. That's what they saw when they spotted my brother, not a person but an object, a thing. They regarded him as something that would bring them entertainment, like a toy, like a video game. We didn't recognize them, but we knew them by their looks, which we'd seen on countless faces all our lives." Ayo nods at the sleeping figure on the couch. "You've seen them, too, many times."

Countless times.

"They thought they'd have fun, and they tried. What they didn't count on was that someone, that I, would stick up for my brother. It was hardly the first time I'd done it. Neither was it the last. But it's the one I remember the most. They made sure of that with their knives. And I, with only my hands, made sure they'd remember us, too."

I give him my best bicep flex.

"I'm not saying it's right to hurt others, even when you're being threatened, like we were. Yet there are times you find you have no other choice. I know this is why you've been having 'behaviors,' why you went after Francis that day at the grocery. Whatever Greg said to deserve the death machine, I'm sure it made you feel like I did when those men approached my brother."

BJ tried to tell them. They wouldn't listen. I had no other choice but to stand up for us both.

"I know. You did what you felt you had to. But fighting back like that has consequences. I'll have this scar forever, and these two, here and here." He points to a couple hidden spots on either side of his abdomen. "I trust you'll never suffer anything like this, but you do have to work with Greg, which might actually be worse, all things considered. If you keep at it, who knows what they'll do? He's still working on that behavior plan of his. Don't give him a reason to add to it. I don't want you to lose anything."

He doesn't need to tell me what he means by anything. It's written all over his face.

"Besides, as long as I'm working with you, I'll fight for you, Cliff. Understand?"

Yes, I do.

"Good. Any questions?"

I think for a minute, not of what but whether to ask, and decide that if I don't, he might not tell me.

What happened to David?

"I thought you might say that," says Ayo. "No, it's okay, my friend. I'm glad you did. See, another way my country's different is that it lacks the resources people here sometimes take for granted. When I said David and I were alone, I meant it. We had no one else who was willing to help. My brother was born with cerebral palsy, but as he grew older he developed several other conditions we found we couldn't manage on our own. Picking up more hours at work wouldn't have come close to covering the cost of his new medications and the procedures he required. Anyhow, I had to be at home with him much more. I couldn't leave for too long without risking that something might happen to him. I might as well have been asleep, like Rip Fran Winkle over there."

"Hah."

"But I couldn't sleep. The stress wouldn't let me. This made David feel guilty, like he was a burden that kept me from living my own life. He wasn't. My life was taking care of him. That was all. I had nothing and nobody else. If I'd given up on him, he would've had nothing, too. I couldn't have lived with that. I tried to tell him, but he wouldn't hear it. He wanted to be sent away, like my family had desired years before. I refused. I'd heard about those places, what went on inside their walls. I wouldn't let my brother spend the rest of his life somewhere nobody knew who he was, much less cared.

"He started resenting me for it. To that point, he'd rarely been upset with me. But soon he was angry almost every day. He only had a push wheelchair — I couldn't afford a death machine on my wages — but if he'd had one like yours, he would've broken much more than my foot. I'm certain of this." Ayo pats the floor beside my wheel and smiles. "I really do see a lot of him in you. I did the best I could to give him a decent life. It wasn't nearly what he deserved, but it's what I had to offer. Unfortunately, what I had to offer wasn't enough. How can a single person take care of all his brother's needs when the whole world jumps up to mock his efforts?"

On TV, the winds blow fiercely through the palms.

"David understood this long before I did. He forgave me, after a while, for my stubbornness. But not until I'd learned the most important lesson of my life. Would you like to know what that was?"

More than anything.

"It was this, Cliff." He accentuates his words with little jabs of his pressed thumb and index finger. "That despite the love I had for him, despite the care I offered him, despite my hardest efforts to make his life a little better, I wasn't listening to David. Because I wouldn't listen, I missed the point entirely. It was his life, after all. For years I'd tried to give him what I thought he should've wanted. I never once considered we might not agree on what that was. I just assumed his and my best interests were the same. Maybe at some point they had been, but things were changing — he was changing — and, for a long time, I'd been unwilling to accept it.

"Slowly, I began to see that our ideas of what made a life worthwhile had diverged. I may have thought I'd known what was good for him, but that didn't mean I was right. Nor did it give me the right to impose my views on his life like the law. The only thing that mattered was what David wanted, even if I opposed it with my whole being." Ayo breathes in deeply through his nose. "Conceding this lifted the burden both from our shoulders and from our hearts. Though it hurt more than losing my family, I knew what I had to do next."

You took him to the hospital.

"I did, Cliff," he says, "because that's what he wanted. Because my role was only to help him obtain it. I admitted him into the hospital, let him live his life, and got on with my own. Not that I had much of one outside him. I worked. I came home. I slept. But I went to see David at least once a week, often more. They wouldn't allow me inside, though. We had to meet out in the courtyard with a staff standing guard not far off."

That's how it was at Sinai Grove, too.

"If I hadn't done this, that place would've killed him. I saw other patients sometimes. They had black eyes and bruises and cigarette burns on their arms."

So would we.

"But my brother was one of the few men who didn't. His staff never touched him that way. They knew what would happen if they did."

I give him another big flex of my biceps.

"It's a living," he smiles. "I think it helped him see why I'd felt the way I had. He seemed to like me better at this point, in any case."

He looks again into the past, his hanky balled up tightly in his fist.

"Because I fought for him — because we fought together — David received the best care they could offer. He got the meds and even some of the procedures he required. But in the long run, these things weren't enough. If he'd had access to the systems you have here, it might've worked out differently. Still, he was a fighter. He persevered as long as his body would allow. Only when it gave up on him did David give up on himself. He started refusing his meals. He'd only get out of bed when I came to visit. Staff said they could force-feed him, if I wanted. I told them it wasn't my choice. It was his. He had already made it.

"The last time I saw him," says Ayo, "he gave this to me. It was something he'd worked on at craft time. It's the one thing I have to remember him by."

Unclenching his fist, Ayo smooths the hanky out on his palm, its shades of tie-dye all subdued under the TV's soft blue light. I've never noticed it before, but in the center of the cloth, against its field of rainbow colors, is a bright handprint even smaller than my own. There are several, actually, layered at different angles to each other. The effect is that of a hand in motion, waving thanks and goodbye, over which Ayo places his own hand and pushes down hard.

"I've shared this with nobody else, Cliff. Before you, I never expected to meet anybody who'd get it. As I've said before, I thought I'd left all that behind, way back at home." As the storm cuts to commercial, he gets up and turns the TV's volume down. "At no point did I think it would be perfect in this country. I'm not that naïve. But neither was I expecting to find the same sad ways of thinking that led people to treat David like they had — at least not in a system like this one, designed to help you flourish."

Putting his hanky away, Ayo steps back beside me in silence. His last thought lingers over our heads like thick smoke in the air after fireworks.

"But it seems like I got through to Mr. Knowland earlier," he says. "What do you think?"

I smile. *I hope so.* On TV, Mean Barry Dean, the personal injury lawyer, slices up a stack of doctor's bills with a katana.

Ayo laughs quietly. "I hope so, too. Still, it could be worse. Being on probation's not as bad as being fired. I'm grateful for the second chance he gave me, and I don't intend to waste it."

I flash him not just one but two thumbs-up. Mean Barry disappears and a spot comes on for apocalypse survival kits, whose gear includes a lantern, compass, hunting knife, can of Pringles, pair of zip ties, the entire *Fast & Furious* saga on Blu-ray, and a camouflaged, battery-powered vibrator that also doubles as a Wi-Fi hotspot.

"But only you can choose what that is, Cliff," Ayo says. "So if you see something you want, you must speak up for yourself and let me know. Whether it takes us twenty years or twenty minutes, I'll help you find the thing that'd make you happier than BJ when he bursts out into song."

The next commercial is for Silver Lining Inn & Suites. All business, as usual, their best customer strides into the lobby, heels clicking against marble. As she brandishes her ArgentCare® Rewards Card, the long line at reception parts like the Red Sea, the clerk's eyes bulge cartoonishly, and the adoring crowd pursues her five floors above the Earth to her accommodations. After shutting the door and locking it tight, she whirls to face me. I dive into the pools that are her irises and swim through their green waters, and when I surface, I take in the only words I've ever heard her speak like a deep breath.

"I deserve better. Why shouldn't you?"

My arm shoots up. I turn to Ayo. My finger's fixed on the TV.

"More like twenty seconds," he says, his smile like another crescent moon upon his face.

Before I can respond, Francis's phone erupts into the rooster's call to wake.

ELEVEN

Last summer, Knowland gifted Angie a poster with the words HEROES WORK HERE emblazoned on a badge flanked by a mask and stethoscope. It's the same one hospitals and clinics displayed outside their main doors for a while, then all took down at the same time, as if they'd been nothing more than props in a big sales promotion. Angie never hung hers up but instead lay it on a small bookshelf in the corner of her office. Ever since, it's been collecting dust alongside her old three-ring binders, nursing manuals, and BM tracking charts. As she takes her purse from next to it and scoops out a pack of Doublemint, the sign slides off the shelf and falls back down between it and her bare wall.

"You did good, BJ," she says, coughing hard. "Here's two sticks for your trouble. Keep in mind those things we talked about that might help with your anxiety. I'd rather reduce your hypertension this way than have to switch to medication."

BJ rubs the arm just freed from her blood pressure cuff. "Easier said than done, as they say. Sometimes the world's more stressful than a game of Operation, but I'll give it my best shot."

He unwraps the gum and pops both sticks in his mouth, then throws his trash toward her wastebasket and misses.

"You can do it. I believe in you. Just remember that you can't control how other people act. The only thing you can control is your reaction to it."

"I know, but life would be a whole lot simpler if I could."

"If only we both could." Angie picks the wrappers up and winks at me through the doorway. "But that's not the way the world works, at least for most of us, including me, as I've learned to my chagrin."

"If it doesn't work for us, then who does it work for, Angie?"

"Great question." She slides behind her desk and starts typing out some notes on her computer. "I guess the answer is, for those fine folks who are in charge — the big bosses and the movers and the shakers of the world."

"But I can move and shake as well as anybody. Why, just feast your eyes on this."

Chewing his gum noisily and pivoting to Ayo, BJ brings his fists up to his chest and cuts a rug to music only he can hear, his tail end swaying like a Swiss ball on a pendulum.

"You've got the moves and the shakes," Angie says as we burst into applause. "A man with skills like that should be the one to rule the roost."

BJ doffs his invisible cap. "If I did, it'd be a much more friendly place, that's for sure."

"You can still make the world friendlier," says Ayo, "even if you don't control it."

The cogs in BJ's head kick into high gear. "But how?"

"By being yourself, of course, and by taking Ms. Angie's advice when you find yourself growing upset. Here, why don't we practice?"

Ayo stands in front of BJ, feet apart, and rolls his shoulders, then his head.

"Are you all right, Yodel?"

"Yes, I'm feeling great. This is helping me relax."

"Hmm. Well, you could've fooled me."

"What do you mean?"

"I mean it looks more like you're trying to dance like me," says BJ, proudly casting his thumbs back at himself. "And no offense, but let's just say you've missed the mark."

"None taken, my friend. I'd never dare to dream I could move and shake like you."

"Well, that's a relief."

"You may rest easy on that front. All I wanted was to show you how to stay calm in stressful situations. It's a skill you may one day find to come in handy." Resuming his shoulder rolls, Ayo takes a few deep breaths and invites BJ to do the same. "There you go. All the way in. Nice job. Hold it there, then breathe out slowly. Excellent. Now, let's try another, this time on your own."

"Here goes nothing." Spitting on his palms, BJ rubs them together, stands up straight, draws in a mighty breath, then starts hyperventilating through his nostrils.

"Not so fast, please. Remember, the goal is to relax, not get ourselves all worked up."

"I'm not worked up," BJ says, his face as red as a stoplight. "I'm as carefree as a cloud on a bright summer afternoon."

"Hmm. Well, you could've fooled me."

"What do you mean?"

Ayo smiles. "Let's try once more. Take one big, slow, deep breath in. Like that, yes. Perfect. Now hold it for a moment."

As he complies, BJ's eyes shut tight, his chest puffs out, his cheeks swell up, and when he finally exhales, he also passes gas that smells like today's lunch, bologna sandwich with a side of cottage cheese and kettle chips. What begins as Angie's laughter soon becomes a terrible, hoarse cough. She spins to the window and wheezes at the lawn where Knowland delivered his liberty speech. The fit goes on so long that Ayo rushes over, pats her on the back, and asks how he can help.

"I'm fine," she manages between gasps. "BJ just caught me unawares, is all. I'll live for now, but thanks."

"Sorry, Angie. It was just a little accident."

"You're okay, dear."

"It was my fault," Ayo says, "but you did good, anyway, BJ. We'll practice more another time. For now, I think Francis is in the breakroom with the other guys. Would you mind joining them while Cliff and I ask Ms. Angie about something?"

"Gee, I'd love to, but we're all friends here. Anything you can say to her, you can surely say to me."

Ayo strokes his chin. "I heard there's a box of oatmeal cookies in there."

"See you folks later," BJ says, galumphing off, "and thanks for the gum, Angie."

"Don't mention it."

Ayo waves me into Angie's office. I plant myself beside the chair in front of her desk.

"We'll keep working on those exercises. I hope he finds them beneficial."

"As do I. Thanks for your help. I'd prefer to stay off meds for his blood pressure, but it's been steadily increasing every month for the last six. If only everyone could be like you, Cliff. Again, your vitals looked real good this go-round. Yours is the cleanest bill of health I've stamped so far this week."

I grin and give Angie two big quivering thumbs-up.

"Thanks for making time for us. May I please shut the door?"

"Have at it." Angie waits for Ayo to sit. "What's up?"

"I've been thinking a lot about our conversation at the cookout. Do you remember?"

"Sure I do. You asked me who Colonel Flattop and Chief Soaring Dick were, and I said it was better if you left that one alone."

"Our week was much too busy to consider it, regardless," Ayo says, his smile faint and anxious. "Perhaps you've heard about it."

"I have. In case you didn't know, word gets around this building like a virus." She scoots up against her desk and whispers, "Between us, I wasn't the only one who relished the news that Cliff had broken Gabhart's foot. I saw Ed Vernon yesterday, and he was downright joyous for what must've been the first time in his life."

"Yes, it was quite something. Afterward, I spoke to Cliff about the risks of lashing out. While it must've felt right at the time — and between us, Greg likely deserved it — Cliff's actions may also bring unwanted repercussions.

But I was referring to another of this week's events, the one which landed me on Mr. Knowland's shit list."

Angie reaches for her purse. "I got that memo, too. Ballsy moves, I must say, both doing what you did and then admitting it to John."

"I wouldn't have done it if I hadn't been sure Cliff would be safe."

"I believe you. Still, as the staff nurse, I can't condone your feeding him by mouth. John has a point. Our clients have support plans for a reason. It can be dangerous to deviate from them. I'd be more concerned if he hadn't put you on his shit list, as he steadfastly refuses to do with your, uh, colleague."

"I understand. I don't mean to make excuses for my —"

"But as someone who cares about this guy" — Angie aims a deep-red fingernail at me — "I was glad to hear you tried to make his night a little better. Nobody else would've done that, and I gather, Cliff, that you enjoyed yourself much more because of it."

You're damn right I did.

Angie dips into her purse and fishes out her smokes. "Just be more careful from now on about who you guys share this stuff with. I'd like to see you stick around a while longer, Ayo. All our folks deserve at least one staff who thinks the way you do."

"Actually, that's what we wanted to ask you about."

"About you sticking around for a while?"

"That, maybe, but also about these men having the staff they deserve."

"I don't have much pull there, but I'd be happy to help any way I can."

Ayo looks to me to give the go-ahead. "Here's the thing." He rests his elbows on his knees and his chin on his clasped knuckles. "I hadn't planned on the barbecue sauce. I hadn't so much as entertained the thought, although the sights and smells were all around us. But then Francis saw fit to mock Cliff for his dysphagia, and —"

"Oh, God. Why am I not surprised?"

"Even worse, he did so right in front of Misters Knowland, Greg, and Brad, and not one of them uttered a single word of reprimand. Either the way he spoke to Cliff was hunky-dory by their standards, or we had just been witness to two separate events."

"Or they were engaged in willful blindness, which only makes it that much more pathetic."

"Whatever it was," says Ayo, "it wouldn't have felt right not to stand up for Cliff. That's when I got the notion to offer him the sauce. I ran it by them first, of course — it didn't seem right, either, to go behind their backs — but they shot it down more quickly than a gun bill in the Senate. And this despite the fact that Cliff had indicated his assent in no uncertain terms."

Angie twirls a cigarette between her red-tipped fingers. "To be fair, it isn't like they had a choice. They don't see Cliff's life from your or his perspective. John's view is different by necessity. He has to think 'big-picture,' which, as far as I can tell, just means the last thing he wants is to be the focus of another breaking story on Channel Eight."

"Yes, he made no bones about that. Probably I would've dropped it had he not then mentioned, in his prepared remarks, that it's our job, as caregivers, to provide our clients with the freedom to make choices and to take risks of their own. I told him as much yesterday. I can't say he agreed with my approach, but he was at least receptive to the sentiment behind it. It's the only reason why I wasn't fired then and there."

"Like I said, ballsy."

"Not as ballsy as I could've been. Not as ballsy as Francis taunting Cliff in full view of his supervisor and the CEO."

"As far as that goes, I'll tell you the same thing I told BJ earlier. Don't get yourself worked up over stuff you can't control. People like Francis, who've been around a while, who've locked themselves into these piss-poor attitudes toward their jobs — they can't change, Ayo. They have no reason to. They've learned how to stay off Knowland's radar while doing no more than the bare minimum. There's nothing you or I can do to help them see things differently."

"But that's just it," Ayo says, sitting up. "What if there is something I can do?"

"And what would that be?"

"After Cliff's meeting, I was feeling thankful, on the one hand, they hadn't terminated me. On the other, I was angry with myself for not having done more to stop Francis from acting like — how do you say — a dickhead."

"That's how we say it, all right. But the question still is, what can you do about someone like —"

"I threatened him."

Angie's cigarette dangles from her lips. "No shit?"

"No shit," Ayo says, then he explains how it transpired — Francis's "question," Ayo's admonition, our vote for what to watch on our TV. "I think I put the fear of God into him. Insulting me was one thing. I could've cared less about that. But I couldn't, and I can't, allow him to continue disrespecting this man here. He's complied so far, wouldn't you say, Cliff?"

So far.

"Well, good for you. That guy's had it coming for a long time. It's just too bad your boss didn't have the guts to give it to him."

"Yes, despite his army clothes and tough demeanor, Brad is a surprisingly weak man. This has got me thinking about the future. I've curbed my colleague's impulses for now. But I don't expect it to remain this way forever. Actually, he fell asleep a while later, last night, on the guys' couch. It seemed their choice of TV shows had bored him half to death."

Angie rolls her eyes. "I'd say he knew better if I liked sticking my foot in my mouth."

"I think he does but doesn't care. We work the same shifts, luckily, so I can keep an eye on him most days. Yet I am just one person. I can only do so much. I'll need help ensuring Francis doesn't make the wrong decisions going forward."

"But the issue is you can't depend on Brad for that."

"Exactly, which is why I'd like to ask you what you think of Mr. Knowland."

Angie laughs herself into another coughing fit, this one more alarming than the last. "Isn't it obvious?" she says, her eyes all wide and damp.

"It's a little clearer, at least."

"I'm sorry." She's wiping her tears with a napkin. "I shouldn't talk this way about the guy with all the power. What I think about him doesn't matter, anyway."

"We wouldn't bring it up if we thought it didn't matter. We trust your opinion, Ms. Angie. We can say the same of no one else who works here." Ayo grabs his knees and squeezes firmly. "But yesterday it felt like I got through to Mr. Knowland, even if only a little. And as you say, he is the one with all the power."

"You think he might be willing to help."

"We wanted to get your thoughts on that. We have no one else to turn to, and the buck does stop with him. You've been here much longer than I. You know the man better. He may be full of hot air, but I think he really does care for his clients. What I don't know is whether my speaking to him would make any significant difference."

"Why not?"

"Well, I am on his shit list, for starters, and Greg is certain I'm the cause of Cliff's 'behaviors.' Already, that's two strikes against me. And then Francis, of course, would deny everything. It would be my word against his, and Knowland might be more inclined to take the latter."

The butt of Angie's cigarette is thick with her red lipstick. She puts it back between her teeth and says, "I think we know where Greg can shove his certainty."

"Yes, but even if I did get through to Knowland, if I were able to convince him of the truth, I'm not certain he'd take any action on it. What I fear is that, at best, nothing would change, and at worst, my efforts would soon blow up in my face."

"How do you figure?"

"That's just it. I don't know. Cliff's team might take it as me trying to deflect or think I'm making up a story to get back on Knowland's good side. If he did nothing and Francis found out, he'd probably feel emboldened to revert to his old ways."

"That would be some shit."

"It would be, indeed. So, you see our dilemma. I want to help Cliff, not cause him more problems. While he wants to be hopeful, he's lost most of his faith in this system. Still, he listened to me and agreed to ask you before choosing one way or the other."

Angie sits back and removes her glasses, her face wrinkling in thought. "I'm glad you did, Cliff. At the same time, I hate that you have to come to me about it. I don't need to tell you it shouldn't have to be this way. Going to John for help shouldn't even be a question. In a decent world, you'd already have approached him with your concerns, and he'd be on them quicker than flies on a warm dog turd." She sets down her cigarette, swivels to the window, and coughs again. "Actually, scratch that. In a decent world, your staff wouldn't treat you like this in the first place. They'd come in and do their jobs like they're supposed to — they'd care for you, care about you — and this would be the rule, not the exception. It doesn't seem that difficult in theory. In practice, it's a totally different story."

"That's what I tried to tell them at Cliff's meeting."

"How did they react?"

"Brad and Greg laughed at me."

"God, forgive me, guys," Angie rasps. "I'm not laughing at you, I'm —"

"I know. I would've laughed, too, if it hadn't made me so disgusted."

"I've been there, sir. I've seen this show a thousand times before."

"This show?"

"The way they respond, or refuse to, when someone brings this stuff to their attention. As far as they're concerned, if it's not on Channel Eight, it's not an issue. And even when it becomes one, when it rises to that level, it's never anything, as Cliff knows all too well, that John can't paper over with another empty promise and the shedding of a couple tiny tears."

"Like what happened with the staff whose place I took."

"Like what happened then and countless times before. Most days, John's up here, not with the guys in their own homes. If it's not great news, or terrible, he'd rather not be made aware of what goes on out in the field. And on those rare occasions when he's confronted with it, as he was with Francis at the cookout, it's much easier for him to simply look the other way. This he does by choice and habit. A problem's not a problem if you don't acknowledge it exists."

"You work up here, too, though, and yet you acknowledge it."

"I made a different choice," Angie says, sliding her glasses back on. "But that's because I can. I don't mean to paint myself as some high-minded hero. I'm not. It's just that sometimes I feel like I enjoy a luxury he doesn't."

"I don't think I follow you."

Angie grins. "You're new to this whole business."

"I'm new to everything," says Ayo.

"And yet you've already learned that good staff are hard to come by.

They can make better money selling me these death sticks at the Sunoco up the road." Angie snaps up her cigarette and holds it out like evidence. "For most people, a job is a job, and that's it. Our staff are no different. That's what these guys are to them: a paycheck, and not a very big one, at that. If John got rid of all the Francises he's ever hired, he'd have no one left to fill his shifts. This would leave him and the Brads and the Gregs of the world to care for these folks by themselves, which is something they're neither willing to do nor capable of. That's why they laughed at you the other day. It's why they choose to blind themselves to what you see so clearly. Think of it as a survival mechanism. It's a lot easier to laugh when you're called out for your shortcomings than to admit them and attempt to make things better."

Ayo folds his hands behind his head. "If I hear you correctly, Ms. Angie, you think speaking to him isn't worth it."

"You came to me for honesty, and I won't lie to you. God knows I've tried to talk to John about these same damn issues, to make him see things as they are and not through rosy glasses. But it's not just staff who've trapped themselves in these abysmal mindsets. They never would've done so if the man in charge hadn't allowed it." Angie comes this close to lighting up her cigarette before she realizes we're still inside. "It wasn't always like this, you know. Years ago, we used to be much smaller, closer-knit. For Cliff and others like him, who'd come from the old hospitals, this place was like a lifeboat. It floated by and picked them up and saved them all from drowning. Those of us who worked here in those days were invested in the company in a way that, looking back from this distance, almost seems quaint. But there was a real sense of community back then. You could smell it in the air, like a garden in spring. Everyone knew and looked out for each other. We felt like we belonged to something bigger than ourselves, something valuable, and yes, even something worthwhile. Things stayed that way for as long as they did because John fostered it. And then at some point he decided not to anymore, and it began to fade until it disappeared completely."

"Why? What happened?"

Angie reflects on this and her unlighted cigarette. "Life," she says. "Life happened."

"How do you mean?"

"The nature of life is to grow, isn't it? That's what we did, as a body. We grew."

"But growth is a good thing, I thought."

"It depends on who you ask. For an agency like ours, growth means expansion — taking on more clients, operating in a wider service area, hiring more staff to meet the increased needs. This looks great on paper, if nowhere else. More service means more revenue. More revenue's what the board is after. But the thing about the board is, their hunger's never satisfied. They're like a dog who won't stop eating even though its belly's full. The difference is their stomach has no breaking point. It just keeps growing, looking ever more formidable on paper. This is all that matters to those who matter most — the movers and the shakers of the world." A sudden sadness fills her eyes like water in two snow globes. "Something changes when an agency like this reaches a certain size. It's not just here I've seen it. Most other residential outfits have gone through a process very similar. My uneducated guess is it's a law of nature: the larger you get, the more the quality of your services begins to stagnate, if not outright decline. But the ship's become too big to turn around, so what you have is ten times as many people who all deserve much more than you can offer."

"The company got bigger," Ayo says, decisively, "at the expense of its own clients."

"Exactly." Angie grabs her cigarette and stands. "That's the way I see it, anyway. Take it with a grain of salt. By no means should you consider me the ultimate authority on anything but these guys' vitals."

"I trust you, Ms. Angie, and I appreciate your honesty."

"Well, thanks for listening, in any case. John sure as hell never did. He was always focused on those bigger fish to fry." Stifling another cough, she steps out from behind her desk. "But that was years ago. Maybe things are different now. Maybe he's changed. You said it yourself. It felt like you'd gotten through to him, even if only a little. That's not nothing. That's a start. And based on that alone, it couldn't hurt to bring it up. Who knows? You might find him more receptive than he's ever been to me."

Ayo stands, too, and moves toward the door. "I guess we'll see. What are your thoughts, Cliff?"

I wheel out of his way and, smiling, I shrug.

"I couldn't have said it better myself," Angie says.

"Think about it, if you need to, and let me know what you decide. I'll support you either way." Ayo makes to open her door, but then stops and turns around. "Actually, Cliff, while we're here, there is something else we can ask Mr. Knowland about. Remember our discussion last night?"

You're damn right I do.

"Oh yeah? What was that?"

"We spoke about Cliff's happiness," Ayo grins. "Another day, we'll tell you all about it. For now, we've taken enough of your time. But thanks again for your help. It means a lot. If it weren't for you, I'd probably feel alone in this big place."

"That's what I'm here for. Good luck with John, gentlemen. Here's hoping he listens. But what I told you last week still stands, Ayo. No matter what happens, no matter what anyone says, don't you dare ever change how you work with these guys."

"I gave you my word, and I meant it."

"Good," Angie says, and all the way to the front she hacks up a lung like someone with a terminal illness.

)

The hallway on the far end terminates in Knowland's room. Through its cracked door come voices, soft and mumbling.

"Maybe you're right, John, but I'm serious about this chair. It's given me a whole new perspective on the issue. Though I'd rather not, I see no better way to —"

"No, I don't think we're there yet. We've still got other options. Remember, our main purpose is to grow these folks' independence, not decrease it."

"I'll remind you that it's equally important, if not more so, to keep them all safe. They can't become more independent if they're putting themselves and others at risk."

"And we're working on it. Look, Greg, I get it. Lord knows your approach would make things that much easier for us. But we didn't sign up for this because we thought it'd be easy. We signed up to help others, knowing full well every day would be a challenge. Not just anyone's up to the task. Shoot, most people cut and run at the first sign things are getting rough. That's not who we are, gang. We live to stare these challenges dead in the face and proclaim, in voices that ring clear as bells, 'Accepted.' Our folks need people like us in their lives. But much more than that, they deserve us."

"Thank you, sir. We won't let you down, sir."

"At ease, Brad. And throw those fatigues in the wash tonight. You reek of that beard balm crap those guys smell like at Axe to Grind."

"Yes, sir. Of course, sir. I went there for lunch. The eggs are fantastic."

"Yeah, well, here's a quarter. Next time, it'd better be on a day we don't meet —"

"Excuse me, gentlemen." Ayo raps on the door and peers inside. "We're very sorry to interrupt, but there's something we'd like to tell you, if you have a moment."

"Ayodele. Please, come in," Knowland says. "Good afternoon, Cliff."

"Speak of the devil." Greg grins in his manual wheelchair. His face is still roasted-brown, his hair's spiked razor-sharp, and he's got his signature-scrawled cast up on Knowland's desk, in between the Old Glory and the clear plaque that reads, in big letters now dusty with time:

LAARP RECOGNIZES YOUR OUTSTANDING EFFORTS
TO PROVIDE BETTER LIVES TO THE DISABLED
JOHN KNOWLAND, CEO
2008

"We were just talking about you, and lo, here you are."

"Here we are," Ayo says. "Hello, Greg and Brad."

"Private. How's everyone doing? The vitals look good?"

"Everything's great from Ms. Angie's perspective, for this man, especially, she says."

"That's wonderful news."

"It sure is, given the circumstances. How goes it otherwise, Cliff?"

I shrug at Greg and wheel in beside Ayo, who's reading one of the walls' several framed posters. It shows a man standing at the edge of a precipice overlooking a body of water, and below this, three words:

TAKE THE JUMP

To its right, in the corner, stands the room's only light source, a floor lamp aimed up at the ceiling. Its dim, circular beam is like a candle at dusk and leaves the three men half-obscured in shadow.

"We've been well," Ayo says. "But I don't think that's the case for everyone. You must've heard about that massive hurricane."

"I saw that. Yikes. How terrible."

"How many cities did it end up wiping out?" Knowland gnaws on a fingernail. "I had it on this morning, but it made me so darn sad I changed the channel."

"Three, last I checked."

"I think it's up to four now." Greg whips out his phone and verifies it. "Four-and-a-half, actually, if you count Jupiter."

Knowland plugs his tear ducts with his thumb and middle finger. "Thank you. That's all I need to know. I'd rather not spend the rest of my afternoon all blue and bleary-eyed."

"Understood," says Greg, silencing his fire horn, "though you may take comfort in knowing the president has dispatched truckloads of toilet tissue to the disaster sites."

"That takes one load off my heart."

"Should I cue up some puppy videos?" Brad asks.

"Not yet. We have our guests to deal with. But first, please join me in a moment of silence for the victims of that dreadful gale."

"With pleasure." Brad bursts to his feet and puts his head down and hands together.

"Gah, just sit, man. This isn't Arlington National Cemetery. There's no need for the theatrics."

Ayo looks at me as if to say, *Oh, brother.*

"Sir, yes, sir."

"Now," Knowland says, "is everyone ready?"

On his count of three, he, Greg, and Brad take deep breaths, bow their heads, and fall quiet for two minutes. Except for Brad, who lacks a smart-phone, they stare at their small screens for the duration, scrolling their feeds, checking their mentions, and smiling when they encounter a dank meme they can relate to. There comes a point, though, toward the end, when Knowland reads a post that makes him lachrymose. I can't see it from here, but my guess is that it has to do with last night's hurricane. He plonks his phone down on the desk and rests his forehead in his hands. When he comes back to himself, his eyes are moist and bloodshot, and his lips quiver like someone on the brink of a total breakdown.

"Thank you, all," he says, checking his watch. "Let's keep those poor souls in our prayers. For now, suffice to say I'm grateful our state remains landlocked."

Greg brushes nothing from the shoulders of his bright-pink paisley button-up. "Well said, chief. It never hurts to count one's blessings."

"Never. It helps us stay humble, grounded, and focused on what matters. Speaking of which, did you guys see we're in the running for another one of these?"

He points to the clear plaque beside which Greg's cast wiggles.

"That's amazing." Brad tries blowing the dust from the award, but it refuses to flake off, clinging to the acrylic like barnacles on an old shipwreck. "Since when?"

"Since Monday. I wrote a piece on it for this month's 'Knowland's Notes,' which I sent out, if my math is right, a whole three days ago."

Greg and Brad regard each other like condemned men on the gallows.

"We knew that. It's just I've been so busy lately, writing Cliff's behavior plan, that I haven't had the chance to read it yet. I'm planning to in full this afternoon."

Both of Brad's legs bounce manically. "Same here, sir. I've been filling open shifts all week, sir, but it is on my to-do list."

"It had better be, and that's an order. It's not every day we get such recognition." Knowland sits up and makes one of those small churches with his hands. "Of course, these things don't matter in the long run. The work we do each day's reward enough. But it is nice, sometimes, to know our efforts to give these folks good lives haven't gone unnoticed."

Brad and Greg nod so hard they damn-near break their necks.

"That's why we've come to see you, actually," Ayo says, clearing his throat in the silence.

Knowland's frown melts a little. His eyes flicker with hope. "You read my 'Notes'?"

"I had a look at them. Congratulations on the nomination. This is a great accomplishment in itself. But I'm afraid that isn't what we'd like to talk to you about."

"If not that, then in God's name, man, what?"

Ayo steps forward. "Something that came up at Cliff's meeting yesterday."

The frown returns to Knowland's face like a sad, recurring dream. "I trust you're heeding my injunction to the letter. Or have you come to admit you've broken it?"

"You'll be pleased to hear I haven't. I understand the rules, sir, and I aim to follow them."

"And not a moment too soon," Greg says, not quite sotto voce.

"I believe there's reason for you to be doubly pleased, though."

"Which is?"

"You might remember that in Cliff's meeting, I mentioned how I think he's acting differently these days because there's something missing from his life, something he desires which he doesn't have at present."

"I remember. Do you have an update?"

"We do. Cliff and I were talking late last night, and —"

"Let me guess. You've found the magic bullet."

"I never said there was a magic bullet, Greg."

"What else would you call it? If what you say is true, you've done more for Cliff in two weeks than we've been able to in twenty flipping years. What's your secret, and are you sure it's legal?"

"Knock it off," Knowland says. "Save your snark and sarcasm for your Twitter replies."

Greg takes this to heart at once. Rolling up his paisley sleeves, he starts tapping away on his phone, tongue hanging out to one side of his mouth like Jordan on his path to the hoop. He stops for a moment and ponders, then adds a parting shot, and after sending the tweet, he sits back and smiles, his eyes gleaming victoriously.

"That's more like it," Knowland nods. "Now, Ayo, what news do you bring us?"

Ayo faces them proudly, hands together in front. "As I was saying, I never claimed to have found a magic bullet. I don't believe such things exist, but I do think being present for someone makes all the difference in their life. In my work with Cliff, I've been patient. I've listened to him. It's quite something, as you must be aware, what you'll hear and what you'll learn if you simply make an effort."

The face Greg makes says, *Duh,* but what he says out loud, so sweetly, is, "And what, exactly, Ayo, are the fruits of your hard labors?"

"Yes, what has Cliff told you? What is it we can give him that'll make him happier?"

Ayo looks to me for my permission. "What Cliff wants," he tells them, "is a companion, a — how do you say — a partner, a significant other. Someone to spend his time with. Someone to share his life with. Someone he can love in ways he never has before." When no one responds, he goes on. "We all want somebody like this in our lives. We search for them, pine for them, rejoice when we finally find them, and grieve just as much if we lose them. Everyone deserves a chance at love. You and I, we've had ours. I see no reason why Cliff shouldn't, either. Do you?"

But Brad, Greg, and Knowland just sit there dumbly.

Ayo sighs. "Hello?"

"Hello," Knowland says, looking down in his lap.

"Hey there," Brad murmurs.

"How ya doin', champ?"

"Did anyone hear what I said?"

"I think so."

"Uh, yes."

"For what it's worth, I did, too."

"So, you have nothing to say in response?"

"I do." Knowland's gaze is still lapward. "I'm just confounded, is all, and I'm trying to work through it mentally."

Brad holds his hand out flat, as if to swear upon a nonexistent Bible. "Same here."

"Here, too." On the desk, Greg's foot boogies like a mummy on the dance floor. "You'll need to give us some time to wrap our heads around this thing."

"How long will that take?" says Ayo.

"Your guess is as good as ours, but I'd estimate it to be anywhere between six to eight hours — for me and Greg, at least. Don't be surprised if it takes Brad twice that."

Brad rockets up, salutes, and goes, "Hooah."

"But why, Mr. Knowland?"

Now it's Knowland's visage that says, *Duh*. "Because he's a knuckle-head, a birdbrain, a clueless and thick-witted doofus. Get my drift? No offense, Brad, not that you'd take any."

"Beg pardon?" says Brad, breathing deep through his mouth.

"I mean why should it take you so long to grasp this? I've been as clear as I possibly can be. Everyone wants to have someone to love. This is the thing Cliff wants most. What more is there for you to think about?"

"I'll explain, but I'm disappointed in you, Ayo, for having forgotten key parts of yesterday's meeting."

"Which parts, please?"

"The ones where we talked about Stella," says Knowland, scratching his beard heatedly, "where it came out that Cliff spurned the poor girl's advances."

"As a result of which," Greg adds with a smile, "she dressed like a spooky tenth-grader who's been voted most likely to shoot up her school."

Ayo drops his hands to his sides. "Are you suggesting Cliff was to blame for that?”

“Who should we blame in his place? The girl adored him, yearned for him, practically salivated over him for years.”

“She loved him,” Greg says. “She saw him as an equal. She made him those hearts, for Christ’s sakes.”

“And, lest we forget, she also took a turd to the face for the guy.”

“How many other women can we say the same about, not just for Cliff, but for any of us?”

Brad shakes his head. “That’s a big fat goose egg, buddyroo.”

“And despite this, he broke her poor heart.”

“Therein lies our confusion,” says Knowland. “Bearing these things about Stella in mind, what more could a man in Cliff’s position, or any other, for that matter, ask for?”

“Go ahead, take your time. Think about it,” Greg says, and he titters and smirks at his watch. “It’s not like we’ve got other things to take care of today —”

“Sarcasm alert,” Knowland frowns. “But what’s the holdup, Ayo? When did the cat get your tongue?”

“We’d ask Cliff himself, but you —”

“I’m sorry, sir,” Ayo says, “but I think now I’m more confused than you are.”

“Why’s that?”

“Because it would seem it’s not I who’ve forgotten key parts of our meeting, but you three. Do you not recall when I mentioned how Cliff sees Ms. Stella as only a friend, nothing more?”

“Of course we remember,” says Knowland, coolly. “What we don’t know is why.”

Greg knocks on the desk three times fast. “I’ll be the first to confess that, in his shoes, I’d be all over that in a heartbeat.”

“Um.”

“What? If someone loved me the way Stella loved Cliff, I wouldn’t take it for granted, is all I’m saying.”

“Greg, you’re a very strange man,” Ayo says.

Greg brushes his shoulders again, then turns toward the wall with the TAKE THE JUMP poster.

“Bizarre as he admittedly is, Greg makes a fair point,” Knowland says. “Most people, and I include myself here, can only dream of having someone so enamored of us. When we, if we, find that person, we shouldn’t write them off or disregard the opportunity altogether, as Cliff has done so flippantly. It’s unlikely we’ll ever encounter another who feels the same way as they do, or did at one point.”

Ayo stands back, feet apart. He rolls his shoulders, then his head, and after closing his eyes, he starts breathing deeply.

“Are you all right?” Knowland says.

"I'm fine. Just trying to relax."

"Hmm. Well, you could've fooled me."

"That wasn't my intention. In fact, I think it's rather I who've been fooled."

"How so?"

"You're insisting that Cliff should be grateful for Stella, that he should've loved her the way she loved him. Respectfully, what you're failing to see is she's not what he wanted, and never was. He wants someone else, someone different. The choice isn't yours, Mr. Knowland," says Ayo, his eyes shooting open like blinds on the night. "It's Cliff's and Cliff's alone. You can't dictate how he feels. You can't make him want something he doesn't. So, what I don't know is why, with your years of experience, you'd find it so hard to accept this."

"Oh, we accept it, all right. It's just that we don't get it. Capisce?"

"This is hardly some great mystery. What's still so confusing to you?"

Greg laughs at the poster. "Everything."

"Everything." Ayo chews the word like a rare cut of steak. "Do the rest of you feel as he does?"

"I think so," says Brad, after painful reflection, "but don't quote me till John weighs in, too."

Knowland rolls his eyes and swivels to face me. "What they're trying to say, gentlemen, isn't easy, but sometimes it must be said, and clearly, so let me handle this. Our system's much better than the one that came before — the old institutions, asylums, and hospitals. I'll spare you their gory details, of course. If you like, you can find them online. I'm impressed by you, Ayo. You haven't been here, in this system, for long, but already you've hit on its great limitation. All our folks were born with unique challenges, which amounted to more barriers to independence than most of us have ever had to contend with. Our job is to knock those barriers down," he says, giving the one-two punch to an imaginary wall, "and in so doing, to provide them with lives that are worth —"

"I'm aware of what the company does, Mr. Knowland. I've been here for almost three weeks."

"Sure, you are. When I preach, it's always to the choir. You know we function as a bridge between the people we serve and their wider communities. You know it's a beautiful metaphor, too, a human bridge spanning a vast ravine that takes our clients from fallow fields to greener pastures. Heck, when it came time to name this little outfit of mine, I had the choices narrowed to two: Knowland Residential on the one hand — obviously — and Bridges on the other. After weeks of deliberation, I settled on the former, and not just because I'd learned another firm had already laid claim to the latter. Speaking of which, they're not doing so well these days, Bridges isn't, if there's any truth to what I'm seeing on my feeds."

"What is your point?"

A small smile appears between Knowland's beard. His blue eyes flash with muted recognition. He sweeps his bangs back into place and says, "My point is, while our bridge brings our folks to lands they would otherwise have never seen, it doesn't lead to every region or into every nook and cranny of the human experience. Sad as it is, its reach only extends so far. Add to that Cliff's own limitations, and you can see how some things, though very few, fall beyond our scope. I hate having to say this, but what you're describing, in terms of Cliff's desires, simply isn't something we're equipped to give him."

"I don't understand," Ayo says, hands trembling at his hips. "What are his limitations? What he wants isn't anything you or I don't hunger for — a deep and true connection with another human being. Why is this impossible?"

"I never said it was impossible. I said it fell outside the scope of our duties. Besides, we do provide him with the chance to make connections every day. Some of them, I know, are very deep. Cliff has made many friends during his tenure with us, and he's had lots of great times along the way." Knowland drums a waltz on the desk as he carefully considers his next words. "But what he's asking for today is much more than those friendships can offer. Please, correct me if I'm wrong, but what he's asking for today, at least in part, is sex."

When Ayo spins toward me, I nod once, slowly and firmly, and everyone but him looks away, feigning interest in the poster with the guy about to jump.

"So what if he is? What's the problem with that?"

Knowland speaks without turning around. "If you don't know already, you never will."

"I'm not asking for myself. I'm asking for Cliff. He needs to know why he doesn't deserve a life as worthwhile as anyone else's."

"He's right, sir," Brad says. "We owe him that much, at least."

Knowland seems to make a mental note to slaughter Brad and his whole family. "The problem's not that he doesn't deserve it. He does. It's that it's not up to us to help him obtain it."

"Why not?"

"Because we don't know how," Knowland blurts, tearing up. "Because it's complicated. Because we've never dealt with it head-on like this before. Because if our folks are looking for sex, they tend to find it on their own, as your Lem does with his mattress." His hands flutter like Rickey's as he rubs the moisture from his under-eyes. "It's easier on everyone this way. It's safer. For their own good and ours, it's the one part of these folks' lives we'd rather not think about in the slightest."

"What about the thing you said earlier, though, about accepting the challenge in voices like bells?" Ayo points back my way. "Here might be your greatest challenge yet. Are you willing to take it, to take him, on? Did you mean what you said, or was it just empty boasting, all smoke and mirrors, little more than a hollow sales pitch?"

"Of course I meant it. I've said it before, and I'll say it again: I'm a man of my word or I'm nothing."

"Then back your word up, Mr. Knowland, with action. Your clients depend upon you for contentment. We're on the same team, yes? We'll work through this together. I'm not trying to fly to the moon, here. I'm trying to give Cliff the life he deserves."

"You might as well be," Knowland says, wincing as if in a fart's aftermath.

"Might as well what?"

"Be attempting to go to the moon."

"I don't think so. Cliff and I, we are grounded on Earth. There's a whole world out there he's aching to see. My job is to guide him through it."

"Your job is to listen to me," Knowland says, "nothing more, nothing less. Understand? You're on thin ice as it is, I'll remind you. Risk his life one more time and you're toast."

"In what way am I risking his —"

"You don't need me to tell you that sex can result in a wide range of issues, not just for our guys, but anyone. There's the potential for diseases, for one, not to mention what could happen if Cliff got somebody pregnant."

Greg's perfect teeth shine in the room's murky light. "That's assuming it's sex with a woman."

"There are ways to prevent these things," Ayo says, his voice soft and his hands linked behind him.

"There are. But there's always a chance they won't work. Condoms break. Birth-control pills sometimes fail. In view of our duty to ensure health and safety, these are risks we're not willing to take."

"And anyway," Greg says, his grin swelling, "being grounded on Earth isn't the same as being grounded in reality."

"What's that supposed to mean?"

"Look, the reality of Cliff's situation is that, as far as sex goes, the obstacles are ominous, if not insurmountable. If you think otherwise, you live in a fantasy."

"Obstacles, huh?" Ayo says. "Such as what?"

"Such as not being able to speak, which would make dating hard, as I see it. It'd be one thing if he could manipulate a keyboard or even point to letters on a sheet of paper, but he's tried these in the past. They didn't work."

"It's true," Knowland sulks.

"More troubling still is the question of physical effort. Let's assume for argument's sake that Cliff somehow found somebody willing to" — Greg throws up in his mouth a little bit — "to do the deed with him — and that's a big, fat if, folks. Excuse me." Knowland hands him a wadded-up tissue, which he uses to dab at his lips, then spits up in. "Taking his condition into account, the strenuous nature of sex would be uncomfortable, if not downright excruciating. Besides, is anyone aware if his — you know — even works?"

"I don't think," Ayo says, "that is any of your goddamn business."

Greg snickers. "You made it my goddamn business the moment you walked in the room. Like it or not, these are critical questions, if Cliff wants what you're saying he does."

"Setting aside that having CP doesn't diminish a person's sex drive — which all of you should know, given your chosen careers — who are you to ask these things, much less demand answers? Who are you to decide what anyone can or can't do with their life?"

"I'm not deciding anything, pal. I'm just laying out the problems Cliff would face in this, um, area. Remaining silent would be a disservice both to him and to the agency."

Ayo stands above him almost like Francis over Brad. "Is that a fact?"

"Why wouldn't it be?"

"Because it seems you enjoy being hostile to Cliff for no reason except to —"

"Calm down," Knowland says, rolling back toward the wall. "This discussion is over. I know it's not what you wanted to hear, Cliff, and I'm sorry we can't help you more. But the truth is that, though he put it crudely, as per normal, Greg makes another point worthy of our consideration. I hadn't thought about these other health concerns, the exertion sex requires and the consequences it might have on your frail body." Tapping his temple, he looks at me with the same pity on his face as when we first met. "Yours is one of the most advanced cases of cerebral palsy I've ever seen. It was bad enough back when I pulled you out of Sinai Grove, and since then it's only grown worse. If you'd been born more recently, you would've had access to better and more sophisticated treatments. The doctors could've addressed your condition much earlier on in your life. If they had, who knows? Eventually, you might've been able to walk."

"But he wasn't born later and didn't have access to all these new treatments you speak of. He's not someone else. He is who he is, and that's why I like him, why I want to help him. So, I'll ask one more time, and that's it. Are you willing to help Cliff find love?"

"Love isn't hard to find around here, as long as you know where to look." Knowland's hand flies to his heart. "I see it in our clients' faces every day. I see it in the hard work of staff like yourself. We run on love, Ayo. It's our fuel, the very gasoline to our engines of caring. Cliff is welcome to fill up his tank anytime — and maybe, just maybe, if the stars realign, he and Stella will come around to each other at last, and he'll know what it means to be loved by someone, even if not in the way he desires."

Ayo sighs, turns to me. "We'll take that as a 'no,' then."

"That's not what I said."

"That's what it sounded like."

"Good God." Greg's cast convulses zealously on Knowland's desk, where it's been gnawing away at its surface like a glacier through a swath of ancient land. "What did it sound like when John said this discussion is over? Why can't you just let this thing go? Short of setting Cliff up with a hooker, what more do you want us to do?"

"Nothing," Ayo says, his eyes bright, "since there's nothing you can do, or want to. Thanks for your time, gentlemen. We'll see ourselves —"

But Greg's already cued up his cute puppy clips. The other two men move in closer to him, the better to see his small screen. In the dimness of Knowland's big office, they smile and watch as if their lives depended on it.

❯

Ayo straightens me up in my shower chair, then scrubs me down with the washrag, being extra careful, as usual, when he reaches my navel and groin. He's barely spoken since we got home and works with a steady and purposeful anger that pulses like hot blood through his veins. Yet there's a soft, pensive quality to it, which has kept me from asking him what's on his mind. Having spent most of my life being ripped from my thoughts for no reason, I'd rather not tear him from his for the same. When he's ready, I figure, he'll share them with me, if he wants. If he doesn't, well, that's okay, too. I doubt it's anything I haven't thought myself over the last several hours, or several years.

What I want to tell him, though, so badly, is that he shouldn't feel like he's failed. No one else has ever had the courage to do what he did today. Hell, no one's ever so much as bothered asking me what I want out of an afternoon, much less out of life. That Ayo has done so means more to me than he could ever know. It's proved me wrong in the nicest of ways. Mediocrity is the gold standard of the system I've fallen into, and I learned to accept it a long time ago. If I hadn't, it would've driven me insane. So just having someone who's as willing to help as he is has been is a great comfort, like a little burst of wind on a hot day. Besides, as much as I hate to admit it, Greg did have a point. The reality is that I was born differently than most people. I'll never be able to walk, or to talk, or even to point to a sequence of letters on paper. Connection with others is difficult for me, if not impossible in most cases. And while my manhood functions like it's supposed to, the rest of my body is beyond repair. Not even the most powerful positive thinking will alter this obstinate fact. Other than Stella before she moved on, albeit for all the wrong reasons, what sort of woman would want me that way? What could I offer her she couldn't find elsewhere, and for a lot less effort, at that? May-be I should be grateful for Greg's honesty, after all. If expressed by the woman I see in my dreams, the truth wouldn't be any prettier.

"Here we go," Ayo says, taking the showerhead down from the wall. "Let's get you cleaned up. Please, when you're ready, close your eyes."

As the water runs over me in warm gushes, cascading down my face and neck, I disappear. In this darkened void, I roam as comfortably as anyone. Like an astronaut untethered from his spacecraft, I blast across broad stretches of infinity and hurtle past whole galaxies of my own making. Here, there are no limitations to control me. Here, if nowhere else, I have unfettered freedom, and Knowland's word — and Greg's — has no power whatsoever. Only mine, which I speak with perfect clarity, carries weight. I say nebula and one emerges in the distance, sprawling and kaleidoscopic. I utter stars and they illuminate the sky. I whisper moon and there it is, a crescent smile flashing on the face of this new universe, reflecting the bright light of foreign suns. I go to it and glissade down its slope, leave my wheelchair hanging from it, and fling myself into the ether as one might into a pool of cool, clear water. Rocketing through space, I've become pure and simple movement, a wave in flux, a consciousness without a body. I explore everything and nothing all at once. My name and diagnosis have burned away from me like meteoric rock in the Earth's atmosphere.

I don't know how long this lasts. For a moment, perhaps, or an eternity. Time's not the same here. Not that it doesn't exist. It's just that you see it differently, like how your friends' faces appear when you're dreaming. It's only when a faint, orange band of light slices the darkness in two that I become conscious again of my body, of the heart sinking fast at its core. If I could, I'd stay here forever. There'd be no one to tell me how I should or shouldn't lead the only life I have. I'd be the one to decide on this question and others as they came to mind. If I wanted some barbecue sauce, I would taste it. If I wanted my staff to respect me, they would. If I wanted a woman to love, I would have her, as long as she wanted me, too.

"We'll find someone, Cliff," says a voice.

The light deepens and grows until it swallows the darkness whole. Ayo stands in its place, at the edge of the tub, the showerhead still in his hand. He rinses the lather from my feet, then turns off the water and slides the nozzle back where it belongs. After he dries me with the towel, he wraps me up inside it and crouches on the bathmat. His anger has subsided, but there's something different in his eyes now, a look I've never seen before on him or anyone else in real life. Quiet, fierce, and intent, it's that of a man who's exhausted his options and has only one left to try.

"Forget them," he says. "Brad, Greg, and Mr. Knowland. Though they talk much, they don't know the first thing about you. If they did, they'd recognize that your desires aren't far-fetched or unrealistic. There's no reason why you shouldn't have someone the way you want. This is your world as much as it is theirs." He lifts the flap of towel that's fallen down across my thigh, covering my nakedness back up. "Make of it what you like. I'm here to help, if you get my drift. I can present you with the choice Knowland is too weak to offer. I'm prepared to take another risk for you. The only question left to ask is whether you are, too."

I answer despite everything, especially myself:

Oh, yes. Oh, hell yes, I am.

TWELVE

It's not often I get out at night. The sight of Tired Oaks at sundown, its restaurants' signs all lit up against the rapidly fading sky, is almost as eerie as Knowland's office seems after-hours. The constant hum of vehicles on State Road 819 has been reduced to a sporadic murmur and the occasional, thunderous groan of a trailer truck. I was expecting to see lots more people down here on the main drag — it is now the weekend — but most have decided to spend it elsewhere than at the mall, DQ, or the furniture place, where the man's still out front dressed up like Uncle Sam. His hair long and unwashed, his face cracked and sunburnt, he plays his top hat like a Fender for an audience of no one.

"At least he isn't humping it," Ayo says, looking back at me through the rear-view.

As we pass, the guy waves, Ayo salutes him like Brad does Knowland, and I catch a quick hint of vodka. I'd need some, too, if I had his job. He's been out here for hours. We saw him both on the way to and back home from the office. Incredibly, his enthusiasm has only increased. He shreds his hat-guitar like Jimi Hendrix at Woodstock, then holds it up to his crotch and begins boffing it, his mouth a big, black, written O on the papyrus of the night.

"It appears I've spoken too soon."

I shake my head, smiling into the mirror. From somewhere far behind us, a police siren wails.

"I suppose I shouldn't blame him," Ayo says, as we stop at a red light. "They pay him to get our attention. He succeeds every time, doesn't he?"

Whether we like it or not.

"That's a man committed to his duties, which, as I'm finding, is a rare thing in these parts."

Well, when you put it that way . . .

"Maybe when his store finally goes out of business, he can come and work for Knowland as a staff."

I try to lift an eyebrow but end up raising both.

"Not yours, of course. Though he'd probably do a better job of it than some people I know."

The light changes to green and Ayo flips the blinker on at the next cross street. There, he turns right, into Silver Lining's lot. The building, though three stories, is much smaller than the one in the commercials. Its white bricks have long gone gray with time and car exhaust. Ayo parks on its far side, out of sight from the highway. Leaving the van's engine on, he unstraps his seatbelt and swings around toward me. Above him, through the windshield, stands the hotel's enormous logo, its dark cloud's gloominess diminished by the counterfeit sunrays behind it.

"Are you still sure about this?" he says.

I wouldn't be here if I weren't.

"All right. I still want to help you. But tomorrow there'll likely be questions. Actually BJ has already asked several. For us to go out at this hour is 'highly irregular,' as he put it. I plan on telling Brad the same thing I told him and Francis — that we went out for a drive, for some fresh air, nothing more."

That still sounds good to me.

"But if you change your mind, and decide to tell the truth, I won't stop you."

I wouldn't worry about that.

"I'm not worried," Ayo says, his scar reflecting the hotel sign's white light. "I just want to make clear my position. But as with the barbecue sauce, I can't promise you this every day. If we made it a habit and managed to not get arrested, I'd go broke in a month, if not sooner."

No, you wouldn't, I say, rubbing my fingers together and bringing my hand near my chest.

"I won't let you pay for this, Cliff. It doesn't come cheap, and it'd just raise more questions we'd rather not answer."

I can't argue with that. Gil the finance guy pores over our books every month with a bird of prey's eye. He'd spot the smallest discrepancy like a mouse in a thicket.

"Well," Ayo says, "are you ready?"

I am.

"Okey-doke, as they say." He twists his phone from his pocket and has dialed half the number on a small sheet of paper when I stop him with a sudden, urgent cry. "Yes, Cliff? What is it?"

What about you?

"What do you mean?"

I mean, what will happen to you if they catch us? You're still on probation. If Knowland finds out what we're doing, it's not just your job you could lose.

"Please, don't you think about that. Remember, I'm prepared to take this risk and to accept its consequences. I know what will happen to me if . . .

The steadfast look he gave me earlier settles back over his face like the dusk falling fast all around us. "But it's not about what happens to me. It's only about you and your desires. If I weren't doing this, if I weren't helping you, I wouldn't be doing my job, and I may as well give my two weeks'."

It shouldn't have to be like this.

"Of course it shouldn't. But much as we'd like to, and though we tried our best, we can't change the way others see things. And the truth is, for that very reason, you may never have another chance at this." He nods at the ashen, brick building. "Let me help you, Cliff. Don't let your worries about me keep you from getting what you want."

I turn to the window. At the north end of the lot, the hotel's dumpster overflows with garbage bags. Its two lids jut open unevenly in the pale, orange glow of a streetlamp. Behind it, above the chain-link fence and untrimmed hedges, Uncle Sam's top hat soars upward, minuscule in the air, pinwheeling for a moment before it sinks and disappears back down below. I think of David, my staff's brother, in his wheelchair, and of Ayo at his back, pushing him through a town not that different from this one, past people not that different from the ones he's finding here. Though we never met, we share something special, David and I. But Ayo's wrong about one thing. It's not only about him helping me. It's just as much about me helping him.

Let's do it, then. But not only for me. For you and me both — and for David.

"Now that's what I'm talking about," Ayo smiles, and he dials the rest of the number.

☽

The lobby floor's not made of marble but mottled vinyl. Its tiles are the kind you'd find in middle schools and hospitals and old clinics and license branches. Study it long enough and you might start seeing patterns, faces even, that you don't recognize from anywhere but which somehow know your deepest thoughts, the ones you keep from everyone, including, and above all, yourself. As they reflect what little light there is in this sterile, empty space, theirs are the only heads that turn and theirs the only eyes that see me.

Ayo stops in the room's center, next to the dingy couch and square end table, where several copies of the same brochure are fanned out, unread and collecting dust. He picks one up and blows on it. On the cover, the woman from the commercials stretches out on a beach chair in a two-piece swimsuit. Holding out a glass of wine, her smile inscrutable, the green pools of her irises smaller but still as deep as ever, she exercises total power over me even from the printed page. But when Ayo winks and lowers her to me, I frown. Someone has spilt their coffee or their soda on the pamphlet, right across her exposed midriff. The stain is umber, old and faded, but no less reprehensible than if it had just happened. I'm struck by the sudden urge to find the guy responsible and make two pancakes of the hands that dropped their stupid drink on —

"How about this one, instead?" Ayo says, showing me another, unbesmirched copy.

That's more like it.

"Good," he says, sliding it into his back pocket. "Anyway, we have business to attend to." He gestures toward reception in the far corner. "Shall we?"

Lead the way.

"No, please, sir." He bows. "After you. I insist."

I give him a thumbs-up and floor it around the table, over the rug with Silver Lining's logo on it, past the elevator, and to the unmanned desk, behind which sits a TV with the news on mute. All it shows are scenes of gray destruction, shots of shattered cities in the wake of last night's tempest. Their streets look like the ones in Venice, water-choked up to the buildings' windows, but their only traffic is inanimate — loose car tires, jagged chunks of Styrofoam, and loads upon loads of garbage, mostly plastic. In closed captioning at the bottom of the screen, in words stripped bare of his solemnity, the anchor tells of the financial toll the storm has taken on the coast — already in the billions, as it stands — and then, almost as an afterthought, of the human lives that have been lost and of those who are still missing.

Ayo leans over the counter, looks one way, then the other. "Must be a slow night," he says, drumming his fingers on a clipboard. "Not that I'm complaining."

Yeah, me either.

"Still, we're on a most important mission, not to mention paying customers." He drags the little bell out from one side and rings it twice. "Hello? Is anyone here? Please, we'd like a room as soon as possible."

The office door behind the counter cracks and a pair of glassy eyes appears, obscured by a wall of thick, white smoke. Dubious and disturbed, they stay suspended there a while, peering out at us from what their owner must think is a secret hiding place.

"We see you in there," Ayo says, "clear as daylight, almost."

The door closes, then opens again. The source of the smoke isn't marijuana. We've had staff in the past who'd go in our backyard and light up. It smelled good, like a forest of pine trees. Whatever this is smells like someone has set a laboratory on fire.

"Just a minute," a voice rasps, and the eyes vanish.

There's a bump, then a yowl, then something falls to the floor, breaks like glass.

"Damn it, Dale," says another voice, higher-pitched and nasal. "That's the second pipe you broke so far this week. I got another out there in my Dodge Intrepid, but be advised, you owe me upwards of forty bucks now for —"

"Shut it, Quinton. I'll pay you back, I promise. But first, I got customers. So, take a good, hard look at me, and tell me true. How's my face?"

"As messed up as it ever was."

After a long, fraught pause, Dale says, "For real?"

"Of course I'm for real. I'm your friend. You want the truth or a lie?"

"I want the truth."

"Well, that's what I'm here for. I'll shoot you straight every time. And the truth is, your face is always messed up. Always has been, always will be. But no, listen, there's no need to get down about it. So's mine. Look here, Dale. Look how messed-up my face is. Look at my pimply nose and spacious chasm of a mouth. I ain't ashamed of it. Hell, I'm proud. You should be, too. There's plenty of screwed-up faces in this crazy world of —"

"I don't care about them faces. I only care about mine." Dale makes a sound like he's trying to push out an unruly turd. "If they see me like this, it's curtains."

"No, it's not," Ayo calls. "It's not curtains. We don't care how messed up your face is. All we want is a room for the night."

"See?" Quinton whispers. "They don't give a shit. Do your job. Make that money. You're going to need it. You owe me fifty big ones."

"You just said forty."

"I said upwards of forty. Aw, hell. I'll figure it out. Go get them a room, for Christ's sakes."

After one more lengthy pause, the door creaks all the way open. Dale stands in the threshold, his bone-bag of a body all atwitch. His face is messed up, to be sure, disfigured by lesions and scrapes. His skin is pallid and yellow, his hair thin, black, and wet, like grease spread over a golf ball with an old, discarded toothbrush. He's either twenty or eighty years old — or both at the same time, bizarrely — and wears a bedraggled black polo with powdery stains on the chest, near the patch with his company's logo.

"How can I help you fellas?" he says, his smile toothless and grotesque.

"We're hoping for a room." Ayo taps the clipboard with a pen. "Just for the night, if one's available."

"Oh, one's available. They all are, actually. You got a floor preference?"

"Yes, and a room preference, as a matter of fact. Three-eighteen, please."

"Well, if that ain't specific as hell."

"I trust we're not your first guests who've been somewhat particular." Ayo nods at the still-smoky doorway, through which Quinton coughs worse than Angie did this afternoon. "We value your discreetness as much as you must surely value ours."

When Dale's glassy, red-rimmed eyes meet mine, they awaken like a man revived from drowning. His tongue parts his leprous lips, then licks them. A tiny laugh escapes his nostrils. He rubs them clean of snot with his cracked knuckles, then raps the clipboard as one might the gates of Hell, or Heaven.

"That we do," he says. "How's it hanging, bud?"

I flash the clerk the biggest thumbs-up I can manage.

"I'd imagine so." Inside the cavern of his mouth, Dale's gums are hollowed-out stalactites and stalagmites. "Go ahead and fill this out, then. I'll grab the key. You're here just one night, you say?"

Writing quickly, Ayo glances out through the front door, where the sun has fully set on the main drag. "One night is all, please, if that."

"Fair enough." Dale goes to the wooden board hanging on the wall beside the TV — still showing its storm-wasted cityscapes — and plucks a metal key up from its hook. "All our rooms are supposed to have cable, but I can't promise it works like it should."

"That won't be a problem for us. Will it?"

We're not here to watch television.

"Yeah, most folks don't complain, either. There's a pool, too, through that hall there, though again, I doubt if you'll be —"

"We won't."

"It's better off that way, believe me. I couldn't tell you the last time it was cleaned. You paying cash or credit, Mr." — Dale squints at the paper on the clipboard — "Ayoddoley?"

"Ayodele. Cash, please."

"Fifty dollars cash, no questions asked," Dale sings, and accepts two twenties and a ten. "I don't suppose you got an ArgentCare® Rewards Card on you."

"That we do not."

"Didn't think so. That's all right. You'll want to take the elevator up. Room's at the far end on the left."

"Thank you, sir. We're expecting someone else, and —"

"I'll let her know you're here. Charlie or Charlotte?"

"Excuse me?"

"Your guest. Which one you waiting on?"

"Her name is Magdalene," says Ayo, "but I think she goes by Maggie."

"Hmm. I ain't heard of her before. She with the same —"

"I thought this was no questions asked?"

"Damn. Yeah, it is." Dale scratches the abscess that used to be his Adam's apple. "Anyway, we do appreciate your business."

"It's our pleasure." Ayo jingles the key on its chain. "All set, Cliff?"

But I'm already halfway to the elevator. Ayo jogs to me and hits the button.

"I got your fifty, Quinton, easy peasy," hollers Dale. "And hey, you, Mr. Yodel —"

Ayo hops in and holds the door open. "Yes?"

"I hope your friend enjoys his stay at Silver Lining Inn & Suites."

"Thanks again very much. You've just made sure his night will be one to remember."

"I don't doubt it a minute," Dale says, and the elevator shuts on a man whose deep secrets he won't even share with himself.

)

The third-floor hall is long and narrow, its light dim and flickering from the uncovered bulbs above us. Its carpet is thin and sickly green, torn in a few spots along the walls' decaying baseboards. Several ceiling tiles have been knocked loose from their grids, exposing stale-pink insulation like rotting flesh below a wound. A flagrant, moldy smell pervades the air in lieu of smoke from Quinton's pipe as Ayo and I race to the far end, and I pretend like I don't know he's let me achieve victory.

"Here we are, then."

He aims his key at the last door on the left, whose number, *318,* is posted in greening bronze under the peephole. The *3* and the *8* have escaped their top screws and hang upside-down from the *1,* as if hiding from it. Ayo tries putting them back into place, but the fasteners are brittle and break at his touch. He lowers the numbers back down where they were, then inserts the key into the lock and swings the door open.

"After you," he says.

The walls inside are bare, save a film-covered mirror over the cabinet with a small TV/VCR set. It's coated with dust an inch thick, and its cord has been gnawed at by mice. At the far end, artificial light from outside sneaks through the window's blinds, which are broken and pointed in every direction. To their right sits the bed — a single, like mine — which is somehow still made, its lone pillow centered on the covers by the headboard. Ayo crosses the floor and looks out at the lot where we parked, at the night, then he turns back to me, softly smiling.

"I don't know about you, but this isn't what I thought this place would look like."

To be honest, I didn't know what to expect.

"It seems much — how do you say — junkier in real life than it does in the commercials."

In its defense, most things do, don't they?

"Not most things. Everything. But for all that, I believe what we've found here is perfect. If it didn't have these flaws, these red flags, even, including its spooky innkeeper, more people would likely be staying here, which would've made this whole night much more difficult."

Count your blessings, as they say.

"Verily." Ayo flips the TV on. A field of static fills the screen, accompanied by white noise at low volume. He turns it off and nods. "It appears Dale was right about that."

That's okay with me.

"Yes, me too." He takes his tie-dyed hanky and rubs the dust from the device and its cabinet, then shakes the cloth out on the floor — there's no wastebasket in here, for some reason — and stands to admire his work. "She'll be here soon, Magdalene. Maggie. I hope she's everything you've been wanting, Cliff, and more."

So do I.

"May I ask you something?"

Sure.

"Are you nervous?"

I'd be lying if I didn't say I am, a little bit.

"That's all right. Everyone is nervous their first time. And yes, anyone who says they're not is lying. You'll be fine, though. I promise. I'll leave you two in here alone, but I won't be far away. I was of a mind to go down to the pool," Ayo frowns, "but then I thought better of it."

"Ha."

"Should I help you get prepared?"

Yes, please, I say, wheeling to him.

Ayo tugs the covers to the end of the bed. Undoing my belt, he picks me up, lays me down gently, and positions my head on the pillow. Less like foam than a large block of cheese, it's hardly the world's most comfortable mattress, but then again, mine at home isn't, either.

"How's that?"

It's perfect.

"Good. And your clothes?"

After my shower, Ayo powdered my rump, threw a clean Depends over it, and dressed me in my nicest PJ's. They're the red silk pair Knowland bought me when I left Sinai Grove for Saltpeter Street. *A housewarming gift,* he called them. I've worn them once in twenty years, on my very first night with the guys. After that, they lay at the bottom of my closet, under a towering heap of my most threadbare sweats, until Ayo noticed them earlier this evening. Freshly cleaned, they make me feel the same as I did years ago: free, hopeful, and, yes, though nervous, ready to take on this new unknown, like someone on their first skydiving trip.

Let's do them, too, if you don't mind.

"Of course."

Ayo unbuttons the top carefully and leans me forward, removing it one sleeve at a time. He slides off the bottoms, folds both articles, and sets them on the cabinet by the ancient TV set. Then he comes back to me and checks to make sure my tube's still rolled up and secure in the gauze and its base isn't covered in mucus.

"Are you still clean? Or do you need to go? There are more Depends in the van."

Nah, I'm good.

"You're comfortable, then, and not cold? I can pull the blanket back up if you like."

Everything's great as it is. I'm ready.

"Very good. I'll wait here till she comes. When she does, if you need me, just holler."

I will. I give him a big smile. *And Ayo . . .*

"Yes, Cliff?"

As I motion downward, he kneels at my side. I hold up my hand and he takes it as he did on his first day with us, his grip warm and more anxious than mine. We shake firmly, our palms dewy with sweat. I bring his hand to my chest, slowly and jerkily, and tell him with a quiet grunt:

Thank you for this. Thanks for everything.

"You're welcome, my brother," he says, his grin mirroring mine like the ocean a sky full of stars.

)

There's a cough at the door, then three knocks, quick and confident, if a little muted. Ayo goes to the peephole, sticks an eye into it.

"Hello?"

The voice that comes is like the knocks — muffled yet self-assured, lush, and sensual. "Hey, there. I'm Maggie. I'm here to see Cliff."

"Yes, please. Just a moment." Ayo removes the rusty chain from its lock and lets her in.

All my life, I've heard the way men talk about women when they're not around, from the staff at Sinai Grove to some I've had with Knowland, up to and including Francis. There's always been such loathing in their tones, sometimes more pronounced than others, but definite and undisguised regardless, even as they've spoken of their so-called love for them. I won't repeat the things they've said — only rarely have they treated us, their clients, so badly with their words — but they've been running through my mind a lot these last few hours. For that reason, and because until now I've never been in their position as far as relationships with women are concerned, I haven't gone into this with any expectations. No, I haven't so much as pictured Maggie in my mind's eye. Part of me, admittedly, was afraid of being disappointed. I knew she wouldn't be the actress in the commercials, the woman of my dreams, a fantasy of mine no one but her could satisfy. I've also been worried that when this moment came, Maggie would laugh in my face, or worse, would regard me with pity.

But she does neither. A leather purse slung over her shoulder, Maggie breezes past Ayo, smiling. She's no taller than he is, and younger than I, probably in her mid-thirties. Her small, round face, with its brown eyes and dimples, isn't loudly made-up, as it'd be in the movies. The brown, kinky curls of her hair conceal earrings that jingle like chimes in the wind. She wears a cream-colored blouse that hangs loosely around her waist and a plaid, crimson skirt that cuts off at her thighs. Her heels are either black or the darkest shade of brown, and they, too, aren't as flashy or as high as one might expect. Her fingers are ringless, but a silver chain hangs around her neck, its pendant shaped like a full moon. It glistens in the artificial light from the window, dotted with tiny, engraved lunar craters.

"You must be Cliff," she says, still smiling broadly.

That's right.

Maggie lays her purse by my pajamas on the cabinet, then comes to me and kneels in the same spot where Ayo was before. "How's your night going?"

Pretty well, all things considered. And yours?

"It's going great. Thanks for asking." She makes to touch my face, requesting permission with her eyes, which I give happily. "Your friend and I spoke earlier. He says there's something you want you've never had before. I can help out on that front, if you'd like."

I'd like that very much.

Ayo grabs his wallet, takes out a stack of bills, counts them with his thumb, and deposits them near Maggie's purse. "The amount we agreed on. I'll be down the hall. Do you need anything else while I'm here, Cliff?"

I'm all set.

"Do you have questions for Cliff or me, Maggie?"

"No, we covered it all pretty well on the phone."

"Good. Then I'll leave you to it."

Wait, please, I say.

Ayo stops on what's left of the room's welcome mat. "Yes?"

I point to Maggie, lay my fingers on my chest, then raise my arms questioningly.

"What is it, Cliff?"

"He wants to know," Ayo says, coming back to the bed, "if you've ever been with anyone with cerebral palsy before."

I grunt doubtfully, put my palm up.

"That is, if you don't mind his asking."

"Of course I don't mind, and yes, I have, a few times."

I pat my chest and lift my arm higher.

"Were they like Cliff?"

"A little," Maggie says, "but not nearly as handsome."

My mouth hangs wide open, my grin big and dumb.

"He says you must surely tell everyone that."

"I don't, actually, but . . ." Maggie massages my neck, near my vocal cords, making more than my cheeks start to burn. "But I'll be honest with you. Before tonight, I've never been with anyone who couldn't — who isn't — who's . . .

Nonverbal.

"Nonverbal?"

"Nonverbal. That's it. Thank you both. Before tonight, I've never been with someone who's nonverbal. So, if you're nervous, it might help to know I am, too."

Yes, it does.

"That said, I'll do everything I can to give you everything you want. This is your night, Cliff. I'm just here to help. If you start to feel strange, if you'd rather I try something different, or even if you want to stop, all you have to do is let me know. You got it?"

I do. And thank you.

Her eyes suddenly shine much more brightly. "You're welcome."

"Any other questions for now?" Ayo says.

I don't think so, no.

"All right, Cliff. Maggie. That's my cue, as they say." At the door, Ayo halts and volte-faces. "Here's to taking risks," he says, and disappears into the hall.

)

Maggie rises and, fixing her brown eyes on mine, takes off her blouse and throws it aside. She reaches back and unhooks her transparent, black bra. Her breasts, below her silver pendant, are two moonlit hills, their nipples hard and hemmed in by gooseflesh. She steps out of her heels, drops her skirt, and divests herself of her underwear, tossing them with the rest of her clothes. She's shaved her pubic hair into a strip as slender as the stem of a forget-me-not. My gaze follows it down to a blooming of petals as ephemeral as it is timeless.

"You want the light on or off?" she says, taking a seat at the foot of the bed.

I'm not sure it makes a difference.

"I think I got that. We'll leave it off, for now, then. I'd close the blinds, though, if they weren't, well, like that."

Yeah, tell me about it.

"Are you comfortable? Do you need to be moved at all?"

I wiggle my head on the pillow, shift a bit on the bed, stretch out as far as I can, then blast her a mighty thumbs-up.

"Perfect."

Her fingertips graze my right thigh. My left. After tracing the shape of my legs and their bruises, she straddles me, knees at my hips, and leans down and kisses my tube. From there, she walks a path with her lips to my chest, through its sparse field of hair, all the way to my neck, then my ear, which she nibbles, her breath warm and light on my skin, her smell, like lavender. As she nuzzles my forehead, I close my eyes. She grins with me from beyond the purple sparks.

"You smell nice. It's a little like oak. Suits you well."

On the way here, and thanks to Ayo's quick thinking, we swung by the pharmacy for a bottle of their best cologne.

Thanks. You do, too.

"Still doing all right?"

I'd say.

"That's great. You're doing great." Maggie's touch is delicate but purposeful. Gently, she tugs at my hair, discovers a knot on the back of my neck, and without hesitation, massages it. "You're pretty tight through here, Cliff. Do you feel that?"

Oh yeah.

"It must be hard work, sitting up straight in that chair all day long, looking out at the world through those brown eyes of yours."

You don't know the half of — oh, hell, yeah, right there. That's what I'm talking about.

Her laugh is pure and unrehearsed. "You like that, huh?"

Mm.

"Then I'll keep at it a while."

She works the muscle like a professional masseuse, kneading with her fingers, knuckles, the heels of her thumbs. The sparks inside my head turn to purple waterfalls that splash up clouds of neon mist with each of Maggie's strokes.

"It doesn't hurt, does it?"

Mn.

"Good. I could do this all night, but there's lots more we still need to get to."

I've thought a lot about what kissing would feel like. This is it, exactly, brought to life and magnified a thousand times over by touch. Maggie's lips are like her laugh, plush and quiet. They taste like I imagine violets might. Our tongues move in unison, exploring at times with subtlety, at others with more emphasis. At one point, though, our teeth knock together. The weirdest, sharpest feeling pulses through me, and through Maggie, too, by the looks of it. We wince and she laughs, says she's sorry. I say it's nothing — it was probably my fault, anyway — and tilt my head up to her face. Her breasts sink to my chest, her nipples tickling my own. Tingling, my whole body shivers, the rising in my groin about to burst through my Depends. Its stiffness raging at her thigh, Maggie reaches down and gives it a deft squeeze over the fabric.

"My goodness, Cliff. What have we here?"

I was about to say the same thing.

"I take it your friend mentioned wearing a condom? That's still okay with you, right?"

Of course.

The light through the blinds falls on her back in broken bands, like the bars of a cage that's been shattered and escaped from — by the blackbird, it seems, tattooed at the base of her neck. It aims toward the sky, wings outspread, its beak frozen open in song. I almost feel bad watching Maggie, tracing her curves with my eyes, but then she looks back from the cabinet and, smiling, just stands there a while longer.

"Nice pajamas," she says, feeling them. "Soft and silky. They look comfortable."

I've only worn them on special occasions.

"I'll bet you look good in them, too."

From her purse, she digs out a small wrapper and throws it on the cabinet when she removes its rubber disc.

"Let me help you out of these."

As best I can, I arch my back and raise my bottom, giving Maggie just the space she needs to slide off my Depends. When she drops them to the floor, a cloud of powder puffs back up into her face. She turns away from me and sneezes twice.

Bless you. And sorry about that.

"Thank you. No worries. Let's take a closer look, shall we?"

She runs her fingers along the shaft's bottom. Bending over, she gives it a kiss. She teases the tip with her tongue, her curls skimming my thighs to her jewelry's faint chiming. My chest rises and falls with her rhythm. My eyes stir in their sockets. Maggie's turned my limbs into noodles, made them soft in her touch's slow boil. I want to hold the back of her head, but my hand won't cooperate, lying as if fastened by chains to the bed. For my whole life, I've been helpless, incapable of all but the most basic of bodily movements, but until now, I've never been completely paralyzed, nor has it ever bothered me so little.

So little, in fact, that it's not until she slips the condom on — its feel slithery and thin, like shedding skin — that I grow conscious of my nakedness. Breaking free, the doubts I've held at bay all night run loose and violent. Just the thought of me in this position was enough to make Greg vomit, and with few exceptions, my staff shudder when they first see me like this. Because it's happened so often, I've always figured I at least partly deserve their disgust. That said, I thought I'd long gotten over it. I had to, or I wouldn't have survived. But as their faces resurface from the depths of my memory, my heart sinks. For the first time since I got here, I don't feel like I belong — not in this room, not on this bed, and especially not with someone as nice or as pretty as Maggie.

Sitting empty on the wall next to the door, my chair agrees. Its cyclops' eye of a headrest stares me down as willfully as Henry Wray or the faces in the lobby's speckled tiles. Its arms point at the bed as the seat's open mouth yawns a laugh. The longer it lasts, the more it sounds like Francis's. Though I whip my head the other way, it doesn't stop. The laughter only grows louder and more hateful. Soon it's amplified by everybody's voice who's ever scoffed at me, beginning with the kids who lived across the street when I was still at home, before my parents gave me up.

Cliff the crippled boy, they'd say.

Though they couldn't have known its implications — we must've been the same age, four or five — years later, it struck me just how easily the word rolled off their little tongues, like the squawking of parrots who've learned a new phrase. Something in their cadences suggested grown-up talk, and my guess is one of them picked it up from his parents. That's why I've never blamed them. They didn't know what they were doing, much less understand the way such words can cut someone like me — or anyone, for that matter. Besides, even if I'd wanted to, I couldn't have clapped back at them. Until tonight, I've never wished I'd had the option. They were the first to call me names, to treat me with something other than humanity. I'd heard the word a lot up to that point. My parents and doctors used it more often than Greg tans. Times were different then, of course. But I'd never heard it spoken with such animus before. I'd known I wasn't the same as most people as far as my body went, but on that day, those kids changed the way I thought about myself. I'm not naïve enough to think that if they hadn't, no one else would've, eventually. School was just around the corner, and when it arrived, things did get worse. Still, I can't help but wonder: if I'd been able to respond in kind, to stand up for myself somehow — though they could've, my parents never did—would things have turned out any differently? Would I have been the one to lay down the terms of my relationships with others? Would it have given me more confidence? More strength? Would it have been easier for me to handle the way most staff regard my body? Or would everything have ended up the same?

I'm not sure why I'm asking. The answers don't exist. All I know is, if I'd put those little bastards in their place back then, I wouldn't be thinking of them now. I wouldn't be so angry and embarrassed. My ears wouldn't be ringing with the laughter of a thousand assholes. And I wouldn't be crying or trying and failing to struggle as Maggie calls —

"Cliff."

She has to say my name a few more times before my body yields to her voice. My limbs are still flimsy and flat, my face hot and wet with fresh tears.

She wipes them away, holds my head from behind, and kisses the shim-mering trails on my cheeks.

I'm sorry. I don't —

"It's all right. You're still doing great." Her brown irises flitter in place. "You haven't done anything wrong. Have I, though? Do you want me to —"

No, please. This is my fault.

"There's no blame to be had here, if that's what you're thinking. There are no suspicions, no judgments. There's nothing but you, Cliff, and me." She brushes my bangs toward my temple. "I like being with you. It feels good. It feels safe. I want you to feel safe with me, too."

I do.

"I want you to feel like you matter," she says. "I see you blushing, but you do. You mean a lot to your friend. I could tell that much over the phone. Not just anyone would take the risk of setting this up." She drops her gaze and bites her bottom lip. "And this might sound weird, seeing as we've just met, but I want you to know you mean something to me."

You're just saying that, I grin through my tears.

"I'm not, but I understand. I'd feel the same in your place. But it's the truth. It seems we've both had people in our lives who've used their words, and sometimes more, to hurt us."

How do you know —

"Your friend told me. I hope that's all right."

Why wouldn't it be?

"He said you're in a program and that he cares for you. My other clients with CP had help, too, so I've heard a little about it. But I'd thought it was supposed to improve your life, not hold you back. Your friend mentioned how sometimes things don't work out like they should, and someone named John, and another guy, Craig, I think. He told me how they refused to help you with this because of what they saw as 'limitations.' They both sounded about as full of shit as men can get without exploding."

Greg. And yeah, Ayo was right about all of it.

"What gives them the right," she says, "to tell you how you can or should live your own life? I just don't get it. It's like they don't care that you have thoughts and hopes and dreams as real as anyone's. They remind me of most of my clients actually, men who treat me like I'm . . ." Maggie trails off, looks through the broken blinds, then back at me. "Though their reasons may be different, their acting the way they do toward you makes them feel powerful. The thing, though, Cliff, is that you're much stronger than they are." She moves down to my battered shins and kisses their permanent bruises, one at a time. "But you don't need me to tell you this. My point is, I see it in you, and I'm pretty sure they do, too."

I don't know if I'd say —what do you mean, the way they've treated you?

"You'd be surprised," Maggie laughs, guardedly, "the way most men act toward me. It's less that they pretend to care for me and more like I'm garbage in bad need of taking out." In our silence, the moon on her chest glimmers. "I got used to it, after a while. I learned not to let it bother me as much. But there are times, whole days, weeks, even, when I forget who I am at my core. When everyone looks at you a certain way, when everything they say and do screams, *You're not as good as me, bitch, you can't help but start* believing them. You begin to see yourself the way you look through their hateful eyes."

I know what that feels like. But why you? You're so —

"It's probably better you don't know. What matters is, you're not like them. You're a good man, Cliff. You've been so sweet to me, and thoughtful, and kind."

How else should I be?

"No other way," she smiles, swinging herself back over me. "Don't be anyone other than who you are, not tonight and not ever. This is your time, and I'm here for you, but you're here for me, too, even if you didn't know it." Maggie leans forward and kisses my chest, chin, and cheeks. "You do now, though. You know how hard it is for us to see ourselves not through the eyes of others but through our own, how much those looks and words can hurt, how we can take those things as truths about ourselves instead of what they really are, which is bullshit. But we don't see how wrong we are until someone comes along and reminds us that, above all else, we're human beings." She grabs me over the condom and brings me back to life. "That's what you've done for me, Cliff. You've reminded me that I'm a human being, that there's a place for me here, in this world, however small and fleeting it is. It makes me happy. It makes me feel like I deserve this happiness. And it makes me feel like you deserve it even more."

I . . .

She sits up, hugging my thighs with her knees, and eases me into her, closes her eyes. Mine, on the other hand, roll to the back of my head. The laughter of Francis and the kids across the street becomes exactly what it should be, a distant memory.

"That's it," she says, going slowly, as if guiding me into the sea.

I try reaching for her breast, but my hand won't comply. Maggie takes it and places it over her goose-pimpled nipple. My leftover fear vanishes as her deep, even breathing grows louder. I close my eyes with her, step into the water. Warm, pink, and rising fast, it laps up against me in smooth, silken waves, beckons me under, bathes me, baptizes me in its blossoming heat. I'd hold my breath forever if it meant I could stay here. I'd swim in these depths for eternity. But my body has limits, and my spirit demands to be freed. In hot, frenzied rushes, it escapes into her, surrenders to her absolutely. She accepts me, all of me, gladly. I go slack in her arms and dissolve like a pillar of salt in her waters, wash away in the ebb of her tide.

"There you are," Maggie says, her voice sleepy and full. "There you are, Cliff. Just like that."

My limbs twitch. My heart swells. I've gone numb in her embrace, but I manage to breathe, finally, long and hard. Planting a kiss on my forehead, she rolls off and lies next to me, rests her head on her palm, rubs my chest.

"How do you feel?"

Like I never want to move ever again.

"Yeah. I get that. It was nice?"

It was the best.

"That makes me happy," Maggie says, and bites her lip. "But it's also making me a little worried."

Why?

"Because if your smile gets any bigger, it's going to fall off your beautiful face."

She's right. I'm grinning so goddamn hard it hurts.

I can't help it. And I don't want to.

"I know. I don't want you to, either."

I reach for her hand. She takes mine and holds it tightly against her full moon.

Was it all right for you, too?

"Of course. It was great. You're great, Cliff. And I'm not just saying that. I mean it. I've meant everything I've said to you tonight. I'm glad I've helped you get what you've been wanting for so long. But it'd make me even happier if you believed me."

I do. I believe you. And thank you.

"No, thank you." She kisses the back of my hand several times. "I know how difficult it was, risky, even, for you to just come here tonight. I'd love to see you again, though, if you're able to sometime, if your friend can make it happen. And if not, I'm still happy we had this."

I'd love to see you again, too.

Over our breathing, a trailer truck sighs its lament.

"Are you ready to get back in those PJ's? I'll grab your friend and let him —"

No, please, I say, *not quite yet.*

Maggie shivers in the darkness. "Is there something else you want? I'm game for whatever. This is your night, after all. What are you thinking?"

I motion at the blanket lying bunched up at my feet.

"Are you cold? I'll cover you up. You can fall asleep for a while, if you like."

I'm not tired or cold. But it looks like you are.

I point to her, then to myself. She smiles. Unfurling the covers, she spreads them across us and lies down at my side.

"Here, you take the pillow. I'll use my arm. It's all right."
We end up sharing it, though. I insist.

THIRTEEN

When morning burst through the blinds, its light fell warm and unbroken on me. I'd been having a dream that I was swimming underwater. A storm was raging up above, and I was trying to go deeper, to avoid it, and because Maggie was down there, somewhere at the bottom of the sea. Knowland was searching for her, too — he had a fleet of three submarines — and if I didn't find her first, he'd execute her. I could hear her calling my name from the depths, her voice troubled and urgent, but a fierce undercurrent kept me from getting any closer. Every time I'd make a little progress, it'd push me back up toward the tempest. Though I fought and fought, my limbs weren't strong enough, and just before I breached the water's surface, I awoke. Everything was soft and golden. There was a tingling in my spine. I remembered last night and I smiled. Then I reached out for her and came up with a handful of my blanket.

)

"There you go," Thomas says, strapping me into my chair. "Come out now for breakfast. It'll be ready shortly."

Would it hurt you to not splash me with it, just this once?

"I don't know what you're saying to me." In the hallway, he turns back. "By the way, Cliff, where'd those PJ's come from?"

I shrug.

"Thin air, I suppose," he says, and smirks, and walks away.

Outside, a car door slams, then another. Three indistinct voices sound in our drive.

"Who could that be?" BJ yawns from his room. "It's not even time for Francis and Yodel."

He's right. No one's ever come by this early in the day. The last time so many people pulled up was when Knowland paid a visit to beg our pardon for Paul's actions.

"It is Mr. Knowland," Thomas says, "and Brad, pushing a wheelchair with a very sunburnt man in it."

"That'd be Greg, of course."

"Who's Craig?"

"It's Gah-reg, with a G. He works with Cliff now, don't you know? He's helping him to not kill anyone with the death machine."

"Oh, yes. I've heard about him. I see he's made a fine job of it, too, hasn't he?"

"These things take time, as they say." BJ stretches in his doorway. "Boy, I sure am hungry, Thomas. What's for breakfast?"

"Your favorite dish, as usual. And two Ensures for Cliff. Get the door for them, then come sit with Lem and have your oatmeal."

"I'll be there in a jiffy." On the way, he calls, "Time for breakfast, Rick, and for the millionth time, no, it's not a —"

"Cookie."

Rickey emerges with one pajama leg hiked up around his knee. He shakes his head and rubs his eyes, then looks at me as if we've never met before. I'm not sure what's thrown him off. He's probably still groggy. Or it could be these pajamas. Maybe he remembers them from all those years ago. But it might also be the look on my own face, which does feel different, somehow, now that I think of it. I wave, but he just cocks his head, smiles, and trudges off, turtle-like, toward the dining room.

"Morning Cap'n, John, Greg with a G," says BJ sleepily.

"With two G's, actually. How ya doin', champ?"

"Better now that breakfast is ready. Come in, why don't you? We're having instant oatmeal, if you're hungry. Thomas, do we have any extra —"

"Thanks, Beej, but no thanks. Why, hello there, Rickey."

"What're you guys doing here, anyway?" BJ says.

After a heavy, too-long silence, someone slams the front door shut.

"We were in the neighborhood," Knowland says, "and thought we'd pop in and see what's new."

"Oh, not much. Another day, another dollar."

Brad's new laptop goes *clunk* on something. "Where's Cliff?"

"Still in his room, I guess."

"I asked him to come get his Ensure, but it seems he's already in a mood."

"Any idea why?"

"I figured I'd leave the answer to you, Craig with a g. But wait until you see his new pajamas. They're quite the sight."

"I'm on pins and needles."

Unless he wants Brad to wheel him back here, Greg will have to stay that way a while. It's too early to be taking in that frizzled face of his. And though it doesn't sound like they're suspicious, I've got to wonder why they've come. I can't rule out that Francis tipped them off to Ayo and I leaving last night. But then, when we got home, he didn't even ask how our "drive" went. He looked exhausted, like he'd been dozing. Because the guys had all retired to their rooms, and maybe, too, because he didn't want to give Francis any openings, Ayo didn't point out that the TV was set to cable news. He just helped me into bed and then we talked some. He offered to put the brochure from the hotel in my closet or dresser drawer — something to remember the night by — but I asked him to take it home with him, as it might raise more questions we'd prefer not to answer. Before he left, I thanked him for giving me the best night of my life. It took me forever to fall asleep, though. I lay there for hours thinking of Maggie, and only Maggie, as Lem sawed the logs of old oak trees.

"When's the shift change?" Knowland says.

"Twenty mikes, sir."

"What the hell does that mean?"

"It means twenty minutes. Sorry, sir. It's army slang. I thought you knew."

"Why would I know that? More to the point, Brad, why would you?"

"I learned it a few days ago."

"From where?"

"From a website."

"Well, from here on out, I want you to say *minutes* in my presence. Don't say *mikes*, don't say *Charlie Foxtrot*, and don't you ever dare say *zero dark thirty* to me. This isn't a war zone. I don't want to hear it. Have I made myself perfectly clear?"

"Yes, sir. Of course, sir. But, sir?"

"What?"

"What if I'm speaking to somebody else?"

"As long as I'm not there, I don't care a whit."

Brad's sigh of relief lasts a whole half a mike.

"Anyway," Knowland says, "how are things going on your end, Mr. . . ."

"Thomas," the staff says, absently, "and things are going fine. Here you go, gentlemen. Breakfast is served."

"My, this sure looks good. Thanks again, Thomas, for your hard work with us."

"Mm-hmm."

"Overnights must be easier, though," Knowland says.

"They are, yes, until morning comes."

"Thomas works two jobs," says Brad. "He goes straight from here to his next shift with Bridges."

"Ah, the competition. I hear they're not doing so hot lately."

"Mm," Thomas says. "We did just have someone pass away. I knew the gentleman. He lived at the site where I work."

There's a chorus of sad, tender *awws*.

"Natural causes, of course. My clients are all in their eighties. We're looking for someone new to fill his spot. But otherwise, the company seems to be doing very well. I haven't noticed any differences, at least."

The next wave of *awws* is much louder and more pained.

"Well, we have to earn our living somehow. I won't hold it against you as long as it doesn't affect your work with our folks."

"It never has, Mr. Knowland. Actually, it's just the opposite."

Spoons clink against their bowls of lukewarm oatmeal.

"Really? In what way?"

Thomas coughs meekly. "It's not such a problem anymore, actually, now that my relief is arriving when it's supposed to."

"We've taken care of it, John. I laid down the law with that staff. It hasn't been an issue for going on a couple weeks."

"That's not exactly true, but —"

"Who're we talking about? Not the new guy, I hope?"

"No, not him," Thomas says. "Ayo always comes in early. It's the other staff, Fran —"

"Again, it hasn't happened since our little chat. If it does, though, Thomas will be sure to let me know."

"I'm trying to, Brad. If I'd had the chance, I would've told you earlier, but the truth is, there've been a few days when —"

"In your opinion, Thomas," Knowland says, "how is Ayo working out?"

"Pretty well so far, as far as I can tell. As I say, he gets in early every day, and everybody seems to like him."

"It's true," says BJ, or at least that's what it sounds like, through his full mouth.

"Good. Sounds like he's taken my warning to heart."

"He better have, sir, if he knows what's good for him."

From the yard comes the shutting of yet another car door.

"Speak of the devil. You're right. Ayo is quite the early bird."

"He's not a bird, Greg with a *G*. He's our staff."

I motor to the window. Ayo's parked out on the street. In his bright-orange dashiki, his head tilted to one side, he inspects the vehicles in our drive with uncertainty. As he heads in, I race out to the front door to greet him.

"Look who's late to the party," Brad says, his fatigues clean and odorless. "Wow, nice PJ's."

Greg's charred cheeks are puffed out in a sneer. "Man, you weren't kidding. They are quite the sight. Where'd you get those, Cool Dude? I might need to buy a pair myself."

"He wouldn't tell me," Thomas says.

"I bought those for him a long time ago. They were my way of saying *Welcome to the agency and your new life here.*" Knowland sips coffee from a Styrofoam mug. "My God, Cliff. That was so long ago. I didn't know you still had them. They look good as new."

Greg wheels himself to me, seizes my shoulder, and twists the silk into my skin. "That's funny. I've never seen him in them before."

I try jerking away. He grips more tightly.

"I haven't, either," says Brad. "They still fit like a glove, though."

"Some things never change. They must've been sitting at the bottom of your closet for decades. Who found and put you in them?"

"I did," Ayo says from the entry, "and yes, that's where they were, at the bottom of Cliff's closet."

"Well, how about that?" Greg leans in and sniffs my neck. "You smell great, too, like old-growth forest. It must've been a special night. What was the occasion?"

Ayo steps in and stands between Greg and me, fingers trembling. "Good morning, gentlemen. There was no occasion in particular. Cliff and I were going through his closet, organizing all his sweats. We found these PJ's and thought they might feel better than his regulars."

"But they're so soft and so, so red — the sort of jammies one wears to impress. You're sure last night wasn't special? Not even just a teeny, tiny bit?"

"As I say, it wasn't much different from any other night."

"You did go on a drive, though," says BJ, squeezing another glob of Quaker Oats into his already jam-packed mouth.

Greg's eyes light up inside their pasty rings. "Is that a fact?"

"It is. We thought it'd be nice to get some fresh air for a while."

"I see. Just you and Cliff, huh?"

"That's right."

"That happen often?"

"Not too often," BJ says. "We don't really go for drives unless it's to the office or the grocery store or Memory Makers or the bank."

"In other words, not without a destination."

"We went around the neighborhood and down the highway a few miles. I didn't think it'd be a problem, Greg. Should we have asked your permission first?"

"No, not necessarily. It just seems a little strange, is all, your taking only Cliff while the other guys stayed here."

"It was later in the evening, after dinner. Things were going pretty slowly. Francis had it under control. Everyone was winding down in front of the TV."

"We watched the Weather Channel for a bit." In his excitement, BJ spills orange juice on the chest of his pajamas.

"That was one awful storm, wasn't it?" says Knowland.

"It sure was. Gee, I hope Jim Cantore's all right."

"When is he ever not," Greg says, "even when reporting from the eye of a cat-five?"

"Anyway, thanks again, Yodel, for helping us to vote on what to watch."

"What's this, now? You guys had a vote?"

"That they did. As it's their house and their TV, it seems only right they choose what plays on it."

"We chose the Weather Channel because we like to watch the storms. They're better than the news, which is too depressing, mostly."

Knowland wipes a tear with his striped tie. "What isn't, though, these days?"

"Pick your poison, pick your poison," Greg sings, tunelessly. "That's what it's all about in a democracy. You might be new here, Ayo, but you're learning fast." He reaches for my shoulder again, but I reverse until I bump against the wall.

"I don't know if I'd say that. All I'm doing is the best I can to help these men. There are still many things for me to learn," Ayo smirks, "such as why you'd try to touch Cliff when he clearly doesn't want you to."

"He's made nothing clear to me except that something happened here last night. Something new. Something different. Something worthy of those bright-red, silken PJ's."

Ayo stuffs his shaking hands into the pockets of his jeans. "I've already told you. We took a short drive, then came home, and I helped Cliff into bed. What more do you want me to say?"

"Nothing, for now." Greg's lizard tongue sneaks through his sparkly teeth. "But I'd imagine that if Cliff could speak, he'd tell us volumes."

It's because I can't, I guess, that Knowland sheds another couple tears.

"I don't know, guys. I think Ayo has a point. It doesn't seem like Cliff's too keen on being grabbed like —"

"Shut up, Brad," Greg says.

"What would you call that," says Ayo, nodding at me on the wall, "if not a message, plain as day, that you should keep your hands off him?"

"I'd call it nothing less than what it is: Cliff and I still working on rapport. As you're aware, it can sometimes take a while for our labors to bear fruit. Patience and persistence are essential. We'll slacken his stiff reluctance to embrace me. You just wait."

"And so I will, with bated breath."

"As will I, evidently," Thomas says, Ensure in hand, "for Cliff to come get breakfast."

"Go on, then, champ," says Greg, as he, Brad, and Knowland clear a path. "Go get that little belly filled with nourishment."

Stomach rumbling, I grasp the joystick and blast ahead, my sights on BJ. He crams another bite into his mouth, drops his spoon to the table, and, per our routine, prepares for impact. Midway through the foyer, though, I slam the brakes — it's best that Greg not witness this — and brace myself.

My hand judders, my wheels screech, and as my body lurches forward, pressing hard against my belt, a small, torn square jolts loose from my chest pocket. It arcs up, above my head, and hangs there for a moment, for an eternity, before falling softly and in graceful spirals to the floor in front of me.

"What is that?"

Bending over, Greg snatches, inspects, and holds it out. "It's volumes, John. Whole volumes. I've got to say, though, Cliff, why Trojan? I've always been a Magnum guy myself."

"Where'd it come from?" says Brad.

My ears burn. My heart sinks. I grunt and try to spin away from Knowland, but Greg kicks my wheel with his good foot and holds it there.

"It didn't come with those PJ's, I know that much."

"Aw," BJ says, "what'd you do this time, Cliff?"

Brad marches to Ayo. "What's the meaning of this, Private?"

"Why are you asking me?"

"You can't be serious," says Greg.

"I'm more serious than your tanning-bed eye protection. It's not for me to decide whether your question gets answered. That choice is Cliff's and Cliff's alone."

"And what, exactly, is he supposed to tell us?" Greg makes his arms go bent and his face all twisted up. "*Ugh?*"

"You are disgusting," Ayo says, "both on the inside and the out."

Knowland tears swaths of hair from his beard. "Be that as it may — and it may, oh, yes, it may — he's not mistaken. Even if Cliff wanted to, he couldn't divulge where he went, what he did, or most importantly, who with. Only you can do that, Ayo."

"Maybe, but again, it's not for me to say, not without Cliff's blessing."

"Well, Cliff? We're waiting."

"Wanna pop."

"Not now, Rick," says BJ. "Can't you see Cliff's in trouble?"

"No one's in trouble — not yet, at least." Greg works his heel into my wheel. "All right, Cliff. Go ahead. The whole world hinges on your blessing."

Resisting the urge to dig my chin into my shoulder, I keep my eyes open and look him in the face. *Why should I?*

"That didn't sound like a blessing to me."

"Yeah, me either."

"I told you he's in a mood," Thomas says.

"Lucky for him, and us, his behavior plan's almost finished. It won't be long before these moods are ancient history."

"I look forward to that day," Knowland says, his cheek exposed through a patch of plucked beard hair, which he caresses as if in apology. "But for the time being, they're still with us. Tell us what happened, Cliff. Who did you see? You can't keep us in the dark about —"

"Why not, though? Why can't he? What gives you the right to ask such private questions of this man, or anyone?"

"It's our job to keep him safe and healthy. That's what gives us the right. It seems you've forgotten everything I told you only yesterday."

"I've forgotten nothing." Ayo comes to and stands beside me. "Look at him. He's healthy. He's safe. And last night he was the happiest I've ever seen him. You would've seen it, too, long before then, had you ever bothered listening to him."

"I don't like your tone," Knowland says, looming over Ayo, "and I don't like your hiding things from me. Not only do I have the right to know. I have the authority. So, I'm not asking anymore. I'm commanding you to tell me."

"I understand." At his sides, Ayo's hands no longer shake. His eyes take on the look they had last night, during my shower. "I understand you think you have the power to command us. Granted, as your employee, I'm subject to your authority. But as for Cliff, he never signed up to work for you. He owes you nothing. You have no power over him. My first obligation is to him — yes, to keep him safe and healthy, but also to respect his wishes. If Cliff would rather keep you in the dark about last night, that's his choice, and I'll honor it."

"How brave of you to hide behind this helpless little creature." Greg's slip-on squeaks against my chair. "You must be so proud, Cliff. It must make you feel so strong."

I try nudging past him. He lifts his foot higher, presses even harder.

"I'm not hiding. I'm right here, out in the open. With or without me, Cliff is stronger than the three of you put together." Ayo steps to and stands above Greg. "I'll tell you what's weak, though. What's weak is how you've treated him. Cliff doesn't work for you, but he did sign up for something else: to receive your care. It's you who owe him something, you who owe him everything. But in this, you've failed at almost every level. You've ig-nored all but his most basic needs. You've dismissed his deepest dreams as unattainable. You've looked the other way when his staff, whose job it is to help him, decide they don't feel like it." Smiling inscrutably, he turns from Greg to Brad, then to Knowland. "Had you heeded your own words, sir, we wouldn't be in this position. Had you listened to Cliff, seen him for who he really is, perhaps he would've trusted you. Perhaps he would've seen no point in hiding. Perhaps he would've felt like he could be himself not just sometimes, but all the time. And perhaps there would've been no need for him to thrive in secret."

Knowland nips at his coffee like vodka. "So, what you've done to him is our fault, then?"

"I've done nothing to him. I've done nothing but help him find happiness. To you, this seemed impossible, even dangerous. But to me, it was my duty. It wasn't very hard, either, because I —"

"Because you what?"

"If you'd let me finish," Ayo says, "I'd tell you it wasn't very hard because I don't just care for Cliff. I care about him."

"Heh," says Greg.

"That's a very nice speech, even if it's all untrue." Knowland buffs his beard's bald spot with a small cloth. "But it still doesn't answer my question. My question was, where'd you take him last night? Who'd you see? Why was there a condom wrapper in his —"

"Save your breath, John. He's not going to tell us. Besides, we're probably blowing this way out of proportion. We may have our suspicions, but if we're being honest with ourselves, do we really think Cliff found someone to be with him" — throwing up in his mouth, Greg holds the wrapper out, then drops it at my feet — "like that?"

I don't move. I don't think. I don't know what this rising in my chest is. I don't realize until after it's happened that I've turned to Ayo and said —

Tell them. Tell them everything.

And before I've even thought to take it back — to say, *No, I didn't mean it, I don't know what just came over me* — he has. He's told them everything. Hands behind his back, he speaks quietly but clearly and defiantly, revealing detail after detail with that same smile, mysterious and bright below his crescent scar. At the Dale and Quinton part, Brad socks the foyer's wall, knocking loose our home's one decoration. The word JOY falls to the floor and breaks in half.

Thomas whistles when Ayo says he paid for everything. As he tells them about Maggie, about how soft she was, and kind, and willing, Greg turns aside and pukes, not in his mouth, but on the floor. Knowland makes *Mm-hmm* sounds as he listens, his arms crossed, his face impassive, and only when Ayo finishes does he nod, check his watch, and have a look through our front window.

"It's past nine," he says. "Where's the other staff?"

Brad unfolds his phone. "I'll give him a call."

"There must be a traffic jam," says Thomas. "Much as I'd love to stick around and see what happens — and congratulations to you, Cliff, on your most special night — I can't be late to my next shift. If you don't mind, Brad, may I leave —"

"No, you may not," Knowland says, typing something quickly on his own phone. "You'll stay until your relief gets here. In the meantime, grab a mop and clean this up, would you?"

Bubbles rise and pop amid the chunks of the orange puddle on the floor.

"But my relief is here," says Thomas, pointing to Ayo.

"He won't be for long. We're going to the office." Knowland's phone makes the swooshing sound of a sent email. "I hate to bring in Linda on a Saturday. I know she'd rather spend this time with her new grandson. But we'll need her there as a formality, if nothing else."

BJ clanks his spoon down like a gavel. "I can't believe I'm saying this, Yodel, but I'm very disappointed in you. You didn't need to lie about where you went, you know, and now look at what you've done. You and Cliff are both in big, big trouble."

"I understand, BJ. I wish I could agree, but I apologize for lying to you all the same."

"I'm sorry," Thomas says, "but I can't wait around for —"

"Go on, Ayo. We'll meet you there. Brad, I want you to bring Cliff in the van. We'll need a statement from him, too."

"I'll ride with you," Greg grins.

"He hasn't had his breakfast yet," says Ayo.

"We'll bring it with us."

"As you wish."

Ayo bends down to my level, his eyes sad, as they were on his first day. But there's also a warmth in them, a wholeness, a sense of satisfaction inexpressible in any language. He puts his hand out and I shake it. His grasp is intent and unwavering. I squeeze back as tightly as I can.

I'm sorry.

"You have nothing to be sorry for. This is your life. These are your choices. Don't you dare regret them for a minute."

But they'll take us up there and they'll fire you —

"Maybe. Maybe not. I don't care. Let them do what they must."

I don't want you to leave.

"I don't, either. But as I say, this was never about me. This was always about you and who you want to be. So, whatever happens next, think only of your future and your freedom. Don't do anything to put those things at risk."

I can't make any promises.

"It's too late for that. You've put him at greater risk than he ever could've on his own." Greg gives him a round of applause. "Nice work, man. Real nice work."

Ayo looks past him to the dining room. "I'm leaving, gentlemen. I hope to see you again. If not, I'm grateful for the time we've spent together."

"I wish I could say the feeling's mutuable."

"If this is how you feel, BJ, I respect your —"

"Cookie."

"I can't get Francis on the horn, sir. The call went straight to voicemail." Brad claps his phone shut and returns it to his fatigues. "I'll try again in a few mikes."

"Damn it," says Knowland, slapping him. "What'd I just say about that?"

"I meant minutes. Sorry. I'll try again in a few minutes."

"That won't be necessary. Isn't that him pulling up?"

"I can think of no one else who drives a neon-green Dodge Challenger with yellow lightning bolt decals on either side."

"Great. Go start the van."

Thomas stands the mop against the wall. "Does this mean I can leave?"

"When he gets in. Why are you still here, Ayo? I told you to head to—"

"And I will, Mr. Knowland, if I can ever get free." He tries dropping my hand, but I grip so hard it hurts us both. "Please. I need to do this."

No, you don't.

"I do, though. I don't have a choice. I'll see you there, Cliff."

I won't let you —

But he's wrong again. He does have a choice, and he's made it. I let him go. He follows Thomas to the door, trailed by Knowland. Francis comes in, smiling through his hangover. He says something about traffic, but they all ignore him, and the last thing I see before everything goes black is Ayo's hand, waving thanks and goodbye.

FOURTEEN

This afternoon, on the Capitol steps, where he'd taken his smoldering stand in defense of free expression, Representative Horner launched his campaign for the presidency. Surrounded by hundreds of his staunchest supporters and almost as many members of the media, he scowled and he jiggled. He jerked and he winced. He punched at the wind and he pounded the lectern, his fist like a spicy ham sandwich. He thundered and swore to lay waste to the forces of tyranny which seek to erase him and those who, like him, are just being themselves. All of us, not only some, Horner said, neckbeard wilting under the weight of his big, cheesy head, should feel free to be who we are at our cores without fear of reprisal or punishment.

The speech, which lasted three hours, was aired by the network in full, without a single ad break. At times, Horner seemed to forget who he was, where he was, and which great state he represents in Congress. At others, he spoke clearly and stirringly as fury flashed in his far-apart eyes. There came a point where, in mid-sentence, he asked to be excused for "just a minute," then turned around and pissed for two. His calls to clobber the news correspondents were carried out by the crowd with clubs and kung-fu kicks, but some, mistaking each other for press, went after and bludgeoned themselves half to death, bringing Firth Bronzer to his first-ever live-TV orgasm. One of his producers offered him a towel and a chance to clean up, but Bronzer, ever the professional, planned to stick to his tight schedule and said he'd have to leave it there.

"Hoh!" Francis slapped his knee. "Get a load of that, will you?"

"In more ways than one," said Brad, next to him on the couch.

BJ wasn't there to share in their laughter. He, Rickey, and Lem have spent most of this week in their rooms, coming out only for meals and bathroom trips, and to leave for Memory Makers in the mornings. They're afraid I might attack them like I did Greg and Knowland — and this despite the fact I couldn't even if I wanted to. To them, it doesn't matter. My continued presence here is a dark cloud hanging heavy over them. The silver lining, as Brad's explained, is that this is only temporary. They'll get back to normal and will be happy again when I'm gone.

"In more ways than one," Francis said. "Good stuff, eh, Cliff?"

"I don't think he heard you."

"No, he did. It's just his hearing is sometimes selective."

"It better not have been when I told him what the plan is."

It wasn't. But he might've waited until the medication had worn off. It might've made more sense to me then. After everything had gone black, I'd come to, weightless and numb, in a bed that wasn't mine, its mattress stiff and clinical, like an article in a journal of psychiatry. The small room had no windows, but a square of light, white as a blank document, burned high above me. The same stink of piss and drying sweat that had permeated Sinai Grove hung in the air. My arms had been strapped tight to the metal bedrails, and a band was on my wrist with my name, blood type, and a bar code on it. I tried reaching for Maggie but couldn't find her anywhere. That's when Brad leaned over me, his hair freshly buzzed, his eyes hidden by tactical shades. Next to him stood a doctor, or at least that's what he looked like, in his khakis and white lab coat. He asked if I remembered what I'd done. I didn't, so Brad filled me in, seeming almost thankful I hadn't smashed his feet, too. As he showed me the notice — Knowland had drafted it himself on his own hospital bed — a tear slid out from under his dark lenses and splashed on the collar of his new fatigues.

"It shouldn't have to be this way," he said, his voice soaked in pity. "But you've left us no other choice. We'll help set you up with a new company. We owe you that much. Then we're finished, Cliff. I'm sorry. After everything you've done, I can't even call you 'Cool Dude' anymore."

☾

"Even if his hearing were selective then," said Francis, "what could he do to change it?"

"To change what?"

"The plan."

"Oh, that." Brad slid on his tactical shades. "Nothing. It's already set in motion. I've just got word Bridges has an opening at one of their sites. It's in town, too, Cliff, not far from here. You'll be moving in tomorrow, by the looks of it."

"Mm. That's sooner than I could've hoped. The gentlemen will be very glad to hear it."

"I wish I could disagree," Brad said, looking at his email. "Actually, this might be the house where Thomas does hours for them. He mentioned how one of his clients passed away recently. Lucky you, Cliff. At least you won't be starting over with no familiar faces."

Or, it would appear, with a clean navel.

"Count your blessings, as they say." Francis leaned back and crossed his ankles on our coffee table. "It's almost too bad, your leaving us now, of all times. You've been so much easier to work with this week. I've felt safer and happier, like I've finally found what I want out of life. I'm going to miss you, or at least what you've become. By the way, Cliff, how's life back in the manual wheelchair?"

Slumped to one side in my old chair, my head hanging limp at my shoulder, I instinctively reached for the joystick and came up with nothing.

"Doesn't look nearly as comfortable," Brad said.

Francis clicked his tongue and bit down on a toothpick. "Them's the breaks. This is what happens when you flout the rules so boldly and so badly. But on the bright side, you'll no longer need Greg's services, now, will you?"

"That's not entirely true. Greg's willing to stay on with you, Cliff, even after the move, and even though you've broken not just one but both his feet. Believe it or not, he doesn't hold it against you. He's certain it wasn't your fault and still wants to help you get through this rough patch." Brad whistled at the dwarf on our back patio. "Talk about compassion and commitment. I sure as hell couldn't do it."

"Nor could I, my friend."

"Who are you kidding? Cliff went after you first, yet you've come in every day since and carried out your duties with flying colors."

"That's only because of that." Francis nodded not at me, but the manual. "And also because I got away."

If he hadn't been blessed with those catlike reflexes, he would've been sitting not on the couch but next to me, in his own wheelchair.

"Either way, I don't know what I'd do without you, so thanks for that, and for making it in relatively on time this week."

"It's my pleasure."

As Horner jabbed and jawed away, Firth Bronzer, his slacks stained with drying ejaculate, brought on a statistician who'd been gauging the public's response to the speech in real time. It had only grown more favorable, he said, as the congressman waxed angrier and his cries for violence got more specific — not just against the press, but also against his political opponents. Topping the latter list was Representative Ploughman, against whom he'd directed the word that'd got him into trouble in the first place. "Don't get me wrong, folks. I'm not asking you to kill him." Horner shook his hulking head and frowned into the camera. "No siree Bob. I'm not asking anything. I'm commanding you to shoot that pussy point-blank in the mouth."

The crowd went crazy, Horner's fists went skyward, and so did his poll numbers among white suburban women.

❯

"I'm still confused, though."

"About what?"

"If Ayo's gone, and Cliff's in the manual, what's left for Greg to accomplish with him? In one fell swoop, all the causes of his behaviors have been eliminated. He hasn't had a single hissy fit since Saturday."

"If they'd just been hissy fits, there would've been no need for any of this." Brad now had his boots on our coffee table, too. Next to his employee's giant sneakers, they looked small enough to fit a toddler. "No, they were much more than that. It was BJ who put it best. What Cliff's committed here are nothing less than acts of terrorism."

"Acts of terror or not, he can't perpetrate them anymore, not in that old thing."

"Yes, but we've only removed the means of attack, not the impulse. Greg's convinced, and so am I, that it still exists inside Cliff, somewhere. It'd be a disservice both to him and his new company not to try and get at the root of the issue, whatever it is, and then to pull it out like so many weeds in a garden."

"Good luck with that," Francis said, laughing with more than his eyes.

❯

If you missed Horner's announcement, if you didn't watch it live, you'd think the only thing he said in it was the *r*-word, which he's adopted as his campaign slogan. Toward the end, he and his supporters chanted it, defiantly, as they'd done at his last speech, for more than seven minutes, uninterrupted, their dukes up and their smiles like curved knives. It's the one part the network has been playing on a loop since Horner finished, donned a superhero cape, and flew away, by means of ropes and pulleys, to the Chipotle down the street for a celebratory late lunch. Firth Bronzer, who's been manning the desk ever since, and who's yet to take a break to change his pants, has been discussing the clip and the word's implications with all manner of experts, including his current guest, the pop star Aughbreighanna Adelaide. She's the first to call the anchor out for airing Horner's use of it so many times these last few hours. At this, Bronzer giggles, then changes the subject to her new haircut.

❯

Drowsily, from down the hall, BJ calls my name. His familiar shuffling gets louder until he appears, in his pajamas, in the darkened doorway, then ambles between me and the TV. He looks different without his glasses, older and slightly wistful, like someone you run into you haven't seen in several years. Bathed in the bright blue light of the screen, he regards me in a way he hasn't all week: with a smile.

"Cliff," he says.

BJ.

"I have something to tell you."

I'm listening.

He reaches up toward the ceiling, a sleepy Seneca sermonizing in the Senate, and speaks quietly, so as to wake no one. "I can't say I'm not still mad at you, because I am, for what you did to us. In case you forgot, Rickey hasn't said 'Cookie' since Saturday — not that I'm complaining — and poor Lem spent half the weekend trying to hide under that broken bed of his. We shouldn't have to live in fear in our own homes, you know."

I know. I'm sorry. I never meant to hurt or scare you.

"Personally, I was over the moon to hear you're moving out. 'Finally,' I said, 'we'll get some peace and quiet around this place. Here's hoping our new housemate doesn't drive a death machine.'" He steps forward and lays a hand on his heart. "But here's the thing. I couldn't sleep tonight. I was tossing and turning around in my bed. I was worried and anxious for me, Lem, and Rickey, and even for you, Cliff, if you can believe it. And then something happened. I remembered those breathing exercises Yodel taught me, and I thought I'd give them another shot. Silly as I'm sure they made me look, they helped me relax and gave me a new perspective. Would you like to know what that is?"

More than anything.

BJ drops his arms to his sides and stands with his feet apart, like Ayo did in Angie's office. He rolls his shoulders, then his head, and as he breathes, deeply and smoothly, calmness and clearness cover him like a blanket. "It's this. You're my friend, Cliff. You always have been and always will be. Though we've had our ups and downs, good days and bad, no matter whose fault they were, we'll always be close, just like this."

He crosses his index and middle fingers, holding them out like a peace offering.

I couldn't have said it better myself.

"But I'm sorry, too," he says, "for not helping you more than I did. I should've been there for you all those times you went crazy, instead of getting mad and yelling a lot. It's just, I didn't know what else to do until I tried what Yodel showed me."

You have nothing to be sorry for. You were just being yourself. You were right to be mad. It was my fault, and besides, I was never your responsibility.

"Well, I'm going to miss you, all the same."

I'm going to miss you, too.

"But maybe we'll get to hang out sometimes, still, like at parties and cookouts and other fun stuff. And who knows? Maybe one day, if you're good, and if it's all right with Laura, you can come visit us at Memory Makers. We can catch up and chat about the old days, and maybe even have a sing-along or two."

I'd like that.

"Everyone will be happy to see you, I'm sure." BJ pulls the waist of his pajama bottoms up over his belly button. "Anyway, thanks for listening. I think I'll sleep much better now. See you in the morning, Cliff. Goodnight."

Goodnight, BJ.

"Goodnight, Francis. Thanks again for all your help."

"Mm-hmm."

BJ putters off and disappears back down the hall, Firth Bronzer thanks the pop star for her time and her new hairdo, and the feed cuts to its twelfth commercial break in the last hour. The first ad's for life insurance, and the next one is for gold. But the third one's not for cash for gold. It's for Silver Lining Inn & Suites. Their VIP strolls through the lobby. Her heels go click, click, click on tiled marble. She checks in at reception, shows me everything she loves about her room, then poses the same question she's asked so many times before:

"I deserve better. Why shouldn't you?"

If only, I tell her, and laugh. I laugh so damn hard I start crying — not at her, but at Francis, who's fallen asleep on the couch. His smile is peaceful and pure, like a baby's, his breathing so soft through his nose. I cry out for him, then I soil myself, front and back. The thing about my manual is that it has a wider seat, one that isn't fitted to my frame, so I can move around more freely side to side. And though it hurts like hell — a sharp, electric shock runs from my wrist up to my shoulder — there's room for me to whip my arm behind my back and, with lots of effort, even slip my hand down my Depends. Grasping my waste as tightly as I can, I wrench it out and hide it at my hip. It's not big, like Alec's, nor will it sail like his Hail Mary, but it'll get the job done. Even if my aim is off, I will at least have sent my message. Squeezing through the pain, I call out for Francis again. And again. This might take a while, but he'll be here for another half an hour. I'll wake him from his slumber soon enough.

About the Author

Josh Cook received an MA in English from Indiana University — Purdue University Indianapolis in 2009 and an MFA in Creative Writing from Lindenwood University in 2021. While earning the former degree, he found work in the Medicaid Waiver program, where he served individuals with developmental disabilities for more than a decade, first as a support staff, then as a program manager, and finally as a case manager. His experiences in these positions inspired the writing of *Another Crescent Moon*, one chapter of which functioned as his MFA thesis. He has presented original scholarship on Shakespeare and F.R. Leavis at research conferences, and his short fiction has appeared in journals including *Across the Margin*, *Fiction Kitchen Berlin*, *Idle Ink*, *Dissonance Magazine*, *Unlikely Stories Mark V*, and *Sage Cigarettes*.

He also teaches college-level writing. It has been his great pleasure to demystify the writing process for anxious students and to see their confidence in themselves and in their own voices grow. In August 2023, he began teaching at Odessa College in Odessa, Texas, where he lives with his wife and two dogs.

His hobbies include reading philosophy and history, and his heroes are Kurt Vonnegut, Franz Kafka, Malala Yousufzai, and Socrates.

www.ingramcontent.com/pod-product-compliance
Lightning Source LLC
Chambersburg PA
CBHW061203210726
48294CB00006B/1737